The Music of Her Life

A Novel

JUDITH M. MCMANUS

Dedication

In loving memory of Virginia...

My mother, my inspiration

.

Acknowledgments

There are so many friends to thank for enduring this long journey with me. First and foremost, to my editor, cover artist, author and friend, Josh Langston, who never gave up on me. If not for his expertise and humorous threats, this endeavor would still be another 'saved' document.

A special thank you to my husband for his patience on this journey and his generous support. Thanks to my first readers, Ginny A., Brenda H., Sherry F., and Emily R., for their time and valuable advice. Deadlines are reached when you have gracious and caring individuals in your life pushing you on to the finish line.

Birmingham, Alabama, my hometown, has always remained in my heart and soul. The trips to the Birmingham Public Library and the Archives of St. Clair County for research, allowed me to meet amazing people and discover a world of invaluable information from the era.

Lastly, to the generation before me which is considered the "Greatest." This book is written for them; their lives, their music, their sacrifice. May their memories never be forgotten.

Part One

Heartbreak and Remembrance

Prologue

Summer 1917
Elyton in Birmingham, Alabama

Lucy Johannsen got out of bed in the wee hours of the night to take a walk. Being in the eighth month of pregnancy, she found this the only way to eliminate the numbness in her right arm and receive the relief she needed. She grabbed her housecoat and quietly slipped out of the bedroom while her husband slept. The upstairs hall was dark except for the glow of the moon and the dim gaslight from the street filtering in through a small window. She used the wall for guidance, and each of her steps was carefully placed so as not to awaken her two young sons. Heading to the lavatory downstairs, she walked to the top of the staircase, stopped, and looked down.

Lucy came down these stairs each day, and many times during the night. Turning on no lights, she held tight to the railing. She could see the dim view of the landing and the next seven steps then started down, taking each step with caution. On the top step of the landing, her slipper caught on a split in the wood, and she started to fall. Her hand grip slipped off the railing, and she tumbled down the seven steps to the bottom. As she lay on the hardwood floor, she felt a throbbing ache in her ankle and a severe pain in her abdomen.

Her unborn son died, but Lucy was forced to carry the deceased child to term. Her husband, Dr. WB Johannsen, delivered the stillborn baby when her natural time came. The infant was taken to her hometown of Clairmont, Alabama, and buried next to Lucy's mother, Ellen.

Mrs. Lucy Collier Johannsen never spoke of or fully recovered from the death of her third son.

CHAPTER 1

The New Baby

March 1919

 $\mathcal{T}$ he attractive, white clapboard house on Tuscaloosa Avenue, was one of the large homes built in the Elyton section of west Birmingham in 1900. It had been constructed on one of the lots divided from the immense acreage of the 1854 Arlington Antebellum Home and Gardens. The house featured a prominent front porch with broad cement steps which led to an ornate stained-glass front door and transom. Two rocking chairs adorned each side of the front door, and white wooden swings hung at each end of the porch. White wicker planters filled with ferns welcomed visitors at the top of the steps. Surrounded by old oak and elm trees, the house stayed cool in the late spring and summer months. On March 4th, the blustery wind continued to blow the wicker planters over, so they had to be tightly secured to the porch railing.

As Lucy Johannsen hung wet laundry on the

clothesline in the backyard, she struggled to keep her balance. Sheets and towels blew back in her face as the strong wind whirled around her thin housedress. Her long reddish hair loosened from the chignon tied at the nape of her neck and long strands became unattached around her lovely face. She watched as her two boys, Bill 6, and Gabriel 4, played stickball close-by. She picked up her empty basket and slowly walked across the yard to sit on the iron garden bench. Two years had passed since the tragic accident, and soon her fourth baby was due.

Lucy loved the smell of spring and the crispness in the air. As she looked around her vast garden, the yellow jonquils and the fragrant purple hyacinths were in bloom. The Confederate Jasmine on the fence was beginning to show-off its new growth, and her favorite pink tulips stood erect in the sunny corner of the yard. Being late afternoon, it was time to light the stove for the evening meal. As she rose from the bench, Lucy felt a strong labor pain and motioned to the boys to come in with her.

"I can't have this baby now," Lucy mumbled under her breath. "I can't."

She and Gabe climbed the few wooden steps to the kitchen door and Bill, as always, took the small wooden wagon to load his choice of vegetables from the food cellar under the house.

As they entered the house, she experienced

another pain, grimaced and exhaled loudly. Soon, Bill unloaded the wagon and placed the vegetables on the kitchen table, then disappeared up the back stairs with Gabe. Lucy sat down and took deep breaths. The pressure grew, and the pains became regular. Trying to massage her lower back pain with one hand, she waddled her way to the back stairs as she guided herself with the other.

"Bill, go next door and bring Mrs. Alexander back with you," Lucy shouted. "Gabriel, I need your daddy. Go quietly through the living room and find him."

This wasn't the first delivery at home so Dr. WB Johannsen's friend and colleague, Dr. Ezra Taylor, would be called. Lucy trudged up the back stairs while holding tight to the railing. As she made her way into the bedroom, Mrs. Beatrice Alexander walked in and assisted while she undressed and got into bed.

"I don't want to have the baby now! I know something will be wrong with it, or it'll be dead!" Lucy cried as she clenched the sheets in intense pain.

Lucy's labor lasted a little over three hours, and the delivery was easy. At 7:04 PM on March 4th, a small baby girl made her appearance. The first breath came with a gentle slap and a loud cry. At 6 pounds 12 ounces and 19 inches long, Lucy barely heard Dr. Taylor say the baby might have been the prettiest newborn he had seen.

"Is it dead?" were the first words Lucy uttered as

she came out of the ether-induced sleep. "I don't want to see it."

Dr. Taylor assured her all was well with the baby, and she had a new daughter.

"I don't believe you!" she cried.

Dr. Taylor motioned for Mrs. Alexander to bring the little bundle to Lucy. When she saw her baby for the first time, she stopped crying.

"She *is* alive, and she's a pretty baby," Lucy said, wiping tears from her eyes. She pulled back the swaddling blanket to see a small amount of dark-brown hair and smooth olive skin. She felt her baby's perfect little hands, counted her toes, and watched as her new daughter slept. "I want to name her Virginia."

CHAPTER 2

Eliza

September 1922

After moving his family to Birmingham from the small town of Clairmont, Alabama, in 1914, Dr. William Boles Johannsen opened his in-home medical office. Since then, the doctor had built a successful practice.

The Elyton section in Birmingham was primarily white middle-class, Protestant and rather affluent. Even with this demographic, Dr. Johannsen's many patients had various backgrounds, occupations, and ailments.

During office hours, the front door of the house served as the entrance, and patients waited in the large parlor. There were three unused rooms on the first floor designated for the practice, and the ornate front staircase remained roped off during office hours. The family utilized the kitchen door of the house during the day, and the four upstairs bedrooms were accessible by the back stairs.

During the influenza pandemic of 1918, Dr. Johannsen closed his practice and stayed at Hillman Hospital day and night. Birmingham citizens stayed indoors since schools, churches, and most public places remained closed for two weeks by order of the governor.

When the long crisis ended, and it was considered safe to come home, Dr. Johannsen hired Mrs. Catherine Bartlett as his nurse and assistant. She worked with great ability at Hillman within those grueling two weeks, and he thought a nurse with her experience would be a great asset to his practice.

In the fall of 1922, Lucy realized the immense need for help with the household. She needed someone to live-in, but would she be able to find someone she could trust? Her fifth baby was due in three weeks, so she put the word out in the neighborhood and hoped for the best.

She asked Mrs. Alexander's girl, Jonnie May, if she could recommend someone trustworthy who could live-in, cook, didn't mind hard-work, and had experience with children. Jonnie May gave Lucy the name of a girl from her church that could easily fill her needs. Lucy asked her to talk to the girl and give her the Johannsen's address.

On a brisk Saturday morning, Eliza Jackson stepped off the streetcar on Tuscaloosa Avenue and double-checked the address given to her. Wearing her old wool coat, brown cloche hat, and carrying an old leather bag, she walked one block to her destination and stopped in front of a large white house.

"*Lawd, Lawd,*" the fortyish, heavy-set black woman thought to herself.

There was a sign in front that read, "W.B. Johannsen, M.D." Not sure if she had the correct address, she walked around to the back door of the house. Noticing the well-kept flower garden and small wagon parked next to the steps, she lightly knocked on the back door.

A younger woman, who looked to be in her thirties, answered the door.

"Miz Johannsen?"

"Yes, I'm Lucy Johannsen."

"My name's Eliza Jackson and I been told from Jonnie May next door you be needin' help 'round here, and I'm hopin' you'd consider me."

Welcomed inside, Eliza saw three young children having breakfast at the kitchen table. She could see that Miz Johannsen needed help. Another baby would be coming soon.

"I need help with cooking, housework, and with the children," Lucy began, "also, my husband is a physician, and his medical practice is here at home.

Keeping his examination room sanitary and the waiting room spotless is another major task."

"Yassum. I be havin' plenty of experience with all that."

"Good, I'm glad. Tell me about yourself."

"Yassum, Miz Johannsen, I'm the oldest of eight kids and just about raised the younger ones by myself. I been cookin' for Mama every day since she worked as help for a family in Powderly, not far from here, and cleanin' just come natural," Eliza replied. "I know Miz Alexander's girl, Jonnie May from the Baptist Church, and she say I should git over here quick and speak to you. Mama can't work no mo,' and she be my reference."

"Are you married?" Lucy asked. "Do you have obligations that could hinder your position here?"

"Nome, I never married but had an ol man once. He run off with some sorry trash, so I still lives at home with Mama. My brothers and sisters are old enough to take care of their selves and help Mama now." Eliza looked down and began to unbutton her coat.

"Let me show you around," Mrs. Johannsen said. "Please, take off your hat and coat. Go ahead and set your bag down."

Eliza had short, black, curly hair touched with gray and wore a floral housedress. Her round, friendly face was smooth, and her dark eyes seemed to twinkle.

She wore brown, lace-up orthopedic shoes with thick stockings. She hung her coat and hat on a nearby coat rack and followed the younger woman. As they walked through the large house, she was amazed at the size of each room.

Both the parlor and dining room had a large, carved wooden fireplace mantel with a built-in mirror. One fireplace burned wood; the other used coal. She followed Mrs. Johannsen into the office and examination room. The doctor was on his way out to make his weekend hospital rounds, and Mrs. Johannsen introduced them.

"So nice to know you, Eliza," Dr. Johannsen said. "I hope to see you again."

As the women climbed the front stairs to the second floor, Eliza noticed a framed photograph of two small boys and another of a young Mrs. Johannsen. She recognized the young boys in the photograph as the two sitting at the kitchen table.

Mrs. Johannsen showed her the four upstairs bedrooms, and each had its own small coal-burning fireplace. The back stairs to the kitchen began at the end of the hall, and Mrs. Johannsen asked her to go ahead. Eliza started down the steps and noticed how slow and careful Mrs. Johannsen took each step.

They walked into the kitchen, and Mrs. Johannsen asked if she would be interested in the job.

"Oh, yes, thank ya, Ma'am," said Eliza, as she picked up the old, leather bag. "Where would you like me to put my overnight things?"

"Follow me." Lucy walked a few steps down the short hall and said, "Your things will go in here." She motioned toward the cloakroom. "And your private lavatory is to the right."

Eliza couldn't believe it. *I never had no privacy or an inside privy.*

"We'll have a bed moved down from the attic, and there should be plenty of rods to hang your dresses."

Eliza followed the younger woman to the sleeping porch.

"You should be comfortable here until your room is ready in the next day or two. The windows are adjustable so make yourself comfortable." Mrs. Johannsen said with a smile. "I'm glad you're taking the job, Eliza. I sensed it the minute you walked in the house. We'll work nicely together."

Eliza looked around as she unpacked a few housedresses, one nice dress, plus hat and shoes for church. Aside from three aprons, unmentionables, hose and the clothing she was wearing, this was the extent of her wardrobe.

She liked that the sleeping porch had a gentle

breeze blowing in from the opened screened windows. A wrought iron daybed rested against the interior wall, and large wooden rockers filled two corners.

How did Miz Johannsen ever take care of this big house by herself?

After Eliza changed her dress and added an apron, Mrs. Johannsen took her under the house to the food storage cellar, showed her the vegetable bin, and told her where the meat hung in the smokehouse. Eggs, butter, and fresh milk stayed cool in the icebox. She stood in front of the icebox and smiled.

"My, my," she said. "I heard about these here iceboxes, Miz Johannsen, but I never thought I be able to have one."

Mrs. Johannsen informed her that the ice wagon came twice a week around 10:00 AM with a new block of ice, and not to expect him until next week. Introduced to the children as their new friend, Eliza, the young woman explained how she would be moving in with them and helping with the house. Gabe smiled while Virginia looked puzzled.

"Hi, Eliza," Bill said with a large grin. "Can you cook pies?"

"Yes, sir, Mr. Billy. I sho can." Eliza then noticed a pained look on Miz Johannsen's face.

"Okay then, Eliza, I'm going upstairs now to lie

down. I'm confident you'll be happy here, and I have the feeling you can run this house as well as I can," Lucy said.

"Don't you worry none. I'll take care of these three." Eliza immediately wiped Virginia's sticky hands and face. She smiled as she took the little girl out of her highchair and watched as her brothers walked with her up the back stairs.

Feeling comfortable in her new surroundings, Eliza thought how nice Miz Johannsen seemed to be. She didn't act uppity and bossy. She was used to loud women barking orders, but Miz Johannsen had a quiet voice and treated her as an equal. *They would get along fine.* Used to an outhouse, she never imagined her own lavatory and bedroom.

She took a moment to look around the well-equipped kitchen. *Lawd, I never seen so many fancy gadgets.*

After exploring the cupboards and drawers, she noticed a pie safe by the back door that could hold at least six pies. The sunny kitchen carried the aroma of hickory and baked cakes from the wood stove. The tall ceiling had one electric light bulb pendant dangling on a long cord and a deep porcelain sink with running water. Hidden behind an open door of a sizeable Hoosier cabinet, was a small shelf holding a candlestick telephone and hanging phone book. Inside the Hoosier, Eliza found a built-in flour bin/sifter, sugar bin, several drawers, a slide-out work table, and more storage. A wall calendar boasting 1922 in large numbers hung on the wall next to the icebox with an "X" marked on days past.

Next to the kitchen, was her new room and lavatory.

"Never in my born days... I git my private place now," she thought as she pulled the long chain and flushed the toilet.

"Eliza!" Mrs. Johannsen screamed.

Eliza hurried up the back stairs to find her new employer in hard labor with a tight grip on the bedpost.

"What do you need me to do, Miz Johannsen?" she asked, unable to disguise the panic in her voice.

"Have Bill run next door for Mrs. Alexander. Then call Dr. Ezra Taylor. His number is next to the telephone."

Just as Eliza opened the front door for Bill, Dr. Johannsen arrived home from his rounds.

Dr. Taylor found Lucy in excruciating pain and performed his examination. Three weeks early, the birth would be difficult because of the breech position and the large size of the baby. Dr. Taylor asked for Mrs. Alexander's assistance.

When Lucy could tolerate the pain no longer, the doctor administered a mixture of morphine and scopolamine which caused "Twilight Sleep." The highly touted drug mixture caused Lucy to flail, scream, and claw violently at herself. She had to be placed in restraints to keep her from injuring herself or others.

After a long, painful, touch and go delivery, Edward Rollins Johannsen, eight pounds nine ounces, was delivered by Caesarean section, a procedure seldom performed except in extreme cases. The doctor gave Lucy another dose of morphine. She would sleep five more hours and remember nothing about the birth, a side effect of scopolamine.

After hours of concern and Lucy's considerable loss of blood, Dr. Taylor seemed to have her stabilized. He worried that because of the scopolamine, the infant might be born drowsy and depressed or with breathing problems. On the contrary, little Edward had healthy lungs and a good, stable heartbeat. The relieved doctor went outside for a smoke, and WB joined him.

"Long night, my friend. You have a big, beautiful baby boy," Dr. Taylor said. "As you know, if the baby hadn't come early, I can't promise I could've saved Lucy. If the boy had waited two more weeks, he would've been nine and a half pounds and too much for her to deliver. I recommend you both call this one the last. She's 36 now, and there is too much risk involved."

CHAPTER 3

A Steady Decline

Summer 1929

*A*fter six years, Lucy found herself dependent on Eliza. She proved to be a master at cooking, running the household, and also became her cherished friend. Eliza understood when she wanted to be alone and in desired silence.

During her silent times, Lucy thought of her loving mother, Ellen. She learned from her the art of sewing, delicate hand-stitching, and how to slowly guide fabric through the old White Rotary sewing machine. When her mother died of consumption in 1907, she had borne eight children, and Lucy's father was left with five minor children to raise, the youngest only ten.

Lucy's father, Otis Collier, was a prominent farmer in Clairmont and owned ten acres of fertile Alabama farmland within the town limits. A husky, jolly man, he grew a variety of vegetables and designated two acres for cotton. He had an apple orchard, abundant grapevines, and plenty of muscadines for making wine. In addition to his regular laborers, his children helped during harvest time.

After her mother passed, Lucy remembered her father almost giving up on life. So distraught, he lost his passion for the land, and in 1908, after twenty-five years, the successful production of the Collier's crops ceased.

With a few long years, and help from Lucy and two older siblings, their father slowly returned to the loving person they knew. With his farming days over, he was asked by the county leaders to try another occupation. Otis Collier ran for Sheriff of Clairmont County and won.

With those memorable days fresh in her mind, Lucy felt the urge to document the summer day when she met WB Johannsen and the unforgettable days in Clairmont. She sat down, dipped her fountain pen, and began to write:

June 1929

"It was a Saturday in the summer of 1910. In my hometown of Clairmont, Alma Teague and I dressed up in our finery and walked to the town square surrounding the old county courthouse. We had a picnic lunch, socialized, and did a little shopping in the small establishments surrounding

the square. My favorite was 'Violet's Millinery,' where I bought my gloves, shoes, and hats.

I had seen William B. Johannsen in town many times, but never had the opportunity for an introduction. He was the new physician in Clairmont and lived at the Teague's Boarding House on Temple Street. As Alma and I walked toward the square, William approached us, tipped his straw boater hat and stopped. He was short in stature, about 5'8", a stout build, well-groomed light brown hair, and had the most beautiful olive complexion. Dressed in a beige pinstriped summer suit, he looked quite handsome.

"WB, I'd like to introduce you to Miss Lucy Collier. Lucy, Dr. William Johannsen, physician." I remember those as Alma's exact words.

I also remember how his gray eyes brightened as he smiled at me and nodded.

"Your servant, Miss Collier," he said with a thick southern drawl as he bowed at the waist and held his hat to his chest. "My friends call me WB."

I nodded with a timid smile, and Alma invited WB to join us. He directed his conversation to me, and I realized how self-confident and comfortable to talk to he was. After a few chaperoned meetings, we would meet in the square each Saturday afternoon. Occasionally, WB would drop in to visit with Daddy at our house on 6th Avenue, or we would sometimes stroll through town, pass old Judge Ingram's large house, and wave. On nice days, the former judge sat on his porch and greeted the passers-by with a broad smile, or a gesture with his walking cane.

My daddy walked the small town daily while on his sheriff duties and usually stopped at the Ingram house when the Judge was outside. Sometimes, the two elderly men swapped stories about their Civil War days, the battles they fought, and how each had been a Yankee prisoner in Ohio. Daddy, at age 19, was a member of Wheeler's Calvary, 51st Alabama Regiment and captured in Tennessee. Judge Ingram, at 27, became a soldier in the Alabama Battalion Infantry and was captured by Union soldiers at Missionary Ridge in Chattanooga. Sometimes, I accompanied Daddy on his strolls through town. I remember how enjoyable it was to listen as the two old men reminisced.

Our wedding day in November, 1911, was one of the happiest days of my life. WB, so imposing in his dark-navy pinstriped day suit and myself, in a white cotton marquisette ankle length dress and long lace veil held in place by a wreath of valley lilies. My sister, Pearl, stepped in and took our mother's place since I was the first girl to marry after her death. WB presented a 'shower bouquet' of valley lilies and roses for me to carry. WB had no family members present at our wedding since both of his parents died years before. His only surviving sister lived in Hanceville and was too ill to make the trip. I loved him so. I fell in love with him on that first summer day we met."

After placing the pen on the table, Lucy folded the paper and placed it in her apron pocket. She walked to the window and looked through the parted muslin curtains. It was a warm summer day much like the one she remembered so long ago.

Lucy walked to her garden and rested on the old iron bench. She looked at her blooming gardenias, and the massive "Alice Hamilton" rose bushes she planted the year Virginia was born. WB provided a good life for her and their four children, but it seemed as if he forgot about their third son.

The accident in 1917 still consumed Lucy. She

blamed herself for falling and couldn't forget the loss of her baby. WB tried to explain the medical reason why he couldn't take the baby, but she always felt that somehow, he could have saved her from the torture of carrying a dead fetus another month. He refused to name his third son, and she couldn't forgive him for that.

The name on the baby's death certificate read, "Unnamed Johannsen," but Lucy secretly named him Walter, after her brother. She gave him an identity. The baby boy deserved that, at least. His life was accidentally taken away, and she would never forget him. Each time she felt the loss, she silently spoke to him.

Lucy's loving memories of WB and their early days seemed so long ago, and now their relationship seemed like crushed particles of lovely old glass swept out into the breeze.

WALL STREET IN PANIC AFTER
STOCK MARKET CRASHES

The headline of the day didn't come as a complete surprise to the Johannsen's. They were one of the very few families in West End who were not hit hard by the October 1929, stock market crash. With Lucy's impeccable business sense and foresight, they paid off their mortgage in early 1929. They never bought into the stock market but invested their extra money in a few real estate deals. Lucy kept their cash hidden in the house because she didn't trust banks.

With the imminent Depression approaching, the Birmingham iron and steel mills closed due to lack of demand. Farmers were hit hard, as was the textile industry. Many local families left the area to find work. Some were long-time patients of WB's.

With Eliza's help, Lucy planted a garden, canned their own fresh vegetables, and purchased what they didn't grow from the local grocer, G. L. Chamblee. Rarely did Lucy buy meat since WB's patients paid him with chickens, and a variety of produce. She and Eliza could make one chicken feed the family for three days.

Eliza's friend from church, Ol Black George, came by once a week to take care of the yardwork and perform odd jobs. He looked to be in his fifties and asked for only two dollars and a meal in return. She didn't know where he lived, or if he stayed at their over-crowded church mission.

George always wore the same dirty overalls and a plaid shirt. His old hat was weatherworn, and his work-boots were caked in mud. Eliza never let George in the house because of his dirty appearance and the strong smell of body odor. Otherwise, he was dependable and showed up for work each Wednesday at 8:00 AM.

Occasionally, vagrants would knock on the back door and ask for food. Eliza always obliged, but Ol

George always stood guard as they ate, and then sent them on their way.

CHAPTER 4

The Secret Organization

Fall 1932

*Y*oung Bill Johannsen entered his freshman year at Birmingham-Southern College, a private Methodist institution known for its high academic ranking. A handsome, studious 19-year-old, Bill made the Birmingham-Southern football team and pledged Pi Kappa Alpha fraternity.

At his father's insistence, he planned to major in Biology and signed up for all the science classes offered to first-year students. Bill tried to stay interested since his father's heart was set on his oldest son also becoming a doctor. Living under the same roof as a medical office, it naturally led to thoughts of blood and sick people, thoughts that turned his stomach. Even though he was exposed to it every day, he was happy to live at home instead of at the men's dorm on campus.

Known for his shyness, Bill seldom dated, but

Southern co-eds followed him around campus and watched as he practiced on the football field. His friend, Joe Phelps, teased him and nicknamed him *"Football Freddie, girl magnet."* He hated that name and the crap he had to put up with. On most weekends, girls hung around the neighborhood hoping to get a small glimpse of him. Most of the time, he ignored it all, but one girl finally stood out.

On an errand for his father, Bill walked into Allen's drugstore and heard loud giggling coming from a group of co-eds at the soda fountain. He paid no attention and headed to the pharmacy counter at the back of the store to pick up the package.

On his way out, he noticed a lovely blonde standing at the magazine rack, skimming through a *National Geographic.*

"Interested in nature?" Bill asked.

"I'm trying to find a science article for a paper I have to write," the girl said.

"Interested in science, then?"

"Yes, I plan to become a doctor."

After she purchased the magazine, Bill walked her out of the store, continuing the conversation. As they walked, he said, "My name's Bill Johannsen."

"Nice to meet you, Bill. I'm Betty Dunn."

The co-eds watched in shocked amazement.

"He never talks to anybody," one girl said.

The so-called "civic" organization WB joined years earlier called an emergency meeting that evening and he would be late coming home. He instructed Nurse Bartlett to call and inform Lucy.

"That's convenient," she mumbled, "he hasn't stayed out late in a good while and then has 'her' call me?" As she hung up, Lucy looked at the only known snapshot of her husband. Virginia and Ed were standing beside him in front of their Model A sedan. *What the devil has happened to him?*

It was late when he got home, and Lucy confronted him. "What kind of secret organization are you affiliated with, WB? Is it something I'll be ashamed of? A club that does good-deeds in society, or bad?" She saw lip rouge smeared on his shirt and smelled liquor on his breath, even though Prohibition remained in full force.

"Ah, Lucy, it's just a bunch of professional men that meet once a month. All we do is drink, smoke, discuss the Depression, and how we can help the community. By the way, the meeting tonight was to discuss our part in the Armistice Day parade on November 11."

Lucy read about a club in the newspaper that consisted of some Jefferson County elite. It provided medical insurance policies, also benevolence for members and their families. The club was financially sound, and being in the medical profession, it seemed only right for WB to join. With the Depression raging, the organization was necessary.

Another "civic" organization also formed a branch in their part of the county; one that took matters into their own hands to rid society of "undesirables." There seemed to be a good bit of enthusiasm for this club from the prominent, high-ranking, and newly appointed members. The pictures Lucy had seen in the newspaper were frightening and didn't show goodwill, only hatred. She hoped to God he hadn't chosen that one.

On the day of the parade, WB left the house early. Lucy thought it an excellent opportunity to sift through the chifforobe where he hung his suits and kept his folded shirts and underwear. Failing to find something that would indicate his affiliation, she shut the doors in disappointment. She would have to wait until the parade.

With the faint aroma of smoke in the air and the leaves on the trees at their fall peak, the family had a brisk ride on the streetcar to 20th Street. Armistice Day, November 11, 1932, wasn't a federal holiday, although there would be a short suspension of business at 11:00 AM. Lucy allowed the three younger children a day off from school since it was a historic day, and they might learn something. Per Lucy's instructions, Bill and Gabe found the right spot for viewing at the intersection of 20th Street and 5th Avenue North in front of the Tutwiler Hotel. To her dismay, there were street vendors with red, white, and blue balloons and Uncle Sam finger puppets. Ed wanted everything he saw, but Lucy would never help someone profit from veterans.

The parade began at 10:00. High school and college bands led the way followed by the city officials. Next were the police and firemen in their full-dress uniforms, with some on horseback. As the Johannsen's watched veterans group after veterans group, they still waited for WB.

Several elderly Civil War veterans marched in their CSA uniforms while others slowly walked with canes or were pushed along in wheelchairs.

Toward the end of the parade, a group of about 80 men dressed in white robes and pointed hoods marched to the beat of the last high school band. Lucy didn't see a banner that gave the name of the organization, but she recognized the all too familiar symbol on the front of their robes. Lucy watched as they marched by, and was shocked to see that their faces weren't hidden.

"There's Daddy!" Ed yelled with excitement as he tried to get his father's attention.

Lucy recognized a few of the men from the neighborhood and some she met through WB's medical practice. She wanted to see his reaction when he saw Ed waving. Lucy and her expression caused WB to raise a stiff hand in a partial wave, then turn his head and continue to walk.

Lucy remained silent when the family met WB after the parade. She noticed the older boys seemed oblivious to the meaning of their father's Klan affiliation. She hoped they were. Virginia and Ed never read the newspaper except for the funnies, so Lucy knew they realized no connection whatsoever.

On the cool ride home, Lucy and Virginia, covered with a lap robe, sat in the front seat with WB, while the boys piled into the back. Lucy sat in silence and looked straight ahead while making no effort to speak to her husband.

"Mama, where does Daddy keep his ghost costume?" Virginia asked.

As they pulled in to the driveway on Tuscaloosa Avenue, the mouth-watering smell of Eliza's fried chicken filled the air. The children ran in and left their parents alone in the car.

"See, Lucy," WB said, "it's just a civic-minded club. We raise money for good works, and back excellent candidates running for political office."

While sitting in the car and listening to her

husband's apparent stupidity, she briefly wondered if he had merely been misled. Either way, it was wrong.

"It's just as I thought; it's the one I am ashamed of," she began. "Do you realize what this so-called 'civic-minded' organization stands for? Nothing but hatred!"

Lucy tried to control herself. She never raised her voice, but this time he would hear what she had to say.

"I'm shocked and embarrassed that you'd let yourself be taken in by such people. I thought you were so much more than this. How much is this mess costing you?"

"Lucy, calm down. As I said, we try to raise money for candidates we think will benefit the community, and we look for people and places we can help...."

She got out, slammed the car door, and left him without saying another word. She gave him no time to finish his sentence.

As Lucy walked in the front door, the appealing aroma of home cooking filled the house. The dining room table was laden with an assortment of fall vegetables, cornbread, and fried chicken, the most substantial meal the family had seen in months. And for what? This day was supposed to be for the veterans. The parade was for the veterans. *Why did those 80, white-robed idiots have to ruin the historical reverence of the day?*

Soon, WB took his place at the head of the table. "Eliza, join us. You're a member of the family, and I want us all together for this incredible meal," WB demanded as they all sat down.

"Oh, no thank ya, sir," Eliza answered with her toothy smile. "I had mine in the kitchen like I always do, but when I serves the coffee, I'll bring an extra plate for the pound cake I made for dessert."

"That's fine," said Dr. Johannsen. "After we finish our meal, I want you ladies to pack up some of this food and take it to the mission at West End Baptist. There're some sad situations down there, and this can be one way we can help. Is Ol George here today? I want him to have a plate, too, and some to take home. Let us pray." He then bowed his head for the blessing.

Listening to her husband pray, Lucy remained in shock and disbelief at how much of a hypocrite her husband was. After twenty-one years, the man she married had turned into a person she hardly knew.

The Depression caused Eliza to cook once a week and on a much smaller scale. The women worked together and always divided the food into meals that would last the family three days. It was an effective system they both devised, and it certainly seemed to work.

"Well, I guess we'll have to cook again tomorrow. I know taking this food to the church is for a good cause, but WB has thrown our system off," Lucy said. But that was hardly the biggest issue on her mind.

Betty Dunn and Bill began a casual courtship, and he brought her home on a few occasions. The girl seemed to be bright, unassuming, and apparently focused solely on her education.

They went to fraternity dances, movies, and frequently studied together, but there were no strings attached. He liked Betty, but the Bank was closed; she wouldn't "put out." He had his pick of girls who would, so he decided to take advantage of it.

Leelee Walther was his pick. Widely known throughout the football team as the "Pride of the Panthers," she was a beautiful brunette with a lovely smile and sleek figure. The guys on the team described her sexual expertise in lurid detail, and Bill was shocked to hear that such a lovely girl was nothing but a quiff. He spoke to her a few times when he was out with Betty, and he had one class with her. She spoke intelligently and had plans to become an accountant. He planned to ask Leelee out to dinner and a movie.

After class, Bill caught up with her and started a conversation. "I hear you're planning to become an accountant," he said while they walked.

"Yes, I am. I love working with numbers."

I bet you do. "So, do I. I'm planning to go into the medical field, but if that doesn't work out, I'll change to accounting. I'm Bill Johannsen, by the way."

"I know."

"Would you accompany me to dinner and a movie this Saturday night?"

"Sure, that sounds nice."

After asking around, Bill found out Leelee recently moved into a small house on Lomb Avenue with her mother. He also heard that her father committed suicide after losing everything in the stock market crash. *He hated the way the guys talked about her.*

On Saturday night, Bill walked to Leelee's front door, and Mrs. Walther answered. A small woman, he could tell she must have been a beauty in her younger days.

He introduced himself politely, and Leelee walked out to meet him. She looked lovely and smiled. When they left, she kissed her mother as Bill took her arm and led her to the car. That loving gesture to her mother impressed him.

After dinner, Bill asked Leelee which movie she wanted to see. She chose "Shanghai Express," with Marlene Dietrich. The theatre was dark, and Bill wanted to sit in the balcony. She didn't mind so they sat in the back where it was dark and they could be alone.

Deep into the movie, Bill wanted to see if the guys were right about Leelee. He placed his arm around her and rested his head on hers. She looked up at him, and he kissed her softly. She returned his kiss, and soon they were making illicit love in the last row of the balcony. Afterward, they began watching the movie again, with no words spoken.

On the way home, Leelee explained that she lost her father after the stock market crash and how she and her mother had to move from Macon, Georgia to Birmingham to be near family. She hadn't made many friends yet, but enjoyed Southern and the change in scenery.

After he walked her to the door, Bill stopped and kissed her on the cheek.

"Let's do this again sometime," he said.

"I'd like that." Leelee said then smiled.

Bill awoke the next morning to the aroma of bacon frying and constant arguing of Gabe and Virginia. He covered his head with his pillow and thought about his date with Leelee.

Knowing all the rumors about her were true, he stayed in bed and felt sorry that he only took her out for a good futz. She seemed warm, with a nice personality, and had a good sense of humor. He might ask her out again, although he wouldn't talk about their date to any of the guys. Never would he listen to that hooey and stoop that low again.

CHAPTER 5

The Ultimate Revenge

Spring 1933

To Virginia's delight, her father, and Dr. Ezra Taylor opened a pediatric practice on the fifth floor in the Brown-Marx Building in downtown Birmingham. The family had the big house to themselves, at last. Now, her father couldn't chase her around the house with a syringe and give her a shot when he caught her. Pain scared Virginia, but she got wise to her daddy. She refused to sit in his lap since it wasn't a sweet father/daughter interaction; he usually had a hidden needle in his pocket. Did he sneak up behind the boys and make them run? Probably not, he only liked to abuse her that way.

On her 14th birthday, March 4, 1933, Virginia's favorite gift was a brand new Philco table radio for her bedroom. It was always tuned in to her favorite local music station. Now she could close the door, turn up her music, and no one would bother her.

On a day after school, she listened to the radio in her room awhile, then came downstairs, and sat at the kitchen table.

Bored and complaining to Eliza, she heard Gabe's familiar whistle as he came in from school and slammed the front screened door. As usual, he was on his way to Holms Drugstore to check out the skirts and meet his buddy, Jack Hammond.

"I want to go! Please, please, Gabe! I'm so bored," she whined.

"Scram! I don't want you tagging along. I have things to do when I get there, and I don't want you around!"

"I won't even go in with you. I have my own money! I want to look at the make-up, anyway."

"Okay, damn it," he said, "but don't even act like you know me!"

The sidewalk on Tuscaloosa Avenue was nothing but a dirt walkway running parallel to the road. Some neighborhood boys had carved shortcuts out of dense brush that grew behind the large homes. With the dust, noise, and exhaust from the rattling motors of motor cars passing them on the street, Gabe and Virginia took one of the shortcuts.

As she walked behind him, Virginia breathed in the spring fragrance of daffodils and noticed the budding dogwoods lining Mrs. Goldman's fence. The crude paths had canopies of trees, and she saw the bright, blue-sky peeking through the branches as the soft breeze blew.

Holms Corner Drugstore opened in 1913 and continued to be the hub of the after-school crowd. The soda jerk knew everyone, and the favorite meeting place was the soda fountain. Rarely a booth or stool stood empty as a mass of youth always filled the store. The black and white tiled floor seemed barely visible as the standing crowd waited to place their orders. The short menu was written on the mirrored wall behind the counter while the rounded chrome handles of fountain dispensers stood amid the shake mixers and glassware.

With a new jukebox installed, the sounds of Duke Ellington, Bing Crosby, and all the popular songs could be heard from the street. "Dr." Holms, a well-respected pharmacist, enjoyed his young patrons as long as they behaved.

Virginia watched as Gabe walked around to the front of the store and met Jack, leaning against the front window. While the boys socialized, she went in, ordered a milkshake, and took it to the glass-topped makeup counter. A magazine with movie star Constance Bennett on the cover advertised a new line of cream rouge, face powder, and enamel nail polish which were displayed under the glass. Virginia couldn't wait to wear make-up and look glamorous. As she walked toward the soda fountain, she heard Jack and Gabe talking about a blonde in a red dress sitting alone.

"I'd like some of that," Gabe said.

"You want some of what? Some of that quiff in the red dress?" Virginia shouted so everyone could hear.

Gabe, pissed off and embarrassed, walked outside. Virginia followed him out as she continued to tease him.

Just as the blonde girl came outside, Gabe walked behind Virginia, knocked in her knees and made her fall. She dropped her shake which smeared across her dress while Jack and Gabe howled with laughter.

After running home, she cleaned herself up and changed clothes. She saw Eliza in the backyard hanging out laundry, and her mother was most likely in her sewing room.

Virginia went to the kitchen and opened a drawer of the Hoosier cabinet. She took out the largest butcher knife she could find and walked toward the front door. Gabe would be home soon, so she went out the screened door to the front porch, sat on the top step with the knife in her hand, and waited.

The longer she sat, the madder she got. Gabe had embarrassed her in front of all those people. After she waited around for an hour or so, he turned onto the sidewalk and walked toward her. Virginia got up and held the knife with both hands.

"I'm gonna kill you, Gabe!" Virginia screeched in her syrupy southern drawl. Like her Mama, she never cried, but this time she came close.

"You're dead!" she yelled as she started down the steps. She made her way to the bottom and raised her knife-wielding arms. Before she got off the last step, Eliza flew out the screened door and grabbed the knife.

"Now Honey, why you want to go and do that fo?" she asked.

Virginia tightened her lips and glared at her brother. "Because he and that drugstore cowboy, Jack, humiliated me in front of everybody at Holms', and then he laughed his sorry ass off! Everybody else did, too!" He was trying to show off in front of some tomato that didn't even pay any attention to him. Ha! He made me ruin my dress!" she sneered. "I hate his damn guts."

"Dry up, Virginia," Gabe yelled. "You, whiney cry-baby! You started it. That'll be the last time you ever go anywhere with me!"

"You're full of bushwa, Gabe!" Virginia yelled as Eliza kept her from tackling her brother.

Hillman Hospital slated a statewide lecture series on infant mortality for March, 1933. Selected as one of the guest lecturers on the subject, WB quickly accepted since Blair County, Alabama was the territory he would cover. He informed Lucy of the plans and that he had friends there who owned a boarding house where he had stayed many times.

"I don't know anyone from Blair County," Lucy said. "What are their names?"

"You've never met them."

"Um, hmm," she thought.

From March 13th to the 16th, WB traveled to Blair County for the medical lecture series for rural doctors. The mortality rate for babies, children, and young mothers was high in this area. He drove himself to Blairsville with plans to stay Monday and Tuesday nights at the small boarding house owned by his old friend and colleague, Dr. Joe Randall, and his wife, Una.

WB always looked forward to the Blairsville visits. The Randall's two-story, white-washed boarding house was built on two acres of prime farmland and Una took pride in her large garden.

He always looked forward to the home-cooked meal that always awaited him upon arrival. He accepted a bundle of mail from Una, and then retired early to his room. After reading through the mail, WB read over his agenda. With the window wide open, he heard the sound of a familiar automobile coming down the boarding house drive.

Tuesday, after a bountiful lunch prepared by the ladies in the community, WB started his afternoon series of lectures to the country doctors. Wednesday, the 15th, and Thursday, the 16th, would have him traveling to various parts of the county to observe the conditions.

After the lectures, he felt a bit dizzy and passed it off as exhaustion. He had to make three stops the next day beginning at 9:00 AM, so he hoped to turn in early. Around 3:00, WB drove down the narrow dirt road to the driveway of the house and parked the car. He wiped his perspiring face with a handkerchief as he walked. "It seems warm, especially for early spring," he mumbled.

When entering the house, WB removed his white straw hat and asked for a glass of cold water. Una obliged and reminded him that supper would be at 6:00 sharp. He nodded and started up the stairs to his room.

WB took off his suit jacket, removed his tie, and unbuttoned his shirt. A breeze blew in through the open window of the sparsely furnished room. The water felt good as he drank, and he then splashed some on his face. He sprawled out on the bed hoping to cool off, and read a small note left for him during the day.

After reading the note, WB thought of Lucy. Why had she turned so cold and aloof to him? He loved her and always would, but she pushed him away years ago. He thought of their wedding day in Clairmont, and how happy they were. They had four beautiful children, but it seemed that her personality completely changed after Edward.

There hadn't been any intimacy in years, and this distressed him to the point of having to find solace elsewhere. WB took a deep breath, "Lucy" he whispered, then closed his eyes, relaxing as the cool breeze wafted through the open window.

The Randall's waited for WB, but he was late for 6:00 supper.

"I imagine he's resting from the long day," Dr. Randall thought since the schedule was tiring, and WB's drive the day before from Birmingham seemed long. They waited on him a few more minutes, but when he still didn't come down, they started without him. Una made a plate for him and put it in the warmer.

The clock chimed 8:00, and WB still hadn't come down. Concerned, Dr. Randall walked upstairs to check on him. He knocked on the door but got no answer, then walked down the hall to listen at the bathroom door. Again, nothing.

Going back to the bedroom door, Dr. Randall knocked again. This time he opened the unlocked door and found WB lying on the bed with a small note in his hand. His face was pale, his eyes closed, and was a little purple around the lips. He tried to get a pulse and then placed his head on the doctor's chest for a hopeful heartbeat. There wasn't one. Dr. Johannsen was dead. Most likely of a massive heart attack, but that was speculation on his part.

Dr. Randall noticed the spilled glass of water and a handkerchief on the floor by the bed. It looked as if he tried to get up but collapsed.

Virginia's favorite radio show, "Amos and Andy", came on every Tuesday night and was one of the family's favorites. She loved to watch Eliza when she snickered and rolled her eyes as the white actors tried to imitate a black dialect. The comedy show aired at 8:00, right after the news hour.

"Phone's ringing," Virginia yelled.

"Johannsen residence," Eliza said. "Yes sir, wait one minute, and I'll get her." She lay the receiver down and called Lucy. "Miz Johannsen, a call for you."

As laughter spilled into the hall, Virginia could barely hear her mother's voice as she came back and stopped in the doorway.

"A Dr. Randall just called from Blairsville where your daddy has been lecturing. It seems he had a massive heart attack and passed away. He was staying at Dr. Randall's boarding house and didn't come down for supper," Lucy said stoically. "Dr. Randall will phone me tomorrow with details about bringing your daddy back home."

The room remained silent except for the static and crackle of the radio show. The boys were in shock. Virginia, sitting on the floor, looked at her mother's face but could see no expression at all. She never saw her mother cry and wondered if she would now. Eliza left the room and could be heard sobbing in the kitchen.

Bill put his arm around his mother and asked, "What do we need to do?"

"Nothing until Dr. Randall calls."

Immediately Lucy turned the radio off and went upstairs.

The next day, Lucy and Bill traveled two hours by train to Blairsville. Dr. Randall was waiting at the station to take them to the boarding house.

"Mrs. Johannsen?" he asked.

"Yes, and this is Bill, our son."

"You favor your father," Dr. Randall said.

The ride to the boarding house was not long, but there was heavy tension in the air, and it was having a strong impact on Lucy. Nothing was said, although Lucy had many questions, and she wanted answers.

When they pulled up to the house, a small, older

woman walked outside to greet them.

"I'm Una Randall. I'm sorry that we have to meet under these circumstances. We thought so much of your husband."

I've never heard of you or your husband. Something about this isn't right. "Thank you," Lucy murmured.

Lucy listened as Dr. Randall began to explain WB's activities the day before, and his symptoms before he retired upstairs. After the postmortem examination, he was sure it was a massive heart attack. Lucy and Bill followed him upstairs to the bedroom.

The county coroner waited in the bedroom for Lucy and Bill. As they walked in, he pulled up the sheet that covered WB's body.

"Mrs. Johannsen is this your husband, William Boles Johannsen?"

Lucy looked at the pale, lifeless body of her husband. She felt his hand. It was stiff and cold. She looked at the handsome face that had aged rapidly in last few years. "Yes," she said softly.

After the identification and all necessary business had concluded, an ambulance arrived to take the body back to Birmingham.

"Here are WB's personal effects, Mrs. Johannsen," Dr. Randall said as he handed Bill his father's valise, straw hat, and medical bag. "Everything should be there. I put his glasses, wallet, and the contents of his pockets in the valise."

Glad to have Bill with her, they drove home in silence in the family's Model A sedan. When they were almost home, Lucy said, "I don't know Dr. Randall or his wife, never heard of them."

"Is that a fact, Mama? I thought Daddy went to Blairsville a good bit."

"I asked him not to go out of town this time since he wasn't feeling well. He always did as he pleased and told me not to worry. I wonder what was always in Blairsville that was so damned important?"

The next few days would be long and hard. Lucy dreaded the arrangements she had to make but was glad of one thing.

WB thought ahead and purchased eight plots in Elmwood Cemetery three years earlier. They made this decision in 1930 after Mrs. Alexander's husband, John, died of injuries from a car crash while on an out of town sales call. His wife, Lucy's friend, Beatrice, was helpless because they hadn't had the morbid foresight. Lucy and WB cared for the Alexander's daughter, Anna, for two weeks since a distraught Beatrice could barely take care of herself.

The funeral service was scheduled for Friday morning, March 18th, at the house on Tuscaloosa Avenue. Lucy scheduled the visitation for 6:00 Thursday evening, and again on Friday morning at 10:00. The service would begin at 11:00 with Rev. George L. O'Connor officiating.

Many messages of sympathy arrived at the Johannsen home after WB's obituary appeared in Birmingham's *Age-Herald* and the *Southeastern Ages* in Clairmont on Thursday.

WB, well known in West End, had also touched many lives through his medical practice. The doorbell constantly rang with flower deliveries and mail by special courier. The funeral parlor would soon bring her husband's body home. Lucy's outward demeanor stayed calm, but with the messages, flowers, visits, and food from the neighbors, the stress was about to overwhelm her.

Eliza understood the stress Lucy was under and took over the house and greeted visitors in her place. She instructed Ol George to clean himself up and be ready to make way for the casket and supervise its placement in the living room. Eliza divided the multitude of food between the storage cellar and the icebox.

The funeral home representatives placed the casket in between two windows as Ol George instructed. Floral wreaths, baskets, and plants filled the living room, and almost consumed the casket. The fragrance throughout the house was almost sickening. Before the family came in, George added chairs to accommodate the expected visitors.

The casket would stay closed until ten minutes before 6 o'clock. Eliza, with tears in her eyes, watched as Ol George opened it and said an inaudible prayer.

Lucy and the three boys were the first to view. The only time their mother would look at her husband, she nodded and let out a long, deep sigh.

"He looks good," Lucy said.

Virginia walked to the casket and stood next to her mother. As she looked at her daddy, she felt a little frightened. She had seen a dead body before, but it was always a wrinkly old relative, not someone as young as her father. He was only 53. The one similarity to the elderly relatives was the full head of white hair. As Virginia looked at her daddy, she noticed the peaceful look on his face, but realized how scared she had become of him.

His hands were placed one on top of the other as his gold wedding ring reflected from the candles in the candelabra that flanked each side of the casket. Tears welled up in her eyes, but she fought them back. She wanted to be like her mother, never cry and never show emotion.

Throngs of visitors and friends began to arrive. Beatrice Alexander, one of the first, pulled up a chair next to Lucy. She grabbed Lucy's hand and stroked it. Lucy looked at Beatrice in annoyance and pulled her hand away. Beatrice seemed a little surprised that Lucy's face wasn't red from crying.

"Lucy, I wanted to help comfort you, I'm sorry. You seem tense and irritable. You need to cry," Beatrice said.

"I will not cry! I have four children to raise," Lucy exclaimed under her breath. "You're trying to help. Thank you. You've been through this, but I am determined to stay strong for my children. I will not go to pieces!"

Lucy greeted each guest, as well as Bill and Gabe. Since Virginia and Ed were so young, she instructed that they go to another room in the house, so they wouldn't have to talk to anyone.

When visitation ended, Ol George closed the casket and turned the lights off. Lucy went upstairs to bed and thought about the long day that awaited them tomorrow.

At the 11:00 AM service at the house, eight of Dr. Johannsen's old friends insisted on acting as pallbearers. There were none selected previously, so Lucy acquiesced.

When the hearse arrived at the gravesite, the

eight men donned their white robes, lined up, and carried the casket to the burial site. They were some of WB's oldest colleagues. Lucy had no idea any of these men were in that organization. She let out a deep sigh of disappointment but said nothing.

When she looked at Liza and Ol George, they turned away, put their heads down, and never brought them up for the entire service. How would she ever be able to face them?

The day after the graveside service, Lucy picked up the valise Dr. Randall had given to Bill. Alone in the house, she took it to her bedroom to clean it out and discard what wasn't needed. She would give her husband's clothes to West End Baptist to distribute to the needy, and to Dr. Taylor, his medical bag.

The valise contained a few dollars held with his money clip, a coin purse with a small amount of change, his gold pocket watch, and a small piece of paper with the name "Elsie Bartlett" scribbled on it with a phone number. That was the name of Nurse Bartlett's daughter.

Lucy looked up from the paper, then continued to rummage through the valise. She found a folded lace handkerchief with the initials EB embroidered on it. At the bottom, she found a bundle of seven letters tied with twine and addressed to WB in care of the Randall's. She opened one, and in a lovely script, it read:

February 21, 1933

My dear William,

I'm looking forward to seeing you in Blairsville on the 13th of March. Mother has given me your lecture schedule, and I'll meet you at the boarding house on Monday evening. How wonderful to be alone with you again. Those times at the convention in Montgomery when we were up with your friends felt like torture. I'm so glad Una is saving my letters for you. I am thinking of you always.

Yours,

Elsie

Lucy put the letter back into the envelope and closed her eyes. Separated from the bundle of letters, she almost missed a small, folded note written in the same script.

Forgive me for being so late yesterday. Our time together is always so sweet, and I feel as if you love me as much as I love you. Leaving this morning was difficult, but we will be together again in a few days.

Elsie

She wanted to read more of the letters, then decided not to and destroyed them instead. It was all coming together now, and her questions were now answered.

The out of town medical conferences and moving the medical practice out of the house gave WB the ability to live a double life. Was this his ultimate revenge for a marriage that virtually ended in 1917? She would ask Bill to take away his father's effects. Should she tell him?

Part Two

The fighting spirit that could never be broken...

.

CHAPTER 6

New Friends

Fall 1938

*T*he news reports of the day brought nothing but the escalating problems in Europe. Adolf Hitler was appointed Chancellor of Germany in 1933, then became der Fuhrer of Germany in 1934. His aggressive foreign policies were causing political upheaval in many countries in Europe. Bill and Gabe tuned in to the radio to gain information on the status of Germany and Europe as a whole. President Franklin D. Roosevelt pledged to stay neutral and had no plans to get our country involved.

Five years had passed since WB's death. Bill graduated in the spring of 1936 from Birmingham-Southern with a Degree in Accounting. After his father's death, he abandoned his science classes since he never wanted to be a doctor anyway. He never got over being sick at the sight of blood and finally admitted it to Lucy.

In his senior year, Bill focused on his math studies and his last football season. He was co-captain of the Birmingham-Southern football team and was voted "Most Popular" in his senior class. With the useless adoration behind him, his attention centered on his new accounting position with Alabama Power in Birmingham.

At twenty-four, his rugged good looks and quiet personality continued to attract college girls and female co-workers. His relationship with Betty Dunn ended soon after his father's death. She transferred to the University of Alabama in Tuscaloosa in her second year and neither wanted a long-distance relationship.

He ignored the immature co-eds, but had a few casual dates with one of the secretaries in the office. Bill liked the girl since she was smart, well-educated, and he could carry on an intelligent conversation with her. Neither wanted a serious commitment, and their relationship was a friendly one with no ties.

After WB died, Bill was forced to take over as head of the household. Since his mother didn't drive, he became her driver. He also had to become the disciplinarian, and it didn't come easily to him. He was stern, yet gentle with his siblings and could handle Virginia and Gabe since they argued constantly. Ed, easy going like his brother, was never a problem, and they respected their brother's authority.

Virginia, now 18, was a first-year student at Birmingham-Southern. Most of her friends had gone away to college, so she knew only a few students. Considered attractive, she had dark-brown, shoulder-length hair, flawless olive complexion, and emerald green eyes. Her lean figure and fashionable clothes regularly brought second looks and whistles.

Her schedule was light, and she had core classes on Monday, Wednesday and Thursday.

In Monday's history class, a student sat next to her whom she had never noticed before. The class was small, maybe twenty-five students, and when the professor called "Susie Langdon," the student's hand went up. Virginia looked over and smiled. After class, the girls walked out together.

"You're new in class, aren't you?" Virginia asked.

"Yes, I'm a sophomore and didn't take the class last year," Susie said.

It didn't take long before Susie and Virginia became fast friends. Susie urged Virginia to consider her sorority, Zeta Tau Alpha, and after a busy rush season, she received a bid to pledge.

Now in college and a member of a sorority, Virginia thought of nothing but socializing and meeting new people. She never dated much in high school because of her shyness, but her timid days were now a thing of the past, thanks to Susie. There was a Pi Kappa

Alpha dance planned after the second football game of the season, and Virginia wanted to go.

Gabe was a member and didn't have a date, so introducing Susie to him might help. Her brother could fix her up, hopefully.

Virginia planned lunch on the quad with Susie and asked Gabe to join them. Just as she hoped, they immediately liked each other. Virginia then brought up the subject of the dance. It was a month away, and she still had no prospects.

Gabe changed the subject and continued to talk to Susie, leaving Virginia as the third wheel. After finishing her lunch, she left them alone, caught the streetcar, and went home.

On Monday, as she expected, an excited Susie came to class; she had been asked to the dance by Gabe.

"Shit, Gabe won't help me get a date. He thinks only about himself," she said.

When Virginia got home she asked outright, "Gabe, do you know anyone in Pi K A who needs a date to the dance?"

"No, and I'm not fixing you up with any of those wolves, either."

Lawrence Abbott transferred to Southern from

the University of Alabama in Tuscaloosa that semester. His family was from Birmingham, and he planned to major in Biology then earn his M.D. from the Medical College of Alabama.

A third-year student, he was still required to take English. He put it off as long as he could and dreaded each Wednesday since that was his only class of the day.

The only upside was a girl in that class he couldn't take his eyes off of. She had dark-brown hair, a lovely face, great figure, and the greenest eyes he'd ever seen. She usually sat alone, but those eyes illuminated whenever she looked his way. He had to meet her.

Getting his courage up, Lawrence followed her out of class after opening the door for her. She smiled, ducked her head, and held tight to her books.

"I've been watching you in class. My name is Lawrence Abbott. Everyone calls me Larry," he said with a smile. "I wanted to meet you face to face and see if your eyes were really that green."

"I'm Virginia Johannsen," she said timidly, then added after a pause, "Well, are they as green as you thought?" She seemed to be concentrating on his own blue eyes.

"Definitely," Larry said.

Virginia liked his smile and his handsome face. He had dark hair with a thick curl that fell over one eye.

She noticed his tailored jacket, pants, and how the argyle sweater vest had been well-coordinated. He had an open collar and a Pi Kappa Alpha fraternity pin on his lapel.

"You must know my brother, Gabe Johannsen," Virginia said. "You're both in the same fraternity."

"Yes, I've met him," Larry affirmed. "I had no idea he was your brother. I was fortunate enough to transfer my membership but haven't met many members."

After the awkward small talk, Larry invited Virginia for lunch at the quad dining hall if she had time. Not sure if she should, she felt comfortable with him and accepted.

He told her that he planned to be a doctor, and like Bill, signed up for the required science classes offered a junior. How she hated doctors. *I've just met him, for heaven's sake, give him a chance. Maybe he could be fun.*

When she got home, Virginia asked Gabe if he knew Larry. He knew him, but not well and never heard anything negative. Virginia knew Gabe would ask around about Larry. In high school, she dated very seldom because of her shyness and the way Gabe had to get the scoop on anyone interested in her.

Virginia learned that Lawrence Patton Abbott

was born to Birmingham attorney William Talbot Abbott and Elizabeth "Bitsy" Patton Abbott. Two years older than Virginia, he was an only child and graduated in the top three of his class from Ramsay High School. Occasionally featured on the social pages of the newspaper, his parents were successful at fundraising, and gave significant donations to the University of Alabama. Larry gave no indication they were his parents.

It had been three weeks since meeting Larry. They sat next to each other in class and had lunch together when they could. He hadn't asked her out yet, and the fraternity dance was getting close. Susie kept grilling her to see if Larry had asked.

Wednesday came, and Virginia couldn't wait to see him in class and hoped he would mention the dance at lunch. How could she not be overly excited if he asked? Was it idiotic to think Larry Abbott would want to go to a dance with her? She always felt so self-conscious.

Larry was five minutes late for class. Virginia watched him quietly slip in, so he wouldn't catch the professor's attention. She smiled at him, but he didn't notice. He sat down next to her and immediately buried his head in his English book. *What's up with him?*

Virginia looked at her English book, then back at him. After no response, she turned her chair, faced the opposite direction, and didn't look his way again. When class ended, she got up and walked out, saying nothing. Her heart pounded as she walked toward the quad dining hall. Maybe he'd explain the problem at lunch.

She waited for Larry at the dining hall, but when he didn't show, she thought what they might have had must be over. *What could be wrong?*

She wondered if it was something she did or was he upset about something else? It didn't matter; it still hurt. She felt sorry they never had a date or even a kiss. She grabbed a small bite to eat then caught the streetcar and headed home.

When she rounded the corner, Virginia saw Larry's convertible parked in front of the house and Larry sitting on the top step of her front porch. Surprised, she smiled and sat next to him.

"How do you know where I live?"

"I asked around. Listen, I apologize for today," he said. "I have a lot on my mind, and things at home are not good. My parents argue constantly. I think they might force me to drop out of college and move to Huntsville with my grandparents."

"Oh no, please say you're joking," she said.

"I'm not, but maybe they'll iron out their differences and put my best interest at heart," he answered. "My father's an attorney here in town and involved with his secretary. It seems my mother found out, therefore, she's drinking too much." Larry put his head in his hands. "It's a game with her. His affairs give her false reason to drink even though she's had her own infidelities in the past. Bitsy Abbott doesn't fool me."

Larry looked straight ahead and squinted in the sunlight. Virginia scooted a little closer and put her arm around him.

"Everything will be okay," she said.

Larry smiled and gazed into those lovely green eyes. He gently kissed her. She had never been kissed with such soft lips or had such a handsome face so close to hers. *Is this real? Can anyone be so perfect?* She tried to control herself. Never had she been kissed with such gentle sensuality.

"There's a dance after the game this weekend. Would you like to go with me?" Larry asked. "I meant to ask you sooner."

"Sure, I'd love to go with you," she answered, while trying to act nonchalant and not too eager.

Larry got up and took her hand. "I'm glad. You're the only girl I want to be with." He started down the steps while still holding her hand. He walked back up and kissed her again.

Virginia thought the rest of the week would never end. She couldn't wait for Saturday night and being with Larry the entire evening. There was no time for her mother to make a formal gown, so she went downtown after class on Thursday and found the perfect dress.

While getting ready for the dance, Virginia thought of nothing but how she wanted to impress him. She wore a long-fitted gown of light green satin, held with rhinestone straps, and draping in the front. The snug dress enhanced her figure.

She parted her shoulder-length dark hair in the middle and pulled it up on each side with combs. A little nervous, Virginia wanted to look perfect. She heard Larry's car outside and slowly picked up her clutch and started down the hall.

Larry arrived wearing black tails, white vest, and a white bow tie. He rang the doorbell and removed his black top hat. Mrs. Johannsen answered the door.

"Hello, I'm Larry Abbott," he said. "I'm here to take Virginia to the Pi Kappa Alpha dance tonight. I'm also a fraternity brother of Gabe's."

"Yes, she told me. So nice to meet you. Come in."

Larry came in with a small box under his arm. Still holding tight to his top hat, he noticed the parlor's tasteful, but simple furnishings. The room was welcoming and warm, not cold and gaudy like his own home. He could tell by this one room that every inch of the house was lived in. The warm fire in the fireplace and the large, worn chair that sat next to it was proof of a loving family.

When he saw Virginia walking down the stairs in a light green, snug fitting gown, he gasped at how pretty she looked and presented her with lavender orchids to wear.

"You're lovely," he said.

"Thank you."

As Larry pinned the flowers on her matching wrap, Gabe hurried down the stairs.

"Hello, Larry, I'm running late," he hurriedly remarked. "Nice dress, VA, a little too snug, isn't it?"

"VA?" Larry asked. "I've never heard you called VA."

"Yes, Gabe calls me that since he's too lazy to say my full name."

"I like it. It fits."

When they arrived at the large, antebellum-style fraternity house on campus, the music could be heard from the street, and couples were dancing outside on the patio. The Freddy Brookfield Orchestra sounded fantastic, and they couldn't wait to go inside.

The clinging satin dress molded to her sleek 5' 4"

figure. Larry stood a lean six feet tall, and she could imagine how their dark hair glistened under the lights. VA held tightly to his arm.

"Dance, VA?"

The Lindy Hop was the new dance craze, and VA was an expert. As Glenn Miller's "In the Mood" played, she followed each of Larry's dance steps. She noticed Gabe and Susie coming in the front door of the fraternity house and waved.

"Look at VA. Her dress is too tight to be doing that dance." Gabe took Susie's wrap and lit a cigarette.

"She looks great out there," said Susie. "Let's get a drink."

As the orchestra played the most popular songs of the day, she loved how Larry pulled her close and hummed the tunes in her ear. He leaned back, took her hand, and placed it behind his neck.

"Having fun, Virginia?" he asked as he stroked her arm. "Do you mind if I call you VA?"

"I am," she softly answered, never taking her eyes away from his. "And, no, I don't mind." She couldn't be falling for him yet, could she? She never had feelings like this. Larry succeeded in sweeping her off her feet.

CHAPTER 7

A Happy Memory

*S*ummer, 1939, continued to bring more unrest in Europe, and it had escalated to epic heights. Hitler invaded Poland on September 1st. The news hinted that the beginning of World War II had begun. President Roosevelt still vowed to keep our country neutral. His focus was the New Deal and getting the US out of the Depression. It had started with Herbert Hoover, and FDR planned to end it.

War news was a constant subject. VA couldn't get away from it. In addition to the news on the radio, the newspaper was full of war and another German invasion. Even newsreels at the movie theater showed the horror of death and gore. Bill and Gabe were consumed with it and said it was just a matter of time before FDR got the US involved.

VA and Larry were inseparable. Eliza always set a plate for him at dinnertime, and Gabe, Bill, and Ed considered him a brother. Larry spent more time at the

Johannsen's than at his own home. To VA's dismay, he stayed glued to the news when he was at the house. She needed to shift his attention to something else. It was all so far away.

Gabe Johannsen and Susie Langdon became engaged in July, 1939. They planned to get married on December 16, in a quaint chapel near Susie's parent's home.

The Langdon's owned immense acreage in a rural area of town considered "over the mountain." The newlyweds intended to make their home in the area since there were long-range plans for much more development in the future.

The small chapel sat on a hill overlooking a vast expanse of cliffs, hogback ridges, streams, and ancient trees. Even though it was winter, VA thought the view was breathtaking and a perfect setting for the wedding.

When Susie Langdon arrived at the chapel escorted by her father, she looked like an angel in white satin and lace. Lucy, VA, and Larry sat in the first pew and smiled as Gabe entered the chapel with Bill, his best man. The guests stood when Susie and her father entered the chapel.

VA watched as her small form floated down the aisle, but her thoughts were on Larry. After the vows were spoken, and the marriage confirmed with a kiss, the guests headed to the reception at the Langdon's home.

The living room was filled with white flowers, and an abundance of wedding gifts were displayed for the guests to view. Congratulatory cards and messages were placed next to the guest book while a spiked punch bowl surrounded by finger foods doubled as the centerpiece on the dining room table.

Mr. Langdon decided at the last minute to engage an orchestra, and fearing the worst, he hired the best. The Stan Johnson Orchestra played the tunes of the day and the orchestra, new to the college circuit, was well known for wedding entertainment. Gabe and Susie danced their first dance to "Moonglow," and soon the other couples joined them.

Larry, keeping his two flasks well hidden, mixed extra hooch into the spiked punch. Gabe looked over and gave him a thumbs up. When VA took a sip, she coughed repeatedly and brought her hand up to her throat.

"How much did you put in there?"

"A lot," he said as he took a long swig straight out of the flask.

As VA danced with Larry, she watched her mother on the sidelines. Lucy looked content, was socializing, and not the elusive, emotionless woman she knew day to day. She was talking to Susie's parents and even laughed at something.

After three glasses of punch, VA looked up at Larry and slurred, "Mama looks happy, doesn't she? I think she does. Do you think she had a few belts of that punch?"

During an orchestra break, a tight Larry and VA walked outside to Mr. Langdon's vast manicured garden. Unusually mild for winter, he guided her beyond the patio to see if there was privacy anywhere on the Langdon's property. He wanted her tonight.

"I want to dance, come on," she said as she swayed back and forth.

In their year together, they kissed, went too far many times, and then it would stop. The frustration for him was overwhelming, but now it was time for the next step. They followed a path that led to a beautiful greenhouse. It was completely hidden by trees and vines.

"Let's stop here," he said.

They went inside to find it fairly warm. Small seedlings, flowering pansies, poinsettias, and plants of various varieties filled up the greenhouse. VA gasped at the beauty of it all.

Larry took her face in his hands and kissed her. He softly moved his lips to her cheek, her ear, and then kissed her neck. He took her hand and walked away from the entrance. He looked around for a soft place. There was a small room in the back that looked to be an office of some kind. They went in to find a bed, dresser, and a small bathroom.

"This must be for Mr. Langdon's caretaker," he said as he kissed her again.

She quietly moaned for more, and he proceeded to lay her on the bed. He pulled down her shoulder strap and his lips found the top of her breast. He pushed one hand up her dress and gently guided it inside her thigh.

"What are you doing? Larry, stop it," VA murmured.

"I've waited for this so long, VA."

"Larry, please don't. We have so much to do while we're young. We can't ruin it."

VA must have forgotten what she had said because his hand found her delicate spot. As she kissed him, he felt her hands unbuckling his belt and reaching in for the part of him she desperately wanted. She found it ready for her. He unzipped her dress and easily let it fall to the floor. They removed the rest of their clothing and lay completely bare on the bed. Motioning for him to come into her, he immediately towered over her and entered at her request.

He had never felt such love and intense sexual

desire in his life. The carnal pleasure overwhelmed him. His strong thrusts into her warm body and feeling every inch of her smooth bare skin caused them to hit the orgasmic heights together.

They lay naked in each other's arms.

"You're the first," she said. "Am I the first for you?"

"Yes," he said between heavy breaths. "VA, please marry me after we graduate, I love you." VA lay next to him with a satisfied smile.

"I love you, too. So much," she said. "Yes, I will marry you."

"Let's plan on December, 1941," Larry said, "but we won't announce it until after Christmas."

Larry looked around and found a thin, pliable twig and fashioned it into a ring. He pushed it onto her finger and kissed it. "You'll have the real thing soon, I promise."

"I love it. I don't need anything else because you made it for me. I'll keep it always."

Still a little tight, the couple returned to the reception where the newlyweds were about to cut the cake. In addition to Susie and Gabe, the photographer snapped pictures of the guests. As VA and Larry danced, the photographer stopped to take a photo of them. A little while later, he stopped them again to pose while slow dancing. They held one another closely with their joined hands clasped to Larry's chest and cheeks touching. They looked up and smiled as the camera bulb lit up the room.

Gabe and Susie were ready to leave for their short honeymoon in Atlanta. Their hotel reservations were at The Georgian Terrace across from the Fox Theater where the "Gone with the Wind" movie premiere was supposed to be held.

"I'll tell Vivien Leigh and Clark Gable hello for everybody!" Susie said as the guests waved goodbye.

Before the newlyweds left, they stopped to thank everyone for being a part of their unforgettable day and for Susie to toss her bouquet. She turned around and tossed the flowers over her head. Applause and loud squeals followed. Susie turned around to see VA holding the bouquet and ran over to her new sister and hugged her tightly.

A happy but wobbly Gabe waited at the door for his bride and blew a kiss toward VA as they ran under a shower of rice and well wishes.

Bill, Ed and a few former fraternity brothers decorated Susie's car with crepe paper, risqué words written on the windows, and tin cans tied to the bumper.

After staying behind and thanking the Langdon's for a lovely wedding, Ed and Bill accompanied Lucy home.

VA and Larry followed close behind and stopped a block from her house.

"Are you sorry?" he asked.

"No," she replied, "but I might be tomorrow."

CHAPTER 8

The Tutwiler

Fall 1940

*E*urope was in turmoil. Great Britain had been preparing for the worst. Men aged 20-21 could be called up for service as "Militiamen" and Civil Defense workers were on alert. The British Army mobilized, and the Blackout began. Great Britain was at war with Germany. Lucy and Eliza kept the radio on all day. The war in Europe consumed the news, and after Chamberlain's numerous debacles, Winston Churchill became the new Prime Minister. Italy, an ally to Germany, had also declared war on Britain.

After work, Bill would sit in his father's old chair, fixated on the news reports from overseas. He casually mentioned to Lucy that he had been thinking about volunteering for service in the RAF, Britain's Royal Air Force, since Roosevelt continued to keep the US neutral. Lucy would not agree under any circumstances. He was

26 and of legal age, but he would never go against his mother's wishes, although it was on his mind constantly.

The BBC reported in July; German forces had begun to occupy Britain's Channel Islands. Bill knew the US would inevitably become involved at some point since Britain was our friend and ally. Germany had bombed Cardiff and Plymouth, and the announcer reported that "The Battle of Britain" had begun.

VA knew Larry was listening to reports on the radio as much as Bill. She couldn't think about him volunteering for British service when he didn't have to. Larry had worked so hard to graduate; she wanted nothing to spoil his ambitious plans, not to mention their future marriage.

With the "Battle of Britain" still raging, the Blitz began in September with massive German air bombings 56 out of 57 days and nights over London and surrounding areas. After decreasing the daytime attacks in October, the Luftwaffe continued the Blitz with a night bombing campaign aimed at seaports and industrial cities.

Larry completed his last semester at Southern in the spring of 1940. He graduated with a Bachelor of Science degree in Biology with a concentration in Pre-Medical studies. He was accepted into The University of Alabama Medical School and his classes would be held in the Birmingham Extension Center as he'd hoped.

Edward Johannsen entered his first year at Alabama Polytechnic Institute in Auburn, Alabama in September, while Lucy urged VA to leave Southern and enroll at Massey Business College in the fall to learn secretarial skills. Her mother assured her it would be much easier to gain employment with this kind of business education.

It didn't matter to her since Larry graduated, and Susie wasn't there anymore. Susie was now busy teaching at "Wee Ones," a kindergarten she hoped to own one day. And, she and Gabe were expecting a baby.

The US inaugurated the first peacetime draft in the fall of 1940. Every male from the age of 18 to 65 was required to register with their local draft board. Each district was given a unique identification, and the draftees names were written on slips of paper and would later be drawn from a fish bowl. Bill and Gabe registered in September of 1940, while Ed had to wait since he hadn't turned eighteen.

So far, the US wasn't involved in the war, but the Johannsen's felt the US would be within the year. VA knew Larry had registered but tried to push it out of her mind.

Larry's pre-med classes began in September, and his studies prohibited him from going out much. Even though she was disappointed, VA understood.

She spent a lot of time with her old friends Gayle Forrester, Sara Nell Ivey, and Katy Parker. They went shopping, to movies, and out to dinner mostly during the week. VA was beginning to dread going to the movies though, since the newsreels showed how the massive bombings targeted not only significant areas of the British government but also civilian neighborhoods. The film clips were devastating and brought the reality of war to the American public.

VA tried to keep the probability of war out of her mind. It seemed so far away, but she couldn't erase her memories of the film clips showing the war-torn communities of London, and the innocent civilians impacted.

Sitting in class at Massey, VA thought how she might be wasting her time. She typed with more speed than her instructor and it was hinted that she might be able to proceed to next year's stenography classes. VA hoped so since she was more than ready to start working.

There had to be something she could do if the US entered the war. Another reason was to earn money for the wedding and honeymoon. The date still hadn't been set, but she and Larry still had tentative plans for a December wedding in 1941.

With this war looming, they wouldn't commit since Larry could be called up at any time.

Jimmy Dorsey and His Orchestra was set to play in the Terrace Ballroom at Birmingham's swanky Tutwiler Hotel on Saturday night, November 8, 1940. Larry finagled tickets somehow, so he and VA planned a night of dinner and dancing to none other than a Dorsey brother.

The dress code was formal for the Terrace Ballroom, and VA found an evening gown in Burger-Phillips' window that would be perfect, since she didn't think Lucy had time to copy it.

The next day during her lunch hour from class, VA walked to Burger's and tried the gown on. It was a black satin, strapless with a floor-length satin skirt topped with soft black tulle. The finishing touch was a long matching tulle wrap accented with sequins. With a little money she had been saving, she bought the gown and arranged to have it delivered to the house.

When Saturday, the 8th arrived, VA slept late. Very seldom did she do so, but she knew that evening would be a late night. She woke around 10:00 AM, and to her dismay, Bill was listening to the latest war news.

"Bill, please let me hear some music for a while. I can't listen to war news today.".

"Okay, but just for a little while. I have to run an errand for Mama anyway," Bill said. "You need to come out of your fairytale and realize how serious the world situation is."

"I *know* how serious it is. Don't you think I worry about you, Gabe, Ed, and Larry every day? Worrying one of you will be called up? I'm trying to figure out a way to help if we do go to war. I might have my fairytale, but it keeps me from thinking about the war every minute of every day!"

Bill gave her a brotherly hug which was a welcome gesture. He understood. "Dance all day if you want to. I'll tune in tomorrow morning since I know you'll be in bed with a hangover." He laughed as he left the room.

VA immediately tuned in to her favorite music station. It was the Glenn Miller hour. She continued to listen but also worried about the war. She sat in her daddy's old chair with her knees up and her arms wrapped around them. After losing her father, she couldn't bear to lose another loved one.

The small radio on VA's vanity stayed on most of the time. She lit a cigarette while drying her hair and sang to the music. Her smooth olive skin needed little makeup, but she would highlight her eyes with black mascara and add a few swipes with the eyebrow pencil. She called for Eliza to help with her dress.

"Umm, umm, gal, you look awfully pretty," Eliza said. "You be the prettiest one there, I know it."

As she looked at her image in the mirror, VA

pinched her cheeks for a rosy blush and applied the subtle light red lip rouge.

"You always say just the right things, Eliza," VA said. "Thank you, I needed to hear that."

Larry arrived at 6:00 sharp. As he adjusted his tuxedo tie in the hall mirror, VA came down the stairs with a smile. He presented a clear box tied with pale pink satin ribbon filled with a corsage of two beautiful gardenias.

"Larry, these are my favorite!"

He knew they were her favorite flower and after she breathed in the sweet fragrance, she pinned them in her hair. Lucy arranged the sparkling tulle wrap around her shoulders.

They pulled up in front of the Tutwiler and Larry left his sedan with the valet. As they came into the lobby, they were one of many couples waiting to experience dinner and dancing to the music of Jimmy Dorsey.

Orchestra music was coming from the ballroom and as VA took his arm, they walked up an ornate circular staircase and stopped on the mezzanine where they greeted a few of his friends from medical school. One of them was Ezra Taylor, Jr., the son of Dr. Johannsen's old friend and medical partner. Ezra's date was Mary Laura Sims, a former sorority sister of VA's and now a senior at Southern.

Larry had reserved a table for two, but they worked it out with the maître'd for a larger table that accommodated four. Larry took VA's elbow and guided her into the ballroom and on to their table.

"Cigarette?" asked Larry after they were seated.

"Thanks, I'd love one," she said as he was ready with his lighter.

VA started smoking the year before, simply because everyone smoked. She thought it a sophisticated and classy vice. The sorority girls learned the correct way to smoke their cigarettes by always holding it between their index and middle fingers. Ring and pinky fingers must point down, even while lighting up. She had to remind herself not to light up before they were seated and never to hold the cigarette between her thumb and index finger; that was social suicide, even though actress Marlene Dietrich did it.

As she looked around the ornate ballroom, she noticed how the arc-shaped stage partially surrounded the dance floor. Behind the stage, sparkling sheer silver ruched draping fell from ceiling to floor. Each orchestra stand boasted a large JD. The ballroom looked beautiful in the soft lights, and the house orchestra was exceptional. They played a great rendition of Glen Miller's popular song "The Nearness of You". VA and Larry danced, and again, he sang the lyrics in her ear.

She rested her head on his shoulder as they danced, and he held her close.

When the song was over, they went back to their table, and Larry softly whispered in VA's ear, "The Nearness of You" will always remind me of you.

Jimmy Dorsey would be on after dinner, so Ezra ordered another round of drinks. The lights were turned up through the four-course dinner.

Suddenly, all the lights went out leaving only candlelight. The draping softly glittered while each musician took his place. The lights slowly came up, and Jimmy Dorsey and His Orchestra came into view.

The spotlight hit the dancefloor, and the orchestra' first number was "Blue Champagne." Patrons not dancing stood in front of the stage and swayed to the music. VA and Larry stayed at the table and listened.

When "Green Eyes" played, Larry offered his hand and loudly sang along with Bob Eberly, the male vocalist, as they danced.

VA wanted to see the female vocalist, Helen O'Connell as she sang "Tangerine," VA's favorite Dorsey song. The Jimmy Dorsey Orchestra sounded as great as their recordings; it was the perfect diversion from the impending war.

The late night turned into the early morning as the two couples left the Tutwiler and continued the evening at Birmingham's infamous Pickwick Nite Club.

Open Wednesday and Saturday nights only, the club's "vibro-cushioned" dance floor was packed, and the bar was standing room only. The swing-band, "Dickie Moreland and His Orchestra," played while patrons danced out into the street.

"This place is... great!" Larry slurred. "Why haven't we been here before? Did you see that mechanical horse bucking everyone off? I'm going to try it!"

"I want to see you try to get on the thing," VA said as she tried to finish her sentence before howling with laughter. "Your ass will never make it."

Larry got on the horse, but the first buck threw him five feet. Nothing was hurt but his ego.

"Let's dance, VA."

VA slept until noon the following day, and since Eliza was off on Sundays, she had to fend for herself for something to eat. The icebox always stayed full of food, so it wasn't hard to put something together. The phone rang, and as usual, VA hoped it was Larry. She answered and heard Lucy's voice.

"Susie had the baby," she said. "She and Gabe have a baby boy. All is well, but you and Bill need to get over here before visiting hours are over. I'm ready to go home."

VA called out to her brother, "Bill, we need to get to the hospital, now."

Steven Collier Johannsen was a beautiful baby with red, curly hair. Gabe glowed with pride as he looked at his son through the nursery viewing window. VA and Bill arrived and marveled at their new nephew. When the brothers began discussing the war, VA left and joined Lucy and the Langdon's in Susie's room. Susie, feeling groggy, smiled and took VA's hand.

"Steven is a beautiful baby, Susie," said VA.

Susie smiled again and closed her eyes.

Lucy said, "I'm ready to go."

CHAPTER 9

This Damned War

December 7, 1941

*B*eing Sunday morning, VA slept late as usual, but woke up to a loud radio announcer's voice and dishes clattering downstairs. She looked at the clock; it was 12:00 noon. She lit a cigarette, inhaled heavily and blew out the smoke.

"Did I sleep that late? Was it noon already? I couldn't have slept the whole Sunday away," she said to herself. VA went downstairs to find Lucy, Eliza, and Bill sitting in front of the radio in disbelief.

"What's happened?" VA asked.

They turned to look at her as Lucy said, "the Japanese have bombed Pearl Harbor. We will enter the war now."

President Roosevelt would address the nation soon. VA felt weak and could think of nothing but her brothers and Larry. They registered in a peacetime draft and now would be called to serve. In a fog of denial, she had visions of her brothers and Larry leaving to fight insane people in some ungodly place.

VA listened along with the others to President Roosevelt's address to the nation. FDR sounded so strong and confident. Even hearing him declare war on Japan eased her mind.

"He'll get us out of this," she said.

After being engaged for two years, VA wondered if the war was the real reason Larry put their wedding plans on hold. She hadn't even met his parents. It was now December, 1941, and he still wouldn't commit to a date.

She'd asked him about Christmas break, but he said it wasn't a good time. She then asked about spring break, 1942, but he still wouldn't give her an answer. VA was beginning to wonder if he'd changed his mind altogether.

They had plans to go to the Pickwick that night and VA would raise the question again.

When Larry escorted VA in to the Pickwick, she asked for a table in the back. She needed to talk to him and wanted no distractions. After he ordered drinks, VA lit a cigarette and inhaled deeply. She blew out the smoke and decided to come out with it.

"How come I've never met your parents, Larry?"

I need to meet them sometime, don't you think?" she asked.

"When the time's right. I need to plan it when my parents are on their best behavior, which is rare. You know Mother drinks, and my father is never home."

VA accepted his answer but felt he was sidestepping the issue. She didn't care if his mother was a drunk or if his father had a mistress. Why did he prolong the meeting? Was he avoiding it all, including the marriage?

"Is it me?" she asked. "Are you embarrassed to introduce me to them?

"Oh, God no," he said. "It's them. I've waited a long time for my parents to put me first and straighten out their differences. So far, that hasn't happened, and I hope you never meet them. They aren't worth the effort. I still live at home because I don't want to spend money on an apartment and I want nothing from them in the way of money."

"What is it then that's keeping us from getting married?"

"I know the inevitable is coming. I'll have to go overseas, and I don't want you to be a war widow. It's hard enough knowing I have to go but leaving you without financial security and alone is more than I can imagine." Larry grew teary-eyed.

"I don't care about that! I want you! I won't be alone, because you'll be back when it's all over, and we will pick up where we left off!" Virginia started to cry the tears she vowed never to shed. Larry was the only one who brought out such feelings in her.

"VA, please don't worry. It'll happen, I promise. I'm not sure what the date will be, but it will happen. You can count on your future with me."

More than a year had passed since they registered, and none of the boys had been called up. Finally, Gabe was notified by mail and enlisted in the Navy on December 18, 1941. He hoped his eyesight would cause him to be rejected, but he passed. Susie, understandably distraught, knew he had to go. Little Steve, a year old now and attached to his father, would be too young to miss him.

Bill knew he was next. How could Gabe be called before him? He had a wife and baby. It was in the government's hands, and when called, he would proudly go. The insane sons of bitches had to be stopped. He saw his friends and neighbors, one at a time, be deployed to Europe, North Africa, or the Pacific. Bill thought of how his mother had three sons ripe for the picking.

Ed came home for Christmas break and stayed glued to the radio. President Roosevelt declared war a year before, but so far Gabe had been the only one called. Was he to be next or Bill? He hoped to graduate from college before being called up.

Gabe, thankfully, was able to spend the holidays at home but was scheduled to leave for training at the Great Lakes Naval Station on December 27. He said his goodbyes to the family on the 26th, so only Susie and little Steve went with him to the bus station.

The Greyhound bus was scheduled to leave Birmingham for Atlanta promptly at 3:45 in the afternoon and then go on to Chicago. There were many other enlistees and their wives saying goodbye.

"I know you have to go, but I can't stand the thought of being without you," Susie said through tears.

"I'll be fine, don't worry," Gabe said. "I'll let you know when I have an address."

He kissed her and then little Steve. Gabe joined the fellow enlistees and boarded the bus.

As the bus rolled away, Susie asked another tearful wife, "how long can this go on?"

For two months, Bill had been seeing Mallory Smith on a regular basis. She was the cute, petite co-worker from Alabama Power he had casually dated a few years earlier. He kept it under wraps since they still weren't serious, and she wanted it to stay that way.

Her personality came across as quiet and casual,

and he liked her company. She wasn't a giggler and wore very little makeup. Her short, curly brown hair matched her short stature and dry personality. She wore practical, tailored suits to the office and tasteful, loose-fitting dresses at night. Mallory was intelligent, and Bill thought she was naturally beautiful.

Bill received his notification on January 15, 1942. He enlisted in the Army as a private on January 21, passed each medical exam, and was scheduled to report to Fort McClellan in Anniston, Alabama on February 1.

After trying not to, he had fallen in love with Mallory. They spent a lot of time together before he had to leave. He knew she wanted no serious commitment but how could he leave without telling her how he felt?

Mallory planned a casual goodbye dinner at Joy Young's Chinese Restaurant with a few of their coworkers. Bill didn't want to say goodbye like this, but he went along with it.

Mallory could act so loving and interested in so many ways, but tonight, she didn't sit next to him at the table. He assumed since they arrived separately, they would leave separately. After being served a great dinner by the family's favorite waiter, Charlie, the group began to disperse with only Mallory and Bill remaining.

"Great night. Glad they're gone," Bill chuckled.

"Me too," whispered Mallory. "I don't want you to go. I'll miss you so much."

He moved in closer and slipped his arm around her shoulder. With lips touching her ear, he whispered, "Why didn't you sit next to me?"

Mallory smiled with tears in her eyes, placed her hand on his handsome face and replied, "I'm afraid I'll lose you. You mean the world to me."

He knew then she felt the same as he did.

On Monday, February 1, Bill got up early to meet the 8:30 AM bus to Ft. McClellan. Lucy and Eliza prepared a special lunch for him the day before so the family could say goodbye.

Ed, away at college in Auburn, spoke to him by phone while Susie wrote Gabe with the news but hadn't gotten a reply. Bill wanted to leave the house alone and without fanfare. Only Mallory would see him off at the bus station.

Around fifty fellow enlistees were boarding the bus, and Mallory shed no tears just as Bill hoped. After they embraced, Bill climbed up the bus steps and found a window seat. As the bus pulled out, Bill opened the window, smiled and saluted Mallory.

When the bus drove out of sight, Mallory experienced an empty feeling she had never felt before. Tears welled up in her eyes as she returned to her car and headed to work.

CHAPTER 10

The Blue Room

Fall 1942

ecause of the war, rationing of gasoline, most food, and even silk stockings brought VA's life, as she knew it, to a stand-still. The family's 1938 sedan remained parked in the garage and would be taken out only for an emergency. The war and the instability of the country preempted the lives of everyone.

Graduating from Massey Business College in the spring of 1942, VA was immediately hired as a stenographer for Southern Bell Telephone Company. She spent most of her time working or going out with friends. With two brothers in the service and Larry waiting for his notification any day, she tried to keep herself busy.

Interning at Hillman Hospital, Larry could seldom get away, but he planned time off the weekend before Thanksgiving and surprised VA with tickets to Artie Shaw and his Orchestra. They would appear at the

Blue Room at the Roosevelt Hotel in New Orleans. The plan was to take the train with their friends, Ezra and Mary Laura Taylor, who were married six months earlier.

VA intended to buy a new evening gown for the trip, but Lucy wouldn't hear of it. With strict rationing, money was spent on allowed necessities, not trivial nonsense. Lucy told her to pick out an older gown and she would re-make it. After a few cross words with her mother, VA reluctantly agreed.

On the night before the trip, VA lay awake in her bed thinking of how her mother had been working all day re-making that old gown. She drifted off to sleep to the sound of the old rotary sewing machine that didn't stop until the early hours of the next morning.

The streamlined train pulled out of Birmingham on schedule at 9:00 AM on Friday morning and would arrive in New Orleans at 8:35 PM. At each railroad crossing the loud train whistle sounded, and the brakes hissed as the train screeched to a stop in almost every little country town in-between. The clickety-clackety sounds of the tracks under them and the smell of some passengers made it impossible to stay in their seats.

VA and Larry spent some of the trip in the club car, where they had a few cocktails and an abundance of hors-d'oeuvres. After two hours, they went back to their seats, opened the windows, and covered their noses.

They tried to relax before they got to New Orleans.

An abundance of cabs outside New Orleans' Union Station eagerly awaited new passengers. The two couples hailed the first "United Cabs" available and arrived at the beautiful old Roosevelt Hotel around 10:00 PM. Ezra and Mary Laura checked in while Larry and VA argued about having adjoining rooms.

"What's Mary Laura going to think?" VA asked. They'd never been in this situation before. When they planned the trip, she knew he had reserved adjoining rooms.

"Who gives a shit, VA?"

"Larry, we can't. What if something unplanned happens?"

He pounded his fist against the wall. "Don't you trust me by now? Look, VA, I want you with me. Please. Put your clothes in the other room. Take a bath in there too. I don't care," he pleaded as he lowered his voice to a whisper. "I want you to be next to me all night."

With nothing else said, Larry and VA checked into rooms 240 and 242. A door separated the two rooms, and it remained locked. They unpacked, changed clothes separately and were ready to meet their friends in the lobby for a late night in the city.

So many times, VA hoped to visit New Orleans but never had the chance, until now. That night, the old city glowed with dim gaslights, and the streets cast a gentle, misty shine from an early evening rain shower. Old hotels and apartment buildings with ornate iron balconies glistened from the humidity while their residents partied on them.

Being there with Larry felt romantic and exhilarating. The couples sipped drinks at the Monteleone Hotel, and Galatoire's. They grabbed a midnight snack at Arnaud's and a nightcap at The Lounge in the Roosevelt.

At 3:00 AM, the old hotel still bustled with activity. Guests checked in while soldiers slept on the lobby couches, chairs, and floors. Bellboys scrambled to accommodate each new guest. Exhausted, VA helped a splifficated Larry to his room and into bed.

"VA, please don't leave," he said, his voice slurred.

"I'll be back in a minute."

VA felt dirty from the train and the long night out. Knowing Larry would need help getting undressed and cleaned up, she decided to start a hot bath for herself and relax. He was probably passed out anyway and likely hadn't moved.

After applying bath powder and slipping on her nightgown, she quietly unlocked the door connecting their rooms to check on him.

To her surprise, he stood next to the bed in his bathrobe. His hair was wet, and his aftershave intoxicated her.

"Come here, Beautiful," he said.

"You aren't soused you stinker!" She smiled and slowly walked toward him. "How could I stay in a separate room?"

Larry gently took her in his strong arms and kissed her with so much passion she had to break away to catch her breath.

"Oh god." That was wonderful. They hadn't had time to be intimate lately because Larry's rigorous schedule. This would be the weekend to make up for lost time.

Larry untied his robe and was bare underneath. Ready for her, he unbuttoned her sheer gown and gently slid it off her shoulders and into a puddle on the floor. His hands wandered and touched each part of her body as he kissed her face, her neck, her breasts.

"You smell so good," he said softly.

He lay her on the bed as they kissed. Their mouths were one as she felt the part of him that she had to have. Suddenly he turned her over and entered her with the passion they both had been waiting for. The climax of their love lasted almost fifteen seconds. All VA could do was to lay there, limp, with Larry on top of her breathing heavily.

"Stay with me," he said.

Larry Abbott watched as his fiancée slept. He had to get up but gazing at her lovely face caused him to pull her close and shut his eyes for a few more minutes. Trying not to wake her, he slowly slipped out of bed and got dressed. The plan was to meet Ezra for breakfast in the hotel restaurant and get an early start. Larry had an important task at hand.

He had a surprise for VA and needed plenty of time to find the appropriate establishment. After walking most of the French Quarter with no luck, Larry and Ezra began to ask around for a shop still open for business. The war dealt a devastating blow to small retail businesses in New Orleans, especially for the item he wanted to buy.

At 3:00 PM, Larry was about to put his plan on hold. While riding the streetcar on St. Charles Avenue, he noticed a small advertisement that read:

Still Open!
Mr. L. Vidrine & Co.
Magazine Street & Felicity
"Dealing in the Finest Antiques & Rare Jewelry."

"Ezra! That's it!" Larry exclaimed.

They exited the streetcar and walked a few

blocks to the intersection of Magazine Street and Felicity. There, they found a small, beautiful old building. It dated back to 1878 and the shop within dealt in exquisite antiques from the 18th and 19th centuries as well as one of a kind pieces of estate jewelry. Mr. Lucien Vidrine greeted them and showed Larry his selection of rare, antique jewelry under glass.

One item caught Larry's eye as it seemed to radiate to each corner of the shop. Mr. Vidrine took it out of the case and presented it to him. The gems were flawless, and it looked small enough for her slim fingers. Larry found what he was looking for.

After learning its history and how the piece was acquired, it took another two hours to agree on a price. It was getting late when they caught the streetcar and headed back to the Roosevelt.

VA woke up at 10:00 AM and found herself alone. *Where was Larry?* She listened and heard no one in the bathroom. The adjoining room was also empty. After picking up the receiver on the room phone, she called Mary Laura to ask if he was with them.

"No, VA, Larry's not here, but I know he's with Ezra. They made plans to do something this morning, but I don't know what. Don't worry; they're fine."

"Meet me in the lobby for breakfast?" VA asked, feeling relieved.

"Sure, see you in ten minutes."

After making herself presentable, VA took the elevator to the lobby. She stopped at the Lounge and ordered a Ramos Gin Fizz as servicemen from every branch of the armed forces filled the bar and lobby. Some had women with them.

"These soldiers must be on leave since the women with them look like whores," she thought.

VA took her drink out to the lobby and bought a newspaper at the newsstand. Mary Laura joined her, and each found cushy chairs to sit in.

While looking around, they marveled at the beauty of the carved mahogany paneling, elegant inlaid marble flooring, and large crystal chandeliers that lined the main entryway. Huge columns separated the registration desk from the lobby area, and large golden eagles carrying the letter "R" embellished the walls over each elevator.

Cigarette smoke, the clinking of glassware, and loud voices filled the elegant lobby while VA and Mary Laura watched as young bellboys paged names for pending messages.

"I can't understand why Larry didn't tell me he had plans today. I hoped we could tour the Quarter today."

"Larry and Ezra went somewhere in the Quarter;

I don't know where. But, not to worry, VA, they're fine," Mary Laura assured her.

With Mary Laura's obvious knowledge of their whereabouts, VA relaxed a little and enjoyed being in the center of excitement in the lobby. She read the war news of the week on the front page of The Times-Picayune, November 21, 1942:

US NAVAL BATTLE OF GUADALCANAL
U.S. VICTORY!

She wondered if Gabe was part of the long Guadalcanal Campaign. Susie told them he was in the Pacific but he didn't say where. *Thank God we had a victory!*

As she continued to read the article, a waiter approached to take their order. VA wasn't very hungry but felt she needed to eat something.

Mary Laura started with a Mimosa, then ordered assorted fruit, biscuits with peach preserves, and coffee for two. The attentive waiter stayed close by and filled their coffee cups five times.

After breakfast, they explored more of the lobby and passed the entrance to the Blue Room where a large sign on an easel advertised Artie Shaw's appearance. A large SOLD OUT banner crossed the sign, and they heard soft music playing behind huge golden doors. After they listened for a few minutes, a security guard shooed them away.

They looked around in the gift shop for souvenirs. The shelves were almost bare, but Mary Laura found a small Cajun cookbook, and VA bought a New Orleans shot glass. There wasn't much to choose from since the gift shop sold off most of their existing inventory and was about to close due to the war. VA suggested they take a walk around the French Quarter and sightsee since they had a free afternoon.

Nighttime was certainly different from daytime in the Vieux Carré. Bourbon Street offered nothing but seedy, exotic, and risqué entertainment. War workers from nearby Higgins Industries and visiting servicemen made up the majority of paying customers.

Mary Laura wanted to see St. Louis Cathedral on Jackson Square, then have a Café au lait with beignets at Café du Monde. After a few hours of seeing nothing but closed shops and very few traditional tourists, the girls decided to go back to the hotel and rest before the night ahead.

The Blue Room opened their doors at 6:00 PM for cocktails, dinner at 7:00, then Artie Shaw and the Orchestra would appear at 8:00.

VA, now extremely anxious about Larry's whereabouts called Mary Laura's room. Ezra wasn't back either, and she didn't sound worried at all. *Hmm... Mary Laura knows something and is keeping it to herself.* She looked at her watch and noticed it was almost 5:00.

After showering, VA expected Larry to walk in any minute. She pinned up her dark hair and slipped on her re-made light blue gown with the sexy low back. Lucy had worked her magic on the dress, and VA was glad she hadn't wasted money on a new one.

The girls met as planned outside the Blue Room and walked in unescorted. They stopped at the bar, and each ordered a champagne cocktail. The waiter showed them to their table on the edge of the dance floor. *How lucky could they get?*

To VA's surprise, Larry and Ezra were standing at the table. Larry, dressed in his blue suit, looked like an advertisement in a menswear magazine. As they seated the girls, he explained how he had been on a special mission with Ezra the entire day.

Piped-in dance music played through large speakers as couples filed in, so Ezra and Mary Laura excused themselves to the dance floor.

"VA, you look lovely," Larry began, "I've been planning this for tonight, and I don't quite know where to begin."

"Planning what?" she asked. "I've been so worried about you. Where were you, and why didn't you let me know you were going somewhere?"

He reached into his pocket and pulled out a small box, placed it on the table, then motioned with his eyes for her to open it. She did, then gasped as the most gorgeous diamond ring she had ever seen sparkled brightly under the house lights. Her hands began to tremble as she picked up the box.

"I'm sorry you haven't had a real engagement ring. So many times, I felt like a failure but had to wait. Since my internship at Hillman, I've saved most of my small salary, and it was all for this ring. I promised you'd have one a long time ago. Never would I accept monetary help from my parents."

Speechless, VA could do nothing but throw her arms around Larry's neck and take in his intoxicating smell and the loving feeling of his embrace. She pulled back and looked into his deep blue eyes. With two fingers, she lined the shape of his beautiful lips. Softly, VA put her hand on his cheek and gave him a slow, loving kiss.

"I love you," she whispered as her lips gently touched his ear.

Returning to the table, Ezra explained how they found the perfect ring at an antique and rare jewelry dealer on Magazine Street. Jewelers were hard to find now because of the war, but with luck and determination, Larry found Mr. Vidrine's little shop. Still overwhelmed, VA watched as Larry slipped the diamond ring on her finger.

"What a romantic way to give me this ring," VA whispered in his ear, "this setting, our friends, this city. It's the most beautiful ring I've ever seen, and I can't believe it fits!"

VA maintained her composure and glanced around the room. She liked the modern decor with the unusual columns surrounding the dance-floor. Behind the stage, sparkling light blue fabric hung and the letters AS appeared on the front of each orchestra stand.

After dinner and dessert, the house lights dimmed, and the room filled with applause. The famous song, "Comes Love" began to play, and bright spotlights illuminated Artie Shaw and his Orchestra.

When female vocalist, Helen Forrest, walked on stage, the whistles were deafening. Larry and VA danced to almost every song as Artie played their favorites. After ninety minutes, the final set ended with "Stardust," and the crowd erupted again while calling for an encore.

Artie in his cocky glory came back out and said, "The only encore for this lively group is…" the orchestra performed "Begin the Beguine." Applause filled the Blue Room as patrons again crowded the dance floor. As they danced, VA looked into Larry's deep blue eyes and she pulled him closer.

"I'm so happy. I'm the luckiest girl to have found you."

Larry took her face in his hands and softly kissed her as they danced. As the song ended, they continued to dance while the other couples left the floor.

"Okay, you two, music stopped," said Ezra.

After the encore and a continuous standing ovation, couples began to leave. Ezra and Mary Laura excused themselves and retired to their room.

A few couples stayed and danced to the piped-in music. As "The Nearness of You" softly played from the speakers, Larry took VA's hand and pulled her close while gently leading the girl of his dreams across the dance floor. This song was their song, and they repeated the words as they looked into each other's eyes.

"This has been the most unforgettable weekend, Larry. You have made my dreams come true. I love you and always will," VA whispered.

Sunday morning came, and they were back on the streamlined train heading to Birmingham at 8:00 AM. The two couples stayed in their seats and drank only ice water.

VA couldn't take her eyes off the ring. The large emerald-cut diamond was set in a silver antique filigree design laden with ten small diamonds.

"The ring dates back to 1886. Mr. Vidrine purchased it through an exclusive 'dealers only' estate sale from the Garden District of New Orleans," Larry said. "The original owner of the ring was a woman by the name of Aimee Dominique Fontenot. At 83, she was the last surviving member of the Fontenot family. They were part of the old New Orleans aristocracy. The only reason it hadn't been purchased earlier was because of the war."

"I'll never take it off. It's the most beautiful ring I've ever seen. You've given me a cherished memory I'll never forget as long as I live."

Arriving back in Birmingham, Larry grabbed a taxi to take VA home. As the cab waited, they both ran in to show Lucy and Eliza her ring.

Lucy looked at it with little emotion, and merely said, "It's pretty."

Eliza loved the ring because she adored Larry. Everything he did was right, in her opinion. As Larry entered the living room, Eliza walked toward him with loving arms outstretched.

"Oh, Mr. Larry, you made our gal so happy!"

Larry called VA the following week to meet him for dinner after work at Joy Young's. He sounded strange, but she shrugged it off. Arriving early, she asked their favorite waiter, Charlie, to select a table for them. He did, and when Larry arrived, Charlie led him upstairs to a small private dining table and closed the privacy curtains behind him.

"VA, my letter came yesterday," he said as he fidgeted in his chair. "I have to go to basic training first and then overseas as an Army surgeon. I leave on

Thursday, December 10th, for Ft. McClellan."

With a shaky hand, VA lit a cigarette. Charlie brought in the cocktails, and she asked if he would also bring her a straight bourbon on the rocks. She kept the existing whiskey sour and toasted Larry.

"VA, I'm sick about it," Larry said.

"I have two brothers gone and may end up God knows where. Now you. I can't bear to think of losing any of you." She felt unwanted tears in her eyes.

Larry spent time with his parents the night before he left for Ft. McClellan. Rarely were William Abbott and Bitsy Abbott in the same room, and it caused the time together at their large house tense and uncomfortable.

"Do you know where you might end up, Son?" William asked.

"No, Dad, I only know Ft. McClellan. After that, we'll probably be sent to a field hospital training facility."

"Oh, Larry, just explain to the Army you're needed heah at home," said Bitsy. "I hate the thought of you traipsing around some horrible, dirty country, and not knowing anything about those people."

"Mother, I have no choice."

Larry shifted his glance toward his father as he rolled his eyes and shrugged. William Abbott wanted a good relationship with his son, and Larry knew it. They met for dinners and occasional lunches but seldom spent any time together at the house. William and Bitsy stayed away from each other for the most part which made life at home empty and unpleasant.

VA met Larry at the downtown Birmingham bus station at 7:30 AM on the 10th. After anxiously looking for him through the vast crowd of fellow enlistees, she spotted him. Standing alone on the platform, he wore his dark-brown suit and carried a small leather valise. When he saw her walking toward him, he removed his hat, and that black curl fell over one eye. Larry smiled as VA ran to him.

I may never see him again. The agony of his leaving overwhelmed her. After holding back her tears, she unloaded them as she sobbed and held him tight.

"Please write and let me know how and where you are," she pleaded. "I love you so."

After a long embrace, he looked at her with tears of his own. "I love you, Virginia. Please wait for me." He then gave her a soft, gentle kiss. "Try to make that one last until I come back home."

Larry boarded the bus to Ft. McClellan, waved and blew her a kiss. Smiling through tears and trying not to collapse, VA waved as the bus disappeared around the corner and out of sight.

CHAPTER 11

Mallory

Spring 1943

Two Blue Star service flags proudly hung in the Johannsen's living room window. The stars represented each son or daughter on active duty. Lucy made them herself and wanted to make sure they were ready and on display soon after Gabe and Bill left.

Bill was coming home for the first time in a little over a year. VA couldn't wait to see him. It was the middle of March, 1943, and Ed would be home on Saturday for spring break. The only one missing would be Gabe. Susie kept the family updated on his whereabouts and brought little Steve over to see Lucy and VA every Saturday.

On Wednesday, the screened door to the kitchen opened to a familiar masculine voice that escalated to "Where's my Mama?"

Eliza dropped the potato she was peeling. "Oh,

Lawd, Mr. Billy, you a sight," she said and tearfully put her hands to her cheeks. "I'll find yo Mama."

"No need, Eliza," Bill said while giving her a long hug. "I know where she is." Bill went to the sewing room and knocked. "Where's my Mama?" he asked as he poked his head through the cracked door.

Lucy looked up and smiled, clearly glad to have him home. "You look so much like your father," she said. "How long can you stay?"

"Only a week, but I have a lot to do in this one week," he replied.

Bill intended to bring Mallory over to meet his family and hopefully, plan a wedding for the fall. He knew his next leave would be the last one before going overseas. They had been corresponding regularly, and he knew she still felt as he did.

It felt good to sleep in his own bed. The barracks bunk passed, but it was nothing like *his* bed. Ft. Benning, Georgia, where he was assigned to infantry school, wasn't far from home.

The ride home on the troop train was long but not unbearable. He planned to bring Mallory to the house Friday night and announce their engagement. Of course, he had to ask her first. If all went according to his plan, she would accept.

The next day, he went to one of the few jewelers

in Birmingham still open and decided on a beautiful engagement ring set with one large diamond surrounded by eight smaller ones. If she accepted his proposal, he would come back for the matching wedding band.

Lucy and Eliza planned Bill's favorite meal for Friday night. He told them that night would be special, and with no questions asked, they went to work.

Even though rationing was in full force, Lucy saved most of her ration stamps. Normally, with just three to feed, they could get by with what they grew in their Victory Garden and what they stored in the food cellar. On this special night though, they loaded down the table with fried chicken, mashed potatoes, green beans, fresh corn, and banana pudding for dessert. It had been a long time since they had dinner quite like this.

Bill opened the front door and ushered in a very cute, petite young lady. "Mama, I want you to meet Mallory Smith," he said.

"I'm happy to meet you, Mallory," Lucy said. "This is Bill's sister, Virginia, and our good friend, Eliza Jackson. Virginia, take Mallory to the dining room for a drink."

As the girls left, Lucy said, "She must be special. I've never seen such a twinkle in your eye."

"She is, Mama."

VA liked Mallory instantly and could see her as a good friend. She wasn't like the girls Bill dated in the past. He, being the handsome football jock, sometimes dated the loose vamps that chased after him. Mallory seemed quite the opposite. Bill stood six feet tall, and Mallory couldn't have been any taller than 5'2". She was soft-spoken, quiet, and sophisticated. *Obviously, Bill is smitten with the smart, well-educated ones.*

Bill announced their engagement at the dinner table. They planned to get married on his next leave, estimated to be in November or December. Everyone was pleased with the news, and VA hoped Mallory would let her help with the wedding plans.

After two helpings of banana pudding, Bill escorted Mallory to the living room, turned down the lights, and turned on the radio. They both lit a cigarette and danced to the slow song, "In a Sentimental Mood" by Benny Goodman.

VA stood in the hall and silently watched them. They seemed to be in their own world, smoke rising as they held their cigarettes. They needed their privacy, so she went back to the kitchen and helped with the clean-up.

Larry had been away four weeks, and his letters didn't come as regularly as she hoped. She'd only received two. VA wrote him almost every day. She couldn't eat or sleep worrying about why he wasn't writing, so she asked Bill.

"He's in basic training. Do you have any idea how busy he is? He has no time to wipe his ass much less write a letter," Bill said, obviously trying to make her feel better. "I guarantee he'll write when he gets a spare moment. I know, I've just been through it."

Ed arrived home from Auburn on Saturday afternoon, just in time to see Bill since he'd received orders to report back to base on the next bus. He didn't know the reason, but he had to leave early on Sunday morning to make it back to Georgia by 6:00.

While spending time with his big brother, Ed informed Bill about the boys they knew from West End who had either been killed in action or were missing. Their neighbor, Bob Ladner, had been shot down in North Africa and left behind a wife and infant daughter.

He learned of the Birmingham casualties from Mallory's letters and silently, he worried his training wouldn't be enough. The war wasn't only a battle for territory and liberation; it was a battle to destroy the devil himself.

The brothers were able to tune in a static-filled Radio Free Europe for war updates. It seemed the Allies needed a lot more training in North Africa. The troops were no match for the German Panzers, so FDR replaced the inept 2nd Corps commander there with General George Patton, and the troops were quickly whipped into shape.

Bill pounded his fist on the table. "The goddamn Krauts are *not* going to succeed with their so-called 'Thousand Year Reich.' They can 'zeig heil' their way straight to hell."

Sunday morning after Bill left, Lucy felt a tremendous sense of emptiness. She went to her room, closed the door, and prayed for her two sons and Ed who would probably be leaving soon. Lucy also prayed for Larry.

She called on "Walter" to help watch out for them. After twenty-six years, he never left her thoughts, and she would quietly talk to him when she felt alone. If he had lived, Walter would have been her fourth son heading off to war.

Ft. McClellan
March 15, 1943

My Dearest VA,

I've been so busy with basic training; I haven't had spare time for anything except to eat and sleep. Please don't worry if you don't hear from me often. I'll write when I can. It looks like we are going to the Medical Field Service School in Carlisle Barracks, Pennsylvania, in the next few weeks. I miss you so and hope to have leave before we go. One of the guys had the radio on the other night and "The Nearness of You" came on, and I missed you so much. Heard Ezra was in North Africa. I'll close now since the only light I have is from my lighter. Please keep writing, and I pray to see you soon. I send much love.

Larry

Bill was right. Hearing it from Larry made her feel much better, even though the letter was short and the misery of missing him was almost more than she could bear. VA felt sure he would be sent overseas after Medical Field School.

Mary Laura told her about Ezra, and that he was attached to the 2nd Corps in North Africa. VA remembered Mary Laura talking about Ezra's last letter and how heavy the casualties were. The terrain was dry, desolate, and hot as hell. He couldn't wait to move somewhere, anywhere. The letter had been dated a month before, so General Patton probably hadn't arrived yet. Ezra told her he thought their commander was a wimp, and the troops had no leadership.

Scrap metal and rubber had become commodities. The entire country was donating unused iron beds, pots, pans, old rusted out cars, bald tires, and anything that could be useful to the war effort. Lucy and Eliza saved bacon grease by the half gallon to donate. Bacon grease was used to make ammunition, and scrap metal was used for shells and bombs.

The four main instructions to civilians were: (1) not to waste anything (2) buy only what was necessary (3) salvage what you don't need and (4) share what you have. The city would come once a week to pick up the donated scrap metal. Every man, woman, and child in America proudly took part in the war effort, even if it consisted of nothing but bottle caps.

Gabe informed Susie he had orders to report to a new battleship in the Pacific, but that was all he could say. The Navy had already taken Japan in the Battle of Midway, and the Marines had taken Guadalcanal in the Solomon Islands. There was still a lot to do there, and he would write as much as he could. He seemed fine, and Susie assured Lucy that if it were possible, he would let her know of any change in location but felt this would be his home for a while.

VA and Mallory kept in close touch after Bill left and met for lunch whenever possible. VA always included Mallory when she and Susie planned a night out or just a dinner and music at home. The three girls liked each other's company and planned to meet as much as their schedules allowed.

Larry was relocated to the Medical Field School in April, 1943. VA went to the mailbox every day with high hopes, but an official letter addressed to Edward R. Johannsen replaced the letter she expected. She ran in and gave it to Lucy who didn't hesitate to open it.

Ed was ordered to go to the local enlistment

board on May 25 to sign up and have all the required medical tests, just as his brothers had. Lacking one semester of his senior year at Auburn, Ed still had five months to go before graduation. He would have to leave it behind and finish when he got home.

At almost 21 years old, Edward Johannsen enlisted in the Navy where he was encouraged to join the Naval Aviation branch. On June 3, he left for training in Memphis, Tennessee, then on to Pensacola, Florida, for flight school.

Carlisle Barracks, PA
May 20, 1943

My darling VA,

We just broke for lunch, and I'm writing as I eat. Believe it or not, basic training is essential to field medicine. If they hadn't forced me into shape, I would never be able to do this job. Being a field medic will be grueling and heartbreaking. It's such a different type of medicine and surgery, and hopefully, I'm up to it. There's a small canteen here with music and local girls to dance with, but Thomas (my buddy from Chattanooga) usually comes with me, and we only drink bourbon and sing to the music. I'm patiently waiting for your next letter. I save each one. Much love is being sent your way,

Larry

VA saved each of his letters, too, and kept them in a shoebox in her cedar chest. When she had nothing to do, she took them out and read each one all over again. There were only a few, but she reserved a large shoebox anyway. Maybe the plans she had made with the girls would take her mind off the war and how much she missed Larry.

Susie and Mallory picked VA up for dinner and a movie at 5:30. They planned to see "Watch on the Rhine" with Bette Davis or "Stormy Weather" with Lena Horne. After cocktails and dinner at Ed Salem's Restaurant, Susie picked "Stormy Weather" since it had nothing to do with the war, and they needed a good musical.

Unfortunately, the newsreel before the movie was full of war news. It showed Europe's devastation plus the arrests and slaughter of innocent civilians in the small towns in France, Austria, and Poland.

The next film clip covered the bombing in England and how London was demolished for the most part. VA put her head down and stopped watching. The Allies had to stop this, but she hated that her brothers and Larry would be in the middle of it.

The news from the Pacific showed older clips of the Allied victory at Guadalcanal and the Aleutian Islands. Susie said she had no idea if Gabe's ship was involved in either of these. His last few letters from the

Pacific had been censored. They had censor stamps in the lower left corner and were taped closed. Some parts of the letters were cut out, so all she could figure was that he was well and how much he wanted to be home with his wife and son.

The war slogan was "Loose Lips Sink Ships" so she understood about the censorship and knew Gabe wasn't stupid.

After the movie, the girls dropped in at their favorite Pickwick Club for a nightcap and to listen to some good music. The Shepard Fleming Orchestra was playing, and the girls remembered them from fraternity dances at Southern.

As they approached the bar, only two seats were available. A handsome soldier politely got up and motioned for VA to take his seat. With a gracious smile, she thanked him. He had been sitting with three other soldiers apparently on leave. The girls were discussing Mallory's upcoming wedding when the handsome soldier tapped VA on the shoulder.

"There's a lot of good music going to waste. Care to dance?" he asked.

She didn't think she should, but Mallory and Susie thought otherwise. They shooed her off and returned to the wedding plans.

"My name is Julian Morley. My buddies and I are on leave before heading to New York. I hope you don't mind my asking you to dance. The other guys are dancing, and I was standing there all alone," he said while motioning a fake tear coming from his eye.

"When are you going?" she asked with a chuckle. She could tell right away this man had a wandering eye and was full of himself.

"We board the train for New York day after tomorrow, and then, who knows?" Julian answered. "I have to say, you have the most beautiful green eyes I've ever seen."

As they danced, VA told him about Gabe being in the Pacific and how Bill and Larry were waiting for orders. She danced two more dances with him before it was time to go.

Susie and Mallory watched VA the entire time. It was all innocent fun, but on the way home, VA felt guilty for having fun without Larry.

Carlisle Barracks, Pennsylvania
August 15, 1943

My beautiful VA,

I've requested leave for September 1 and let's pray to God I get it. The war newsreels are getting us all down, and I'm beginning to worry about not having enough knowledge to help the wounded. The film clips are showing so many devastating injuries and since I'll be in the line of fire myself; I worry I won't be able to treat them. Oh, by the way, I got a promotion to Captain since I had more hospital and interning experience from the get-go. I will be second in command of our field unit when we arrive overseas. Hoping you and Susie are having fun planning Bill's wedding and wish I could be there. I miss you so much, and I plan to see you in September.

With all my love,

Larry

She tossed the letter in the air and caught it while jumping on her bed like a child. She couldn't wait! Only two weeks away, she would have to take a few days off from work while Larry was home, hoping to get married.

Maybe she would meet his parents after all these years, although she didn't care if she ever met them. Larry was all she needed from the Abbott family.

The doorbell rang and Bobby Ames, the Western Union delivery boy, stood at the door.

"Telegram for you, Miss Johannsen," Bobby said.

VA's heart sank. She gave Bobby a tip and shut the front door. She knew about telegrams and how they were bringing bad-news every day. They now had three blue star flags in the window.

VA, alone in the house, decided to open it when Lucy or Eliza got home. She put it on the table and went out to the sleeping porch and basked in the breeze blowing in. Rain was predicted, so everything seemed to be cooling off. Too nervous to wait, VA went back inside, picked up the telegram, and took it back to the porch to open it.

```
August 25, 1943

CHATTANOOGA, TENNESSEE

VA AM ALMOST HOME (STOP) MEET
ME AT THE TRAIN STATION
(STOP) 930 PM ON 25TH (STOP)

LARRY
```

She dropped the telegram unable to believe he would be there in a matter of hours, and she had just read his last letter! He must not have had time to call.

VA waited on the platform as the Southern Railway passenger train No.1 chugged in from Chattanooga in the rain. The train arrived right on time, and she watched as soldiers, families, and businessmen stepped off.

Suddenly, she saw the handsome face with short, black tousled hair trying to pop out from under his uniform cap. And that beautiful smile. She perched on her tiptoes and waved. He had already spotted her when the train pulled in. She pushed herself through passengers and porters pulling heavy luggage until she had him in her arms. Larry kissed her in front of everyone, but neither of them cared. No one else paid attention, anyway.

"I got the telegram four hours ago," she said as her voice broke. The damned tears were trying to flow again, but she fought them back.

"They granted leave a week early. The army surprised me," Larry said with tears of joy in his eyes. His emotions were about to take over, too.

Larry drove the car straight to the house on Tuscaloosa Avenue. Eliza had a late snack waiting and prepared Bill's downstairs bedroom for him. Larry had lost some weight but looked like he had gained a good bit of muscle.

VA couldn't wait to be alone with him, but he looked tired, so she thought they should just say good night. Larry reluctantly agreed, took a double shot of bourbon and kissed VA one last time for the night.

The next morning after a huge breakfast, Larry took VA to meet his parents.

The Abbott's large estate was "over the mountain" and close to Susie's father's vast property.

Borrowing Lucy's car, VA and Larry drove up to the large, black iron gates. He got out of the car, opened the gates, and then drove up a long driveway surrounded by large trees, beautiful gardens, and a perfectly manicured lawn.

When they stopped in front of the triple garage and carriage house, Larry peeked in a window to make sure his car was still there. VA nervously straightened her dress and checked the seams in her only pair of stockings. Larry told her how lovely she looked and how proud he was for his parents to meet her.

The house, built of grey limestone, looked three stories high. She could live comfortably in the carriage house apartment over the garage.

Larry didn't want to take her in the back door but rather through the front. As he opened the large heavy wooden door, a beautiful collie greeted them. VA quickly stepped back. She was afraid of dogs, but this one seemed friendly enough.

"This is Tallulah," Larry said as he briskly petted her head and neck. "She's named after Tallulah Bankhead. My mother knew her back in their younger days."

VA reached down, petted Tallulah and quickly lost all fear. She was a sweet dog and even licked her hand.

"Larry is that you, Honey?" a loud, aristocratic

southern female voice called from the drawing room.

"Yes, Mother, and I brought Virginia with me."

"Won-da-ful, Darling. Come on in!"

VA was amazed but also amused at the massive double staircase. It wouldn't surprise her if Cinderella floated down in a huge ball gown to meet Prince Charming. Heavy credenzas and large family portraits consumed each wall in the entryway as well as ornate mirrors.

The walls in the drawing room were painted light peach with floor to ceiling French doors surrounded by drapes in heavy green brocade fabric. More portraits and mirrors filled the walls while puffy upholstered sofas and chairs dared someone to sit on them.

An attractive middle-aged woman with dark hair and heavy, caked makeup greeted them. She stood next to the huge fireplace and wore a colorful silk kimono. She held a champagne glass in one hand and a cigarette holder in the other.

"Hello, Fa-gin-ya! I am so glad to meet my son's girl!" Mrs. Abbott said in a sickeningly sweet voice. "I am 'Bitsy' Patton Abbott and I wondahed when I would evah meet you."

"Mother, this is Virginia Johannsen, and we are engaged to be married," Larry said.

She sauntered toward VA and greeted her with a limp handshake.

"What? Do tell! When and whea?" she asked. "I'll certainly be thea." She held her arms out for Larry to come to her for arm's length hug and an air kiss.

"We haven't set the date, but soon," Larry answered. "I'm home for a week, so we don't have the time on this leave."

VA suddenly felt disappointed, but not surprised.

"Well, Fa-gin-ya, what do you have to say about that?" Mrs. Abbott asked in what struck VA as a snooty and bitchy sort of way.

"I can't say anything. The war is dictating all of our lives for now," VA answered. "When Larry gives me the word, we'll start the simple plans."

"That damned woah. That's all I evah hear about. You'll have a big wedding at our church, won't you? I insist. But of course, it's your wedding." Mrs. Abbott grimaced and took a long drag from her cigarette.

I doubt that bitch has donated anything to the war effort. One of those damn curtain rods could make a thousand rounds of ammunition.

"We'll see, Mother. I can't make any definite plans yet. I wanted to tell you both at the same time; I'm shipping out to England in four days." Larry looked at VA. "That's why I got my leave so early."

All VA could do was look back at him with surprise. She felt sick and thought she might faint. Larry had to steady her.

"How could you be so mean not to tell Fa-gin-ya?" Bitsy asked.

"Because I wanted to tell the most important women in my life at the same time, and I wanted VA to meet you before I left." Larry's voice conveyed his irritation. "Where's Dad?"

"At the office or somewhere with who knows what," Mrs. Abbott replied. "I see him on rare occasions." She checked her empty glass. "How about a drink?" Without waiting for an answer, she opened a beautiful cabinet filled with every kind of liquor, soda, champagne, and wine imaginable. Plus, crystal glasses in every shape and size.

Has she ever heard of rationing? Black Market, definitely.

"Mother, it's only 11:30 in the morning. Too early for us," Larry said as he lit a cigarette for VA and himself.

"Well, sit down and tell your Mama about Fa-gin-ya and her people," she said. "I want to know who her daddy is and whea they're from."

"Mother, we have to go, but I'll fill you in later in the week. I'll be back because I want to see Dad."

They said their polite goodbyes, and VA had never been so ready to leave a place in her life. *What a fake, alcoholic bitch!* She didn't seem to care if Larry was going overseas at all. From now on, VA vowed to herself, she would secretly call Larry's mother "Bitchy" Abbott, not "Bitsy."

VA said nothing the entire way home. She couldn't believe Larry kept this from her until now. They would have to wait even longer to get married. *What if he never came back?* She couldn't bear that thought.

Larry finally connected with his father but only for a brief lunch, so she didn't have a chance to meet him. VA was glad Larry stayed at her house since he had no real home to go to. From what she could tell, his mother was a snooty bitch and his father, a slimy asshole.

The last night of his leave proved to be a solemn one. Larry wanted to take VA to Joy Young's restaurant and sit at their favorite private table. He had so much to remember while he was gone. VA wanted to hold on to his arm and stay as close to him as she could. She never wanted to let him go. When they arrived at the restaurant, Charlie was waiting for them, had their table reserved, and ready with a bourbon on the rocks and a whiskey sour.

"I hope this be satisfactory, Mister Larry," he said with a smile.

"Yes, this is perfect, Charlie. You always know what we need." Larry tipped him a five-dollar bill. After sitting a few minutes, Larry swallowed and shook his head.

A look came over his face she'd never seen before. "I can't imagine the horror I'm going to see," he confided. "We've trained for the worst, but I'm afraid I won't be up to it."

"You will be up to it because you have the knowledge and experience. That's why you were promoted to help lead the field unit," VA said.

He nodded, but the task at hand clearly terrified him. After saying goodbye to Charlie, they took a drive through the Southern campus, passed Holms Drugstore, and then parked the car in the driveway of the Johannsen house.

"Let's walk," Larry said.

He took VA's hand as they strolled the moonlit block lined with large old homes. Larry always felt this was his neighborhood. The full moon kept disappearing behind clouds, but they had enough moonlight to see the canopy of oak and elm trees lining Tuscaloosa Avenue. A faint smell of smoke filled the air as embers continued to glow from burned leaves. Larry spent more time on this street in his adult life than he had with his parents.

"As long as you're by my side and waiting for me,

I can endure the horrors I will see and the battles I will witness," he said.

"Don't worry; I will always be here waiting for you."

"VA, please love me tonight before I leave."

"Come to my room later," she said.

They walked back to the house to find Lucy in the living room listening to the latest war news.

"I want to thank you for everything, Mrs. Johannsen," he said. "If I don't see you in the morning, please keep me in your thoughts, just as if I were your son, too."

Lucy nodded, and to VA's surprise, she got up and hugged him.

"Don't worry, Larry," Lucy said. "You *are* part of this family, and I will pray for you just as I do my three sons."

VA smiled. She had never seen her mother act so tenderly.

VA had been in bed for two, long hours before she heard a quiet knock on her bedroom door. She got up and answered it. Larry stood there in his bathrobe, elbow propped on the door frame while thumping his temple with his fingers.

She pulled him in, shut the door, and kissed him while untying his robe. She wanted him in every way imaginable. He wanted her every bit as much, and she gave him all she had. They rocked with sexual delight which lasted until they peaked with a feeling of intense orgasmic pleasure. VA had been waiting for this since New Orleans. She had almost forgotten the feelings he brought out in her.

"VA never forget how much I love you. No matter what happens."

Larry stayed in her room all night and rose at 6:00 AM. He tip-toed down to Bill's old room and grabbed his uniform. After a quick shower, he realized there wasn't much time to get to the station by 8:00. As he tied his shoes, the aroma of breakfast filled the house.

Eliza, already in the kitchen, offered Larry a weak cup of coffee and homemade toast.

"Thank you, Eliza," he said. "This is hard for me."

"I know Mr. Larry. It be a hard day for us all. Miz Johannsen is sewing a blue star for you to add to the three she already have."

He was never so touched. No one, not even his own mother, cared enough to place a blue star in a window for him. The sound of VA running down the back stairs added a touch of frenzy to the previously tranquil kitchen. He couldn't be late for the train. Stealing a glance at VA's worried face, he smiled at her disheveled look.

VA grabbed a cup of coffee and grimaced after taking a sip.

"I'll be so glad when we don't have to dilute the coffee anymore. I might as well be drinking hot water."

"I'll see you when I get home," Larry said to Eliza as she brushed a tear from her cheek. "Take care of my girl."

The Birmingham Terminal Station was crowded with servicemen. VA couldn't begin to guess where they were all going. The #2867 troop train stretched as far as the eye could see as passengers waited to begin boarding. It appeared almost full, which made sense since its point of departure had been San Antonio, Texas, and then through to Atlanta. The final destination was Newport News, Virginia, at the Hampton Roads point of embarkation. From there the troops would be deployed overseas.

"Please write," he said. "I'll send you my address when I have one; I love you."

"I'll never forget last night," VA whispered in his ear. "Please come home to me. I have no life without you."

The train whistle blew, signaling time to board. They hugged, kissed and hugged some more. Larry boarded the train, and VA watched as he found a seat. Lowering the window, he waved. As tears streamed down her face, VA whispered, "I love you."

CHAPTER 12

A Sad Goodbye

December 1943

Mallory's last letter from Bill said he would be home on December 15, 1943. He had been stationed at Camp Miles Standish in Massachusetts for winter training. His outfit would leave for Boston on January 4th before shipping out to England on January 18. Bill instructed her to plan the wedding because while he was home, they would be married. Now she had a wedding to plan.

Mallory's mother, Mrs. Edna Smith, and VA accompanied her to a quaint bridal shop in Forest Park, close to her home.

The shop featured a small selection of wedding gowns and bridal accessories. Light green walls with a border of hand painted white and pink rose bouquets provided a lovely backdrop for the white gowns.

Being petite, Mallory selected a simple, long-sleeved white satin gown with a heart-shaped neckline. The matching tulle veil had a small mesh tiara attached.

"You look beautiful," said VA as Mallory looked at her reflection.

Mrs. Watson, the proprietor, would personally alter the gown since the war had caused her to dismiss her alterations staff. War brides now seemed to be the basis of her clientele.

Larry had been in England for almost three months and was training in one of the British General hospitals. Soon he would be transferred to a field hospital, but he couldn't give more information than that. VA received a few letters sporadically from London. He couldn't say where he was but reminded her how much he loved and missed her. She tried to keep up a good front, but she missed him terribly.

VA stayed busy with wedding details since Bill would be home on December 15th, a few days away. *Thank goodness she had that to keep her busy.*

When she wasn't at the office, she stayed home making wedding favors and planning the reception. Susie headed up the church details. The ceremony would be at West End Baptist and the reception at the house on Tuscaloosa Avenue. A small, intimate affair was planned with family and close friends, including some of Mallory and Bill's former co-workers.

Knowing the terminal would be crowded, Mallory and VA were early to meet Bill's train. It was running late. They found an empty bench and waited on the platform. Hundreds of servicemen and women stood with their families while waiting to ship out to who knows where. VA watched them and wondered if they would ever come back. That thought stayed in her mind constantly.

"Do you know why the train's so late?" Mallory asked as a porter walked by.

"Nome, I sho don't."

"It should've arrived an hour ago," VA said. "They should tell us if anything's wrong."

Another hour passed, and Mallory paced the platform while holding her handkerchief and continuously twisting it tightly.

There were so many uniforms in the crowd with their loved ones. Would they be able to see him when and if he arrived?

"I'm worried," said Mallory. "I've heard a lot about sabotage and German spies carrying out orders in this country. With so many troops on trains, they'd be a prime target."

"Not here, Mallory," VA said. "I could see New York or somewhere on the west coast, but not in

Alabama."

"Haven't you heard about the German U-boats off the coast of Louisiana?"

After they waited four hours, the loud whistle of the "Birmingham Special" could be heard. The train finally came into view amid a cloud of steam and slowly rolled to a stop. VA climbed up on a wooden bench to catch a glimpse of Bill, but too many people blocked her view.

"I don't see him," VA said. "I hope he didn't miss the train."

Suddenly that familiar low-voice came out of nowhere.

"There's my girl," Bill said to Mallory with a cool and calm demeanor.

Mallory turned to him with tears in her eyes. She cried as he picked her up and kissed her.

"We were so worried," she said. "Why was the train so late?"

"Some kind of mechanical issue," he said. "We were stopped on the tracks until the problem was repaired. I was pretty burned up."

VA quickly walked up to an older looking, more distinguished Bill.

"Hello, baby sister." Bill gave her a tight hug.

His hair had been cropped very short, and he sported the casual army uniform and boots while carrying a large duffel bag.

"I'm so glad to see you," VA said. "We've missed you."

"And I missed you, too, VA," he replied. A small tear sparkled in his eye. "We have a lot to do this week, don't we? Let's go home, I'm starved."

When they turned into the driveway of the house, Bill could already smell the tantalizing aroma of his mother's kitchen.

He walked into the house to find Lucy and Eliza setting the dining room table. When Lucy saw her son, she stopped and wiped her hands on her apron.

"Hello, Son," she said. "I'm glad to see you."

"Hello, Mama."

Bill walked over to her and gave her a gentle hug. His mother placed her hands on his shoulders.

"I'm so glad to have you home. You look good. Wash up and let's eat."

Eliza finished setting the table and brought in bowls of fresh vegetables from the garden and Bill's favorite fried chicken.

Mallory and VA sat down as Bill took his place at the head of the table. Lucy and Eliza brought the pitcher of iced tea and a Chess pie for dessert, then both sat down.

"This looks so good, Mama," he said. "Eliza, you and Mama have outdone yourselves."

"Oh Mr. Billy, it's all for you," she said with her toothy white smile.

"The food in the mess hall is awful. After a long day of strenuous combat training during the day, I have to eat the slop."

"Doesn't anything taste good, hon?" asked Mallory. "You look so healthy."

"The coffee isn't too bad, but it gives me the shits," he answered. "Sorry, Mama and Eliza for the words, but that's the only way to describe it."

The wedding date was set for Sunday, the 21st of December, 1943, at 2:00. VA and Susie had completed most of the details except for calling the guests with the date and time.

VA heard her mother talking on the phone.

"That's good news, Susie. That'll be a great surprise for Bill," Lucy said.

Gabe had been granted a seven-day Christmas leave and hoped to be home in time for the wedding. VA wondered how he worked that out. It didn't matter. He would be home for Christmas and hopefully the wedding.

December 21st arrived and the house on Tuscaloosa Avenue was ready for the wedding reception. VA and Susie pressed the linens for the dining room and decorated the front porch with white paper bells and an abundance of red poinsettias and green magnolia leaves, cut from the yard.

Even though she'd used up most of her sugar ration, Lucy was able to bake a small wedding cake. Her neighbors helped by compiling their ration, and she ended up with more than enough.

Eliza prepared the simple refreshments for the reception ahead of time, and the fine china, silver, and crystal were cleaned and polished. After placing a few flowers in vases for the reception, every detail had been addressed.

Suddenly the front door opened, and the loud booming voice of Gabe Johannsen filled the living room.

"Where's everybody?"

Susie screamed with delight and ran over to him with open arms. Lucy came out of the kitchen and instantly stopped. She saw him and dropped her gloves. He came over to her, picked them up, and gave her a tight hug.

"How are you, Mama?"

"I'm fine, Son. I'm glad you were able to make it for the wedding. Bill will be pleased." Lucy said in her quiet, unemotional way, though she still smiled. "You made it just in time."

The family would be leaving for the church in five minutes. Bill hurriedly ran down the stairs whistling and tying his tie. He looked distinguished in the dress uniform of the United States Army. The brass "U.S." and "crossed rifles" insignias on the lapels shined brightly as did his regulation boots. He looked at his mother and saw Gabe.

"What the hell? You SOB! You *did* make it!"

The brothers shook hands and gave each other a brisk hug. Gabe had to wear his dark blue naval ensign's service uniform since he had no time to change. Bill offered his arm to Lucy and escorted her to the car.

VA and Susie greeted the guests as they arrived. Since there were very few men available to escort the ladies, they were instructed to seat themselves. The most obvious absentee was Edward. Susie's parents arrived with little Steve, and he squealed with delight when he saw Gabe.

VA remembered Gabe and Susie's wedding and how wonderful it was. Bill's would be just as wonderful but under different circumstances.

Susie motioned that Mallory had arrived. Mrs. Smith emerged from the sedan while Mr. Smith helped his daughter out. Mallory looked beautiful in her white satin. She held a small white Bible tastefully covered with lily of the valley, and stephanotis tied with long, flowing thin satin ribbons. Her father guided her up the stairs to the sanctuary entrance.

Mallory saw Bill with Gabe, grinning and waiting for her. A large smile filled her small face as she said to VA, "What a way to celebrate our marriage by having his brother here."

Susie and VA proceeded the bride to the front where Mr. Smith gave his daughter away. In VA's opinion, Bill was the best, most genuine person she had ever known. How lucky Mallory was to have a man like him fall in love with her.

After the reception, the photographer took a beautiful picture of the newlyweds in their chauffeur-driven sedan. Their honeymoon to New Orleans would last six days.

December 21, 1943

Dear Larry,

Bill and Mallory were married today. I wish you could have been here. Believe it or not, Gabe made it just in time to be Bill's best man. I am missing you so, now that the holidays are here. Christmas hasn't been the same since you left. So many are overseas, and no one feels like celebrating. When I go to the movies, I look for you in every war newsreel, but always leave disappointed. The clubs and ballrooms have virtually closed since there are so few men. Please send me a note so that I'll know you're safe. My life has been put on hold until you come back home to me.

With love,

VA

Looking up from the letter she'd just finished writing, VA heard a loud crashing sound. She ran to the kitchen to find Lucy bending over Eliza, who was lying on the floor.

"What's happened?" VA tearfully asked.

"I don't know. She was talking about the wedding and just fell off the chair," Lucy was trying to take Eliza's pulse the way WB had taught her.

Without hesitation, VA ran to the phone to call an ambulance. "Come on, come on! Get a line, damn it!"

"Do you need the line, Virginia?" VA heard the voice of Mrs. Goldman on the party line.

"Yes! Mrs. Goldman. I need an ambulance for Eliza!" The woman immediately hung up and VA was able to get the emergency call through.

Lucy continued to wipe Eliza's face with a soft damp cloth and talk to her. "Her pulse is weak," Lucy said over Eliza's unconscious body. Lucy's worried expression spoke volumes; Eliza was the best friend she ever had.

The ambulance arrived quickly, and the attendants checked Eliza's vital signs. They prepared her for the ride to the hospital and Lucy stayed close-by. Eliza slowly opened her eyes and when she saw Lucy, she tried to speak. Lucy held her hand as they rolled the gurney to the ambulance. VA saw her give Lucy's hand a weak squeeze. Lucy bent down to listen as Eliza slowly mouthed, "I love all."

"It looks like she's had a stroke, Mrs. Johannsen," the attendant said. "We'll get her to Hillman as soon as possible."

As they lifted the gurney into the back of the ambulance, Lucy asked to ride with her. Reaching for her hand, she wanted Eliza to know she was there. When the ambulance left, VA followed in the car.

They waited a few hours in the family waiting room for the doctor.

"Mrs. Johannsen, Eliza suffered a massive stroke, and we lost her," the emergency room doctor said. "We did everything we could to stabilize her and bring her blood pressure down. Had she complained of dizziness or headaches or possible blurred vision? Did you notice if she had any difficulty speaking?"

"She never complained about anything," Lucy said. "I'll notify her relatives."

Lucy, visibly shaken, walked out of the waiting room and toward the parking lot. VA stayed quiet since she knew her mother wanted no conversation and only to go home. *How could they go home without Eliza there?* When she needed a small compliment, a little comforting or just motherly affection, Eliza was always there. The beautiful woman who graced their lives for 21 years had left them suddenly and without warning.

December 28th was bitterly cold in the Baptist cemetery at Eliza's church. Her graveside service was attended by many friends, family, and fellow members of the congregation.

Neither VA nor her mother had ever seen a service quite like this. Singing, praising, loud affirmations, and an "Amen" followed almost everything the pastor said. It had been considered the celebration of Eliza's life, not a sad goodbye.

When they returned home from the funeral, the house felt lifeless. Eliza's sweet spirit had filled every room, and Lucy felt a wave of sadness from the loss of her closest friend. Eliza always seemed to understand when Lucy felt alone and stood by her when WB died. Lucy remembered the day of WB's funeral and the Klan members Eliza and Ol George witnessed there. She remembered the sweet words Eliza said to her.

"Now Miz Johannsen, no need to worry none 'bout

those people at the doctor's funeral today. They's just ignorant folk and you didn't know they was going to be there. I saw the look on yo face. We's just gon forget about it and go on and raise these children."

VA helped Lucy clean out Eliza's room. She could discard some things, but most of her clothes would be donated to the church.

They found a small box in her dresser drawer that said "for Miz Johannsen" written on the top. Lucy looked at VA with tears in her eyes. She opened the box, and a small locket with Eliza's picture lay inside. A card said:

To my friend, Miz Johannsen,

I know you are my best friend. The best day of my life was the day in 1922 I came to yo back door. This family is my family too.

Love, Eliza Jackson

Lucy took the locket out of the box and had VA put it on her. She would wear it for the rest of her life.

After Bill's wedding, Gabe and Susie took little Steve and spent Christmas in Gatlinburg, Tennessee. They returned to Lucy's house the day of the funeral and were informed about Eliza. Gabe, so much like his mother, turned around, removed his glasses and began to dab his eyes with a handkerchief.

Bill and Mallory returned from their honeymoon in New Orleans on the 29th and described how cold it was down there, but they had a glorious time.

They came home to Lucy's house and would stay there until Bill had to leave. Lucy and VA broke the news about Eliza, and all he could do was sit down and put his head in his hands.

"Mama, have you thought of selling this big house?" Bill asked as he inhaled deeply. "With just you and VA here, it's too much for you without Eliza."

"Yes, I've thought about it, and I might," Lucy said. "It's a big undertaking, but I'm thinking about it. When this war is over, I'll discuss it with all of you and make a decision."

December 23, 1943

My dear VA,

Merry Christmas! We'll make up the Christmases we've missed very soon. I won't lie, this is hell. The letters have been slow because working in this hospital is continuous. Sometimes I'm in the operating room for 10 hours straight. Trying to sleep is impossible. New casualties arrive two to three times a day. I keep your picture in my wallet to show the new medics when they talk about their girls. They don't believe me when I tell them the color of your eyes. We have no time to find Radio Free Europe for music. I grab all the sleep I can get. Sending my love,

Larry

Captain William B. Johannsen, Jr. left for New Jersey on January 4th, 1944. His duffel bag carried army issued essentials and a new photo of Mallory taken in New Orleans. He would miss his wife and could think of nothing but desolation and tragedy where he was going. Well trained in every type of ground combat, he had no idea what was coming, but he was ready. He wanted to be a part of ending the madness.

A tearful Mallory accompanied him to the train station where fellow servicemen were also going overseas. Mothers were sending their young sons off into oblivion for all they knew. Small children were hugged and kissed by their young fathers.

Many tears were shed that day at the station, but the less visible were the ones felt so much. Mallory hugged and kissed her new husband goodbye.

"Come home to me. I love you so," Mallory whispered in his ear.

He smiled and boarded the troop train. Like before, he found a window, smiled and saluted his new bride. Servicemen were hanging out of the windows to get a last glimpse of their loved ones.

"I love you," Bill mouthed as he looked at his new wife from the window.

Mallory watched the train slowly leaving the station. Before she turned to leave, Bill popped his head out the window and waved one more time.

CHAPTER 13

Home Front Devastation

January 1944

Al thought Mallory should live with them while Bill was overseas. It sounded like a good situation and Mallory would be closer to Alabama Power where she worked. They could help each other stay busy. If Lucy decided to sell the house, Mallory would move with them. Lucy agreed. They didn't have to do much persuading because Mallory liked the idea right away.

Gabe's leave ended two days after Bill left. He had to report to the USS *Essex* in the Pacific and await further orders.

Ed, now a Naval Aviator, flew missions over the Gilbert and Marshall Islands but hadn't been assigned to a permanent battleship.

Mallory received a letter from Bill before he left the states. His unit would be departing Boston on January 18th for England. He couldn't say any more than "I love you, and I'll be home as soon as I can."

VA and Mallory went to movies, and met after work for drinks, anything to keep their minds off their loved ones overseas.

Susie joined them for dinner and spent time at the Pickwick Club when all three were bored out of their minds. It seemed to be the only club still open, although they heard it might close. The atmosphere was quite different since there were so few men for the unattached to dance with.

Many women had war-related jobs, and all three discussed if they should, too. Susie quickly dropped the idea and opted to stay with her kindergarten duties since she could bring Steve to work with her.

Mallory decided not to leave the power company since she had built up so much time there. The telephone company was essential to the war effort, so VA wanted to stay put. Just because they were not working in a steel or armament factory, didn't mean they weren't helping the war effort.

On an early spring Friday night, Mallory and VA were restless. They took in a movie then went to the Pickwick for a nightcap. They heard the club would close in the next few days and they wanted to get out of their rut and listen to some live music.

There were a few servicemen there and a good orchestra. While at the bar, a couple of soldiers asked them to dance, but they refused. They only wanted to listen to music and talk.

"May I have this dance, Virginia?" The voice came out of nowhere.

She turned around and there stood Julian Morley. She looked at Mallory.

"Well?" he asked.

Mallory nodded. "Go ahead."

"Where did you come from?" VA asked.

"From New Jersey. We're about to go overseas."

"So is everyone else. I thought you went to New York."

"It was actually New Jersey for extra training in communications. I'm on leave before we ship out."

She agreed to the dance. As the orchestra played a slow song, Julian held her uncomfortably close, and she pulled back. When the song ended, she thanked him and walked back to the bar.

"Wait," he said. "We have more dancing to do."

"Not tonight. We're just here for a nightcap."

"Please," he asked with a needy look on his face.

"Okay. Just one more dance."

The orchestra played their rendition of Harry James's "I Remember You," and VA had to pull away again. Julian danced well, not like Larry, but close. She seemed to follow him easily and enjoyed dancing with him when he wasn't pressing her too close.

"I enjoyed our dance, Julian, but I have to go. Best of luck to you."

She felt a little sorry for him as he stood there alone. *Very handsome indeed and he said and did all the right things.* If she wasn't in love with Larry, she could go for him.

"I feel guilty dancing with someone else," VA said to Mallory. "It's like I'm cheating on Larry in a sense."

Mallory told her to forget it and write Larry when she got home. She didn't do anything wrong. After all, it was only two dances.

March 10, 1944

My Dearest Larry,

I miss you so much. Mallory and I went to the Pickwick Club tonight, and they played "I Remember You." Every time I hear that song I think of you and how I hope you remember me in your thoughts as I keep you in mine. Mallory is living with us, and it works for all. We go out after work sometimes, and it helps us not to miss you and Bill so much. He is on his way to England. You might see him though I hope not. We don't want him in a hospital. Mama is thinking about selling the house. Since we lost Eliza, we don't need this much room since there are only three of us. Please stay safe, and I can't wait for your next letter. Sending all the news I have on the home front. I will love you until the end of my days.

Yours always,

VA

Mallory's latest letter from Bill was dated February 5th. He couldn't say much of anything except how much he loved and missed her. He wanted to let her know he was okay. VA hadn't heard from Larry in 3 months. *What the hell?*

March brought nothing but blustery winds, cool temperatures and the Germans occupying Hungary. *What would they occupy next?* Mallory hadn't heard from Bill in almost six weeks. She kept writing to him at the address he had given her before he left. She hadn't heard from him, so she assumed he transferred to another section.

VA waited each day for a letter that didn't come. Finally, one arrived.

Somewhere in England

March 16, 1944

Dear VA,

I hope you and the family are well. I am spending each day covered in blood and death. It seems it will never end. I never sleep. The doctors and nurses here are some of the hardest working people I ever met. I have probably lost 15 pounds since I'm constantly on my feet and have no time to eat. The only solace I have is a girl named Nancy Britton. She is a British nurse with the Red Cross stationed here at the field hospital. She brings a joy to my life I thought was lost. I became a lonely shell of a man, but I have fallen in love with her. I couldn't help myself and can't continue to do my duty without her. You were my first love. Now I have my last love. Please never forget me and please forgive me.

Larry

When Virginia crumpled up the letter and collapsed, Lucy hurried to her. She couldn't understand what her daughter was saying through loud sobs and confused deportment. She and Mallory read the crumpled letter on the floor.

"VA talk to me!" Mallory screamed, trying to help

as she hugged VA in an attempt to calm her. She couldn't do anything but hold on to her as she sobbed.

"Let's get her off the floor and on to the sofa," Lucy said. "Then I'm calling Susie."

They were able to lift VA off the floor and when she was settled on the sofa, she began to calm down. Lucy noticed a strange look on her daughter's face as her limbs went completely limp and she became completely unresponsive.

Mallory kept trying to talk to her, but VA was like a cold block of stone that would never crack.

"How could Larry do this?" asked Mallory. "How convenient for him, a woman at his disposal. I wonder how long this has been going on. I hope I never see him again."

Susie came over the next day and tried to get through to her. VA had been in the catatonic condition for 24 hours.

"I think we need to call Dr. Taylor." Lucy said. "I thought she'd pull out of this, but if she stays like this, she'll become dehydrated. She probably is already."

As Lucy opened the front door for Dr. Taylor, he didn't seem concerned about her health, just her frame of mind.

Dr. Taylor gave VA a sedative, so she could sleep and would check in on her the next day.

"So many of these 'Dear Jane and Dear John' letters are going out and coming in," Dr. Taylor said. "VA isn't the first and certainly won't be the last. Make sure she gets plenty of liquids."

Lucy and Mallory sat by her side at intervals hoping one of them would be there when she came out of the psychotic state.

After three days, Lucy tried to get her to eat. She ate nothing and only drank when forced to. Lucy, concerned for her daughter, called Dr. Taylor again.

"Lucy, I understand your concern, but this is something Virginia has to work out," Dr. Taylor said. "This is a life altering blow to her and time is the only healer. Keep making sure she has plenty of liquids and give her one of the sedatives at night, so she can sleep."

How Lucy missed Eliza right now since she seemed to be the only person who understood her complex daughter. Visibly in dire straits, she and Mallory noticed VA's weight loss and how her face had become sallow.

Thinking it might help, Mallory turned on the radio in hopes a little music would bring VA out of her dire condition. When "The Nearness of You" played, she blinked and started to cry. Mallory ran over and grabbed her; holding her while she sobbed. Mallory cried with her, and the two friends stayed together in VA's room the entire night.

"How could he do this?" VA asked. "I've waited for him, and he just pissed our four years together away for some whore."

"You don't know the circumstances," Mallory said. He's in a hellhole, and this woman batted her eyes and twitched her ass. All he could think about was his dangling prick."

Mallory never said words like that, and they had a good laugh. VA didn't laugh long though and almost went back to her catatonic state.

"I've loved him for four years. I didn't pursue him; he pursued me! This war is ruining everyone's life. I hope the bitch is blown up!"

VA leaned back on the bed and soon fell asleep while her closest friend stayed with her.

The following morning, VA got out of bed, went downstairs, and yanked Larry's Blue Star flag out of the window. She rolled it up and planned to take it to the local enlistment office to donate it. It was too special and represented too much to be wasted on him. She sat down in her father's old chair and sobbed as she thought about how much he had hurt her. All the plans they had made were destroyed. All her dreams were burned to ashes. She had suffered an emotional air strike, and her life had been blown to pieces.

CHAPTER 14

When the Lights Go on Again

Summer 1944

$\mathcal{T}$hree months had passed since Larry's letter, and VA tried to go about her usual routine. She never socialized even though her friends and co-workers begged her to. Lucy always had supper ready at 6:00, never faltering from Eliza's schedule. Mallory would be home around 5:30, and the girls would have a cocktail and then dinner.

The radio comedies seemed to be the only escape from war news. The three women always tuned in after supper and especially liked Bob Hope. One of Bill's favorites, the comedian was on a USO tour in Europe, and Mallory hoped Bill would be close enough to see a show. The broadcast from overseas would air at 7:00.

Music softly played as Mallory read the newspaper, VA smoked while perusing a magazine, and

Lucy sewed. "When the Lights Go on Again (All Over the World)" by British singer Vera Lynn came on, all three stopped what they were doing to listen.

"That song is so appropriate for the way the world is feeling right now," Mallory said. "When she sings, '… and the boys are home again,' I think of how I miss Bill and want him home."

As VA listened, she thought of Larry and hoped he realized his mistake. Maybe he would write a letter to her for forgiveness. She had already thrown his picture away and placed the engagement ring in her jewelry box. *No way in hell was she giving that back.*

Then the radio played, "I Remember You." VA went upstairs, fell on her bed, and sobbed. She had cried more in the last three months than she had in her entire lifetime.

Her last letter to Larry must not have arrived before he wrote his infamous one to her. She promised herself long ago never to show her true feelings, just like her mother. That promise shielded her heart, but the protection stopped when she met Larry. He brought out in her every emotion imaginable.

June 1, 1944
Somewhere in England

Dear Mallory,

I must make this short since we're shipping

out tomorrow and lights out in 10 minutes. Mail is coming to the US from London, so I need to send this before we leave. I miss you and love you so much. Your picture from New Orleans is in my pocket close to my heart. I can't wait until this is all over and I can be home with you. Please tell Mama and VA how much I miss them and I'm glad you're living with them. I've been thinking about Ed and Gabe and hoping they're safe. They aren't infantry but are in as much combat and danger. If you all hear from them, let them know I can't wait for us to be all together again.

Yours always,

Bill

Mallory placed the letter in her top drawer with the others. There weren't many since he had been in route somewhere most of the time. They were postmarked from Ft. Benning, Georgia and somewhere in Tennessee, desert maneuver training in California, and from Boston before sailing to England. She wondered what was brewing but could never ask. It seemed his outfit received a lot of extra training

On Tuesday, June 6, 1944, the headlines read:

INVASION!
ALLIES STORMING FRANCE!
GREAT INVASION IS UNDERWAY

Mallory consumed the newspaper and immediately turned on the radio. It broadcast "Invasion" news on every station. The Allied forces had come ashore in Normandy on the coast of Northern France. They stormed the code-named beaches of Utah, Juno, Omaha, Sword, and Gold to take out fierce German positions.

Mallory prayed Bill hadn't been injured or worse. Lucy and VA joined her shortly and brought in some weak coffee. Mallory filled them in, and they listened to every major news network.

CBS would broadcast for 34 hours straight and included General Eisenhower's 'Order of the Day,' part of the "Great Crusade" to eliminate the savage Nazi tyranny that saturated Europe.

"The invasion has to be the reason for so much extra training," Mallory said.

All VA could think about was Bill and Larry. She still loved him and hoped he was at a hospital in England while his scheming female went to the front. VA encouraged Mallory to take a vacation from work and stay by the radio. VA went to the office, but the news was broadcast on the company loudspeaker all day. Her eight-hour shift felt like an eternity.

Mallory couldn't relax. She ate very little but smoked a lot. She would light up and pace in front of the radio. Lucy tried to get her to eat, but she wouldn't. If she did, her nerves would send it right back up. She kept a glass of water close by simply to avoid dehydration.

Mallory's mother came to the house to persuade her to come home for a while, but she refused. She didn't want to leave Lucy and VA. Mrs. Smith understood and planned to stay at the house with Mallory for two weeks.

The newscasts reported that the Allies had broken through the German artillery and taken the beaches of Normandy. They were on the way to Cherbourg, France, and beyond. France's liberation had begun, and Mallory Johannsen felt intense worry and pride at the same time. She hadn't heard from Bill but wasn't expecting to. He was in the middle of hell.

By late July, the Allies had made their way deep into France. Liberation from the German occupation was well underway.

Bill's outfit, the US Army's 8th Infantry, 4th Armored Division, was one of the major players in France. It had been mentioned in the war news, especially at St. Lo. That meant Bill must be on the ground in major combat with the enemy in strange terrain.

News reports indicated that German Panzer divisions hid in hedgerows, and the Sherman tanks couldn't penetrate them unless modified with hedgerow cutting equipment. Bill once told her the tanks were death traps.

On Saturdays, VA and Mallory were in the habit of walking to Holms Drugstore, sitting at the soda fountain reading magazines while they had one of their specialty Lime Rickeys.

VA showed her the spot on the sidewalk where Gabe knocked her knees in and recounted how she planned to kill him. She frequently remembered that day so long ago. Now her brother was fighting in the Pacific, and she worried he might never come home.

As they rounded the corner to the house, they saw Bobby Ames, the telegram delivery boy, parking his bicycle in front of the Johannsen house. Mallory stopped and waited until he left. VA remembered the telegram Larry sent her, and the news had been good. It could be addressed to either Lucy or Mallory. Slowly they walked to the house, and with a shaky hand, Lucy gave Mallory the telegram.

```
WASHINGTON DC 845 PM 8-05-44

MRS MALLORY JOHANNSEN
508 TUSCALOOSA AVE BIRMINGHAM,
ALA

THE SECRETARY OF WAR DESIRES
```

```
ME TO EXPRESS HIS DEEPEST
REGRET THAT YOUR HUSBAND CAPT
WILLIAM B JOHANNSEN WAS KILLED
IN ACTION TWENTY FOUR JULY IN
FRANCE

LETTER FOLLOWS
THE ADJUTANT GENERAL
```

Mallory let out a loud mournful scream and fell to the floor. She began to shake her head and crawl like a baby as she cried, "No! No! Not him!"

Lucy and VA read the telegram and hurried to her aid. Lucy shook all over as she picked Mallory up and led her to the sofa.

VA couldn't hold back the tears and anguish. *No! It couldn't be true! Her brother had been too strong to let something like this happen. He had the extra training!*

Lucy called Susie and asked her to try to get word to Gabe and Ed. VA stayed at Mallory's side while Lucy notified Mrs. Smith. That night her mother moved into the house to stay with Mallory indefinitely. Susie came over to try and help. Mr. Langdon and Alma would care for little Steve as needed.

After the initial shock, Mallory calmed down and quietly went to her room. She kept the curtains drawn and only came out when necessary. Mrs. Smith made sure she drank plenty of fluids. Mallory let no one in, and her bereaved loved ones agreed to leave her alone.

Not knowing what to do, VA paced the floor and listened for Mallory to call out. Still denying the death of her brother, she kept listening to the radio for news of lost troops being discovered in the deep forests of France or paratroopers being found alive in trees. She knew it was only a fantasy. Things like that didn't happen, especially in this damn war. Her big brother was gone and would never be back.

A prominent gold star replaced Bill's blue one in the living room window as they waited a long ten days for the letter from Washington. Finally, it came by certified US mail.

Washington DC
August 15, 1944

Mrs. Mallory Johannsen
508 Tuscaloosa Avenue
Birmingham, Ala.

Dear Mrs. Johannsen,

My sincerest regrets from the War Department on the death of Captain William B. Johannsen. From our close sources on the ground, Capt. Johannsen was targeted by a German sniper. An outstanding officer, he was a courageous leader and friend to his company. He is buried in the Blosville Cemetery near St. Lo, France. Please contact my office if I can be of further assistance.

In deepest sympathy,

Henry L. Stimson, Secretary of War

"At least we know where he is," Mallory said tearfully. "With so many soldiers buried overseas, I'm glad they documented his burial, and Mr. Stimson could tell us his location."

After weeks of trying to stay strong, Lucy retreated to her bedroom and sat on the bed with her hands folded in her lap. She thought about her quiet little boy with a heart of gold who grew up to be a wonderful man. Oh, how she would miss his smile, his shy disposition, and unassuming intelligence.

She and WB raised a fine son who proudly gave his life for his country. Tears rolled down her face. Lucy reached into her pocket, brought out her handkerchief and gently wiped her eyes.

Many times, since the telegram, she quietly slipped away to her room. She would have her moments alone to cry, and to pray that her two surviving sons would soon be home. She must try to stay strong for Mallory. "Walter" and Eliza were never far from her thoughts. "Please watch over him. I know he is with you," she whispered.

Mallory spent weeks in a fog. She lost weight and didn't care. She didn't cry again. VA tried to get her out of the house on the weekends, but she refused. Lucy, never an alarmist, grew worried. Mrs. Smith wanted to take her out of town to visit relatives in Florida, but Mallory declined. Lucy sent for Dr. Taylor, who made a house call that afternoon.

"Mrs. Smith, your daughter is still in a state of shock," Dr. Taylor began, "there is nothing I can do. She will get on with her life when she's ready, so let her grieve in her own way. There is no medicine for this. If she can keep liquids down and start back to work, she'll be fine. Time is the only cure for her condition. I see many wives and mothers going through this. The war is taking so many of our young men and women and will take even more until this mess is over."

Dr. Taylor prescribed a sedative, so Mallory could sleep, but that was all. VA agreed with him and knew it was grief. She knew how Mallory felt.

VA didn't lose Larry in the same way, but he might as well be dead. She would never see him again. It had been six months since the disastrous letter arrived, and she almost felt ready to get on with her life.

Susie welcomed her second son, Andrew Langdon (Andy), on September 1, 1944. Lucy and VA noticed soon after Bill's death that Susie was expecting and understood why she hadn't announced it. Being petite, she didn't show until mid-July.

"There didn't seem to be an appropriate time," Susie said. "You and Mallory were going through so much, and I didn't want to seem elated about anything. Maybe I should have told you."

"Susie, don't worry about it. Andy is here and healthy, and I'm doing much better. Mallory's slowly getting her life back in order," VA said with a smile. "Mama hopes Mallory will bring Bill back to the US for burial at Elmwood with Daddy. She wants her son to be home."

CHAPTER 15

It's All Over

Spring 1945

*I*n February, Roosevelt, Stalin, and Churchill met in Yalta to demand Germany's unconditional surrender and begin post-war planning. VA and Mallory were startled to see the picture of President Roosevelt at the Yalta Conference on the front page of the newspaper. He didn't look well. He had always been so strong and confident, but now he looked sickly and frail. Even with so much fighting on both fronts, the Allies seemed to dominate.

Europe continued to be in turmoil in the spring of 1945. The horrific Battle of the Bulge finally ended in January with a great American victory.

Soviet troops liberated two concentration camps, Auschwitz and Birkenau, where they discovered thousands of people barely alive, hundreds of corpses recently killed, and the remains of almost one million. The US and Britain liberated more camps with the same findings, all by the hands of the Germans.

The Americans and the world were horrified. The victims were law-abiding citizens but didn't fit into the Nazi's "Master Plan." Hitler and his cronies succeeded in only one thing; showing the world the devil, his disciples, and the gates of hell.

The Allies knew they had to be wiped off the face of the earth. Hopefully, that was about to happen.

The headlines on April 13, 1945, read:

PRESIDENT ROOSEVELT DEAD
TRUMAN TAKES OATH OF OFFICE

The country was in shock and disbelief. FDR had been the power behind the re-emergence of the USA during the Depression and now the imminent victory over the Axis powers.

The country loved and trusted him, and his election to a fourth term as president was unprecedented. He died of a cerebral hemorrhage in Warm Springs, Georgia, at only 63. The headlines shocked the world.

The newsreels showed the presidential funeral train carrying his flag-draped coffin back to Washington accompanied by his wife, Eleanor. Throngs of mourning citizens along the way waited to get a glimpse of the train while on its journey north.

The Allies were closing in on Berlin. They

wanted to capture Hitler and his aides, but this was not to be. While in his bunker, Hitler and his bride, Eva Braun, committed suicide on April 30, and his top aides did the same or fled. A slimy coward's way out. All of this happened while allied bombs ravaged Berlin. A handful of aides were captured and imprisoned.

The headline on May 7 read:

UNCONDITIONAL SURRENDER OF ALL GERMAN FORCES TO ALLIES

The war in Europe was over. More concentration camps were liberated, and the news coming out of Europe was nothing but death, devastation, and the shattered lives of human beings.

Victory in Europe was celebrated all over the country, but with the Pacific war still raging, Birmingham celebrated in a somber way. VA, Lucy, and Mallory took the streetcar downtown and quietly celebrated with dinner at Bogue's Restaurant. Lucy rarely went out to dinner, but she wanted to that night.

The last four years of war had taken normal life away from most people in the US. Each citizen in the United States was touched by the war in some way.

Women entered the work force in armament factories replacing the men sent overseas, many businesses were negatively impacted, and most of all, the supreme sacrifice given by at least one member of most families.

The number of casualties was significant and already severely wounded veterans with life altering injuries were returning home.

Hopefully, the Japanese would surrender soon, then Gabe and Ed would be home. That's when the nightmare would finally end.

The headline on August 15, 1945, read:

AFTER ATOMIC BOMBING
OF HIROSHIMA/NAGASAKI
JAPAN'S UNCONDITIONAL SURRENDER ENDS WAR

"It's all over!" VA jumped up as she read the headlines. "I can't believe the nightmare's finally over. Look Mama, read this!" Tears streamed down VA's face.

As Lucy read the headlines out loud, her voice broke, and she began to cry. She pulled a handkerchief out of her apron pocket and sobbed into it. Mallory ran to her and held her mother-in-law as both shed uncontrollable tears held back for so long.

"Bill didn't die in vain," Mallory cried, trying to catch her breath. "He died as he lived, protecting all of us. He was a proud soldier who helped eradicate the evil that most certainly would've impacted us and future generations."

"Mama, this country has a fighting spirit that will never be broken. Just think how the home front came through for the war effort in every way imaginable. You, included. We all did everything humanly possible to help win the victory," VA said through tears.

Lucy continued to cry and nodded. Her three sons went off to war too young. It was hard to understand why one of them had to grow into manhood a half a world away. It wasn't fair. One didn't come back, and his beloved image would stay young forever.

Now the only thing to do was pray that Gabe and Ed got home safely and soon. Some boys were already home from Europe and some from the South Pacific.

VA had already seen Leon Stevenson at the office. They worked together before the war, and he returned from Europe a month earlier. Southern Bell kept Leon's job open, but many other former employees weren't so lucky.

Many of the previous positions at Alabama Power had been dissolved. Mallory told VA how the current employees had to take on more responsibilities, but she didn't think it would last long though. It would take a while for the country, and its workforce to return to normal.

20 SEPT 1945

MRS. SUSIE JOHANNSEN
3245 ROSEMONT ROAD
BIRMINGHAM ALA

SHOULD ARRIVE BREMERTON
WASHINGTON 7 NOV THEN HOME
(STOP) WILL NOTIFY YOU (STOP)

MUCH LOVE

GABE

CHAPTER 16

New Lives in Mexico

Spring 1946

Mallory needed to get away. After losing Bill, her life was empty, and her future looked dismal. It had been almost two years since he was killed, but time hadn't healed her sorrow. As former servicemen returned to the office, she felt jealous of their wives. *Why did Bill have to die?*

Waiting for the streetcar after work, Mallory browsed the window of a small travel shop that had recently opened. There were posters in the windows advertising far away places and ones close-by. Some heavily promoted excursions by air and others advertised the current "glory days" of rail travel.

One colorful poster caught her eye and a smile replaced her usually joyless face. Maybe this was the answer. Having a few minutes to spare, she went in and picked up a few travel brochures.

Reading through the brochures on the streetcar, she was ready to leave as quickly as possible. She planned to ask VA and a few friends, but if no one else wanted to, she would go alone.

When VA came through the front door, she found a smiling Mallory waiting for her. "What's going on?" she asked. Noticing the travel brochures spread out on the coffee table, she picked one up that read "Escape to Mexico." An attractive couple was featured on the cover listening to a mariachi band. Another one featured the Gardens of Xochimilco. She smiled immediately.

"Mallory, let's go! When do you want to leave?"

"The sooner the better."

With friends Gayle Forrester and Dorothy LeVoy on board for the trip, the plans were made. The train to Laredo, Texas, was scheduled to depart from Birmingham at 9:00 AM on April 10th and arrive at 1:30 AM on April 12th. In Laredo, they would board the daily Pullman sleeper train to Mexico City and arrive by 6:00AM on the 14th.

The long trip by train wasn't comfortable, so VA planned to stay in the lounge car most of the time. With larger windows and plenty of comfortable seating, she would enjoy the scenery since it was beautiful this time of year. While reading a magazine, she thought about the trip to New Orleans with Larry. She put the magazine down and lit a cigarette. Resting her chin in her hand, her eyes filled with tears as the train passed through the bayous of Louisiana.

Watching as the Spanish moss dripped and swayed from the cypress trees, VA felt as if her love for him would never go away. She closed her eyes and slowly shook her head.

"VA, I needed to get up and walk. Gayle and Dorothy are asleep. Are you all right?"

Mallory sat down next to her sister-in-law and noticed VA's tearful demeanor.

"I know how you feel. The last two years have taken a devastating toll on my life. Work and otherwise."

"Mallory, I can't keep my mind off him. Riding through the bayous while remembering our New Orleans trip, makes it hurt even worse."

"Maybe it's time we both start over. I'm ready if you are. Let's try."

The Pullman sleeper arrived at the Mexico City train station at daybreak. The four girls awoke to the conductor announcing the arrival. Scurrying to get dressed and retrieve their belongings, they felt rested and grabbed a porter to help with the luggage. After a bumpy cab ride, the girls checked into the historic Hotel de Cortes in Mexico City for four nights. Instead of separating, they pooled their money and reserved a suite.

The first night, they went to dinner at the famous Ciro's nightclub where a good Latin orchestra provided the music.

Mallory watched as the others turned away dance partners. She had no desire to dance. The Latin music was great, but she didn't know the Rhumba. After two rounds of drinks, a younger Latino man came out of nowhere and extended his hand to her. She guzzled the last bit of her drink and said, "What the hell?" The Rhumba wasn't a difficult dance to learn and she was a pro after a few different partners.

An older Latino gentleman asked Gayle to dance, and she finally accepted. The man looked to be in his fifties and Gayle seemed comfortable with him. He taught her the Samba and the Rhumba, and his manners were impeccable. She caught on fast, and the gentleman bought food and drinks for them the rest of the night.

VA and Dorothy stayed at the table, and two greasy-looking Latino men sat down with them.

"Excuse, por favor, we would like for you to dance. Por favor?" one of them said as they looked at Dorothy and VA.

"No thank you. I have a broken ankle, and my friend is staying here to keep me company since I can't dance," VA lied. Thankfully, the men got up and left, and VA assumed they understood. They looked slimy, and both smelled like tequila and stale cigarettes.

"Thank you, VA," Dorothy said. "I wouldn't dance with that if my life depended on it."

"I wouldn't want to smell like that if my life depended on it."

Mallory and Gayle came back to the table, and the drinks and food had been well taken care of. They didn't have to pay a peso for anything!

"This is too good to be true," they all said.

Everywhere they went, men would ask them to dance or to accompany them to view the sights. Naturally, they all declined. These four women were not on the take. VA wanted nothing to do with these wolves nor did the other three. They were there to have fun, drink, and listen to good Latin music.

On the second night, Xavier Cugat played at Ciro's. With luck, the girls got in, but with a stiff cover charge. They didn't care; they loved his music. Cugat's famous song "Brazil" was the first one played, and couples got up to dance the Samba.

As VA listened to the music, she noticed a Latin man with slicked back, black hair and a thin mustache approaching her. He ran his hands over his greasy hair, then awkwardly danced over to her in time with the beat. Stifling a laugh, she had to look away.

"Senorita, you be my pleasure, por favor," he said in broken English. "Mi nombre Bernardo fuerte como oso."

She looked at her friends with a facial expression that said, "What did he say?"

"He says he's strong as a bear, and his name is Bernardo," said Dorothy.

"I'm sure," VA said as she rolled her eyes and accepted. After showing her a few Samba steps, he started rubbing her back and sliding his nasty hands up and down her arms in a creepy way she didn't like.

She continued the dance but at a distance. He danced the Samba well and even though he turned her stomach with his skin-tight pants and short bolero jacket, he was a great dancer. When the dance ended, VA nodded and said, "Gracias."

"Oh, no-no, Senorita, we have more, por favor."

"No, muchas gracias. Mis amigos," she said as she gestured to her friends waiting at the table.

Surprisingly, he got the message and followed an older woman to her table. "What a gigolo," VA murmured under her breath.

The girls paid plenty for the evening and Cugat.

Turning down more suitors, they stayed, watched the local patrons as they danced the Rhumba and Samba, and enjoyed the authentic Mexican cuisine. They left Ciro's after paying their bill and went back to the hotel lounge.

They found an empty booth for four and waited to place their order. VA kept thinking about that grease-ball, Bernardo.

"His skin-tight pants were disgusting," VA said as she lit a cigarette. "He was a good dancer, but did you see how huge his bulge was? It could've been a roll of pesos, for all I know. It didn't look real."

They all were laughing so hard, they couldn't place their order.

"How do you know, VA?" Gayle asked. "How close were you looking?"

"I'm serious. I had to get a foot away from him," VA said with a straight face. "I couldn't help but see the disgusting thing." She finally cracked up.

"Did you see the one I danced with?" Mallory asked while gasping with laughter. "There was hardly a bulge like that, but his skin had fine glitter sprinkled all over it, and his mustache was penciled on. I think he was looking for the guy with the bulge."

"Okay, listen," Gayle said. "Remember that Diego person I danced with after VA went off with Bernardo?

His slicked back hair was dripping from the crap he put on it. He was nothing but a goof out for some nookie."

"Did he say that?" Mallory asked.

"I got the message when the fool rubbed his johnson against my leg then winked at me. I immediately gave him the brush-off and came back to the table."

Loud laughter erupted again, except from Dorothy.

"It's all disgusting," Dorothy said.

The girls spent the next day at the ancient Aztec "floating gardens" of Xochimilco. What a wonderful way to push the war and all the heartbreak out of their minds for a little while. They took loads of pictures while floating through the lavish gardens on colorful boats called *"traginera."*

Their last day in Mexico City was spent at the Museo Nacional de Historia housed in the Castillo de Chapultepec, a beautiful old castle built in 1775, then dinner at "El Taquito Bullfighting Restaurant."

The 1923 restaurant was charming and had a bullfighting theme. They sat outside on the terrace, ordered margaritas, and listened to the Mariachi band. Since the atmosphere was authentic Mexico, the girls ordered Caldo Tlalpeno, a flavorful chicken soup, and Tampiquena, a Tampico styled steak.

As they enjoyed their last night in such a beautiful location, Gayle asked, "Let's go home by way of New Orleans. Wouldn't that be fun?"

VA glanced at Mallory. She smiled.

"I think that's a great idea. Let's take a vote," said Mallory.

The Mexico trip was everything they expected and more. After experiencing new dances, great music, excellent food, and beautiful sights, the girls were ready to head back to the states. They all needed a large glass of ice cold American water. They boarded the train in Mexico City and headed home via New Orleans.

Arriving in New Orleans at 3:00 PM, and without making prior reservations for two nights, they were fortunate the Roosevelt Hotel had a vacancy. Happy memories returned to VA and Mallory, but the feeling of great loss seemed to outweigh those memories.

With no war, the old hotel was alive again with tourists. Again, the girls pooled their money left over from Mexico and checked into a suite. Exhausted from the long train ride, they relaxed in the elegant lobby, catching up on current news, and each had a "Sazerac" in the lounge. The night would be for relaxing, the next day would be for sight-seeing and shopping.

As the group toured the old streets, jazz music

played, plenty of shops and cafés had re-opened for business, and the Mississippi River tours were up and running again. Rues Bourbon and Royal were much cleaner, and families walked the old streets now since blatant risqué entertainment wasn't as visible.

VA, remembering the last time she strolled these streets, stayed quiet. As she walked, the memories took her back to the happiest day in her life. That day was gone; that time in her life was gone, and even seeing the name "Magazine Street" on an advertisement filled her with emotion. She looked at that advertisement again.

Mr. L. Vidrine
Magazine Street & Felicity
"Dealing in the Finest Antiques and Rare Jewelry."

"I have to run an errand," she said. "I'll meet ya'll back at the hotel at 5:00."

Making her way to the streetcar on Canal Street, she caught the first one heading down St. Charles Avenue. She asked the operator when to get off for Magazine Street and Felicity.

VA's heart pounded as she found the lovely old building. The prominent sign "L. Vidrine" hung from the porch. As she opened the door, the loud tinkling of a bell sounded. An elderly gentleman came into view.

"How can I help you?"

"I saw your advertisement and wanted to see

your rare jewelry."

"Of course, what are you looking for?"

"I'm not sure. I'll know when I see it. My fiancé was here a few years ago and purchased Aimee Fontenot's beautiful diamond ring. Do you remember?"

"Oh, yes. Your fiancé was adamant about finding the perfect ring for his wife to be. I have never seen a man so enamored. I don't see that you're wearing it."

"No, I lost him during the war."

"Mon cher, I'm so sorry for your loss. He was a nice man and very handsome."

"Thank you. I miss him."

VA looked in Mr. Vidrine's glass jewelry case. There was a lovely antique brooch in the form of a crown.

"What's the story behind this brooch?" she asked.

"Ah, yes. This brooch came into my possession recently. A former Mardi Gras King of Rex passed it down from his late wife to his daughter in 1900. Her name was Desiree Bordelon. It's a lovely piece. She passed away ten years ago and I was able to acquire it through family connections."

"I love it. Can I afford it?"

"For you, yes. I will part with it for fifty dollars. It is costume, not genuine."

"I have thirty dollars. Will that do?"

"For you, mon cher, it will do."

VA left Mr. Vidrine feeling as if she took a piece of Larry with her. Even though the brooch wasn't made from genuine stones, she would always remember the quaint shop and the sweet Mr. Vidrine.

Meeting up with the girls at 5:00, VA felt satisfied. She and Mallory took this trip to try to put their sad past behind them and start fresh.

"VA, where did you go?" asked Mallory.

"I revisited my past. Now I'm ready to start my future."

VA heard that Larry Abbott was home. *So, he survived and came back home, that's great. What should I do? Run to him? Did he bring the British wench with him?* He wants to see me. For what? He can forget it since he made his choice.

She also heard that "Nancy" didn't come to the US with him. *Well, too damn bad. That ass can reel in his sorrows.* What nerve he had after the months she spent in despair, struggling to bring herself out of a deep state of depression and wanting to die. That bastard would never get a second chance from her.

Mallory begged her to see him. "If nothing else, maybe it would officially end the wondering and explain the reason why he broke your heart."

"I don't know if I should. What if seeing him breaks my heart all over again?" VA asked. "Why is Larry doing this to me?"

"VA, see him. Ask the questions you've wanted answered for two years. I'll get in touch with him and make the arrangements."

She reluctantly agreed. "I'm only doing this for you, Mallory, although my mind's made up."

VA didn't want to go, much less talk to him. Curious though, she wondered what kind of bullshit he had to offer. VA ran late but couldn't care less. She made it to Joy Young's by 6:30, and Larry was waiting. Charlie led her to the table.

"Hello, VA, I'm glad to see you. You look wonderful," he said as he stood up. "I'm broken up about Bill. I felt like he was my brother, too."

"Hello, Larry," VA replied over the roar of her heartbeat. "Thank you. I can't believe he's gone. The loss is almost more than I can bear. Mallory is trying to get her life back to normal, if there is such a thing now. You knew about Eliza, too, didn't you?"

"Yes, I'm so sorry. Mallory told me." He pulled the chair out for her, and when she was seated, he began to speak.

"What are you drinking now? Still the whiskey sour?" He nodded to Charlie. "We have a lot to discuss, and I don't know where to begin."

VA noticed a little greying at his temples and a few tiny wrinkles on his face. Undoubtedly stress from the war, but he was still handsome, although she didn't want to admit it. Charlie brought the drinks and she paused a minute, trying to choose her words carefully.

She took a sip of her drink, lit a cigarette, and said, "We have nothing to discuss. You broke my heart. I was faithful to you from the beginning to the end, and all you needed was a convenient female to make you send that letter."

"It wasn't that way, VA. She happened to be there when I needed someone. I missed you so much, and she was a shoulder to cry on, a person who would listen. I still love only you. I always have, and I always will."

"Apparently not. You weren't strong enough in that regard. You wrote how you 'fell in love with her' in your final letter. Believe me, I'm thankful you made it back," she said as she crushed her cigarette out in the ashtray. "I know you went through hell, but you're crazy if you think I would take you back after what you did to me. Maybe you should persuade your 'Nancy' to come to the US. That would be the best for both of us."

VA got up, left Larry at the table and never turned around. As much as she still loved him, he would never hurt her again.

She sobbed as she ran to the streetcar stop. *What have I done? Did I just ruin my entire life?* "No," she told herself. "He broke my heart. Did he expect me to take him back as if nothing happened?" The war changed everything, she admitted, but did that warrant forgiveness for writing such a letter to her? *Must I regret this the rest of my life?*

VA found Mallory eagerly waiting at home for her. With tears in her eyes, she sat down and said, "I think I just ruined my whole life."

"Why do you say that? I hope you were nice to him."

"I tried to be. But all I could think about was what Larry said in the letter--the last love of his life had been her. He had the nerve to say he still loves me, but I got up and left."

"Oh, VA, people changed so much during the war. He did, too. We didn't go through what they did. He came home, and Bill didn't. Think how lucky you are."

VA cried again because Mallory was right. She lost her entire world; Bill and their future together died at the same time. VA decided Larry was on the rebound, and he thought she was the only one he could come home to. She almost felt sorry for him.

As Larry watched VA leave the restaurant, he knew her feelings were justified. How could he let her know sending that letter was a huge mistake? He never loved Nancy but realized it too late. He felt alone. He wanted VA, although she made it clear she didn't want him.

On the drive back to his parent's estate, he tried to think of a way to get her back. Now living in the apartment above the garage, he remembered how she liked the old carriage house. If he could get her to understand what happened to him in England, he would propose again. If she agreed, they could live in the carriage house apartment until he finished his residency.

Larry called VA every day for two weeks. He wanted to clear things up, but each time he called, Mrs. Johannsen would answer with an excuse for her daughter.

"Larry called twice today, Virginia. I'm tired of making up excuses," Lucy said.

"Tell him I'm not home, or that I just don't want to talk to him, I don't care!"

Lucy shook her head. "You should at least talk to him."

"Mama, he's on the rebound. Why does he keep torturing me?"

The next time he called, Lucy made VA come to the phone.

"Larry, please stop calling. It only makes things worse."

His voice sounded slow and hoarse. "I have to see you again. My life is crumbling around me, and I have no desire to go back to work. You're the only one I can depend on to help me."

Damn it, why is he doing this to me? "I can't, Larry. I thought I made myself clear at Joy Young's. You made your choice in England. After all our plans, our letters, and most importantly our love, you threw it away after some nurse paid a little attention to you."

"VA, please! I need to see you," Larry pleaded. "One last time, okay? Just in memory of old times?"

"I can't do it. I may not be able to recover if we see each other again."

"Do I have to beg, VA? Is that what you want?" he asked. "Okay, I'm begging you."

With a long sigh, VA finally gave in. "Okay, Larry, where do you want to meet? I'm free on Saturday."

"At the Greenwood Cafe. It reopened in the same location."

"I'll meet you there at 7:30." VA hung up the phone, determined not to back down. *I will not be responsible for what comes out of my mouth. Why should I cut him any slack? Being hurt so badly and wanting to die is not something I can just push under the rug and forget.*

After a grueling work week, Saturday finally came and she was tempted to call Larry and back out, or just not show up. VA had to focus though; this was Larry, the only man she ever loved. But he had found a substitute overseas. She would never forget that. With a hint of devilish payback, she'd make sure he didn't forget it either.

VA found just the right dress to show off her figure and dazzle him. Just what she needed to make him realize what an asshole he had been. *Am I being too mean? Hell no!*

After a few drinks at home, VA caught the streetcar to Greenwood's. She walked into the restaurant looking like a million dollars and feeling no pain.

As she walked to the bar, she could feel the patrons noticing her, especially the men. Larry stood as she approached him and as he looked around the restaurant, she could tell he was fully aware of the attention. *I hope you realize what you threw away, mon amour.*

"Hello," she said with no enthusiasm.

"You look lovely."

"Do you have a table or are we staying at the bar?"

"Oh, I have a great table. It's in the back so we can have some privacy."

She struggled to be friendly. Larry was going out of his way to be the man she knew a few years ago. Her pride always got in the way. She didn't know if this was a battle she wanted to win, or if she just wanted to make him beg. They ordered a champagne cocktail and a bourbon on the rocks.

Larry lit a cigarette and said, "I can't get you out of my mind. You intoxicate me with your beauty, and we were so good together."

What a stupid line. She didn't respond, opting to wait and see what happened. There would be no way she could feel for him the same way as before, so why not make the best of it? As much as she hated to admit it, she knew she was lying to herself.

As the jukebox played one of VA's favorite old songs, "I Remember You," Larry stood up and extended his hand.

"Dance with me. I know you love that song."

"I'm surprised you remember," she said as he took her hand. He pulled her close as they danced next to the table. She held him tight. *Oh, Larry, you feel so good to me. I've missed you so much and want to take you in my arms and tell you how much I love you.*

"Please let me back in your life," he whispered. "I never stopped loving you."

At that moment, they accidentally bumped into a couple walking to their table. "Virginia?" It was Julian Morley with an attractive blonde. "How are you?"

"I'm well, Julian. I'm glad to see you made it home in one piece. So nice to have seen you." She acknowledged his date with a smile.

Larry looked at VA with a question in his eyes. "Do you know him?"

"I danced with him a few times at the Pickwick Club when Mallory and I would go for a nightcap. He left for overseas soon after, I think. It's funny; we keep bumping into each other."

As they sat back down at their table for coffee, his expression must have revealed his unhappiness with her answer.

"Why didn't you bring Nancy home to the US with you?"

VA could tell the question jolted him. She couldn't wait to hear his answer.

"I got caught up in the moment of death and gore. For twelve hours straight I'd be in the operating room with no break. There were so many devastating deaths and life-altering injuries. Some I didn't think I could fix," he lit a cigarette. "There were times I had to go outside and puke. I had never seen such suffering. Nancy brought food and coffee or whatever else I needed. I thought I loved her, but I didn't."

Listen to him. He's so nervous by having to answer *that one question.*

"She was in love with me and wanted to come back to the states with me, but I refused her because of you. I didn't see her again after I broke it off. This war made me a damn son of a bitch to two women. I lost the one I loved and rejected one who loved me."

Listening to his lame excuse, VA thought, "Rejected the one who loved me? Really? Did I not love you? You lost *and* rejected me, you ass!"

She wanted him back, but what he just said only poured more salt into the existing open wound. She couldn't forget how she felt after receiving the letter and how long it took to feel like she wanted to live again.

VA began in her slow drawl, "When I got your letter, and after you completely broke my heart, I wanted to die. I never thought I'd ever have the chance to tell you that in person. I counted on getting married when you got home. That was our plan, remember? I saved my salary for our honeymoon and pictured in my mind our own home and children...."

"VA, wait. Let me explain," he said.

"No," she continued. "I knew I wouldn't see you most of the time, being a doctor's wife, but it didn't bother me. It took almost a year to want to live again. Mallory lost Bill forever, and I lost you forever, too. She tells me how lucky I am that you came home, but what she doesn't realize is that you died, too."

VA watched as he closed his eyes then looked away.

"Is it over for us, then?" Larry asked.

"I'm afraid so. I'll always love you, but not in the way you want. I won't be hurt again because a nurse might bring you coffee after a long surgery or might develop a crush on you. I'm going on with my life, and it will be without you."

Larry's shoulders slumped, as did his voice. "Let's go, VA. I'll take you home."

As they walked out of the restaurant, VA let him take her arm and lead her to the convertible. The ride was quiet until Larry reached over and gently took her hand in his.

"You're right," he said. "I understand. I had no right to even think you'd forgive me and immediately pick up where we left off."

"What are you going to do now?"

"I'm going to get myself together and finish my residency. Then I can take a stab at making a good life for myself."

When they walked up to the familiar front door of the big house on Tuscaloosa Avenue, they turned and looked into each other's eyes. Larry bent down and softly kissed her cheek then held his cheek to hers for a few seconds.

Larry, please beg me again, I'll say yes this time. I love you.

"Goodbye, VA," he said. "I hope our paths cross again sometime."

CHAPTER 17

New Surroundings

October 1946

$\mathcal{L}$ ate in 1946, Lucy decided to take Bill's advice and sell the big house. They didn't need all the room, and she hadn't the energy to clean it anymore. With VA and Mallory at work most of the time, she decided to look for a small house with no stairs.

She still enjoyed the walk to Chamblee's market for groceries. Normally, VA would drive her, but on that cool October day, Lucy wanted to take her time.

The fall leaves were at their peak and the crisp morning air had that familiar faint smell of chimney smoke. She took the long way past Elyton Elementary School, walked the lovely tree-lined sidewalk of Monroe Avenue, and then turned onto 6th Street.

Lucy noticed a "For Sale" sign in front of the Parker's little house on 6th Street. Only a few blocks away from Tuscaloosa Avenue, she was familiar with the house and met Mrs. Parker some years earlier. Katy Parker had been a sorority sister of VA's, and they both had visited the house on a few occasions. She instructed Gabe to get specifics on it and make an appointment to see it the next day.

Arriving at 806 6th Street at 9:00 AM, Lucy wanted to see it quickly and leave. She didn't like the idea of poking around someone else's house.

The quaint, pale green house had a small front stoop, a screened-in porch on the side, and a detached garage at the end of the driveway. After Mrs. Parker welcomed them in, Lucy quickly asked why she was selling the house.

"Since my husband died last year, and losing my son in the war, I don't need the house anymore. My daughter Katy got married and lives in Gadsden, so I plan to move there to be near her and the grandchildren," Mrs. Parker said.

"I understand," Lucy said as she looked around at the simple furnishings in the nice-sized living room. "May I look at the kitchen and the bedrooms?"

"Of course. Make yourself at home."

As Lucy and Gabe walked through the house, she found that the three bedrooms were large enough and the full bathroom in the hall would be plenty for three people. The well-equipped kitchen had plenty of counter space and the back door led to a lovely backyard.

The small patio had a large brick grill and the nice yard was planted with rose bushes, flower beds, and shade trees. The detached garage seemed large enough for storage and the car.

"This will do fine," she told Gabe, "make the arrangements for purchase."

"We can meet with the mortgage company tomorrow," Gabe said.

"Mortgage company, hell! I don't need a mortgage company. I'll pay cash."

Lucy felt good about her choice. She, Mallory, and VA would move in as soon as Mrs. Parker was ready to vacate the property.

For weeks, Mallory had been struggling with the thought of moving into a place of her own. The last two years with VA and Lucy had been a godsend for her, and she never could've survived without the love and support they all shared during the war, especially after Bill died. After all, they lost him, too.

Dreading the thought of moving, she realized it was the only way to come to grips and go on with her life. The memories of Bill in the large house were sometimes more than she could bear.

Reading through the want-ads in the newspaper, Mallory found a listing for a small apartment in the "Highland" area of Birmingham near historic Five Points South. It was within her budget, and she made an appointment after work to see it.

The streetcar line was only one block away from the address and fifteen minutes from the office. Mallory walked to 1254-A 12th Avenue South to find a beautiful old house that had been renovated into two duplexes. She loved it already. An elderly gentleman stood on the private porch.

"Mrs. Johannsen?" He said with a welcoming smile.

"Yes," she said as they shook hands.

"My name is Wilfred Riddle. I own the house. Please come in."

Mallory knew right away this would be her new home. It was just the right size and had everything she needed. Best of all, it was one block away from shopping and the streetcar line.

She was excited for the first time in a long while, but it would be hard breaking the news to VA and Lucy. They were family, and all three had been through so much together.

"Mama, I can't believe you made the decision!"

VA said with excitement when she heard the news. "I always liked Katy Parker's house. You made a good choice."

She had seen the "SOLD" sign in front of the little house but had no idea it was her mother who bought it. The decision was long overdue, and she was looking forward to her new surroundings.

VA couldn't wait to break the news to Mallory since they both needed a change. It must have been hard on Mallory living in a house that held constant reminders and memories of Bill. When Mallory walked in the front door, VA noticed her big smile.

"I'm glad you're in a good mood. Mama bought the small house on 6th Street! We're finally moving! We're both ready for a change. Aren't you?"

"That's great! I have some news, too. I'm moving into a place of my own in three weeks," Mallory said. "This has been on my mind for a while, and I found a place in Southside."

"Really?" VA said as her excitement lost its enthusiasm. "Have you told Mama yet?"

"No, I'm going to tonight. I just signed the lease."

In September, 1945, Edward Johannsen was assigned to post-war duties in the Pacific Theater. First, Okinawa for seven months and then Honshu, one of the main islands of Japan. In November, 1946, and on the last leg of the voyage to the states, he spent a week of R and R in San Francisco with a few buddies in his unit before returning home.

```
SAN   FRANCISCO   CAL   11-15-46
10:07 AM

MRS. LUCY JOHANNSEN
508 TUSCALOOSA AVENUE
BIRMINGHAM ALABAMA

MAMA - WILL BE HOME BY TRAIN
NOV 20 (STOP)

LOVE ED
```

When Ed's train pulled in to Birmingham at 4:00 PM on the 20th, Lucy, VA, Gabe, and Mallory met him at the Terminal Station. Seeing his family waiting on the platform brought a mournful sense of reality he had yet to experience.

Realizing Bill's absence immediately created a void in his life that would never be filled. The war took him away for almost four years, and during that dreadful part of his life, there was never time for grief.

"I'm home," he said out loud as he stepped off the train. He walked to his mother with a tear rolling down his cheek.

"I'm glad to see you, Son. We've missed you. You look thin," Lucy said as she placed her hands on the handsome face of her youngest child. She pulled him down and kissed his cheek.

After hugging a smiling VA and Mallory, Ed walked over to Gabe and extended his hand as more tears began to fall.

"I know, I miss him too," Gabe said as he brushed the proffered hand aside and hugged his little brother. "Let's go home."

When they rounded the corner to the big house, Ed noticed nothing had changed since he left, and he was coming back to a neighborhood frozen in time.

Seeing the horror of death during the war and participating in the devastation afterward gave him pause to think how lucky was. He couldn't wait to walk the old neighborhood and breathe in the sweet fragrance of home.

After four years away and one month at home, Edward Johannsen left for Auburn, Alabama, in January 1947, to finish his senior year and obtain his business degree. He regained the ten pounds he lost while he was away, due to his mother's home cooking, and vowed to come home to stay after he finished his last year at Auburn. He had no plans to leave home again.

Like Mallory, VA was starting a new life. A few of the men from the office had asked her out, but she wasn't interested. She wanted to have fun although no one seemed to appeal to her. Lucy told her she was being snobbish and to go out, anyway. It didn't have to be serious, just fun.

Tom Hastings, a fellow in the communications department interested her. He had a high-ranking position in the company and had always been cordial and friendly.

She wanted no relationship now, and after speaking with Tom a few times, he didn't seem to either. *He could be fun.*

Tom impressed her since he was the Vice President of Southern Bell's long-distance communications, nice looking, and a smart dresser. Each time she had a conversation with him, he seemed calm, cool and collected. She liked him.

VA's office door was ajar, and Tom poked his head in.

"May I come in?" he asked. "Not taking you away from anything urgent, am I?"

"Heavens no," she said. "Just typing a little dictation to mail out today."

"The Pickwick has re-opened and their house orchestra is playing Friday night. Would you like to go?"

"Yes! I would love to," she said. "Sounds like fun."

"Great, I'll pick you up at 7:00."

Tom rang the doorbell and greeted Mrs. Johannsen with a smile. "How do you do? I'm Tom Hastings."

"Hello, Tom. So nice to know you."

At that moment, Tom saw VA coming down the stairs. He couldn't help but smile.

"You look wonderful, VA."

"Thank you, Tom. Ready?"

Tom handed VA a clear box tied with a pale pink ribbon. A small nosegay of light pink sweetheart roses was inside, and she gasped with delight. She took the flowers out of the box and immediately smelled their light fragrance.

"Tom, these are beautiful, thank you!"

He bowed slightly as he said goodnight to Mrs. Johannsen. Taking VA to the car, Tom looked forward to an evening with a lovely woman with whom he could be himself.

The Pickwick Club had come alive once again. The music drifted out of the front doors and into the street. Tom valeted his sedan and escorted VA in with her arm in his.

The house orchestra was playing their first set of dinner music. Tom and VA sat down at a table one back from the dance floor. They each lit a cigarette and ordered drinks.

The orchestra played Tommy Dorsey's "The Night We Called It a Day," and Tom stood as VA took his hand, and he led her to the dancefloor.

As they danced, he said, "I'm glad we're here tonight. I meant to ask you out months ago, but I heard through the grapevine you weren't dating."

"That time of my life is over. It took a while, but I've decided to start my new life and have fun. The last four years took a toll, but those days for me are over."

"Glad to hear it. I know what you mean. The war also took a lot away from me, but I'm putting it all behind me. Let's have fun tonight."

Also known for its food, the Pickwick's specialty and VA's favorite, was Trout Almandine. The last time she had it was before the war. The drinks flowed, she had her trout, and a handsome escort. She needed nothing else.

Feeling no pain, she and Tom danced while he held her close. Following his every step, she put her arm around his neck and looked behind him. Dancing a few yards away was Larry Abbott looking at her as he did that first day in English class.

"Oh, god help me, this can't be," she mumbled.

Larry danced with a short, lovely redhead while watching VA's every move. He noticed that she saw him and smiled his beautiful smile. When the dance ended, Tom took VA back to the table, and she could barely speak.

"Virginia are you okay?" he asked.

"Absolutely, the orchestra sounds great. That last song just made me a little weak in the knees."

"I know, me, too," he said as he lit a cigarette for both and ordered coffee.

As VA sipped her coffee, a familiar voice said, "Hello, Virginia. It seems we have the same Pickwick schedule."

"Hello, Julian. It seems we do," she said with a chuckle as it occurred to her he was perfectly gorgeous.

"Tom, I'd like to introduce Julian Morley, an old Pickwick friend."

Tom stood as the two shook hands, and VA invited Julian to join them.

"Thank you, but I have a date waiting at my table. I just wanted to say hello."

"So nice to see you," she said.

VA looked around for Larry and finally spotted

him. He and his redhead were on their way out of the ballroom, and he never looked back. VA's heart pounded, and she felt a bit jealous. It had been a year since their last meeting. It was fine seeing him, just unexpected.

As VA and Tom left the ballroom, she told him what a lovely time she had.

"Would you like to go to another club? It's still early."

"I'm really tired, Tom. I need to go home and sleep late in the morning. This week has been rough at the office for me, and I know it has been for you, too. May I take a rain check for another night?"

"Sure. This week has been brutal for me as well, and I look forward to cashing in that rain check. I'll take you home."

They rounded the curve to Tuscaloosa Avenue and stopped in front of the house. VA couldn't stop thinking about Larry and how good Julian looked.

"I'll see you on Monday at work," Tom said. "It's been a great night."

"Thank you, Tom. I had a wonderful time. And yes, I'll see you at work on Monday."

Glad Tom didn't try to kiss her, she felt he could be a good casual date from time to time.

It seemed odd to see Larry with another woman, though. She wondered if the woman had been the British nurse, and he brought her to the US after all.

Mrs. Parker moved out of the little house on 6th Street on Friday, February 21, 1947. Lucy was packed and ready for the movers first thing Saturday morning.

The house was built in 1933, but it would be new for them. Lucy had to give away a lot of furniture since it couldn't all fit in the smaller house. Gabe and Susie got a good bit of it since Ed and VA didn't need it. Lucy gave the rest to West End Baptist Church for the needy.

After living in the house on Tuscaloosa Avenue for almost thirty years, Lucy felt a bit emotional since this had been WB's house, and they had raised their four children there.

The memories of Bill and Eliza were some of the most precious memories she had, and they would have to be locked away for now. She would make new living memories and Lucy was ready to accept the changes.

The date for Edward's graduation was Saturday, May 22, 1947. Preparations were being made for Lucy and VA to take the train to Auburn on Friday. The three of them would return home on the following Sunday, the 23rd.

Lucy proudly watched her son graduate with honors with a BA in Business Administration. He had gone to war at age 20 in the middle of his senior year, made it through four long years in the Pacific and miraculously survived. Lucy thanked God every day for sparing two of her sons.

After graduation, Ed settled into the new house and realized he hadn't been home for any length of time in almost seven years. He left for Auburn in the fall of 1939, and then after three and a half years, the war. The last time he had been home before entering the Navy was spent with Bill discussing the war. The next morning his brother had orders to leave sooner than planned, and he never saw him again.

Edward Johannsen, 25, had grown to be six feet tall with piercing brown eyes, the trademark olive skin, and a head full of thick black hair. He parted it on the side and combed it back like Clark Gable. He seemed to be the catch of the year.

"You attract girls like Bill did," VA said. "Go outside and give 'em a thrill."

"Bushwa, VA," Ed said. "He was much better looking than I am. Anyway, they're nothing but jailbait."

He ignored the silly female behavior and concentrated on gaining employment with Mutual of Omaha Insurance Company. He had one interview so far and hoped for another.

Ed walked to Holms Drugstore with VA for old time sake. She needed a few things and walking with her would be bittersweet. They had always been close, and he missed his sister for four long years.

While they were at Holms, a lovely blonde walked in and sat down at the soda fountain. He couldn't take his eyes off her.

"You know who that is, don't you?" VA asked.

"No, but I think I might marry her one day."

"That's Mary Ladner. Her husband was shot down in North Africa, and she has a four-year-old daughter. Don't you remember Bob Ladner from school?"

"I remember him, and it was the Pacific, not North Africa. A nice fellow. I somehow remember Mary, but it seems so long ago," he said. "She's a few years younger than we are, isn't she? I want to get to know her if I can."

"You should," VA said. "Mary is a nice girl from a good family. After Bob's death, she moved back in with her parents on Monroe Avenue and had the baby while Bob was overseas. He never met his daughter."

Ed waited until VA made her purchase. Mary Ladner remained at the fountain, and VA motioned Ed to come with her in the direction of Mary.

"Mary, I saw you come in. Do you remember my

younger brother, Ed?" VA asked.

Mary smiled. "Hello, Ed. I remember you, but it's been a long time. I recall seeing you and your brothers playing football at the high school from time to time."

"You have a great memory. We played a good bit. The war took me away for a while, but I'm home now," Ed said in his soft and shy voice.

Taken in by her lovely smile, he began to blush. Ed sat down beside Mary at the fountain. They talked about the neighborhood before the war and all the mutual friends they had, and the ones they lost.

Ed didn't even see VA leave the drugstore. He and Mary were so deep in conversation, they didn't see the soda jerk waiting for Ed's order.

VA left her brother in good hands. As she walked in the house from the drugstore, she overheard Lucy talking on the phone. That was a rarity, so she stopped and listened.

"Mallory, as a favor, would you put in a request to the War Department to bring Bill's body home to Birmingham? I would appreciate it."

VA knew her mother was a person of few words. She made her point quickly and hung up. No goodbye, no time for Mallory to say anything. Mallory knew Lucy almost as well as VA did.

Part Three

Gardenias are a Girl's Best Friend...

CHAPTER 18

The Pickwick Club

Fall 1947

*H*onorably discharged from the Army in early 1946, Julian Charles Morley moved to a small apartment on prestigious Highland Avenue in Birmingham. A Transportation Inspector with Southern Railway by day, he proved to be a definite ladies' man by night. Julian stood around 5'9", had deep hazel eyes, broad shoulders, and a slim waist. He parted his light brown hair on the side and combed it back from his face. In addition to being handsome and a smart dresser, he had a notorious black book with each page filled.

One name wasn't included in this black book. He wanted to add the name of the beautiful girl with emerald green eyes to the top of the first page, but he hadn't had the chance. The times he'd seen her, she always had an escort or the fiancé overseas.

He wondered if she was engaged to one of the

men he last saw her with at the Greenwood Café and the Pickwick. Tom Hastings hadn't been the name of the fiancé she told him about the first night they met a few years ago, and the other one wasn't introduced.

He was intrigued with this woman and wanted to know her status. They danced a few times, but he couldn't get her out of his mind. She was a beauty with class. Most of the girls he went out with were trashy and drank too much. She had grace and poise but in a snobbish way. He liked her style, but he only knew her as "Virginia."

Julian wanted to see her again but had no idea where she lived, where she worked, or if she was even available. Now that the Pickwick Nite Club was open again, he would have to go there on a regular basis. That way, and with a little luck, he might catch up with her.

On a Saturday, after a long work week, VA, Mallory, and Dorothy LeVoy planned to do some shopping, have dinner out, then grab a quick nightcap at the Pickwick.

Birmingham offered plenty of other nightspots, but the girls could go to the Pickwick unescorted, and they liked the atmosphere.

"Why don't we go to the Tutwiler tonight for dinner and drinks? It's a change," Mallory said. "We haven't been there in a long time, and I heard the

Continental Room Lounge was renovated and enlarged. If we don't sit at the bar, we can have dinner there, and it won't matter if we're unescorted."

"That sounds great, what about you, Dorothy?" VA asked.

"It sounds good, but I think I'm ready to call it a day. I'll go next time, though."

After dropping Dorothy off at her apartment, Mallory said, "I don't think she has a very high opinion of us, or she doesn't know how to socialize."

"She's the spinster type, and I think men make her nervous. She's a great dancer, though. Remember in Mexico? She's a great conversationalist, but not much of a social butterfly."

After walking into the lobby of the Tutwiler, they immediately noticed the crowded lounge. They saw a large sign posted in front of the Terrace Ballroom that read "PRIVATE PARTY."

"Oh, well," Mallory said. "Let's find a place to sit in the lobby, and get a waiter. Hopefully, we can snag a table."

They sat down on a vacant couch not too far from the entrance to the bar. The unrelenting sound of loud voices, and the clinking of glasses in the hotel lounge caused the usual calm atmosphere to be unpleasant. The smell of cigar smoke made it worse.

Shortly, a waiter walked up to take their order.

Plugging her ears with her fingers, Mallory looked at VA and then at the waiter. "What's going on?" she yelled.

"Tallulah Bankhead is in town and reserved the Terrace Ballroom for a huge wing-ding. Most of the patrons in the lounge are part of the Alabama Dental Association Convention, though their party is in another ballroom. I guess they're starting off the evening here," the waiter said.

"Let's go to the Pickwick, instead," said Mallory.

VA splurged and valeted the car at the Pickwick. She didn't want to ruin her new shoes walking on the gravel parking lot. After she and Mallory entered the club, they couldn't help but notice how crowded it was.

"What in the world is going on tonight?" VA asked.

They didn't recognize the name of the orchestra, but they were fantastic with their "Harry James" sound. Still early for VA and Mallory, they found a table next to the orchestra so they could listen to the music without interruption.

"Well, what do you know? What is it about this club that draws us both here on the same nights?" Julian Morley asked VA as he approached the table. "May I refresh both of your drinks?"

"Mine is fine, thanks, but VA could use a refresher," Mallory said.

VA quickly turned her head and glared at Mallory.

"Okay, sure. I can use another. It's a gin and tonic."

"I'll be right back," Julian said as he left for the bar.

"Mallory, what the hell?" VA said through her teeth while pretending to be mad.

She could never be mad at Mallory. As they laughed, Julian quickly reappeared with three drinks.

"I know you said you didn't need a refill, but I took a guess and thought it could save me another trip later. I might be dancing or talking or who knows?

"Well, thank you, Julian. I appreciate it," said Mallory. "It looks like your guess was correct."

VA fumbled in her purse and brought out two cigarettes and a lighter. She gave one to Mallory and Julian stood by ready with his lighter.

"Mallory, would you mind if I danced with your friend?" he asked while lighting her cigarette.

"She's my sister-in-law, and no, I don't mind."

VA felt vulnerable when she gave in to the fact the man was absolute perfection. It looked as if he had put on a few pounds. *I'm staring. Stop it, you fool.* She couldn't help but notice his skin was flawless, and he had a very nice profile. His nose was straight, and the right size for his face, not like hers which was a little large. She wanted to get a closer look, but quickly turned away.

When he took her by the hand and led her to the dance floor, VA felt goosebumps. Never did his eyes leave hers as he placed his hand firmly around her waist, and ever so gently, pulled her close. She didn't mind this time as she got the closer look she wanted.

Julian had plenty of hair with a slight curl and a good hairline. His lips were not large, but on the fuller side, and he had the most attractive deep dimple in his right cheek.

VA continued to study his face, and strange chill went up her spine. It felt as if she had seen him for the first time.

As they danced, he placed his cheek on hers and whispered, "I was hoping to see you here tonight. I don't even know your last name."

VA leaned back to look at him, smiled and said, "I'll tell you later."

She had never been swept off her feet quite like this. As they danced, Julian never took his cheek off hers, and when she drew back to look at him, he smiled.

"Virginia, I've been waiting for you to come back to the Pickwick. Since our last meeting, I haven't been able to get you out of my mind. Tell me you aren't still engaged."

"Why don't we sit?" she asked.

VA took his arm, and they returned to her table. After they sat down, VA watched as Julian lit two cigarettes and motioned for the waiter.

"We'll have a gin and tonic and a scotch on the rocks."

Oh lord, that sultry drawl. It sounded authoritative, self-confident, and commanding. Julian impressed her, and never did she think anyone could get Larry Abbott out of her mind, but Julian did.

After she told him about the broken engagement to Larry, Mallory returned to the table. VA listened as she told her about seeing Ben Gravlee, an old attorney friend of Bill's.

VA completely changed her train of thought and listened as Mallory updated her on Ben's family, and his law practice after the war.

While she gave Mallory her undivided attention, VA rested her hand on Julian's thigh and squeezed. His look of desire made her blush, and she asked to be excused.

She hurried toward the patio in the back of the club. She stopped and turned around. There he was, standing in front of her. He took her face in his hands and kissed her in a way she had never experienced. Her hands rested on his chest as he pulled back and looked into her eyes. She smiled, he kissed her again, and then they retreated into a dark corner of the patio.

Hidden by bushes and large urns of flowers, they sat down on a fancy garden bench where she wanted to look deep into his soul.

"You are the most beautiful girl. Please let me see you again."

"You're full of it, but I'd like that," she said.

Am I over Larry completely? VA didn't want to think about Larry because she wanted to embrace the moment and go with her instincts. It had been so long since she had a desire for someone other than Larry.

When they stood, Julian took her hand, and leaned in to kiss her again. She thought her emotions would never come back, but this seemed like it could go too far. She had to stop it.

"We can't do this, Julian," VA said, as she remembered saying the same thing to Larry so long ago.

"Why not? No one's around."

"This isn't even a date. We coincidentally met at the same nightspot," VA said. "Let's go in."

Waiting for him to agree, he pulled her close and gently kissed her neck, shoulders and the palms of both hands. Though almost distracted from coherent behavior, she was right. If she gave in, anything they might have together could be ruined.

Disappointed, they returned to the table and found Mallory sitting with a very handsome, distinguished older man.

"VA, I want to introduce you to Peter Moore. I think I've mentioned him to you."

"Yes," VA said as Peter stood up. "It's so nice to meet you, Peter. Julian Morley, an old friend," she gestured.

The orchestra began playing Dick Haymes' version of "Mam'selle."

"Please excuse us; this is a great song. We'll be right back," Julian said.

VA looked back at Mallory, and they both smiled. Peter seemed to be a great guy, and Mallory looked genuinely happy. She deserved it.

As they danced to "Mam'selle", Julian pulled her so close he could almost feel her heart beating. The song reminded him of her every time he heard it. *After the dance ends, I'll take her outside to the car.* Hesitating, he realized she didn't want that. Virginia wasn't like the other girls he knew. They always gave in to him, and where were they now? A regretful distant memory. She was different.

Do I want to fall in love or keep my independence? He'd seduced his share of ladies; they would succumb, and then he would have his way, but there was hardly an emotional attachment. He had plenty of money, but what good was it when he couldn't share it with someone close?

He tried to deny his feelings for Virginia and give it a while. If he still felt the urge to see her, then he would call. *How does she feel about me?* She mystified him.

As they walked back to the table, Julian apologized for expecting too much from her. He didn't want her to think him a complete SOB or that he did that sort of thing all the time, even though he did.

"May I see you again sometime?" he asked.

"Of course. You and I dance well together," VA said with a sensual smile as she gave him her phone number.

"You're not like the other girls I've known. I felt nothing for them, but you make me feel like a different person. I'm glad you'll see me again."

His hazel eyes never strayed from hers as he leaned in to kiss her gently on the lips.

"I'm glad, too. Call me when you have a chance. Tonight is the beginning of some good times together."

"Oh yes-it-is," Julian thought. "By the way, what *is* your last name?"

CHAPTER 19

Changes

November 1947

Ed and Mary Ladner had been seeing each other exclusively for three months, and he knew she was right for him. Even though they hadn't been dating long, Ed knew his feelings for Mary were genuine. He wanted to propose but wanted it to be special, something to remember. Gabe, Susie and the boys were coming over on Sunday, and he would ask for advice from his brother. After a huge Sunday dinner and a touch football game, Steve and little Andy passed out on the living room floor. Ed asked his brother to take a walk with him.

"I want to propose to Mary, but I don't know how she might take it. She says she loves me, but I'm afraid she'll turn me down because of Tricia. I love that little girl, too."

"I wouldn't worry too much about it. If Mary does love you, she'll say yes. If you make sure she knows you love Tricia too, then that's all you need to do. Just ask her in a way that lets her know your feelings are genuine," Gabe said in a fatherly fashion.

He took his brother's advice to heart, and after a week, Ed bought the ring and planned a romantic dinner for two at Lucy's house.

His plans were set. He asked Lucy to bake his favorite cake and prepare the baked potatoes. Then he would toss a salad and fire up the brick grill on the small back patio.

The dining room table was set for two with Lucy's beautiful 24-carat gold trimmed china, crystal champagne glasses, and sterling silver flatware. Two silver candlesticks were placed on the table, and some late-season roses from the garden were arranged in a crystal vase by VA. He wanted this night to be perfect.

After Bob died, Mary was miserable in the small apartment alone and would need help with the baby. She was persuaded by her parents to move back in with them and let them take care of her when the baby came. Tricia arrived five months after Bob died.

Mary's husband, Bob Ladner, had been based on the same aircraft carrier as Gabe Johannsen. Mary called Gabe a few times when she found out he was home on leave. She wanted information on Bob's death, but couldn't get Gabe to open-up about anything pertaining to the war. Mary finally realized how difficult it would be for Gabe to describe details, especially to his buddy's widow. All she knew was that Bob had been shot down flying maneuvers over the Solomon Islands by a Japanese warship.

After getting to know Ed again, Mary felt as if he had come into her life by divine intervention. Her life had become hollow, and her only happiness was four-year-old Tricia. Her parents were trying hard to make a life for them, but she and Tricia couldn't stay there forever. Bob's death left a place in her heart that was empty until Ed came into her life.

Being with Ed made her feel loved, safe, and happy. He was a sincere, genuine person, and she had fallen in love with him. She didn't mind his quiet shyness, and she loved his great dry sense of humor. To her delight, Tricia took instantly to Ed, and Mary thought it had to be because of his calmness and soft-spoken manner. How could she have ever known that day at Holms drugstore would change her life?

VA and Lucy were going to Mallory's on the evening of Ed's proposal dinner. VA had to talk her mother into it since Lucy didn't think it was necessary.

"Mama, they need to be alone, don't you think? Ed certainly doesn't need his mother around on such a special night."

When they got to Mallory's, VA showed Lucy around the charming duplex. She liked it very much and thought her daughter-in-law chose well. They had a cocktail, and VA noticed that her mother seemed agitated. They'd been at Mallory's for an hour, and Lucy appeared ready to go home.

"Good lord, Mama. We haven't even eaten dinner yet. Ed's fine. We have to give them some time." VA looked at her watch. "It's 7:00, and Mallory prepared a great dinner. Calm down."

After dinner, VA looked at Mallory and rolled her eyes. "Let me help with clean-up."

"No, no, not necessary," Mallory said knowing Lucy was ready to go.

"Well, I expect we'd better go then," Lucy said. "Dinner was very nice. Thank you."

Getting into the car, VA immediately piped up. "Mama, you were rude to her. She went to a lot of trouble fixing dinner for us! I'd be ashamed."

"I'll do as I damn well please. I don't need you to tell me how to behave and I can't see that you could do any better. If you weren't so snobbish, *you* might have a husband by now."

That last remark cut deep into VA's soul. *It wasn't my fault Larry found someone else. I would have been married, but the last four years denied me of that happiness, that full life. Why are you being such a bitch? Do you want me to take up with just any man? I can't do anything right in your eyes.*

VA stayed quiet the entire way home, and Lucy placed her hands in her lap and looked out the car window.

When they drove into the driveway, the lights were out, but they could hear music playing from the open windows.

"Uh oh," VA said. "We can't go in now."

"I'll be damned if that's so," Lucy said. "I'm going to bed."

They parked the car in the garage and went in the back door. All the dishes were washed and dried. The dining room was set again in its usual way with the china and crystal carefully placed back into the china cabinet. No one was there.

"Ed must have forgotten to turn off the radio before they left," VA said.

"Well good," Lucy said. "It must have gone well."

"How can you tell? It's only 9:00."

VA vowed to stay awake until Ed got home. She changed into her pajamas and got comfortable in her daddy's old chair. By 2:00 AM he still wasn't home. She felt like his mother waiting up, but finally, she heard the key in the front door and Ed came in.

"Well? What did she say?"

"I'm getting married to the most gorgeous girl in West End!"

"I knew it! When?"

"Not sure yet, we have to take time and look at the calendar. In a month or so but maybe after the first of the year. We talked in depth about Tricia, and I'll adopt her if that's what Mary wants. I would in a minute, but that's her decision."

"Mama went to bed a long time ago, but I couldn't wait to hear the news. I'm calling Mallory now. She wanted to know when I did."

Julian Morley couldn't stop thinking about Virginia. It had been two weeks since he'd seen her at the Pickwick. He tried not to call her and get her off his mind, but it was no good. Nothing worked.

He went to work every day and did his job thoroughly, but couldn't get those eyes, that body, or the feeling of her skin out of his head. The 1947 Southern Railway Christmas party was coming up, and he would call and ask her to go.

"Virginia, this is Julian Morley," he said with a trembling voice. "It's been a while, and I apologize for that, but I'm calling to ask if you're free on Saturday, December 13th? That's in two weeks. I have a company Christmas party at the Terrace Ballroom, and I hoped you'd be able to accompany me."

"Yes, it's been a while. My brother is getting married on the 14th, and I'm not sure of all I need to do, but I think I should be able to go with you. Sounds like a great night."

"Great! I'll pick you up at 7:00, and it's formal. Tell me your address." After writing down the address, he felt like a complete idiot. He hoped she didn't hear the tremble in his voice. No woman had ever caused that to happen.

The next two weeks went by quickly. Julian, eager to see Virginia again, purchased a new, black tuxedo and formal patent leather shoes. He went to the barber the day of the party for a clean shave and haircut. He wanted to look his absolute best tonight.

He rang the doorbell precisely at 7:00 and adjusted his bow tie. It felt like he tied it too tight. The door was opened by a short, middle-aged woman with greying hair. He noticed the resemblance.

"Good evening, Mrs. Johannsen. I'm Julian Morley."

"Come in Julian. So nice to meet you. Virginia is expecting you."

At that moment he saw VA coming out of her bedroom wearing an emerald green gown and holding a matching cape. She smiled, and when he opened his mouth to speak, he stammered a little.

"V--Virginia, you're lovely in that color." It was all he could say.

Julian had seen some beautiful girls in his time, but none as lovely as Virginia. He noticed how her hair was pinned up with a few curls falling on each side, and how her deep green eyes were illuminated from the emerald color of her dress. He handed her a beautifully packaged white box. Inside were three perfect gardenias fashioned into a corsage and dotted with rhinestones for a slight sparkle.

"Oh, Julian, these are beautiful! I can't believe you found gardenias in December. Thank you!"

He took the cape and placed it around her shoulders. As he pinned the gardenias on the cape, she said with a smile, "You look very handsome in your tuxedo."

Julian opened the door of his black, 1947 Chrysler convertible and helped VA in. He couldn't wait to show her off to his co-workers. "Virginia, I'm speechless. You look so pretty tonight."

He turned on the radio and the song, "I'll Get By (As Long as I Have You)," came on. VA leaned her head back on the seat and hummed to the music for a minute or so, then stopped.

"Why did you stop?"

"I can't carry a tune; I wish I could."

"It sounded fine to me," he said with a chuckle.

He caught her looking over at him and then pulled her over to sit beside him. He took her hand and brought it to his lips and kissed it. He looked at her, and she seemed to be impressed with the move.

In a few minutes, he turned the car into the Tutwiler valet parking lane. He walked around and opened the door for her and helped her out.

As usual, the hotel bustled with patrons and party goers. He took her arm as they entered the building. The lobby was decorated with lavish pine garlands, holly wreaths with red ribbons, and a beautiful floor-to-ceiling Christmas tree next to the circular staircase.

Julian led her up the steps to the mezzanine and then into the Terrace Ballroom where they found their reserved table. Some of Julian's co-workers and their spouses dropped by for an introduction then moved on to find their tables. Julian ordered drinks and lit two cigarettes.

"This room is beautiful with the decorations, isn't it?" VA said as she looked around the room. There were two, large, decorated Christmas trees on each side of the orchestra stage, and each tree held a multitude of brightly colored ornaments and sparkling silver icicles. Each guest table had a large arrangement of Christmas pine and poinsettias.

Julian had requested a table for two near the dance floor. There were other couples with a small table like theirs, and others with larger tables for a group.

Several large food stations had been placed at each corner of the vast ballroom. Each station had a chef who created his specialty and described it to the guests. Julian and VA weren't ready to eat, so they ordered another drink and carried on an intimate conversation.

He moved his chair next to VA's and placed his arm around it.

"Why does everyone call you VA?"

"That's the nickname my brother Gabe came up with because he was too lazy to say, Virginia."

"Well, I like it. May I call you VA?"

"Of course, everybody does."

"May I also say that you are the loveliest girl at the party? And that I'm so proud that you're with me?"

The orchestra started to play, and VA felt a little edge. With the excitement of tonight and the wedding tomorrow, she hadn't eaten a thing all day.

"Let's get some dinner," Julian said. "I think we

both need something to eat."

As he pulled out her chair, she said, "Thank you for inviting me to your office party. I'm having a wonderful time." She realized she had slurred her words but continued. "My office party is next weekend. Would you like to come with me?"

"I'd love to," he said. "No more drinks for you."

After lighting a cigarette, VA ordered hot coffee and dessert. She needed a clear head and wanted him to know she didn't ask him to the party out of gratitude. She simply wanted to see him again. "I'll let you know about the party. Not sure of the details yet."

"Let's dance," he said as he took her hand.

The orchestra played a slow number, and VA melted in his arms as they held their cigarettes while dancing. He hummed in her ear. *Why did she feel so comfortable with him? Was she imagining it? He felt good as he held her.* She rested her head on his shoulder as they glided across the floor. They seemed to mold into one another as each dance step was in sync. She was so at ease with Julian. *Was she ever this relaxed with Larry? Stop comparing every man to Larry, damn it!*

When Julian took her hand and brought it to his lips, their dance was almost over. He didn't want to let her go. His other hand was placed firmly around her waist. The movement of her body excited him, and he wanted to get her out of there. He had to be in love with her. When the music ended, they left the dance floor and noticed that other couples were leaving.

The coffee must have helped; VA didn't appear so tight anymore.

"Ready to go?"

"The party has been so nice, Julian. I hate to see it end."

"We can have many more nights like this, if you want them."

"I do," she replied.

He leaned down and gently kissed her cheek before he put the wrap around her shoulders. He led her to a chair in the Tutwiler lobby, then stepped out to retrieve the car from the valet.

On the way home, the radio played a slow Harry James song. It was cold outside, and the heater in the car had yet to warm up. Julian tried to drive as she shivered and snuggled in even closer. That did it. Julian pulled the car over into a dimly lit parking lot close to her house and parked the car. He turned to her, put his arm around her and pulled her close.

"VA, I can't stop. I have to have you."

He kissed her with an eagerness that seemed to overwhelm her. His heart raced as he took his jacket off and began to remove her cape. The heater wasn't warm but he was on fire.

"Julian, wait! Not here. Keep driving and I'll show you where."

The heater finally warmed up, and he followed her directions. She directed him to the back of the old Elyton Elementary School where it was quiet and dark. He parked, then turned off the lights and the engine.

Being so aroused, he thought he might bust. He couldn't let that happen. It would be disappointing to them both. He tried to contain himself but she had already ignited the flame.

He unzipped her dress and guided her down to the seat while never taking his eyes off hers. She seemed so willing and he kissed her warm lips while exploring every curve of her body. His mind went blank as the need drove him to find a welcoming entrance. The part of him he wanted to give her found its opening. She almost welcomed him in.

"Julian, stop. We can't."

"Oh lord, VA, please! I want you so much."

"It's not right. Not now, not...yet."

His frustration overwhelmed him. He hit the steering wheel with the palm of his hand and looked out the window to nothing but darkness. He got out of the car, walked around the parking lot, and came back in about five minutes.

"We've only had one date. I'm not easy," VA said. "Help me with my zipper?"

Julian complied and after sitting quietly for a while, he broke the silence. "VA, I'm in love with you."

Her look betrayed some suspicion. "Are you sure it's not just lust?"

"Yes, I'm sure. I've never known anyone like you! No one ever excited me so."

"I doubt that," she said. "After tonight, I'll probably never hear from you again."

"We have a date to your office party next Saturday, remember?"

"I know. I was hoping you hadn't changed your mind."

"Never. I'm your date, like it or not."

Julian started the car, and VA held tightly to his arm as he took her home. He walked her to the door and kissed her, then gave her a gentle hug.

As he walked back to the car, he made the decision. She was going to be his wife. He had been in love with her ever since the second or third time they danced at the Pickwick. He hoped it wouldn't be a one-sided love.

December 14th, 1947, was cold, with light snow predicted, and it was VA's little brother's wedding day. The Ladner's charming house was a perfect setting for the wedding.

The front parlor, set with chairs facing the fireplace, had been decorated with red roses and large, shiny magnolia leaves. Every flat surface in the dining room was filled with food and refreshments for the reception. The two-tiered, white wedding cake was embellished with white roses and topped with a bride and groom.

VA could smell the icing as she helped to set out the wedding favors. As the pastor gathered everyone together, the pianist played a variety of lovely melodies on the piano. At 11:30 sharp, she played, "Here Comes the Bride."

VA watched Gabe lead Lucy to her seat then take his place next to Ed as best man.

Mary Ladner slowly stepped down the staircase in a champagne ivory, satin suit with matching hat and carried an arm bouquet of white roses and Lily of the Valley. VA thought she looked like Ginger Rogers coming down the stairs with her slim figure, lovely face, and blonde hair.

Mary's mother, Selena Ladner, sat with her five-year-old granddaughter, Tricia. Mary made sure her mother and daughter had a small nosegay of white sweetheart roses, and Ed, a white rose boutonniere. Mr.

Ladner met her at the bottom of the stairs, and presented her to Ed.

After the short ceremony and wedding pictures, the newlywed couple greeted every guest. VA had never seen Ed so content. She knew Mary would be the perfect wife and partner for him.

"Well, VA, how is your love life these days?" asked Gabe while passing a piece of the wedding cake to her. "Mama says you've been seeing Julian Morley."

"So, what? It's none of your business." VA replied as she tried to find someone nearby to talk to. She knew he'd start poking around about Julian.

"I'm just asking. I hear he works for Southern Railway. What does he do?"

"I'm not exactly sure of the exact title, but I know he's an inspector of some kind. We've only had one date. Julian is a nice fellow, and I like him."

As Gabe continued to probe, Mary and Susie grabbed her for a group picture, and she got away from him as fast as possible. *He always gets in my business. Why can't he leave me alone?*

While posing with Ed and Mary, she thought of how her wedding could have been like this. Today, as much as she fought it, her thoughts were on nothing but Larry Abbott.

CHAPTER 20

Highland Avenue

Summer 1948

*J*ulian and VA had been seeing each other regularly for three months. They went out after work and on the weekends. He hadn't invited her to his apartment yet, but he wanted to have her over for dinner. His sister, Dorothy, suggested he have the place deep-cleaned and fumigated before that happened. She told him the place "...looked and smelled like a nasty, dirty man."

After three months together, VA learned a lot about Julian. He proved to be more than a guy out for a good time.

Born on Christmas Day, 1905, Julian was one of six children--three girls, and three boys. Raised in Seddon, Alabama, his father, John T. Morley had been tragically killed in 1922, from injuries caused by a construction accident at Mitchell Dam in Verbena, Alabama. James, his older brother, remained overseas after the Great War, so Julian automatically became the man of the house at age 17. His father's death caused him to give up his college plans to provide for his mother, younger brother, and three sisters. He then began his career with Southern Railway.

John T. hadn't been a wealthy man, but he owned his home in Pell City and left a small pension, and a life insurance policy to his widow, Lena. With Julian's wages, in addition to the life insurance, they lived comfortably.

Julian admitted to VA that he was 14 years older than she, and how he had to go to work after graduating high school. With all the hardship, he and his siblings still had a good childhood.

John T. had been a kind, devoted father and was well-read. Their stern mother saved every extra dime that came into the house, especially during the Depression. His sisters jealously commented on how Lena was overly kind, and spoiled Julian since he gave up college for his family.

When he told VA his age, she didn't care that he was 43, since she thought he looked ten years younger.

Her 29th birthday was in a week, and Julian asked her to meet him for dinner at the Bohemian Bakery and Delicatessen on 4th Avenue South. The quaint patio, and outside bar would be an ideal setting for an early dinner. They found a private table on the patio, and Julian pulled his wrought-iron chair close to hers.

"I want you to meet my family," he told her. "I know they'll love you. First, though, I'm inviting you to my apartment for dinner this Saturday night. I'm planning a special birthday for you."

"Okay," VA said with a slight question in her voice. "I'm looking forward to this, I think."

"Don't worry. I've been planning this for weeks. I think you'll like it."

VA smiled as she leaned over and pulled his tie, so his face stopped right in front of hers. She lightly kissed him on the lips and whispered, "I can't wait."

Julian instructed VA to come to his apartment, so she could fully experience what he'd planned. He gave her his address, and when she arrived, she should knock on his door at 6:30 sharp. Excited, she grabbed her purse and headed to the apartment.

She had been on Highland Avenue many times, and Julian's apartment building was one of the charming old ones from the early 1900s.

The stately old structure, built of beige-colored limestone, had turn-of-the-century scroll detailing and was quite exquisite. Each apartment had a lovely covered balcony, accented with ornate cement spindles. She parked on the street and went to the front entrance.

After opening a heavy glass door, she saw a beautifully carved wooden staircase. Built-in to the wall, each brass mailbox had a tenant's apartment number and a buzzer. VA found Julian's and pushed. She looked at her watch, and it said 6:29.

"Come on up!" said a familiar male voice.

VA climbed the stairs and immediately found his apartment. A savory aroma seeped through the apartment door. She lightly knocked, and the door slowly opened to a small violin trio playing "Mam'selle" on the balcony.

As she walked into the living room, she quickly noticed a beautiful table set for two in the dining room. Candlelight lit the entire apartment. The bronze chandelier was illuminated with flames; apparently never wired for electricity.

VA stood, rooted in amazement at the charm of it all. *Who opened the door for her?* The trio continued to play as she looked for Julian. Behind the front door stood the familiar maître d' she recognized from Ed Salem's Restaurant.

"I'm Robert, your waiter for tonight. May I offer you a champagne cocktail to start?"

"Yes, thank you," she said as he took her purse and jacket and gently placed them on a chair.

As VA looked around the living room, she noticed

tasteful furnishings including a dark blue couch, built-in bookcases filled with model trains, and a grouping of framed pictures. Each picture seemed to contain an attractive woman.

Robert brought her cocktail and slowly slipped out of the room. The aroma of steak made her mouth water. As VA took a sip of her cocktail, she slowly swayed to the soft music of the trio. Julian came out of the kitchen with hors-d'oeuvres.

"Good evening, Virginia," he said with his beautiful drawl and seductive smile.

Watching as he placed the hors-d'oeuvres on the table, she took another sip of her cocktail before he took it and set it down. Already swaying to the music, VA took his arm and they danced to the soft strings.

"I love you," he whispered looking into her eyes.

"I love you," she murmured as she kissed him.

"Care for an appetizer?" he asked, gesturing to the tray.

Sitting on the dark blue couch, they tasted the stuffed mushrooms and shrimp cocktail. Julian took VA's hand and raised his glass.

"To the loveliest woman I've ever known and *will* ever know. I hope this is one of the happiest birthdays you will ever have." He took her hand again and brought her close, and they danced as they held their drinks.

They toasted as Robert quietly entered the room and announced, "Dinner is ready."

VA was led to the dining room and the beautiful table of candlelight and red roses. In awe of the romantic glow of the room, she was enamored with this man. She felt so touched that he had planned so long for tonight--and all for her! No one had ever expressed feelings for her in such a way. The strings softly played as they were seated.

VA liked her steak well done, and Robert made sure it was perfect. Few people could grill a steak to her liking. A few times during dinner, Julian took her hand and raised it to his lips. Overwhelmed, she thought he couldn't top this evening if he tried.

Robert brought in the most beautiful birthday cake she'd ever seen. Small, white and expertly decorated with pale pink and white trimming. The orchestra played while Julian sang "Happy Birthday." There were nine lit candles. VA made a wish and blew them out.

"I hope that wish included me," Julian said.

"Maybe," she said with a timid smile. "I have to say this has been the most wonderful birthday I have ever had. No. It's actually the most wonderful *night*."

"It's not over yet."

"You can't possibly have anything else planned!"

"Wait and see."

After Robert and the orchestra left, Julian re-lit the burned-out candles, then went to the record player to put on some soft instrumental music. He sat down beside her and leaned over to kiss her. It was a loving kiss, not a sensual or passionate one.

"VA," he said as he dropped to one knee. "I love you. I'm sure I have loved you since the second or third time we saw each other at the Pickwick. You were on my mind while I was overseas, and when I returned home and saw you at the club with Mallory, I knew. Will you marry me?" he asked as he handed her a small box containing a ring with a large, beautiful diamond.

She gasped and said in a timid voice, "I've loved you, too, much longer than I thought. I realized it the last time I saw you at the Pickwick. Yes, I will marry you."

With that, he placed the ring on her finger and kissed her with gentle affection. Suddenly, the doorbell rang, and Susie, Gabe, Mallory, Peter, Ed, and Mary all popped in.

VA laughed as they all came in. "Julian, you SOB, they all knew?"

"Well, you needed a real birthday party, didn't you?" He turned to the others and announced with excitement, "She said yes!"

Mallory ran over to VA and hugged her tight. "I knew it!"

Gabe shook his hand, and Susie hugged Julian while Ed and Mary hugged VA. The people she loved the most were celebrating the beginning of her new life.

CHAPTER 21

Cheers to a New Life

Spring 1948

*T*here was a wedding to plan, and Lucy searched wedding dress patterns that would suit VA. She always wanted to create a wedding dress, and now she could. She wouldn't need but a couple of months and was surprised at the excitement she felt.

"Mama, we haven't set the date yet. It might even be next year," VA said.

"It takes a long time to make a wedding gown. I'll need to start on it as soon as possible."

"We're looking at the calendar this weekend. I'll know by Sunday. Julian needs to plan it around his vacation days, and so do I. Maybe we can settle on a date in June."

"That's only three months away, but it'll still give me plenty of time."

Wanting to get married soon, they decided on June 27, 1948. Being on a Sunday, each could take the following week off from work for the honeymoon.

VA never wanted a big, fussy wedding, and hoped her mother wouldn't be too disappointed not making a lavish gown. All she wanted was a simple, but elegant, white satin suit. She found a beautiful one featured in *Bride's Magazine.*

"Mama, this is what I want to wear," VA said as she showed Lucy the photograph in the magazine.

"Are you sure you don't want a long wedding dress?"

"I'm sure. I want the whole affair to be simple, and that includes what I wear." To VA's delight, her mother seemed fine with the choice.

With the magazine photograph propped next to the sewing machine, Lucy replicated the satin suit. The jacket and straight skirt were more difficult to sew than she expected. The satin tended to move while cutting, and it was difficult to keep a neat edge.

After breaking two sewing machine needles, Lucy's frustration almost caused her to take the streetcar downtown and buy a white suit. Glaring at the white satin, she calmed down and gingerly pumped the treadle of the sewing machine. After one month, four machine needles, and three fittings, the suit fit perfectly.

Knowing how hard her mother worked on the suit, VA was determined to find the right accessories to wear with it. At Loveman's Department Store, she found a small, white bridal hat with a birdcage veil, and white satin shoes. She also bought a beautiful crystal corsage brooch that she would pin on the lapel of the jacket.

VA protested when Susie, Mary, and Mallory wanted to give the couple a reception after the wedding. VA wanted no fanfare, just Julian. The faster they could start their honeymoon, the better, but she finally gave in.

When June 27th finally came, VA's nerves got the better of her. *Were they second thoughts?* She called Mallory and was assured it was only nerves. Feeling better, she got dressed in her white satin suit. She put her hair up, and curled it around the new white silk hat, then unfolded the small veil, so it rested just below the tip of her nose. When she came out of her room, Lucy was waiting and smiling.

"Virginia, you look beautiful. Oh, and you have a delivery."

A large box sat on the table by the front door. VA opened it and found a beautiful bouquet of white gardenias tied with long, white, satin ribbons. VA read the card enclosed:

"To my beautiful bride. I can't wait to spend my

life with you. Julian."

Never had VA been so touched. She took the flowers and inhaled the sweet fragrance. Taking them to the dining room mirror, she looked at her reflection, and almost cried. Fighting back the tears, she realized Julian had succeeded in restoring her emotions.

"It's time to go," Lucy said.

When they arrived for the 12:30 ceremony at West End Baptist, Ed was waiting to escort Lucy in. Already in the chapel were a few family members from Clairmont, Julian's family, and a few of VA's co-workers.

Gabe wanted to take VA in, walk her down the aisle, and give his little sister away. He hoped this would be a good marriage. She'd been hurt badly by Larry, and he didn't think she had fully recovered from it.

Julian's younger brother, Phillip, stepped up as the best man.

After the short ceremony, the pastor uttered the long-awaited words, "I now pronounce you man and wife. You may kiss your bride."

Julian raised the small veil and gave VA a gentle but loving kiss that lasted about 15 seconds.

Ed let out an ear-splitting whistle while Mary looked at him discouragingly.

Everyone laughed, including the newlyweds.

Lucy walked over to Lena, Julian's mother, and began a quiet conversation. All of Julian's siblings were there except for his brother James, who remained overseas. Phillip and his sisters Dorothy, Mildred, and Martha introduced themselves to VA..

"Your eyes *are* emerald green. I didn't believe you, big brother," Phillip said as they all laughed.

"We're so glad to finally meet you, Virginia. Julian has said so many wonderful things about you," said Mildred.

"I'm glad, too, although I hoped we would've met before now. I haven't met your mother yet," VA said as she glanced at her new husband. She liked his sisters right away, and they all seemed to be friendly.

"I'm sorry, I'll get her," Julian said quietly.

VA, a little nervous, watched as he gently took his mother's arm, and brought her over for the introduction.

"Mother, this is Virginia," he said.

"I'm happy to finally meet you, Mrs. Morley. I'm so glad you're here."

When Mrs. Lena Morley slightly nodded to VA, she had a small twitch in her almost undetectable smile.

Oh please, not another Mama. She immediately felt as if his mother was disappointed with her son's new wife.

Susie clapped her hands and announced, "Everybody, head to the Pickwick Club for a celebration to remember!"

Julian asked VA to stay behind a few minutes. "You've made me so happy. I can't wait for our honeymoon and the rest of our lives. This day is the happiest of my life," he said.

"Mine too. You've brought out in me something I thought I'd lost. But it's found again, and I want to make you happy. I'll do my best."

The newlyweds made their way to the Pickwick Club, and the girls hadn't forgotten any details. The Freddy Brookfield Orchestra played the songs of the day, and a long table held a buffet fit for a king. VA and Julian couldn't believe their quiet nuptials had turned into a party to end all parties!

"Mam'selle" was the first song played. The newlyweds danced their first dance as man and wife. More couples joined them, and when the orchestra played "The Nearness of You," VA sat it out. She was glad Julian was too busy socializing to notice. Mallory came over and apologized for that song.

"It's fine. Today's the happiest day of my life, and sentimental feelings for old songs went away a long time ago."

When the small wedding cake was rolled out, Julian took VA's hand and headed to the cake table. They toasted each other with champagne Gabe provided, then cut the cake. The Alabama "Blue laws" prohibited the club from selling alcohol on Sunday, so it had to be discreetly brought in.

Julian began, "VA and I want to thank each one of you for this perfect day. Mallory, Susie, and Mary, this is a reception fit for royalty. Thank you. I've married into a fine family, and I feel like VA has as well. All I can say is, thank you, and if VA wants to say something...."

"I want to thank my mother for understanding our wishes, and my sisters for demanding this reception. I couldn't have planned it better myself."

After the laughter and applause, VA and Julian headed for the door and waved goodbye amid the rice being tossed all the way to his waiting car. The honeymoon to Atlanta was about to begin.

The drive to Atlanta would take four hours since Highway 78 went through every small town on the way. He thought they'd never get there. He pulled her close and told her to be patient, and he would be, too. He tried to drive as she rubbed his leg and kissed his neck.

"Stop, VA, or we'll have to pull over." He didn't

want to since this was their wedding night, and he wanted it to be special.

"I can't help it. I want you now," she softly whispered in his ear.

He finally talked her into waiting until they checked in to the hotel. Reluctantly, he let her slide to the other side of the bench seat in the car. The radio was on, and Julian watched his wife's foot tapping to the music while she sat pushed against the car door. After a few minutes, she slid over and cuddled him.

"Don't be mad. I'm just going to sit by you and go to sleep."

"VA, you don't understand. When you're close to me, I lose control."

"Well, control yourself."

VA slept the rest of the way and woke up as they pulled into the historic Georgian Terrace Hotel in Atlanta. A young bellboy took their luggage, and the valet parked the car.

After they checked into their room, VA went directly to the bathroom, and put on her new negligee. Dinner would have to wait. She only wanted her husband.

Opening the bathroom door, she walked to him as he stood next to the bed. She threw her arms around his neck, and kissed him with so much passion, it took his breath. She was so ripe, so ready. "I'm going to give you everything you want," she whispered.

Julian was dressed only in his bathrobe. He was ready for her. They fell onto the bed, and he stripped away every bit of sheer cloth she had on. He touched every part of her and kissed her as she moaned for more. The golden part of him that seemed to dictate his every move found her without guidance. He was on fire and needed to douse it. As he made that entrance, she moaned loudly with pleasure. He caressed every soft, yielding inch of her body and rocked with her in excitement. Never had he felt such sensual pleasure.

"You're unbelievable," she said between breaths. "You're like something out of a lurid magazine."

Each lit a cigarette and decided to clean up for a late dinner. VA started the shower and stepped in. The warm water felt good, and Julian was an amazing lover. She hadn't experienced anything like him. A few seconds later he joined her in the shower.

"What *are* you doing?" she asked.

"Joining you."

She delighted in the sexual way he lathered soap in his hand and washed each part of her body. She, in turn, lathered soap in her hand and washed every inch of him. They kissed, and the soap caused their bodies to slide into more lovemaking. *Was this possible?* She felt so inexperienced with him since only one other man had made love to her. There were many sexual things she read and heard about, but never had the desire to do. Some things seemed disgusting, but she was willing to see if Julian could change that opinion.

The newlyweds got dressed and made their way downstairs and stopped at the lobby bar for cocktails before dinner.

Julian pointed out the classic hotel lobby's crystal chandeliers, marble columns, and Italian tile floors. They ordered steak and champagne in the Terrace Garden Grill Room, and with coffee, the maître d' presented a lovely tray of assorted desserts. Each selection had *"Congratulations"* written on the fine china dessert plate.

After dessert, they went to the Terrace Garden Lounging Room for a nightcap. The lounge, almost completely enclosed in glass, was blackened with the night sky but illuminated with a multitude of stars.

They sank into a soft, oversized chaise lounge and held hands while looking at their wedding rings. Julian raised her hand to his lips and kissed her ring. She pulled his arm around her, and they lay gazing at the stars.

CHAPTER 22

A Big Surprise

Fall 1948

With the honeymoon over, the newlyweds reluctantly found themselves back in the real world. After their return, Julian was informed his daytime schedule as a railroad inspector would have to change to evening hours, effective immediately. As much as he protested, his boss wouldn't budge. The existing evening inspector was forced to take a leave of absence due to medical reasons but would be back on the job in about a month. Julian seemed to be the only man capable and experienced enough to take his place. He unwillingly accepted.

Julian left for work at 5:00 PM and got home around 2:00 AM. VA would hurry home from work, but usually missed him by about 5 or 10 minutes. She didn't cook much but would always have a dinner in the icebox when Julian got home. They had their weekends though, to do anything they wanted.

Many a Saturday night, VA turned on the record player, and they would dance for hours. Other times they met friends at the Pickwick, although the last few times they partied there, VA noticed a strange woman sitting alone at the bar. Normally it wouldn't get her attention, but each time, the woman wore the same deep burgundy dress with fur trim, and Julian always stopped to talk to her. She assumed the woman had been an old friend or acquaintance, so she let it go and never brought the subject up.

VA and Julian celebrated their three-month anniversary with dinner at Joy Young's and dancing at the Pickwick Club afterward.

Being late September, 1948, cool fall air had arrived. VA seemed quiet during dinner, even when Charlie brought them drinks on the house to celebrate. She hadn't been feeling well but kept it to herself. She picked at her dinner and asked Charlie if they could take it home.

Julian worried that something could be wrong. *Had he done anything?* "Let's go," he said after settling the check. "Do you still feel like going to the club? We won't if you're not up to it."

"Yes, I want to. I'm just not hungry."

The Pickwick, always crowded on Saturday nights, seemed warmer than usual. VA felt the cool breeze blowing through the windows, so she requested a table by the back door. That way she could walk outside if she got nauseated.

She noticed Mallory and Peter sitting at their usual table and waved. The orchestra sounded good and played all the old favorites. A little hesitant, she let Julian lead her to the dance floor, and she tried her best to keep up. She felt okay although she'd pass on the next dance.

VA joined Mallory and Pete at their table while Julian went to the bar, ordered their cocktails, and waited for them. VA kept her eyes on the bar to see if that woman showed up. He came back to Mallory's table and brought her a gin and tonic, then sat down. She lit a cigarette and took a sip of her drink as the orchestra began to play Glenn Miller's "Moonlight Cocktail" and Julian jumped to his feet and held out his hand for her.

"Excuse us, we'll be back," Julian said.

VA seemed to know just what dance move he was about to make, and she asked him to take it slow. She noticed him looking at her with concern.

"Are you okay? You don't look so good."

"Yeah, just a little tired," she lied.

The music continued to play as he led her back to the table. *I made it through this dance. I need to sit down.*

"I'll get you a glass of ice water. Be right back,"

Julian said.

While catching her breath at the table, she glanced around the club to see if she recognized anybody. She spotted that woman at the bar again and got up to walk to the ladies' room. Taking a closer look, VA noticed something oddly familiar about her. The short cropped, dark hair enhanced her somewhat exotic facial features.

Without his knowledge, VA caught Julian about to take a stool next to the woman. *Who is this person?* On the way back to the table from the ladies' room, she noticed the woman was gone, and Julian waited at the table for her with the ice water. *Where have I seen her before?*

At a table next to the stage, she saw Ezra Taylor and his wife, Mary Laura. Across from them sat Larry Abbott and a very attractive woman.

"Well, I'll be damned," VA said under her breath.

"What is it?" Mallory asked.

VA motioned with her eyes to look at the table across the dance floor. Mallory saw Larry and rolled her eyes.

"Who gives a shit, VA?" she whispered so Julian couldn't hear. "You don't have to talk to him."

VA laughed out loud. "Mallory! You're cursing!"

"I'm shocked," Julian said with a laugh.

"I always have. Just not in front of anybody. I learned a lot of terrible words from your big brother," Mallory said as she looked at VA.

"She does it all the time," Peter said as they all laughed.

VA didn't look Larry's way again. She felt better and hoped a good song would play so she could slow dance with her husband.

The orchestra's rendition of Artie Shaw's "Dancing in the Dark" played next, and VA offered her hand to Julian. They danced close gazing into each other's eyes until the song ended then returned to the table and said goodnight to Mallory and Pete.

On the way out, VA passed Ezra, said hello and introduced him to Julian. Ezra seemed thrilled to see her, congratulated them on their marriage and how he would love to catch up. Knowing it would never happen, she agreed how nice that would be.

On the way home, VA felt nauseated again. She dismissed it as having too much to drink on an empty stomach. Julian helped her up the steps to their apartment and put her right to bed. He took her temperature, and it was normal, but shortly thereafter she threw up and immediately felt better.

VA continued to feel ill throughout the weekend.

She vomited a few more times and couldn't keep anything down. She was never an alarmist but worried she'd contracted diphtheria or something horrible like that. As much as she hated to, she would have to go to the doctor. They would only draw a little blood and give her penicillin.

She made an appointment with old Dr. Taylor who still occupied the office he shared with her father. When she walked into the office, it hadn't changed. Chills ran up her spine when she remembered the day when her daddy brought her in and Dr. Taylor "yanked" her tonsils out. Right there in the office!

She sat down amid the other patients and hoped the wait would be short. People coughing, children red-faced with fever, and one patient held a barf-bag under his mouth.

Thankfully, it wasn't long until the doctor came out and greeted her personally. He wanted to know all about her life now and asked about Lucy. She updated him on her marriage, and how she had seen Ezra, Jr. the week before.

"What can I do for you, Virginia?"

"I'm nauseated all the time, and I'm afraid I've contracted some awful disease from eating seafood or drinking too much without eating. I have no appetite."

Dr. Taylor smiled as if he already knew the problem, then took blood and urine samples. He eased her mind and told her she would get a call from him in a few days with the results. If she felt nauseous or dizzy, she should nibble a soda cracker and sip some hot tea or a Coke. She thought that was an odd prescription, but would do as he said.

Two days passed and the crackers and Coke seemed to help. VA's phone rang at her desk at work, and it was Dr. Taylor.

"Virginia, I have good news for you. You don't have a dreaded bacterial disease. You're going to have a baby!"

"What? That can't be. Really?"

"You're a newlywed, aren't you? Surely you didn't keep your husband at arm's length on your honeymoon."

"Well, no, but I didn't think it would happen so soon."

"Your body is on a schedule. When things happen at the right time, babies are conceived. Your immediate plans have nothing to do with that schedule. Didn't your mother explain anything to you before you became sexually active?"

"She'd never talk about anything like that. She'd forbid it. I learned about sex from my sisters-in-law and reading books. Yes, of course, I know about the female cycle, but we were on our honeymoon."

"Well," he said with a laugh. "I think you'll know what to do after the baby is born. It looks like you should be due around the middle of March."

VA hung up the phone in disbelief. *We've only been married for three months. How am I going to tell Julian? How will he take it?* "Oh Lord, help," she prayed.

After work, VA stopped at Hill's Grocery Store and picked up fresh eggs, vegetables, bread, and milk, things the doctor told her to buy to begin a new diet that would be healthy for the baby. He told her to stop eating a lot of sweets, but she didn't like sweets that much, anyway.

She continued to worry about telling Julian but felt excited. The pregnancy also meant she would have to go to the doctor on a regular basis. If he didn't have to probe her much, it'd be fine. He'd probably take her blood pressure, temperature, and deliver the baby when it was time. She'd talk to Susie since she'd delivered two babies.

Julian, back on his daytime schedule, came home a little late since he had to wait for the night man to check in. He walked in the door and kissed her. He mixed a strong drink for her and himself.

"I'm tired. I think I'll go to bed right after supper," he said. "There've been problems with some railroad equipment, and I had to delay three routes today until the problems were corrected. The boss rode my ass all day; we got it fixed but, I'm drained. I also stopped at Bobby's Bar for a drink."

"Uh oh," she thought. VA noticed he was stopping at Bobby's a lot lately. *We have liquor here. Why does he go there?* Maybe he was tired or just needed casual male conversation.

He paused when he saw a lot of vegetables but little meat for dinner. He asked her why the change from the regular kind of meals.

"I thought we should vary our diet. It's much healthier for us, and it'll keep our weight down."

"That's not necessary, VA. You're so slim. Have I gained weight?"

"No, but I want to keep it that way."

"As long as I'm not still hungry after I eat, it's fine with me."

How in the hell am I going to tell him? She cleaned up the supper dishes and went to bed. She nuzzled close to him and whispered, "I love you."

The alarm clock sounded at 5:30 AM. They both got up and began their usual routine. VA fixed breakfast while Julian showered and got dressed. While he ate breakfast, VA took her bath and got ready for work. The schedule seemed to work for them. Both left the apartment at 7:15, and arrived at work promptly at 8:00. Julian drove the car, and VA rode the streetcar. Their jobs were in different areas of town, so this seemed to be the only way.

That night, Julian came straight home and in a much better mood. Relieved, she planned to break the news to him after supper before they turned on the radio.

They both liked "Suspense Theater" and it came on at 8:00. Before the radio show aired, VA went into the living room with the newspaper. She handed it to him, and he slowly began to flip through the pages. VA mixed drinks and sat down next to him on the blue sofa. She lit a cigarette.

After a long drag and blowing out the smoke she said, "It seems like your day came out better than yesterday."

"Yeah, it did. No equipment problems today. No boss on my ass." He chuckled.

"Well, I have some news you might like to know."

He put down the paper and VA began by reminding him of how she hadn't been feeling well and how tired she'd been.

"Are you sick? What's the matter?" he asked with concern.

"No. As a matter of fact, I--I'm going to have a baby."

She feared he would slam down the paper, be furious, and blame her for letting it happen. Instead, he sat straight up on the sofa, faced her with a big smile, and put his arms around her.

"Really? That's great! Now I know why you're feeding me rabbit food! When did you find out? When is it due?"

"I found out yesterday. I would've told you last night, but you were in such a shitty mood. It's due in the middle of March. That means it happened on our honeymoon."

"I wonder which time it was, the first time or one of the ten other times?" he said with a sinister laugh as he grabbed and kissed her.

When "Suspense Theater" came on, VA stretched out on the sofa with her head on a pillow in Julian's lap. He stroked her hair, and it wasn't long before she relaxed and went to sleep.

CHAPTER 23

Welcome Home

Spring 1949

On February 1, 1949, VA looked at her reflection and was concerned since she wasn't showing much and hadn't gained a lot of weight. Dr. Taylor assured her that it being her first baby and with her slim build, she would pop out soon enough. She'd been going to work as usual, but Dr. Taylor advised her to take a leave of absence at the end of the month and rest as much as she could.

She began to experience a few back pains early on March 16th. She thought it was nothing but overexertion from cleaning the apartment, yet by the time her husband got home from work, she was on the sofa in labor.

Julian called an ambulance that took her directly to Lloyd Noland Hospital. "Damn it, VA, why didn't you call me at work? I would've come straight home!"

"I thought I did too much today," she said while taking short breaths, "and because the last few times I've called you at work, you haven't been there."

On March 17th, at 6:45 AM, Virginia "Ginger" Rebecca Morley was born weighing 6 pounds, 8 ounces. Still under anesthesia, VA didn't see her baby until late that afternoon. When the nurses brought baby Ginger in, VA's eyes filled with tears.

She marveled at the small amount of brown baby fuzz on her head and her beautiful eyes. Her little face reminded her of Julian. And what a beautiful face! VA hoped the baby's eyes would be greyish blue like WB's.

"She's the most beautiful baby born so far this year," Julian said. "I made *that* clear to all the fathers-to-be while we looked in the nursery window."

VA and Ginger would be in the hospital for five days. During that time, a nurse guided her through what to expect and everything newborns demanded. Julian stopped in for a quick visit each morning before work and a longer one before he went home at night.

VA couldn't forget those times he hadn't been at the office, though. He could've been out of the office because of an on-site mechanical issue, but each time she called, she was never given the explanation for his absence or his whereabouts. *It couldn't be anything else. I'm not about to ask questions. Not...yet.*

Having just given birth, VA was tired, sore, and weak. It was difficult to walk, and she dreaded the flight of stairs in the apartment building. She would be discharged Saturday and couldn't wait to rest in her own bed. She felt as if every major organ in her body had been relocated and was now trying to move back to its original location.

Ginger was sound asleep as VA held her. She and Julian were on their way home with their new daughter, and she was still exhausted.

Noticing the blustery March wind blowing through the trees, VA loosely pulled the blanket over Ginger's little face. Parking in front of the apartment building, she waited as Julian ran around the car to help them out. VA smiled at him as he opened the door.

"Here we are. Welcome home," he said.

"We missed you," she said as she kissed him. *Look at that smile. He looks so happy.*

The Highland Avenue apartment proved to be large enough for the extra baby furniture and supplies. In February, VA borrowed Susie's crib and had it placed in the dining room next to their bedroom door. They also purchased a small dresser for baby clothes, and all of Ginger's necessities.

A few days before Julian was to bring his wife

and new daughter home, he planned a small "Welcome Home, Ginger" get together at the apartment. He invited Lucy and asked if she'd also extend the invitation to Gabe, Ed, and their wives.

"I'll let them know," Lucy said, "but I have a feeling we'll all give it a few days before we come over."

He asked his mother, Lena, and his three sisters to whip up a few refreshments and get the apartment cleaned-up and ready for Ginger.

"That's fine," said Lena. "We'll be there early Saturday morning to get started."

Julian helped VA up the stairs. He hoped she'd be pleased by the surprise he'd planned and then opened the door to their apartment.

"Welcome Home, Ginger!" Lena and her daughters said loudly in unison.

VA jumped with a start and wasn't smiling. Lena hurried over to VA with her arms outstretched. Julian thought she would hug his wife and just look at their daughter.

Instead, she took the baby from VA without saying a word. His three sisters surrounded their mother holding their new niece. Not one acknowledged VA.

Ginger began to cry loudly.

"This is too much for her," said VA. "I'm going to take her to the bedroom."

"Wait before you do. See if Mother can quiet her down."

Julian knew VA wasn't happy as Lena tried to pat and rock Ginger. The baby continued to cry. His mother reluctantly gave her back to VA and glared at her in the process. Ginger calmed down quickly once she was back in her mother's arms.

"I'm going to settle Ginger down then go to bed," VA said.

"Didn't you notice how much thought your husband put into this little party for you today?" Lena asked, her lips drawn tight.

"Yes, I did," she said as she looked at Julian, "and I appreciate it. Everything looks so nice and I can't wait to have some of the sandwiches, but right now, I *have* to lie down."

VA's sullen attitude embarrassed him and made him mad. After all his mother and sisters did for them today, she just grabbed the baby out of Lena's arms and headed off to bed. Julian stayed silent but noticed as his mother narrowed her eyes while watching her daughter-in-law leave the room.

As VA tried to get Ginger back to sleep, the loud

voices in the living room continued. Nothing VA did would calm the baby down. *Is it the noise in the other room? What's wrong with her? Is a diaper pin sticking her?* She checked, and the diaper was fine. Ginger continued to scream as she looked at the clock. *It's not time to feed her.*

VA sat on the bed, bounced Ginger, and softly rocked her. Finally, she quieted down and went to sleep. Just then the bedroom door opened, and Julian walked in. VA quickly motioned for him to be quiet.

"Shh, she's almost asleep," she whispered over the loud laughter coming through the wall. VA put the sleeping baby on the bed and covered her.

Julian walked toward her with a scowl. "What the hell's wrong with you? Why were you rude to Mother?" Julian said in an angry whisper.

"What? You've got to be kidding!" VA quietly replied. "Our baby was screaming because of the loud voices in there. Would you please ask them to come back another day?"

"They did all of the cleaning and made the refreshments just for you!"

"Hardly. Didn't you notice how I was ignored by each one of them? They didn't even have the decency to speak to me!"

The stiffened demeanor and the angry look on

his face surprised her. She had never seen a look like that on his face, in fact, she hadn't ever seen him angry. She followed him as he went back to the living room and did what she asked.

"VA asked if you all could come back another time. Thank you for all you did for the party," Julian said through gritted teeth. He shot an angry glance toward VA.

"Yes, thank you," added VA. "Please come back soon." Never in her life had she been through such a scene. VA realized the obvious. *Why does Lena hate me so?*

They all walked out the door with Lena having the last word. "We'll come over here to see my granddaughter when we please. Don't ever forget that, Julian."

He knew his mother hadn't been keen on the idea of his marriage to VA but hoped she would change her mind. It didn't look like that would happen for a long time.

Lena's statement prompted Julian to confront VA. "Why did you want them to leave?"

"My body has been through a great deal, and I'm tired. The baby doesn't need all the excitement. Their loud voices scared her."

Julian became even more irritated. "She's too

young to be scared! I'm going down to Bobby's Bar. I can do what I want there, without anyone controlling me. I'll be back in a couple of hours," he stated as he slammed the door.

VA didn't like him to frequent that place. In addition to the booze, there were usually a slew of unescorted, slutty women hanging around. If Julian wanted to get drunk, she didn't care, although he seemed to be acting strangely; especially where his mother was concerned. *Is he a Mama's boy?*

Maybe his odd behavior was because of having a new baby in the house and getting comfortable as a new father. But, after Ginger's 8:00 PM feeding, Julian still wasn't home. She realized he'd been gone six hours. She called Bobby's and asked to speak to him.

"I'm sorry Mrs. Morley, but Mr. Morley left here two hours ago."

Where in the hell did he go? She waited until 2:00 AM for him but finally went to sleep after Ginger's feeding. Asleep on the sofa, she finally heard the key in the lock. It was 4:00 AM. VA watched a rough-looking Julian stagger in, slurring his words, and stumbling over the furniture in the dark living room.

"I'm home if any damn body cares."

VA got up, helped him to bed, and told him to be quiet, so Ginger wouldn't wake up. She got an overwhelming whiff of cheap perfume and noticed smeared makeup on his shirt.

"What the hell is this stink on your clothes?"

"What are you referring to?" He slurred his speech and swayed.

She undressed him and told him to get in the shower and be quiet. There was no way she would sleep in the same bed with that filth on him.

"You'd better have a damn good explanation," she said.

She put him in the shower as he protested loudly, but slowly cleaned himself up. While he showered, VA hung up his jacket, and placed his trousers in the dry-cleaning stack. After getting a strong aroma of liquor and cigarettes, she put his jacket in the stack as well. She cleaned out his pockets and found a slip of paper inside of one.

"Loved your company, as usual, today and tonight. I hope you'll call me again so that we can recreate this day all over again. Here's my phone #."

VA felt numb. Standing in the bedroom with her new baby five feet away, she realized her mouth was wide open and thought she might go into shock. She went back to the bathroom and yanked him out of the shower. Julian seemed more coherent and less unstable. After she dressed him, she went to the kitchen and put on some strong coffee. No way would she go to bed without an explanation.

"What's this?" she asked as she showed him the slip of paper.

"I don't know. Whoever this is must've put that slip of paper in the wrong jacket."

"How did you know I found it in a jacket? The stench on you before your shower came from nothing but some sorry whore. Ginger and I are leaving in the morning! Your ass is sleeping on the sofa. Stay away from me and never touch me again!"

The next morning, Julian watched as VA packed his new daughter up for Lucy's house on 6th Street. He tried to talk to her, and explain he did nothing wrong. After she called a taxi, he continued to plead and apologize for his behavior the day before.

The taxi arrived, and the cabbie helped VA with the suitcases.

As VA and their newborn daughter walked through the door, she glared at him and stated, "I want a divorce. I will not live under the same roof, much less sleep with a womanizing cheater!"

Julian couldn't believe what she just said. "What are you saying? You'll regret that decision! I love you, *and* Ginger. All I did was sit at the bar and have a couple of drinks. I was angry and getting tight, but not to the extent of taking up with some woman! Don't leave me!"

Julian, trying to remember the night before, sat down on the blue sofa, and put his head in his hands and murmured, "What have I done?"

VA looked in the phone book and wrote down Ben Gravlee's phone number. Ben was Bill's old attorney friend whom Mallory had seen at the Pickwick a year before.

She made an appointment with Ben the next day with no second thoughts. She and Julian hadn't been married a year, and he began to cheat. She would have none of that even though she loved him deeply.

Ben advised VA to think about her accusations carefully and to consent to a separation for six months. After that, the divorce should be granted unless there was a reconciliation. She told him that wouldn't happen. There was no way she could reconcile with someone who knowingly ruined the love and life they shared. Now a precious baby was in the picture. Adamant and angry, she would not budge.

VA refused to talk to Julian when he called. Finally, Lucy recommended that she see him and get a sober explanation.

"Hell no, Mama. He made his choice to go to Bobby's and pick up a slut just because I told him to ask his mother to leave and come back another day. Ginger screamed because of how loud they were. What was I supposed to do on our first day home?"

"Okay, then. I understand," Lucy said. "But you need to talk to Julian in person, anyway. He calls every day, two and three times. I hope you didn't jump to conclusions."

"I didn't, Mama. There were some tell-tale signs I noticed way before Ginger came, but I ignored them. I tried to not think about the times he wasn't at work, and that strange wom--"

She stopped mid-sentence. *She'll think I'm making that part up since it's so unbelievable.*

"You'll make your own decisions," Lucy began, "I'll watch Ginger only until you get your affairs in order, that's all. I strongly advise that you see Julian. I'm tired of answering the damn phone."

VA didn't want to see him, much less talk to him. Again, she felt betrayed and hurt but called and agreed to meet him at the apartment that afternoon after he got home from work.

It had been two weeks since she and Ginger got home from the hospital and moved out. *I don't want to do this. What am I supposed to say? What kind of pathetic line is he going to throw me?*

Julian waited for her at the Highland Avenue

apartment as planned.

"VA, I need you to be home," he pleaded.

"You made your decision. Apparently, I'm not enough for you. Bobby's seems to attract the type you want."

"VA, stop. DAMN! I love you. I did nothing wrong. This person must have put the note in my pocket without my knowledge. I don't even know who it was. There were a lot of people at Bobby's that night, and I pissed a few off."

"It's best we remain separated. Maybe then you can decide whether you want your independence or a family. You have a daughter now. That little girl needs a father. If you aren't willing to do this, then we're through with you. All I know is what I read in that note. I don't believe you're innocent, and if you need to get in touch with me, call Ben Gravlee."

With that said, VA turned and left. She got in the car and cried the entire way home to Lucy's. *Why is it that when I love someone so deeply, my heart is completely broken?*

She remembered speaking to Larry the same way when he wanted her back, and she realized too late it was probably a huge mistake. When she fell in love with Julian, he melted away the shield that protected her heart. He had become the center of her life, but now he ruined it.

Oh Lord, am I making the same mistake all over again?

The divorce was granted in October, 1949, and Julian remained at the apartment on Highland Avenue. He continued to call VA, but she wouldn't talk to him. He was granted visitation rights to see Ginger every other weekend, and VA made sure she was never home when he came to the door.

CHAPTER 24

A Little Girl without a Father

December 1951

*L*ittle Ginger was almost two years old, and VA was miserable. She missed Julian and heard he had moved on with his life. She wanted to go back to work and thought about renting a small apartment for herself and her daughter, but after putting her plans on paper, she realized her small budget wouldn't allow it.

The last eighteen months brought her former life to a screeching halt. Lucy refused to let her go out with anyone, and only babysat under extreme circumstances. VA stayed in contact with Julian's sister, Mildred, and squeezed out every detail of each chaperoned visit Julian had with Ginger.

Julian missed VA and their daughter. The full and happy life she selfishly stripped away, caused him to become lonely and miserable. He hadn't seen VA or talked to her in over a year, and his scheduled visits with Ginger were made through Lucy.

Months of heavy drinking and careless womanizing led to reckless behavior that finally took its toll. His job with the railroad was on shaky ground, and he went for days without showering or shaving. The Highland Avenue apartment was filthy, but he didn't care. The only thing on his mind was his wife and daughter and how to get them back.

"You'll never get them back unless you clean yourself up and straighten yourself out!" Mildred shouted. "I didn't come over here to listen to your sorry excuses. I'm here to help you!"

"Help me, then," he said as he lit a cigarette and poured a shot of whiskey.

"Listen, I apologized to Virginia for the way we all behaved when you brought them home from the hospital. I told Mother we shouldn't go, but she wouldn't listen. She had to blast her way in and show your wife she was still in charge of her 'precious' son! Virginia hesitated, but accepted my apology, and now we're on friendly terms. I'll help her any way I can."

"I'm glad you did that. What should I do? I want her back."

"This place is a rotten disgrace, and I wouldn't blame Virginia if she never stepped one foot in this apartment again! First of all, you stink. This whole place stinks! When's the last time you showered?" Mildred put her handkerchief to her nose and walked to the kitchen. "This is awful," she said. "I can't even count how many empty whiskey bottles you have in this cabinet."

"I need my wife," he said. "I want her to come home."

"Which wife?" she asked. "Julian, have you lost your mind? What the hell is this?"

Mildred brought out the basket filled with dirty laundry. She held up a bra, tap pants, and a garter belt. "Whose are these? I know they aren't Virginia's."

"Somebody I picked up last week," he said.

"You're lying. I know who you've been seeing, and if you don't put a stop to it, Virginia *will* find out, if she hasn't already. Gabe Johannsen knows a lot of people, and has spies everywhere."

"I ended it. I haven't seen the woman in weeks," Julian said as he drank the shot. "Give me the phone number of your cleaning woman."

"You're going to have to clean up a lot more than this apartment. That means that sorry woman had better be completely out of your life. I'm serious!"

Mildred threw the laundry basket down. "She caused you a lot of trouble before, and you'd better make sure she doesn't do it again. If you convince

Virginia to come back, and I hope you do, that woman had better not interfere with your lives again!"

Julian picked Ginger up every other Friday at 6:00 and took her to his mother's apartment for the weekend visit. He never missed the time with his daughter, though he knew VA wouldn't be home when he came. Although, one night he caught her off guard and arrived early. He wore a suit and made sure he was freshly shaven.

"Hello, VA. I'm here to pick up our daughter."

"I'm sorry you caught me. I was on my way out."

"Why? Why do you make it so difficult for all of us? I love you, and you are so convinced that I did something horrible, but I didn't. We need to discuss our daughter and hopefully, our life together."

"I've heard you've been seeing someone named Catherine. Is that true?"

He remembered Mildred's warning. "A few times, yes. We're divorced, remember? That was your idea. I'm free to see anyone I please, but she means nothing to me. Go to dinner with me, right now, and let's discuss our pathetic life. It's almost Christmas, and I miss you."

"I can't. I have plans," she said.

"Please. This is our life we're talking about," he

tried not to sound pathetic.

"I don't want to go anywhere with you."

"Stop it, VA! Are you going to continue punishing me for something I didn't do?"

VA stayed hesitant but thought about how her whole life could change if she didn't give him a chance to bear his soul.

As she thought a few minutes, she said, "I'll check with Mama and see if she'll watch Ginger for a little while."

Lucy reluctantly agreed since this fell under the category of extreme circumstance.

VA let him take her arm and lead her to the car. *How much she wanted him, how much she loved him.* Despite her desires, she remained determined not to let him sweet talk her into anything and would hold her ground.

They walked into the beautifully decorated Ed Salem's Restaurant, he tried to lead her to the dance floor.

"Take me to a table, please. I don't feel like dancing."

"Come on, dance with me. For old time's sake? Our table will be ready in a few minutes."

"Just one dance," she said.

His gentle embrace, his masculine smell, and how he placed his cheek so close to hers made her feel such deep love for him. She'd never lost that love.

So many times, she told herself not to let this happen, but he captured her heart years before. Julian had taken Larry Abbott completely out of her mind. *How could she let him go again?* They had a beautiful daughter, so she would give him one chance and listen to what he had to say.

"VA, I can't spend any more time without you and Ginger. You both are my whole life. I've tried to go on, but I can't. Please come back. I love you."

"Julian, we have been all through this. It's impossible," she said. "I don't trust you."

"Please, VA. I did nothing wrong! How am I supposed to keep a happy relationship with Ginger if you won't even speak to me? Please come home."

As they danced, VA looked up into those hazel eyes; they glistened with tears.

"Don't get your hopes up," she said hesitantly.

He smiled and gently kissed her cheek. "I can't ask for any more than that. You didn't say no. I miss you, Virginia Morley," he said as he softly kissed her lips.

When he tried to kiss her again, she turned her head. Julian quickly got the message and didn't try again. They continued to dance until the maître d' motioned that their table was ready.

"Gin and tonic?" he asked as he seated her. "You haven't changed again, have you?"

She realized at that moment how damned confident he was. She had almost forgotten his sensual swagger. VA gazed at him while taking a long drag on her cigarette.

"Spend New Year's Eve with me?" Julian asked.

"You're taking a lot for granted, you know."

"I think you're fighting the feeling of wanting to be back with me."

"No. Just thinking how you are too damned cocksure for your own good."

After dinner, the orchestra played as Julian took her hand and guided her to the dance floor where she wanted to be. After that dance ended, he motioned to Shep Fielding with one index finger in the air and a nod. Immediately, "Mam'selle" began to play.

VA's emerald eyes looked up to a sincere smile.

"I love you," silently formed on his lips. He leaned in to kiss her again, and this time she didn't turn away.

"Merry Christmas, Virginia."

VA and Julian rang in 1952 with a quiet dinner at home. It felt good being on Highland Avenue again. She missed the beautiful old apartment.

She always envisioned taking Ginger out on the covered balcony and rocking her to sleep in the old glider, while taking in the view of beautiful old homes, ancient trees, and Caldwell Park. She loved to watch the mothers strolling their children while the area residents fed the squirrels from the park benches.

Reconciliation was constantly on her mind, but she still resigned herself to the fact that she couldn't trust him. He constantly denied the note in his jacket. Being drunk that night, he thought he probably pissed the wrong person off, and that's how they got their revenge. VA wasn't sold on that story, but somehow it didn't matter now.

After dinner, Julian put on some soft music. He took her hand and pulled her close as they swayed back and forth.

While they danced, VA felt the familiar chills that had surprised her years before. She pulled away from him and stopped.

"I can't."

"What? What do you mean?" he asked.

"I know where this is going. I can't risk it."

"VA, damn it, stop it! You love me. I know you do.

Quit fighting it and let me love you again! Stop thinking about what you thought things were. Think about how things are now!"

After taking VA in his arms and kissing her, Julian made her come to. She backed away from him.

"I'd better be going," she said. "I can't let this happen again."

She grabbed her purse and headed for the door. "I guess I'll see you on your next visit with Ginger."

He stood in the living room saying nothing. He looked at her and smiled.

"Don't look at me like that, Julian."

"Come here. You're not going anywhere."

Knowing she wasn't going to leave, she threw her purse down and ran to his awaiting arms. He consumed her with his sensual kiss and soon she completely gave herself back to him. He was still the skillful lover and she the awaiting prey.

VA stayed the night in the arms of the man she loved. She felt as if the huge mass of hurt, loneliness, and distrust had lifted.

She awoke and looked at the sleeping man who continued to make up her world. He woke up to her gaze and smiled.

"Please marry me again."

"You're kidding," she laughed.

"Nope, I'm serious."

"I don't think I'm ready for that, all over again," she said while remembering how she rejected the second chance with Larry. "I can't live with the fear of the same thing happening again. Ginger deserves a happy life, and I am determined to have that for her even if it doesn't include you."

"You don't really mean that, do you?"

"Yes, I do. I'm tired of being the one who gets hurt," VA said as she got out of bed. "Every bit of happiness I've ever had has been destroyed by someone who thinks only of themselves, not me! They come running back thinking I'll take them back!"

"Don't compare me to that other guy you knew before you met me," he said under his breath.

"This is much the same but under different circumstances." She flipped her hair out of her face and began to cry unwelcome tears. "I can't live with someone I can't trust."

"Come on, what do you say?" Julian asked as he reached out to hold her. "I'm begging you. You have always been able to trust me. I know you love me."

"I do love you," she said as she snuggled close to him. "Let me think about it, but don't get your hopes up."

Ginger reached out happily for her daddy as he walked into the house on 6th Street. Julian grabbed her and danced around the room as Susie and Gabe came into the living room.

"We're getting married again," VA announced. "We decided two weeks ago."

"What? You're kidding," Gabe said with a scowl. "After all, he put you through?"

"That's great, VA! I'm so happy for you!" Susie said excitedly. "When?"

VA took Susie to the side and told her their tentative plans which would be with little fanfare. Susie always listened and never judged. VA loved that about her, and she was one of the best friends she ever had.

VA noticed Gabe's attitude with her decision. *He thinks I'm making a mistake. I can feel it.*

"I know you'll both be happy this time," said Susie.

"I hope so, but I doubt it." Gabe said under his breath.

Ed and Mary moved to New Orleans a year before and VA hated the fact that they weren't there to join them for the good news.

So many times, before the reconciliation, she thought about packing Ginger up and moving to be near them, but her plans were always belittled by Gabe and her mother. But now, it didn't seem to matter since her life was falling back into place.

Julian's position at Southern Railway continued to be uncertain. Before the reconciliation, his life was in the tank. He didn't care if he showed up for work or not. After receiving a severe reprimand and warning from his boss, he was forced to get himself together and set his priorities straight.

Now, with VA and Ginger back in his life, he had a reason to demonstrate a good work ethic, improve his job performance, and hope for advancement with the company in the future. The last year of reckless behavior had taken a huge toll and now his life was taking a new turn.

On the morning of Thursday, February 21, 1952, VA got up quickly to prepare for her second wedding day. She went through her closet and picked out a short-sleeved dress suitable for the nuptials, then decided it wasn't appropriate since it was cold outside.

Finally deciding on a pale blue wool suit with a matching hat, she went through her jewelry box and put on the diamond ring Julian had given her before. VA also kept the wedding ring and put it in her purse. After winning the struggle of keeping the seams of her stockings straight, VA slipped on her high-heeled black pumps and felt pleased as she looked at her image in the mirror. A far cry from the beautiful white satin suit she wore last time, the pale blue was appropriate now.

VA, Lucy, and Ginger were to meet Julian at the courthouse in downtown Birmingham at 10:45. She kept asking herself if she was doing the right thing and the answer was always yes. They got off the elevator on the fourth floor, and Julian was waiting. He stood there with a big smile and a small box in his hand.

"For you, VA. You look lovely," he said as he handed her the box.

She opened it and found a beautiful corsage of three white gardenias. She felt her smile widen.

"So many times, I've thought about the first flowers you gave me. They were just like these, and it was also in winter. The florist evidently likes you. Thank you."

Julian turned to Lucy and took Ginger in his arms. "Thank you, Mama Lucy, for being here."

Ginger beamed as Julian held her while Lucy pinned the corsage on VA's lapel. Lucy, being the only family member present, would be a witness as well as one of the clerks in the office of the Justice of the Peace.

The ceremony again was short, and afterward, Julian took everyone to lunch at Bogue's Restaurant.

After taking Lucy home, the small family made their way back to the apartment on Highland Avenue. VA felt happy and at home again. Ginger, getting a little fussy after such a long day fell asleep on the sofa. Julian turned on the record player as he and his bride danced, and their daughter slept.

Little Ginger's third birthday came on Monday, March 17, 1952. VA planned a small family get-together for her at Lucy's house after church on Sunday, the 16th. Sadly, Ed and Mary couldn't be there. They had a new baby boy, Billy, just six weeks old.

"We have news to announce while everyone is here," Julian said. "I've been given the opportunity for a good promotion and a substantial raise. VA and I have discussed this over and over, so we'll be moving to Atlanta in May."

"Really?" Susie said. "Are you all happy about the move?" She looked from one to the other.

"It's a great chance for Julian," VA said. "In a few weeks, we'll look for a small house. Ginger needs a yard to play in, and a house will give us more room, anyway."

As May approached, VA started packing and waited for information on available houses in Atlanta. Gabe had recommended Bobby Jim Gordon, a successful real estate agent in Atlanta. VA hated that stupid name, but he was very successful and eager to help. Bobby called with every potential prospect, and finally, one house fit the criteria she and Julian were looking for. It was in a southern suburb of Atlanta close to the airport called East Point.

While Lucy and Lena cared for Ginger, VA and Julian drove to Atlanta to meet with Bobby. VA refused to call him Bobby *Jim*, and sneered each time she heard it.

The name sounded so ridiculous to her. She hated to sound snobbish, but every time, Julian purposely added the "Jim," and it made her cringe.

Bobby showed them a cute little white house with two bedrooms and one full bath. It was in a neighborhood of affordable houses built after the GI Bill was passed in 1945.

VA liked the neighborhood, and the house looked well taken care of. It had a nice, shady fenced backyard, a fireplace, a small kitchen with an eating area, and was well within their budget. The house would do nicely for their needs, and moving day was scheduled for June 1.

CHAPTER 25

Three Happy People

June 1952

$\mathscr{G}$abe and Susie invited VA and Julian out on the Saturday night before the move. Susie's parents offered to babysit the children, Ginger included. Susie told VA to dress up because they were going to a swanky new supper club called "THE Club."

VA had heard of it and read about the architectural design in a local magazine. "THE Club" would be the perfect send-off, and she couldn't wait to tell Julian.

The occasion meant a new dress. Moving day would be in two weeks, so maybe Lucy had time to make her something suitable. VA found a photograph of a dress in an old Vogue magazine that didn't look too fancy.

Julian came home from work in a horrible mood; a co-worker blamed him for a near-fatal miscommunication with the engineer of a locomotive. All problems were quickly resolved, but Julian's boss took the guy at his word and didn't even bring him into the conversation.

"I can't wait to get to Atlanta and away from that son of a bitch. He never let me say a word. He reprimanded me in front of the worm that caused the problem and blamed me," he continued. "The incompetence of that idiot caused the miscommunication. I know he's after my job when I leave. Damn it; this move can't come soon enough." Julian went to the liquor cabinet and poured himself a straight bourbon. He quickly drank it and poured another.

"Daadee! Me up!" Ginger saw her daddy and ran to him.

"You're talking so well--I can't believe it!" Julian quickly changed his tone of voice and picked Ginger up.

While VA packed dishes, the radio stayed on, and she watched as her husband glided and twirled their daughter around the room. She hoped this would get him in a better frame of mind. She was excited about "THE Club" and hoped he would be too.

"Gabe and Susie want to take us to 'THE Club' on Saturday night for a going away dinner. You didn't make any plans, did you?"

"No, I haven't. That'll be great! I've wanted to

take you there. And they're supposed to have an illuminated dancefloor!"

VA couldn't take her eyes off her new dress. Even though it was a simple style, she thought it might have been the prettiest dress her mother ever made. Made from blush pink taffeta, it fell a few inches below her knee. It had a halter top, a low-cut bodice, and a thin matching bow in the front at the waist.

"Did Mama Lucy make that for you?" Susie asked. "She outdid herself this time."

"Don't you think it might be a little low cut, Julian?" Gabe asked.

"Hell no! It looks great!"

Driving to the top of Red Mountain, the valet greeted them at "THE Club's" main entrance. The front lobby was decorated in black and red while the lounge had been done in pinks, greens, and purples.

VA thought it garish, especially with the turquoise ceiling. What a beautiful place to be decorated in such horrible colors. She wasn't an interior decorator by any means, but she knew what looked good.

VA glanced over as Susie rolled her eyes. She must have thought the same thing. Julian leaned over, about to whisper something into VA's ear, when a familiar voice came out of nowhere.

"Virginia! How are you? It's been so long since we've seen you," said Mary Laura Taylor.

"I'm fine, so good to see you both. You remember my husband, Julian Morley, don't you?"

The men shook hands as Gabe and Susie returned from the bar and chatted for a minute.

"Our table's ready. So good to see you, Ezra," Gabe said.

Gabe reserved a table next to the dancefloor, and to VA's delight, Susie had placed a beautiful bouquet of flowers on it. While reading the card she found tucked inside, VA fought back tears.

VA and Julian,

Birmingham won't be the same without you, and neither will we.

Please come home often...We'll miss you so.

With much love, Susie & Gabe

Handing the card over to Julian, VA looked at Susie and Gabe. "I don't want to leave, now."

Soft dinner music played as some couples danced. Gabe got up and extended his hand to her, and VA accepted. She hadn't danced with her brother since they were kids. She remembered how they used to turn up the radio at the house on Tuscaloosa Avenue, and he would teach her the newest dances of the day.

"Are you happy?" he asked with a serious tone in his voice.

"Yes, everything's fine."

"I hope so," Gabe said.

After dinner, the lights were turned down, and the multi-colored illuminated dance floor lit the room. The house orchestra began to play, and couples headed to the dance floor.

The foursome joined the mass, and Julian held her close as they danced. A few couples stopped to watch them as he whispered something in VA's ear that made her laugh out loud. They knew they were in the spotlight but didn't care. She never wanted this night to end.

When they got home, Julian turned the radio on to the all-night music station out of Atlanta. As they danced, he took VA in his arms and gave her a loving but seductive kiss. She returned the kiss, and soon they were making love on the blue sofa that soon would move to Atlanta.

They awoke to sunshine coming in through the front window of the apartment. VA looked at the clock, and it was 10:00 AM.

"Julian, wake up. We have to pick up Ginger."

"Okay. Did you have fun last night?" he asked.

"It was one of the best nights I've ever had. You?"

"Oh, yeah."

Since Gabe and Susie lived across the street from the Langdon's, they stopped by to thank them again for the unforgettable night.

Susie tearfully hugged VA goodbye and kissed little Ginger. Eleven-year-old Steve hugged his "Auntie" and told her to come home soon. There were tears in little Andy's eyes when he told his Virginia goodbye.

CHAPTER 26

Atlanta

July 1952

*B*obby Jim Gordon was very helpful with the GI loan and had all the paperwork ready to sign when they arrived. VA couldn't wait to move in and get their small house in order. The house was just right for her little family. Ginger had a tiny bedroom and they had theirs. Being no good at decorating, she found floral café curtains and venetian blinds at Sears-Roebuck that would be fine for their windows. She didn't care if they weren't perfectly coordinated, just so no one could see in.

VA and Ginger met their neighbors and seemed to connect with the couple next door.

Julian and Richard Richmond had a mutual interest in locomotives, and both were veterans of the war. Richard had been a Navy Seabee assigned to build bridges for the Allies and was now an architect for a private construction company.

Chloe Richmond and VA hit it off immediately. Alice, their daughter, and Ginger played together, but both were spoiled and the center of attention. VA and her new friend shrugged it off and knew they'd get along eventually.

Chloe was a petite girl with a short curly haircut and always wore brightly colored sundresses with sandals. Richard was tall, had longish black hair, and a goatee.

VA and Julian were happy to know Chloe and Richard had a mutual admiration for good music. The two couples would frequently put the children to bed, play their music, and dance until the wee hours of the night. VA hadn't missed Birmingham at all since they met the Richmond's.

Summer seemed to drag for VA but having Chloe next door made the days bearable. They would take the children to the Grant Park public swimming pool to get a little sun while they watched the girls play and swim.

VA had no complaints and knowing she had a friend in Atlanta made her feel good. Chloe would tell her gossip about the neighbors but never anything scandalous, except the time a wife was caught by her husband, in the middle of the day, sleeping with a knife salesman.

That woman was considered "sorry trash" and snubbed by most residents of the neighborhood. The house was sold soon after, and a nice family moved in.

"I'd hate to be on their shit list," VA mumbled under her breath.

A neighborhood Fourth of July cookout and dance was planned, so VA volunteered her services. She was assigned to decorations, not her specialty, but would do what they needed.

After looking through magazines and thinking back to V-E Day, she bought red, white, and blue fabric and tried to make bunting for the planned dance floor.

VA and Julian seemed to be the happiest they'd ever been. The Fourth of July celebration went off without a hitch. The children went to bed around 8:00, and the dance floor opened immediately after. A babysitter stayed at each house, so the parents could let loose and celebrate.

The men set off fireworks, and Julian volunteered to provide the music. He played his favorites which seemed to be everyone else's, too. The entire neighborhood danced into the early morning hours.

VA brought Julian home while he was still in an alcohol-induced stupor. They made passionate love while Ginger slept in the next bedroom.

A few hours later with a slight hangover, VA trudged into the kitchen to make Ginger's breakfast.

In rare form, she screamed from her bedroom,

"Mommy, bekfast!"

That's just what I need this morning. Why did I have that last drink?

Julian strolled into the kitchen looking rough. "What a night," he said.

"Daadeee," Ginger said. "Bekfast."

"Yes, I know, baby," he said as he lifted his little girl out of her bed. "We'll have no more mornings like this, I promise."

The "dog days of summer" proved to be the hottest August VA had experienced in a long time. Georgia's sticky humidity seemed to be at its worst. She opened the windows--top and bottom--and had fans going in every room of the house. Poor Ginger played with ice to keep cool.

The Grant Park pool felt like bathwater, and Atlanta hadn't seen enough rain in two weeks to help. If it sprinkled, the steam from the pavement caused more unbearable humidity.

VA, with no energy, sat on the screened porch in a pair of shorts and a halter top. Even with the fan blowing directly in her face, she felt uncomfortable and miserable to the point of nausea.

Suddenly she had to run to the bathroom and

throw up. Ginger stayed on the small screened porch and played. After losing her lunch, VA felt better and returned to watch her wet little girl playing with nothing but a pan of ice and a spoon.

Three and a half years had flown by, and VA realized she and Julian had celebrated the third anniversary of their first marriage in June. The first anniversary of their second would be in January. VA quietly laughed and fanned herself with a magazine. With a dish towel from the kitchen, she wiped herself off with some of Ginger's ice water and closed her eyes.

VA woke up to a sweet little voice saying, "Mommy, I'm hungry."

She jumped up and looked at the clock in the kitchen. It was 5:00, and Julian would be home in roughly ten minutes. She had completely forgotten about dinner. The heat had gotten the best of her, so she got up and ran into the kitchen. Her feet were wet, the linoleum was slick, and she slipped down hitting the floor hard. She landed on her left thigh.

Julian walked in and found her on the floor with Ginger sitting next to her.

"What happened?" he asked.

"Daadee! I played with ice and Mommy did too!"

"Damn it; I fell," VA said. "I slipped on the wet floor."

"Are you okay? Do you hurt anywhere?" He hurried over and helped her up.

"No, but I'll have a huge bruise on my thigh tomorrow."

Julian went to the bedroom to take off his sweaty clothes. When he returned, he told her about a trip to Savannah he had to take Monday of the following week. His new position with the company forced him to travel frequently and she hated it when he was out-of-town.

"I think I'll take Ginger home for a visit while you're gone."

"That sounds fine," said Julian. "I should be home Wednesday of next week. Stay longer if you want to."

She hadn't been home since they moved, and Ginger had grown so much in two months.

She looked like Julian's side of the family except her hair stayed dark-brown like VA's, and her eyes were a striking blue-grey like WB's. Ginger was a little beauty with that combination. All three of Julian's sisters were attractive, so taking after them was a streak of luck.

VA's feelings for Julian's mother hadn't changed though. She hadn't seen Lena in a few years and made no effort to contact her. His sisters were loud but nice, and had become friendly, especially Mildred. Lena had always seemed distant and jealous of her. At the first wedding, and gatherings after that, Lena stayed on the other side of the room and barely spoke to her.

The last encounter they had was at the 'welcome home' party. That's when VA knew Julian's mother seriously disliked her. *What have I ever done to cause her to hate me?* She never mentioned it to Julian, but if it continued after this visit, she would have to.

Julian took VA and Ginger to Atlanta's Terminal Station on the following Monday morning for the 8:00 AM departure to Birmingham. After saying goodbye, VA watched him as he walked back to the car.

A woman stopped him and they had a short conversation. He quickly turned away from her but she followed him to his car. VA couldn't get off the train and get a closer look, but it looked like the same woman who sat alone at the Pickwick bar. *What the hell was she doing in Atlanta?*

VA watched as her husband and the woman drove away together from the station and out of sight. Her stomach churned, and she thought she might be sick. She found their seats and settled in for the four-hour trip. VA couldn't get the vision out of her mind. *Who is that woman and why did he let her get in the car?*

After an hour, Ginger fell asleep while VA smoked and read a magazine. The cool morning temperatures changed into scorching ones, and her clothes were soaked with perspiration.

She was restless, couldn't concentrate on the magazine, and felt sick to her stomach. It had to be the heat and the stench of some of the passengers. *Hadn't they ever heard of deodorant?* She wanted to go to the dining car and get a Coke but couldn't leave Ginger. The vision of Julian and that woman consumed her.

It was only 11:00 AM, and they wouldn't arrive in Birmingham until 12:30 or 1:00. VA felt miserable and suddenly had to get to the bathroom and puke. Thank God it wasn't occupied.

When she returned, Ginger woke up, and they went to the dining car. The nausea subsided some after snacking on peanut butter crackers and drinking a Coke.

The train pulled into the Birmingham Terminal Station at 1:35. VA never experienced a trip so god-awful. She still felt sick to her stomach and her thigh hurt. When they departed the train, VA imagined she looked as if she had been hit by one. Holding Ginger's hand, she slowly took the steps out of the train car and saw Gabe waiting to meet them. She breathed a huge sigh of relief. The porter grabbed their bags and followed the trio to Gabe's car.

"I'll never take the train again in the summer. I don't know how, but if possible, I'll get back to Atlanta by other means," VA said.

They pulled into Lucy's driveway, and Susie ran out to greet them.

"I'm so glad to see you! Look how much Ginger has grown! What happened to you?"

"Don't ask. This has been the trip from hell," VA replied.

"Mama Lucy," Ginger said.

A big smile came to Lucy's face, and that alone made the shitty train ride worthwhile. After Susie and Gabe left, VA went to her old room and plopped down on the bed. She felt as if she smelled like the train car and its sweaty passengers, but she needed a rest. The nausea, now gone, left her feeling weak.

She woke up to the aroma of Lucy's famous pot roast. She got up and slowly made her way to the kitchen. Ginger had pots, pans and bowls spread out on the floor and copied her grandmother while she cooked.

"Mama, do you have any bourbon?"

She went to the old china cabinet in the dining room where liquor was kept. Gin, bourbon, vodka, and a few bottles of tonic water filled a small shelf in the cabinet.

"I keep it for Gabe and Susie when they come over," Lucy said.

It wouldn't surprise her if Lucy nipped from time

to time. *Why not?*

VA told Lucy about the dreaded plans to visit Lena. "Mama, please go with me. That woman hates me for some reason."

"Lena's the least of your worries. She has a soft spot for Julian since he had to quit school and go to work to help support them," Lucy recalled. "Lena told me a while ago that after her husband died, the family was in dire straits. Julian, being the oldest boy at home, had to take on the responsibility."

"I know, but she proved her feelings for me at the 'welcome home' party. She hasn't said twenty words to me since I met her, and most of them were hateful."

After two drinks, a cigarette, and a phone call from Mallory, they had dinner and turned on the radio. Lucy had all the windows open, and the steady breeze cooled off the little house on 6th Street.

VA glanced at the newspaper and with eyes widened, noticed an ad for a new doctor's office opening in the Medical Arts Building in Southside. It was in the same location as the Pickwick or next door.

NOW OPEN
DR. LARRY ABBOTT, MD
SPECIALIZING IN FAMILY MEDICINE
MEDICAL ARTS BLDG.
SOUTHSIDE 4-7812

Really? She wondered what he looked like now. It had been almost seven years since she'd seen him. VA continued to skim over the paper and found the obituaries. A familiar name was listed. She read Dr. Ezra Taylor Sr. had passed away after a lingering illness. He was 72 years old.

"Mama, did you know he'd been sick?"

"Yes, I heard, but I didn't know he'd died. He was a fine man."

A graveside service was to be held for Dr. Taylor at Elmwood Cemetery at 11:00 AM on Wednesday. In a matter of minutes, she read that two significant parts of her past life had been printed in the same section of the newspaper.

The next morning, VA got up dreading the visit with Lena, and felt the familiar nausea again. After throwing up three times, she counted back on her fingers. She must be pregnant again. She wouldn't tell anyone until she was sure. It had to be early in the pregnancy, but as much as she and Julian made love, it could have been anytime within the previous two months.

As they pulled up to Lena's old apartment building, VA tried to remember the number, but there was no need. Lena met them at the front door of the building, grabbed Ginger, and spoke to Lucy. VA, almost ignored, shrugged as she looked at Lucy and went in. They climbed the old marble stairs to the second floor. The hallway was dark and smelled like moth balls and enamel paint. Lena opened the door to her apartment and fussed over her granddaughter in her usual loud, irritating voice. Ginger's little chin began to quiver.

"What's the matter?" Lena asked. "Would you like to see a surprise I have for you?"

VA held Ginger and her little face brightened when Lena came back with a beautiful doll.

"Thank you, Mama Lena," little Ginger said softly.

"How's Julian?" asked Lena as she looked at VA with a smirk. "I haven't talked to him in a while."

VA ignored it. "He's traveling a good bit now. That's why we came home to visit. He's in Savannah until tomorrow. I wanted to bring Ginger home to visit her grandmothers." *Be nice, VA, even if you can't stand her!*

Lena turned up one side of her mouth in a half smile as she asked, "Would y'all like something to drink?"

"Thank you, no," VA said as she looked at Lucy.

VA was ready to leave, but they couldn't yet--it'd only been five minutes. Knowing she would have to endure another hour at least, she walked around the apartment and stopped to look at old, framed family photographs, including ones of Julian when he was small. He was a beautiful little boy. His hair was light blond, with a slight curl, and his large hazel eyes were encased in long, black eyelashes. As she continued to look, there were pictures of the sisters in their younger days and a lovely old wedding picture.

"Mama Lena, is this your wedding picture?" VA asked, as she picked up the old metal frame.

"Yes, that's Julian's father and me on our wedding day. That picture was taken on April 7, 1902."

"It's a lovely picture. Your wedding dress was beautiful," VA remarked. "Julian looks a lot like his father."

As VA continued to look around the room at the photographs, she came across one that made her stop.

Her mouth dropped as she saw a picture of Julian and a woman in a wedding dress holding a large bridal bouquet. He had a broad smile on his face and wore a white boutonniere. *She looked like that damn woman!* Now she knew where she'd seen her! Julian had a picture of her in the apartment on Highland Avenue before they were married.

"Who's this with Julian?" VA asked as she held up the picture.

"That's Julian's first wife, Catherine. I think that was taken around 1937. They divorced before the war. I still miss her and try to keep in touch."

"Oh…I see," VA mumbled. *That bitch is Catherine! It's all clear now. She's that odd woman and I know now why you hate me. You still think of her as your daughter-in-law!* She put the picture back and didn't say another word to Lena. *What's Julian's connection to her now?*

"I think we'd better go, Virginia, since Gabe, Susie and the boys are coming over. We need to get supper started." Lucy lied.

"Let Ginger stay here with me tonight," Lena said.

VA didn't expect that. What should she do? *No! Hell, no!*

"Ginger, would you like to stay with Mama Lena tonight?" Lena asked, reaching for the little girl.

Ginger's chin quivered again, and she reached for VA.

Thank goodness.

"She won't stay with me either, unless her mother is with her." Lucy said.

VA breathed a sigh of relief, glad the loathsome duty was done. She would have nothing to say to her mother-in-law again.

When they left, VA wanted Lucy to hold Ginger and say good-bye. *I'm through with that woman.* VA was out the front door of the apartment building and waiting in the car for Lucy and Ginger.

As Lucy approached the car, VA saw the look of concern on her mother's face.

"What's the matter?" Lucy asked as she got Ginger settled in the car.

"He was married before and didn't bother to tell me, Mama."

VA planned to go back to Atlanta on Wednesday, but she wanted to go to Dr. Taylor's funeral and pay her respects to Ezra, Jr. He had, and would always be, a good friend. Susie planned to pick Ginger up that morning, so VA and Lucy could go to the funeral and spend some quality time together.

Being late August, the weather felt surprisingly comfortable. VA and Lucy walked in the shade most of the way to the cemetery.

"Mama, I still can't believe Julian was married before. I can't stop thinking about it. Something didn't feel right before we remarried, but I ignored all the signs."

"Keep your head, Virginia. Don't bring it up unless you're forced to because it won't do you any good. You're both happy now and hopefully she's out of the picture entirely."

VA kept thinking about that picture. By the look of the wedding dress, the marriage took place in the late 30s, and Julian must've been in his late twenties. He looked like a boy in the picture.

He *was* fourteen years older than she was and certainly old enough to have an ex-wife, but why didn't he tell her? Her thoughts became consumed with his deception.

Almost to the cemetery, they passed Mary's mother's house and Selena Ladner stood on the front porch and waved. VA missed West End. The neighborhood held so many wonderful memories, especially the images of Bill, and her beautiful Eliza. *Are the memories of Julian ones to forget?* The mass of hurt, and distrust was once again building deep in her soul.

As VA and Lucy walked through the main gates of Elmwood, automobiles filled with mourners began to arrive. They followed the cars until the graveside tent became visible. VA estimated at least a hundred people attended.

She recognized a few from her childhood and then saw Ezra, Jr, an only child, and Mary Laura. Mrs. Taylor passed away a few years earlier, so only a handful of family members were present. Twelve chairs faced the casket under the tent for the family.

After the short Methodist service, the minister shook each family member's hand, then stood aside as they filed out. They greeted each guest, so it took a while for VA and Lucy to make their way to Ezra and Mary Laura.

"VA, we're glad to see you. Mrs. Johannsen, my father would be so happy knowing you're here," said Ezra.

Mary Laura wanted to know all the latest about VA, life in Atlanta, and Ginger. They had a daughter of their own and another baby on the way.

When VA and Lucy stepped back to leave and make their way through the crowd, they noticed a familiar face walking toward them.

"Hello, Mrs. Johannsen," he said as he tipped his hat, smiled, and looked at VA.

There stood Larry Abbott. Lucy smiled and nodded. He was alone, and VA searched for something to say.

"Hello, Larry. It's been a long time since we've seen you. I came into town for a short visit and read about Dr. Taylor. It was nice to see Ezra and Mary Laura again. What have you been up to the last few years?"

She wanted to know everything about him but would take whatever he wanted to divulge. She realized she spoke too much and too fast.

"I have my practice up and running after living abroad for a few years. Although I missed the US, I stayed and gained some essential medical skills over there. All of that took about seven years. If you'll both excuse me, I'll pay my respects to Ezra. So nice seeing you."

Larry's hair had greyed a little more on the sides, and he was still the handsome man she had known years before. His beautiful smile was the same and so were his impeccable manners. *Am I over him? I don't think so.*

Watching Larry walk away caused VA to experience the old familiar feeling of loss. She hadn't seen or talked to him in seven years and it felt as though she just watched his bus to Ft. McClellan turn the corner and take him out of her life for good.

In a matter of minutes, Larry Abbott had taken Julian Morley completely out of her mind and replaced him with a gentle feeling of worry-free calmness.

VA and Lucy walked in the direction of the "Johannsen" gravesite. Shaded by a large dogwood tree, the marble monument was flanked with two boxwoods, and red begonias were planted at the base.

The grave of Dr. William B. Johannsen was on one side, and on the other side was Captain William B. Johannsen, Jr.

Mallory brought Bill's body home from France in 1948, and it was comforting to VA to know Bill's final resting place at Elmwood would always be well-tended and close to her mother. While they walked back to the house, her thigh began to throb.

The next day, VA was set to return to Atlanta, but awoke to intense pain in her leg. Getting out of bed, she almost fell and called for Lucy.

"Mama, I can't walk. My left leg hurts." She lifted her gown to a horrific bruise and intense swelling.

"I think we'd better call a doctor," Lucy said. "That looks bad."

"Since Dr. Taylor's gone, we don't even have a doctor now," VA said.

"I'll call Larry Abbott."

"No! Mama, I can't see him. Especially as a patient!"

"You'll do as I say. I'll call Larry now."

Larry Abbott rang the doorbell at the little house on 6th Street. It felt odd seeing VA as a patient, but from the description Mrs. Johannsen gave him, it was a necessary house call.

He greeted Mrs. Johannsen and found VA sitting with her left leg up in one of the chairs he remembered from the old house. He saw a beautiful little girl playing on the floor and smiled.

"Hello, VA. What seems to be the trouble?"

"I told Mama not to call you, but she insisted. I fell last week and landed hard on my left thigh. It's painful, and now there's a nasty looking bruise."

"Let's take a look," Larry said.

VA slowly lifted her gown to expose her leg, and the swelling had increased.

"When did the intense pain begin?" Larry asked.

"This morning. It's been hurting for a few days, but it didn't worry me. I couldn't put any weight on it after I got up this morning."

Larry felt the bruise and VA flinched, but he tried to be gentle.

"A hematoma has formed within the damaged tissue on the injury site. You'll have to stay off the leg until the swelling goes down. You're doing the right thing by elevating it."

He opened his medical bag and rummaged through it. "Continue to do that; wrap ice in a clean cloth, and apply it to the contusion for 20 minutes. After that, lightly compress the affected area in the bandages I'm leaving here for you. Make sure you rest, VA. You may need crutches if it's not better in 24 to 48 hours."

"I have to get back to Atlanta," she said.

"I suggest you wait a few days to make sure the swelling is going down. I feel sure you'll be able to go back to Atlanta the first of next week."

Larry gently patted and squeezed her shoulder then smiled. As he got up, he asked, "Who's this pretty little girl?"

Ginger looked up at him and grinned. "I'm Ginger," she said.

"Hello, Ginger, I'm Larry, an old friend of your mother's."

Lucy walked him to the door. "Thank you, Larry, for coming over on such short notice. With Dr. Taylor gone, I guess we don't have a doctor."

"Call me anytime, Mrs. Johannsen."

Larry got in his car and started the engine. He sat for a few minutes and thought how he wanted to take VA in his arms as he had so many years before. She had been his, that little girl could've been his daughter, and he threw it all away with the stroke of a pen and a few words written in a letter. He couldn't blame that on the war, only his inability to cope.

As he drove off, the feeling of her soft skin stayed on his fingertips. He wanted to stay with her and help guide her through the healing process. Why hadn't he been stronger and not let that female in England lead him on? He was desperate then, and desperate now. He still loved VA, but she was married, had a little girl, and seemed to be happy.

Now, his life was nothing, meant nothing. He had a successful practice, made plenty of money, but spent most of it on psychiatric help for a wife he didn't love. His outer façade was nothing but a lie.

Larry couldn't focus on his work and reconnecting with VA consumed his thoughts. He wanted to see her again before she went back to Atlanta. It had been two days since the house call. He was restless and couldn't sleep. His wife was already in bed, so he picked up the phone.

"Hello, Mrs. Johannsen. I'm calling to check on Virginia. Is she able to get to the phone?"

"Yes, Larry, I'll get her."

He felt nervous, but why should he? She was his patient and he was concerned about her recovery.

"Hello? Is that you Larry?

"Hello, VA. I wanted to check on your bruise. I know you're going back to Atlanta in a few days, so your doctor needs to be able to release you to travel."

"It seems better. I'm doing as you said, and it looks like the swelling's going down."

"That's good. I'll drop by tomorrow and check it, and then you'll be free to go home. I'll see you around 5:00."

When he hung up, Larry felt a little excited, but a little guilty. *I still love her. What am I doing?*

Larry parked his car in the driveway of the house on 6th Street. A little anxious, he knocked on the door.

"Hello, Larry," said Lucy. "Come in."

He walked in and VA's leg wasn't elevated. She was sitting in the chair and dressed. This scenario was much different than a few days ago when she wore only a nightgown.

"How's your thigh?" he asked. "Let's take a look."

She lifted her skirt to expose the bruise, and never took her eyes off him.

"It looks much better, VA. Get up and let me see you walk."

She got up and walked slowly. There was no limp and she seemed stable.

"Are you experiencing any pain?"

"No," she said.

Larry looked around, and Lucy had taken Ginger to the kitchen.

"VA, how would you feel about going to dinner

with me? Just for old time's sake."

She hesitated and looked into his blue eyes. "Are you sure? What about your wife? Won't she get a little worried if you come home late? I don't know if I should."

"She won't know if I'm home or not, believe me."

"Okay, I'd like that," VA said.

VA walked slowly to Larry's car and he helped her in. This was a new car. The old one she knew was probably in a junkyard somewhere. She smiled as she thought about that old convertible.

"What are you grinning about?" he asked.

"Just thinking about your old car. Whatever happened to it?"

"It's in the garage at my parent's house. I couldn't part with it. That car holds too many special memories and I still drive it from time to time."

VA looked over at him and smiled again. So many times, she thought about the mistake she made by letting him go. Their lives could've been so different.

"How does Joy Young's sound?" he asked.

"Great. I haven't been there in years."

As Larry helped VA into the restaurant, Charlie was the first person they saw. He appeared delighted to see them.

"Mr. Larry, it's so good to have you back again. And you, too, Miss Virginia."

Charlie led them to a private, upstairs table and even remembered their favorite drinks. It had been so long since they'd been there together.

Larry lit two cigarettes and asked, "Are you happy?"

"I miss Birmingham, but other than that, I'm happy. You?"

"Oh, sure. My wife and I have a nice old home in Southside; she has a lot of friends to keep her busy while I'm at the hospital or the office."

"How are your parents? Did they ever work things out?" VA asked but didn't care.

Larry explained that his parents finally got a divorce, and his father remarried. Bitsy still lived in the big house all alone with her beautiful cabinet full of liquor and her "pretty things." He knew his mother was beginning to lose her mental capabilities and had been forced to hire a live-in companion for her.

As VA listened, she couldn't help but look at the outline of his face, hear the sound of his voice, and experience a huge feeling of regret. They both made mistakes and each of them were paying for those mistakes in much the same way. She could tell he wasn't happy.

Larry took her home, helped her to the door, and said, "Thank you for going with me tonight. I'm glad we could be alone and talk. Take care of your thigh and have a safe trip back to Atlanta."

"I'm glad we went. Thank you."

He bent down and softly kissed her lips.

"I'm sorry, VA. I shouldn't have done that."

"Please don't apologize. I'm glad you did."

She started to go inside, and before she closed the door, she placed her hand softly on his cheek and smiled. "I'll never forget you as long as I live."

CHAPTER 27

The Problem with Daddy

Spring 1953

VA prolonged her trip back to Atlanta and stayed in Birmingham four more days. She spoke to Julian on the phone, and explained the reason for the delayed return. Just hearing his voice made her want to stay away from him even more.

Her thigh began to swell again, so she continued Larry's instructions. Morning sickness and the painful thigh proved to be a constant challenge. When she elevated her leg, a barf bucket stayed next to the chair. She was tired of being immobile, and wanted to help Lucy around the house, but her mother wouldn't hear of it.

While they were in Birmingham, her mother had taken over the care of Ginger, and Lucy let the little girl help with baking, took her on walks to the grocery store, and watched as she played on the old swing set next door. This gave VA a chance to recuperate.

VA and Ginger stayed in Birmingham for a total of ten days and when they got back to Atlanta, Julian was out of town again. Chloe picked them up at the station at 5:35 and VA described how the return train trip back to Atlanta wasn't quite as bad as the trip over there. Even though she had to find a way to keep her leg elevated, it was much better.

They pulled in to the driveway, and the little house was dark. Chloe told her they didn't see much of Julian while she was away. They hadn't seen any lights on in the house over the weekend, and rarely heard the car. Chloe informed her they hadn't been home much, though.

"Hmm," VA muttered to herself while she put the suitcases away. *"What the hell has he been doing?"*

With morning sickness, the thigh, and seeing Larry again, VA's thoughts had temporarily abandoned the apparent deception, but that "Catherine" woman was back in the forefront of her thoughts. *That damn woman is about to be brought out into the open.*

VA didn't know how or when she was going to do it, but she would make Julian explain that third wheel in their marriage.

The phone rang, and it was Julian checking to make sure they got home safely. He told her he was in Charlotte, North Carolina, and should be home the next day. Since VA and Ginger were still in Birmingham, he decided to drive to Charlotte on Saturday and work through the weekend. That eased her mind a bit, but VA couldn't forget the woman and Julian at the train station, leaving together.

That vision would remain engraved in her mind. *Keep your head, VA. Don't bring it up unless you have-to.* She remembered her mother's words.

Julian returned home to a happy Ginger and a lukewarm VA. She noticed his hesitation after she turned her head when he tried to kiss her.

"I missed you both," he said. "Are you feeling okay? How's the thigh?"

"Better, I can put weight on it without so much pain," she answered. "I'm making an appointment with the doctor tomorrow. I'm pretty sure I'm pregnant again."

"Really? Great!" Julian said happily.

"You don't mind?"

"Hell no, VA," he answered with a puzzled look on his face. "What's the matter with you, anyway?"

She answered the last question with a shrug. No way was she going to get into it with him now. She would wait and see how he reacted after they went to bed.

Ginger had been asleep for a while, and VA decided to take a long bath and relax. In a few minutes, Julian tapped on the door and brought her a cocktail.

"Thought you might enjoy this after the long train ride, and all you've been through the past week."

"Thanks, I needed it. I'm going to bed in a few minutes," VA said. *You have no idea what I've been through.*

Julian was still up watching TV when she finally got into bed. She dozed off and woke up to her husband kissing her cheek.

"I didn't mean to wake you," Julian said.

"I wasn't asleep. I dozed off."

Julian leaned over and gave her a soft kiss. She turned to him and gently stroked his face with her fingertips. He tenderly kissed her neck and shoulders as his desire for her overwhelmed him. The past ten days without her left a longing that had to be addressed. After they brought that longing to an explosive end, they lay together exhausted, and covered in beads of perspiration.

"I missed you so much," he said.

She lay there as he held her but didn't return the statement. *Keep your head, VA.*

Julian noticed a change in VA but couldn't figure out what was wrong. Could it be the pregnancy that caused her to be so quiet and moody? She was eight months along now, and her attitude toward him continued to be cold.

She hardly spoke to him during the holidays. He wanted to take his daughter to Birmingham for Ginger's birthday in March, but VA refused. "We just need to stay home," he remembered her saying. That was fine with him, since he didn't want to drive four hours and only stay a couple of days.

Finally, after another month, he'd had enough. "What's the matter, VA? You've barely spoken to me in seven months," he said. "Have I done something to make you mad? What is it?"

"Nothing." She was surprised he waited this long to ask her.

"That's nothing but bullshit! There must be some reason for your behavior towards me! I haven't done anything but be here for you and Ginger!"

"This baby has taken a lot out of me," she said. "I'm tired and my back hurts. I'm 34, you know."

"That's not it, don't lie to me!"

"Hmm, I'm trying to keep my head, Mama, like you said. After that last statement, it's getting harder and harder."

"Talk to me, VA, damn it!"

"I think I need to go to the hospital," she said.

Julia Marie Morley made her debut at Crawford Long Hospital on Friday, April 15, 1953. A healthy baby, she seemed to have been a little on the small side at six pounds, two ounces. VA finally decided to name her after Julian but thought Julie didn't sound sophisticated enough. She always liked the name Julia, so the decision was made.

VA stayed in the maternity ward for five days. Her recovery remained on schedule, but Julia needed to gain a little weight before she could be released. In those five days, Julian came to the hospital only twice.

Chloe and Richard helped with Ginger during the day while Julian worked. Lucy planned a visit to help with Ginger after they were discharged from the hospital.

VA returned home on Sunday, and the next day Julian headed out of town again.

Savannah, Birmingham, Chattanooga, and Raleigh seemed to be the trouble spots for Southern Railway since each location had become short staffed.

He left on Monday for Chattanooga and wouldn't return until Friday. It looked to VA as if Julian did nothing around the house while she was in the hospital.

Before she and the baby came home, Ginger stayed with Chloe most of the time, and was told he wouldn't let anyone in the house, not even to help with cleaning.

Lucy arrived by train in Atlanta on Tuesday. After a long cab ride, she came into a mound of dirty laundry, and the stench of garbage filling each room of the little house. Lucy found VA in bed, Julia in the crib, and Ginger watching cartoons on TV.

"What in the world?" Lucy asked.

"Julian went out-of-town yesterday and left me with this mess. I don't know what's going on. There's a woman involved--I'm almost sure. I tried to clean up some, but I'm weak and I can't ask Chloe to help. She and Richard have done more than enough."

Lucy said nothing, put her suitcase in Ginger's messy bedroom, and started for the kitchen.

The small kitchen had a lime green, metal dinette table covered with open cereal boxes. The white porcelain sink was filled with dishes, the garbage can was running over and looked as if it hadn't been emptied in a week. Lucy walked to the sink, and two cockroaches scurried out from under the mass of dishes. The floor needed to be swept and mopped, and another cockroach flew by her head. She didn't want to see the bathroom.

"When has Ginger had a bath?" Lucy asked. She noticed the child's dirty face when she walked in the house. Walking toward the bathroom, the unrelenting odor of dirty cloth diapers filled the hall. She opened the door to a neat and tidy sink, toilet, and bathtub.

"I'll get this place back in order, but as soon as you're able, you'll come to Birmingham and stay until you get your life figured out."

VA noticed the apparent change in Julian's demeanor after they brought Julia home. The baby was now three months old, and he never fussed over her like he had with Ginger. He didn't try to be affectionate, and his attitude had become resentful. She knew he really didn't want another baby.

"What the hell's been wrong with you?" she asked.

"What are you talking about? Nothing's wrong with me. You're a fine one to talk. The one who hardly spoke to me for seven months."

Julia started to cry, and VA left the room. VA checked on Ginger, and she was still asleep. Bringing the baby back with her, she sat down and bounced Julia on her knee.

"Let's go out this weekend," she said. "It'll be the first time in a while, and I think we need to get out of the house. We can call Chloe and Richard and get a sitter."

"Do you think I'm made of money?" he asked as he glared at her.

"Go to hell," VA replied as she got up and put Julia back to bed.

VA went to the bedroom and separated the clothes for the washer. The girl's clothes in one pile, her clothes in another. Julian's clothes were neatly folded on the chair, and it looked as if his pants and shirts needed cleaning. She always went through his pockets, so dollar bills wouldn't be washed, and fountain pens were taken out.

In his pants pocket, she felt a book. She took it out, and it looked to be a bank book. It wasn't from their bank. She opened it, and it read C & S Bank.

Hoping it was a new savings account, VA turned the pages to find several large deposits and many withdrawals. The dates were June, 1952, to the present. The bank account had been opened when they first moved to Atlanta. *I haven't seen any of this money.*

She turned another page, and large checks had been made out to Mrs. Catherine Morley. The amounts ranged from $200 to $750. She dropped the bank book and said, "That bitch!" She picked it up again and noticed her husband standing in the doorway.

"What in the hell, Julian?" VA asked as she threw the book in his face.

"What're you doing going through my pockets?"

Now was the time she'd been waiting for. After all these months, he'd finally extended the invitation....

"What're *you* doing giving huge amounts of money to that bitch? I know who she is. Did you really think I'd never find out?"

She pushed him out of the way and closed the door. She wanted an explanation, and as she turned around, he stood in front of her.

Never had she gotten physically mad but at that moment her hand was raised to hit him. He caught her hand and pushed her back toward the dresser filled with perfume bottles and a lamp. VA grabbed the lamp and threw it at him as tears filled her eyes. These were tears of rage, not hurt.

She looked straight into his eyes, kept her voice down because of the girls, and spoke through gritted teeth.

"Your ass is in a world of shit, Julian. Catherine Morley has finally come out in the open even though I've known about her for a long time! Why are you giving her so much money? We could use that money, you sorry son of a bitch! I saw the woman all those times at the Pickwick Club and again at the train station. I also saw your wedding picture at your mother's apartment. I wanted to give you the benefit of the doubt because you begged me to come back and because of the girls. I kept thinking you would voluntarily tell me about her. You said you still loved me, and that I needed to come home. What bullshit!"

VA's anger caused her to pace the room like a wild animal. When she turned to look at her husband, that huge mass of hurt and distrust came out in the form of a hand raring back and slapping the hell out of him. Her force of anger almost sent him to the floor. With a shocked look on his face, he held his hand to his red cheek.

"Do you think I'm stupid?" she asked. "I'm through with you, and I mean for good!"

"I love you, VA. Let me speak! She's my ex-wife, a thing of the past. I have no feelings for her. We have a son, and I am supporting them. Those were the terms I agreed to, or she would contact you."

"Terms? Are you kidding? What right does she have to demand terms? How old is the son?"

"He was born before we got back together."

"So, just as I thought, you were messing around with your ex-wife, right after we separated the first time? You wasted no time, did you? You didn't even have the decency to tell me you were married before and now you have another child? That's just great. Let me tell you something. Your daughters and I will vacate these premises as soon as possible, and you can be with her all you want. I'm through and it wasn't any fault of mine! I'll see an attorney tomorrow, and that'll be the end! Get out and never speak to me again!" she said as she slammed the door.

"Hell, no, I'm not leaving!" Julian said through the door. "You'll hear me out! Open this door!"

Suddenly, Julia began to cry, and Ginger walked out of their bedroom with tears rolling down her face.

"Daddy?" she said.

VA opened the bedroom door, took Ginger's hand, went into the girl's room, and shut the door. She *never* said another word to him.

"Please, VA, listen to me," Julian begged as he sobbed outside the door.

VA knew it wouldn't last. She was never meant for true happiness. Julian led her on again with his charm, and she fell for it. She felt like a damned fool, but now two little girls would have to suffer from the mistakes she made.

She contacted an attorney friend of Chloe and Richard's and met with him the next afternoon. Chloe watched the girls as VA filed for divorce a second time on the grounds of fraud.

The attorney, Carl Thomas, advised her to stay in the Atlanta house for six months, and then she could move back to Birmingham. That was Georgia law in 1953. He would draw up the papers and be in touch.

She didn't know or care where Julian lived. She heard he had moved in temporarily with some friend from work.

Julian never had the chance to explain to VA that Catherine had been blackmailing him for almost two years. It had cost him a fortune to keep her quiet since his two daughters would be the ones to suffer for his recklessness. The boy would suffer as well since he would never know his sisters. VA would see to that.

Julian loved VA and his daughters, and always would. He realized the mistake he made by not telling her about Catherine.

What he couldn't understand was why she never spoke up when she saw them at the train station or the Pickwick? Was she trying not to cause a scene, or did she just not care? Her silent treatment toward him before Julia came was finally coming to light.

He'd temporarily moved in with a co-worker and felt his entire world had been jerked out from under him. He couldn't go home since VA threatened to call the police if he came close to her and the girls.

Over and over, he blamed himself for ruining both their lives.

Catherine wanted him to move in with her, but she had been the cause of all of this. He could have her arrested for blackmail, but what good would that do? It would only ruin the life of the innocent boy.

Delighted with the news, Lena called and begged Julian to bring Catherine and their son home to Birmingham permanently.

"Mother, I will not bring them to Birmingham or anywhere! I have no contact with her anymore. That woman ruined my life with Virginia! I should've listened to Mildred. She warned me this would happen. The only time I'll come to Birmingham will be to see my daughters! If you want to see me, you'll have to get on a train!"

With her life in shambles, VA endured a grueling six months alone in Atlanta with her daughters in the close-knit neighborhood she had grown to love. She thought her little family would live there for years, but the new 'friends' she made turned out to be fake and shallow. Even Chloe and Richard had distanced themselves from her.

VA thought they all had so much in common, but a divorced woman was considered damaged goods. Now she was labeled an outcast, never invited to parties, or neighborhood functions. She couldn't get away from there fast enough.

The final divorce decree was issued in January, 1954, and the settlement left Julian with the house, the car, and a monthly visit to Birmingham with Ginger and Julia. VA was awarded everything else but a rocking chair and the TV. She never spoke to Julian again without an attorney present.

Chapter 28

Back In Birmingham

April 1954

A few months after VA and the girls moved back to Birmingham with Lucy, Gabe suggested to his mother that she consider building a house "over the mountain" called Shades Crest so they could be nearby.

The beautifully developed section of Birmingham was growing by leaps and bounds. Families from the old neighborhoods were moving from the west side of Red Mountain to the east because of its natural beauty and to fulfill their ideals in a country atmosphere close to the city.

Lucy, never one for change, agreed to think about it.

When VA expressed an interest in going back to work, Lucy wouldn't hear of it and told VA she would have to raise her own children. Gabe told his mother the only reasonable thing to do was move. After a lot of tall talking, Lucy finally agreed with him.

The small, brown, three-bedroom house on Mabry Drive in Shades Crest, would be move-in ready late August, 1954. A large black walnut tree stood proudly in front of the large picture window and had branches as wide as the house itself.

Since the house faced west, the tree would shade the front of the house in the afternoon. The small street was lined with large trees, nice homes, and plenty of neighbors. Lucy bought the house on sight and instructed Gabe to put the 6th Street house on the market.

The little green house on 6th Street sold in one week. Lucy and VA had two weeks to pack and move out. Thinking back, Lucy remembered how she and VA moved out of the large house on Tuscaloosa Avenue and into the smaller one that couldn't hold all her furniture.

Now it seemed quite the same since the furniture from Atlanta was stored in the garage. VA wanted none of it. She called a mover to take it and throw it in the garbage if they wanted to. Lucy settled her down and talked her into keeping the nice pieces she and Julian had purchased.

After the move, VA and the girls met a few neighbors. The Barker family, next door, had three children, two girls, and one boy. Two houses down, the Phillips family had two boys, and there were a few war widows with no children.

Susie now owned the "Wee Ones" kindergarten in Shades Crest and picked Ginger up every morning for school. VA had one more year before Julia went to kindergarten and then she planned to go back to work. She needed the money.

The Shades Crest area was growing rapidly, and new neighborhoods were sprouting up everywhere. The real estate business was booming "over the mountain" and Gabe's company, HJHome Realty, gave cocktail parties almost every weekend and VA was always included. She loved the parties since they were business functions and she already knew most of the guests.

Being invited to a party at the Country Club meant you were affluent, successful, and escorted a wife with social connections. Most of the prospective clients were successful old friends from West End who were part of the mass migration.

A party was planned for the next Saturday evening, and VA was chosen to fill in as hostess in Susie's place. All she had to do was greet the guests, point them in the direction of the bar, and the abundant spread of hors-d'oeuvres. The rest would take care of itself. It was nothing but a "schmoozing fest in dressy clothes," as Gabe described it.

The last ten, turbulent years had taken a toll, but VA's looks hadn't changed. She still had thick, dark hair, a lovely figure, and her beautiful emerald green eyes were still as bright as ever. She greeted all the guests, most of whom were prominent figures in the finance community and leaders of other real estate companies, and their wives.

Susie's shoes were hard to fill, but VA felt comfortable in the temporary role. Her life of worry, distrust, and heartbreak were gone, and she was enjoying her life, finally. That shield of protection covering her heart was back in place and would remain there. A man in her life didn't fit into her plans now, or possibly ever.

Two welcome faces came into view in the form of Dr. Ezra Taylor and Mary Laura. They had plans to move over the mountain and were looking into a few new areas under construction.

VA couldn't wait to talk to them in depth, and she planned to join them after all the guests had been greeted. After she welcomed the last guest on the list, VA grabbed a cocktail, and found Ezra and Mary Laura.

"I'm so glad to see you both," VA said. "I think you'll like it out this way. We moved over here about six months ago."

"Did you and Julian move back from Atlanta to this area?" Ezra asked. "Gabe sure made a good move when he left West End."

VA's demeanor quickly changed, and Mary Laura noticed at once.

"Ezra, get me another drink, please."

VA told her all about the previous six years. Mary Laura had no idea, how could she?

"I wish you would've called me. We have two girls too, you know, and we need to get them together. You heard Larry Abbott opened his practice in Southside and is doing well, didn't you?"

VA nodded and hoped she could hear more about Larry, but Ezra walked up with the drinks. VA thought she'd better mingle.

As she walked away, she said, "Make sure you speak to Gabe about the areas you're interested in."

Fall, 1955, began VA's new life. Ginger started first grade at the nearby elementary school. Susie let Julia start kindergarten at two years old to help VA out, and picked her up every morning. This allowed VA to work part-time so she would be there when the girls got home from school.

Gabe's friend, Elias Steadman, the owner of TSBB, Inc., a growing book publishing company, needed a part-time assistant payroll clerk three days a week. VA, without hesitation, accepted the position.

The only social interaction she had was helping Susie with the cocktail parties on the weekends which kept her busy and helped her stay up to date with her old friends.

A few times when she visited the kindergarten, VA noticed some of the teachers looking at her and whispering. Even at special occasions at the elementary school, the young mothers from Ginger's class completely ignored her and whispered. This was the same treatment she received from her so-called good friends in the neighborhood in Atlanta. Why was she being treated like an outcast or worse?

"Why are they talking about me?" she asked Susie. "I've known most of these girls for years. What did I do?"

"I don't know. I wish I did. Don't pay any attention to those 'little women.' Believe me, they're not worth it."

VA's shield of protection had now been forced to carry over to her social well-being. She had never been an extrovert, but now she felt like retreating into a shell and not coming out except for going to work. VA made good friends at TSBB and HJHome. She also had her old friend, Gayle, and her beloved Susie and Mallory. She had no use for anyone else.

She wasn't interested in dating or meeting anyone. The real estate parties were work, and there wasn't time for anything but "schmoozing."

Another party was planned, and VA had to fill in for Susie again as hostess. This time though, the location was "THE Club" and formal. The last time she had been there was the going away dinner before moving to Atlanta. She remembered that night as amazing.

There were times she wanted to cry over Julian and their life together, but the memories of the last six years of her life had become a bad dream, and now it was time to wake up.

The formal party at "THE Club" would be the last one VA would host. The hours of preparation took time away from Ginger and Julia. Lucy became adamant about not raising VA's children, so she brought the subject up with Gabe.

"You'll need to find someone else to take Susie's place. Virginia has obligations here, and I'm not their mother! Since I don't drive, I won't live on her schedule!" That was all she had to say. Gabe agreed, so that was that.

Since this party would be the last VA would host, she made the most of it. After the guests had checked in, VA noticed a few spots reserved with no names. Those were guests personally invited by Gabe who had yet to show up. The reservation book closed at 7:00, but she waited at the entrance to the ballroom a while longer, so she could add their names when they arrived.

After fifteen minutes, VA closed the reservation book and headed to the bar for a bourbon and water. There were seventy-five guests, and the small club orchestra took their places on the stage.

The first number played was "Papa Loves Mambo" and the colorful dance floor illuminated just as VA remembered. A few couples danced but most watched on the sidelines and looked to be snickering at the couples. *What was wrong with these people? Don't they know how to have fun?* The blatant snobbery was uncalled for and a slap in the face to Gabe.

As VA stood at the bar, she noticed four guests entering the building. They must be the ones on the list that Gabe invited at the last minute. She hurried to the ballroom entrance to check them in.

"Hello, VA."

In her haste, she hadn't looked up. When she did, there was Larry Abbott and a short, attractive redhead. With them was another couple by the name of Mr. and Mrs. Dell Vandenberg.

"What a surprise. Good to see you, Larry," she said as her heart began to pound.

"This is my wife, Nancy. This is an old friend of mine, Virginia Johannsen. I don't remember your married name."

"So nice to meet you, Nancy. My name's Virginia Morley now."

The little woman said nothing and seemed to be tipsy. VA let the snub go since she really didn't care. The Vandenberg's seemed very nice, and VA directed them to the bar. Of all people, Larry. He evidently brought Nancy over from England. She never spoke, so VA didn't know if she was "the" Nancy or if she had an accent.

She knew her love for Larry hadn't faded, especially after the dinner they had almost two years ago. She could thank Julian for helping her to forget him in the beginning, but now seeing him again conjured up so many feelings.

He looked so nice in his open collar and sportscoat. The black curl over his eye, now streaked with gray, made him look even more distinguished. VA immediately changed her train of thought. *He's married, for heaven's sake.* Out of the blue, Gabe appeared, and thanked Larry and Dell for coming.

"Larry, how long has it been? Five, ten years? I understand you're interested in moving to our neck of the woods," Gabe said.

"If I can persuade Nancy. She's partial to Southside since we own a house on 11th Avenue South, and it's convenient to my office," Larry said. "But we're interested in a lot near here. Shades Valley Creek runs the length of it, and I'm sold," Larry said as he glanced at VA. "Does this part of town have a history?"

Gabe went into his spiel. "The town was incorporated in 1939. The original plans in 1929 were the brainchild of Mr. James Garrison to create an immense residential area along the ridges of Shades Mountain and Red Mountain. Our long-range plan is to build on his original ideas, and to provide park-like subdivisions. We also plan to keep 95% of the existing tree cover intact," Gabe said proudly.

Larry glanced at Nancy with a pleading look on his face. VA could tell he wanted to move.

Nancy shrugged and said, "we'll think about it. 'Tis getting a wee bit late, dear, but we want to thank you awfully for the lovely party."

She *was* British! VA also felt Nancy knew who she was. She didn't utter a word at all except to say it was time to go, and it was only 7:30.

She didn't look at all like VA expected. She pictured his nurse taller, beautiful, and with dark hair, like the war posters. Her shade of red looked mousy brown, straight, worn short, and parted on the left side. VA noticed Nancy's eyes were also green.

As the Abbott's met up to leave with the Vandenburg's, Larry looked back at VA with a sincere smile. *I wish he hadn't done that.* She had an unpleasant suspicion of what could happen. Her love for him never went away, it had just been put on hold.

Only being allowed to work three half days a week, VA felt stagnant and bored. She was never allowed time to meet her old friends for lunch or god forbid, go out on a Friday night. Only 36, she still looked damn good.

Out of nowhere, Mary Laura called and wanted her to have dinner with them at Dale's Cellar the next Saturday night. Ezra had a friend they wanted her to meet. She hated blind dates, but hell, she was bored to tears. Like a child, she had to ask Lucy for permission and if she would watch the girls. To her shock, Lucy agreed. While sitting at her vanity table preparing for the date, Ginger wanted to know where she was going.

"I'm going out with some friends of mine for dinner."

"Mommy, you can't go out. Daddy's not here."

Ginger didn't understand why her daddy wasn't living with them anymore, and VA never explained. She didn't try. Whenever Julian's name was mentioned, she would only murmur, "jackass", under her breath.

Ginger seemed to live in her own little world and rarely spoke to her mother. She would try to carry on a playful conversation with Julia, but that was all. A worried VA brought it to Lucy's attention, but as always, Lucy said she would grow out of it.

CHAPTER 29

The Rumor Mill

Summer 1956

Payne Brown was a furniture salesman based in High Point, North Carolina. He and Ezra had become good friends three years earlier when Payne was rushed to the hospital for an emergency appendectomy while on a sales trip to Birmingham. Since then, Mary Laura and Ezra met him for dinner when he came into town.

VA looked great when she left the house. The silk floral dress fit snuggly and in just the right places. She looked like pure class, and when she arrived at Dale's Cellar, the hostess led her to the reserved table for four.

Ezra and Payne stood as she approached the table and Mary Laura had a drink waiting for her. Ezra introduced them, and VA wasn't disappointed. He was tall, nice looking, not like Larry or Julian, but in a sweet and boyish sort of way. By the pleased look on Payne's face, he seemed happy with his date. Dale's had recorded music playing and couples were already on the small dance floor dancing to the slow melody of "Only You" by the Platters.

"Shall we?" Payne offered his hand to VA.

Being cautious, he didn't hold her too close. He asked the obvious questions, and she answered truthfully. She was divorced, with two children and worked at TSBB, Inc.

Curious about his travels, Payne told her he lived in High Point, North Carolina, employed by a high-end furniture company, and sold to upscale furniture stores around the Southeast. With no marital status mentioned, she didn't ask and assumed the obvious.

The dinner ended around 10:00. Payne walked VA to her car and took her hand and raised it to his lips.

"I hope to see you again, Virginia. May I call you when my next trip to Birmingham is planned?" he asked.

"Yes, I'd like that. Thank you for tonight. I thoroughly enjoyed it."

When VA got home, Lucy and the girls were asleep. She lit a cigarette and turned on the TV. The stations were about to sign off, so she sat in silence, and thought about Payne and how he might bring her back to life.

VA was originally hired as the part-time assistant to Bill Cunningham at TSBB. She thought he was a smart ass, little weasel but she always performed her job well, did what was expected, and stayed out of his way. She didn't like the way he looked at her. He always got a little too close when giving her a project or just talking to her.

With an office to herself, she wanted to keep her door closed, and Cunningham out. She couldn't do it, though, since employees constantly came to her for an advance in their salary for a variety of reasons, and she had to be available. She'd been working there a year and needed a raise. As much as she dreaded it, she had to go to Bill Cunningham to ask for one.

"Bill, I've been here a year and I need a raise in salary. It's essential for me now since I have two growing daughters and their needs are getting expensive."

"You live with your mother. She has plenty of money, and you receive child support, do you not?"

She had to plan her words carefully. "If it's any of your business, I don't ask her for money. My salary takes care of my girls and their needs. She doesn't."

"Well, let me think about it. We've been working together for a year. What's in it for me?"

"Kiss my ass, Bill. Never mind."

"I would love to, VA."

She left his office humiliated. Her response could have been much worse, but she controlled it. She had to work. Gabe helped her get this job, and she liked Elias Steadman, the owner. No way would she quit. The only upside could be if she complained about Cunningham to Mr. Steadman. *Maybe then that ass-wipe would be fired, the slimy weasel.*

Payne Brown came into town on average once a month. He called VA each time a trip was planned, and their dating pattern began. Lucy didn't mind keeping the girls since VA seemed to like him, and it was only once a month.

He always stayed at "Motel Birmingham" in Irondale which wasn't too far from the house, and they would always go to the familiar "Gulas Club" for the food and good music.

Payne wined and dined VA, and she had developed some feelings for him. She never voiced those feelings since he could have a woman in every city throughout the Southeast for all she knew.

Gabe got wind of the relationship and in no uncertain terms he would tell VA she needed to stop it before it became serious. On his weekly visit to the house, the conversation became heated.

"Why? I have the right to a relationship if I want one! He's nice, a friend of Ezra's, and we have fun! That's all!"

"Look at your track record," he said, "you have two children, you're divorced and live with your mother. You're giving the appearance of a tramp. My friends have seen you out with him, and it seems you two are publicly showing affection. Your affair with him seems to be the major topic of their conversation. Being divorced twice in four years stokes the fire of the rumor mill."

"I don't care! It's not an affair, and it's none of their damn business--or yours! Now I know where the 'little bitches' at the school and kindergarten get their information," she yelled. "Don't you think I've noticed them talking about me behind my back? Who are they to dictate my life? Most of those women are slobbering drunks and would screw their next-door neighbor if they felt like it. They're spreading rumors that just aren't true!"

"Just think about what I said. It's for your own damn good."

Payne would be in town that week and VA looked forward to it. He always informed her of his day of arrival, and that helped plan her schedule. He would be there Wednesday, and Lucy would watch the girls only if they were bathed and ready for bed when she left.

When Payne picked VA up at the house on Mabry Drive, he met her mother for the first time. VA introduced them, and being her normal, stoic self, Lucy's demeanor wasn't friendly. *Oh no, she's been talking to Gabe.*

"What did I do?" Payne asked. "Is your mother always that cordial and friendly?"

"She never fusses over anyone. Don't waste your time thinking about it."

As usual, they went to Gulas's and the house orchestra played with "Lola" as the featured vocalist. After dinner and dancing to most of the old familiar songs, Payne was ready to go. VA wanted to stay, but she succumbed to his seductive charm.

He drove her to "Motel Birmingham" and enticed her to have another drink in his room.

"That's fine," she thought, "I'm a grown woman." She still felt a little tight from the restaurant and after having the drinks in his room, Payne took VA's hand and led her to the bed.

"It's time, VA. I want you and have for a long time."

VA didn't know if she should stop him or let him. *Go with your instincts, VA.* She stood as he started to undress her and then kissed her roughly. She returned the kiss, then pulled away. She didn't like the vulgar way he kissed her.

"Payne, I can't. I'm sorry. I'm not in love with you," she said.

"It doesn't matter, VA. I'm not in love with you either, but don't you think it's time?"

With that said, VA knew his intentions. She thought he might have been different, but he was the same as all men. He wanted to see how far he could get and at that point, he wasn't getting any farther. Payne drove her home and left her at the door.

"I'm sorry it didn't work out for us, VA," he said as he walked to his car.

Running late for work the next morning, VA drove to the office in record time. Never would she let Bill Cunningham have a reason to discipline her. She hated to think what the cost would be. The thought of him made her cringe. The phone rang in her office, and it was Ezra Taylor on the other end.

"VA, I have tragic news. Payne Brown had a massive heart attack last night and died. The motel housekeeper found him early this morning. He must have been in ill health but never mentioned it. I don't know what to say, VA. I'll talk to you later when I get a little more information. Were you two together last night?"

"Yes, we went to Gulas's for dinner and dancing,

and I got home around ten." She hung up, closed her office door, put her head on her desk, and sobbed.

"Why can't I find a sincere person I can spend my life with? My life is doomed to fail," she said out loud as she tried to catch her breath. As she wiped her tears, she said out loud, "Oh lord, what if I'd slept with him?" She couldn't help but chuckle.

After speaking to Ezra later, VA found out that Payne Brown was married to an alcoholic wife in North Carolina. Why wasn't she surprised? She should have asked him on their first date, but when Ezra said nothing about his status, her assumption leaned to his being unattached.

"When they're not married, they're sorry asses. If they are married, they have mentally ill, alcoholic wives, and are just looking for an escape," she told herself.

VA Morley was through with men, period.

CHAPTER 30

Only the Good

Summer 1959

*J*une, 1959, consisted of a trip for the girls to Gulf Shores, Alabama with Julian, and the annual long drive to Dallas, Texas for a visit with Ed and Mary. Julian and his new wife took the girls to the beach, even though VA loudly protested.

VA loathed driving with Lucy to Ed's. It would take fourteen hours, without stopping, and then her mother expected to drive back to Birmingham the next day. Lucy had never been one for long visits, but VA and Ed usually talked her into staying three nights, at least.

VA could always relax in Texas. Something about Ed and Mary brought a comfort to her she didn't have at home, and they never judged her.

Lucy also seemed relaxed there. Lucy enjoyed her time with her grandchildren, Billy 7, and Tricia 17. She usually saw them twice a year, but this trip gave her the opportunity to give them her undivided attention since Ginger and Julia were with their father.

Ed and Mary's friends, the Cornell's, planned a weekend pool party, for adults only, and every couple from the neighborhood was invited. The party would begin at 5:00 in the afternoon on Friday, and end at 5:00 on Sunday.

The Cornell's pulled out all the stops. Each guest brought their favorite appetizers and sides, while the hosts provided all the liquor and meat for the grill. VA couldn't believe how much liquor there was, and it was a dry county!

"Joe Cornell's been buying booze all year for this," Ed said.

Loud music played late into the night, and VA danced with anyone who asked her. It was all in good-fun. If she'd been in Birmingham, she'd have been labeled "the husband-stealing tramp", and rumors would fly, especially in Gabe's crowd.

The favorite songs of the party were, "Personality" by Lloyd Price, and "Since I Don't Have You" by the Skyliners. VA was in her element, but by 2:00 AM, she was partied out and ready to go to bed. Ed and Mary joined her, and all planned to head back to the ongoing party the next afternoon.

VA heard the phone ring at 4:00 in the morning. She heard Ed talking, but went back to sleep. Then she heard a knock on her door.

"VA, it's me," Ed whispered loudly. "Come to the

living room."

"I'm coming," she said.

She found Ed and Mary in the living room talking to Lucy.

"Susie suffered a major stroke earlier tonight and was rushed to the hospital," Ed said. "She complained of a headache and immediately collapsed. Gabe said it doesn't look good."

Lucy was ready to leave as soon as she could pack. VA, stunned, could only think of her best friend, and if she would still be alive when they got home. They planned to leave at daylight, but it would be impossible to get any sleep.

The fourteen hour drive back to Birmingham was tough. Lucy didn't speak except to say she was hungry or needed to stop for the restroom. VA tried not to cry. She kept the car radio on and listened to music or the latest news. She *had* to break the unrelenting silence.

VA already missed Susie. She had always been her rock to lean on, and gave advice without judgement, unlike her brother. Susie went through everything with her, good and bad. The fun times at the house on Tuscaloosa Avenue, the weddings, the war. VA was going through a different kind of grief. A grief she had never experienced before.

Susie had undergone major surgery to relieve bleeding in the brain and survived. Still unconscious, her prognosis was unknown since it was still early. Susie's condition was stable, and she would be in the hospital for a while.

Susie remained in the hospital for a month. She suffered brain damage due to the stroke and was paralyzed from the waist down. She only had partial use of her left arm. Her speech had also been affected, but she seemed to know Gabe, Steve, and Andy. The master bedroom became a hospital room, and Gabe hired round-the-clock nurses.

From the time Susie got sick, women began to come out of the woodwork to get Gabe's attention. VA was again filling in for Susie at the HJHome cocktail parties. When she hosted the parties, she had to laugh at those fake bitches throwing themselves at him.

There was always one who would latch on and stick to him all night. It didn't matter to them if he was married or if they were married. With Susie at home, and unable to communicate or go anywhere, he became the catch of the Country Club. VA heard that one woman planned to divorce her husband for him. The hypocrisy of it all was unbelievable. *And he appeared too stupid to notice. Or was he?*

Having to be in the same room with these women at school functions made her sick. They would see her across the room and saunter over and try to start a conversation. They'd ask about Susie and how Gabe was doing. She would force a "doing fine" out of her mouth, then walk away. VA received more luncheon invitations in one week than she ever had in one year.

"They've got to be kidding," she told Lucy. "The way they talked about me and treated me? They're only trying to get to him through me." She threw each invitation in the garbage.

"Like hell I'll RSVP."

CHAPTER 31

Passing the Torch

July 1961

*J*uly 7, 1961--another day that would live in infamy for the Johannsen family. Now that Ginger and Julia were older, Lucy enjoyed being home with them while VA worked. They played outside, rode bikes, or walked to Shades Crest Village without supervision. Julia was 8, Ginger 12.

The girls walked in from being next door and turned on the TV. Julia sprawled on the sofa and Ginger sat in her favorite chair in front of the picture window. It was hot, and Lucy had all the windows open with fans blowing in every room. They tuned in to "As the World Turns" and Lucy sat down on the sofa with Julia to watch it with them.

The show stayed on fifteen minutes, and then she would go back to her bedroom to sew. Suddenly, a loud blast shattered the window where Ginger sat, and Julia started to cry.

"What was that?" Julia screamed. "Ginger, are you alright?"

Lucy jumped up from the sofa and went to Ginger.

"Are you hurt?" Lucy asked as Ginger began to cry.

"No, I'm okay."

Lucy, visibly shaken, told Julia to call the police. It sounded like a gunshot to her. Ginger continued to cry as the police arrived to investigate. It had been a gunshot, but where it came from, they couldn't speculate. They found a small caliber bullet lodged in the chair Ginger had been sitting in and if it had been any higher, the bullet would have struck her head.

Lucy calmed the girls down, and after the policemen left, she went to her bedroom to lie down. VA came home quickly from work and soon Lucy began to complain of chest pains. She called the ambulance, then Gabe.

Lucy was admitted to St. Vincent's Hospital that evening and placed under observation. The next morning, there were still no leads on the shooter. Lucy was getting restless and didn't like having tubes and probes attached to her.

"I'm ready to go home. Tell the nurse to help me with my clothes," Lucy said. "I feel fine. How is Ginger?"

"She's fine and worried about you. You can't leave yet, Mama," said VA. "The doctors still want to keep you under observation, and make sure your blood pressure returns to normal."

Lucy took it on herself to start disconnecting the IV and the cuff to the blood pressure monitor.

"Mama, stop! You have to keep it all connected. They're trying to regulate your elevated blood pressure," said VA. "Don't you remember when Eliza died? We can't let that happen to you."

"She had a stroke, just like Susie," Lucy retorted. "I had chest pains. They're gone now."

Lucy fidgeted with her covers and kept her usual furrowed brow.

"The doctors want to make sure there isn't any other reason for your chest pain." Gabe said as he prevented his mother from disconnecting her blood pressure cuff.

"I don't care what they want. I'm going home."

VA and Gabe stayed at the hospital the remainder of the day while their mother slept. The doctor said Lucy's prognosis was good and she would be able to go home in a day or two.

Finally waking up around 3:30, Lucy seemed in good spirits and still planned to go home. Smiling, and in a good mood, she told them she felt fine. Visiting hours were over at 4:00, so VA and Gabe left, but promised to be back around 7:00.

When they returned, Dr. Ted McGuire was waiting for them. It seemed Lucy suffered a massive heart attack around 6:20. Code Blue had been announced, and the on-call cardiac team rushed in to begin immediate resuscitative efforts but to no avail. Lucy Collier Johannsen's time of death was 6:26 PM.

"Mama!" VA cried as she brought both hands to her mouth. She walked into the room where she found an orderly trying to pull out her false teeth.

"Stop it! All of those teeth are hers!"

After taking care of all the required paperwork, they left the hospital and went home. VA caught Gabe quietly crying as he drove. It shocked her to see the successful man about town not be in control of his feelings. She had never seen him cry and didn't think he knew how. He was a carbon copy of their mother, and his visual display of sadness wouldn't be witnessed again. VA thought the last two years with Susie, and now his mother, had finally taken its toll. She said nothing the entire way home and let him grieve.

While in town for the funeral, their visit to see Susie gripped Ed and Mary. They felt as if they were seeing someone they never knew. Susie, no longer the happy and beautiful girl who did more for others than her own family, was now a small, frail, sickly figure who could barely move one arm. Her beautiful face and perfectly shaped full lips had thinned, and her graying hair had been brushed away from her face. Mary stood beside the hospital bed and took Susie's hand.

"Susie, it's Mary. I've missed you so. Look, here's Edward and we've come to town to visit."

Susie glanced at both, not knowing who they were. Gabe caught her eye, and she gestured to him with her weak arm. He bent down to hear her speak.

"She's trying to remember. She knows your faces are familiar but can't place you."

Mary squeezed Ed's arm and sat down in a chair close by. Ed talked softly to Susie and suddenly her eyes widened.

"Edward," she murmured.

"Yes, it is," Ed said softly. "I've missed seeing you. My brother keeps you all to himself." Susie could barely smile, but she remembered him. Just knowing she knew him meant so much. He turned away and looked at Gabe with tears in his eyes.

VA walked into the bedroom to see her two brothers, Susie, and Mary. "We're all together again," VA said as she stood next to Susie's bed. "It's been so long."

The scent of mimosa trees and gardenias filled the air at the small house on Mabry Drive. The matriarch of the Johannsen family would be laid to rest at 10:00 AM. It was a cloudy, but warm day, and VA perspired in her sleeveless dress as she helped the girls get ready.

Many calls, cards, and flowers had been delivered to the house, and it brought back to VA the memory of her daddy's funeral in 1933. The doorbell rang nonstop, and she was ready to leave for the funeral home in Southside. Deliveries would just have to be left at the door.

The smell of flowers overwhelmed the visitation room at the funeral home. The simple silver casket, covered in roses, was one Lucy would have selected. Gabe and Ed made all the funeral plans, and a soft blue gown and robe set was selected by VA and Mary for Lucy to wear.

VA walked to the casket with Julia and Ginger. Lucy's short gray hair had been curled. She never wore it that way, and she also had makeup on.

"That doesn't look like Mama Lucy," Ginger said.

VA tried to explain why Lucy had makeup on. The funeral home wasn't trying to change her appearance, but to help it since she wasn't alive. Ginger understood, but Julia looked at her grandmother without saying a word.

Suddenly, Julia turned and grabbed her mother

around the waist and sobbed. The family and a few friends were entering the room, so Ginger and Julia sat down on a sofa and stayed quiet.

Lucy Collier Johannsen was buried next to her husband, Dr. WB Johannsen on July 9, 1961. The short graveside service was well attended. VA felt lost without her mother while Gabe and Ed were stoic and unemotional. Mary and Mallory stayed close to VA while she greeted old friends and relatives from Clairmont and West End.

As the family headed for their cars, a voice came out of nowhere.

"Hello, VA. I was sorry to hear about Mama Lucy. I was always so very fond of her." It was Julian. "The girls are growing up, aren't they? I'll not let them see me today. I'll be back in a couple of weeks for our visit."

Not knowing how to react, VA said, "Thank you, I know you were fond of her."

He stepped back and let her continue to the car. Ginger and Julia were already in Ed and Mary's car with Billy and Tricia, and never saw him.

After a long day, VA and the girls found themselves home alone. The lost, empty feeling consumed her. She walked down the hall to her mother's closed bedroom door. VA opened the door and found it was still the way her mother left it. Her sewing machine was open, and cut-out pieces of a skirt were waiting to be sewn.

On her mother's bedside table were her glasses, and the treasured clock radio she listened to every night before going to sleep. The bedspread still held the outline of her mother when she went to her room to rest after the shot shattered the window. VA couldn't bear the thought of knowing her mother was gone.

After Ginger and Julia went to bed, VA went to their small den, sat on the sofa, and lit a cigarette. The tears began to flow, and she couldn't stop them. She looked up, and Julia stood in the kitchen.

"Mama, can I sit down by you?" she asked. Julia had never seen her mother cry.

VA held out her arms, hugged Julia, and said, "I want my Mama."

The police report was filed, and the findings were that a retired Air Force veteran, Mr. Joseph Hall, one street over from Mabry Drive, had been shooting at squirrels on July 7, and a stray bullet shattered the Johannsen's picture window.

It had been accidental, no charges were filed, but VA made it clear that she lost her mother because of some old fool shooting at tree rats. Gabe told her there was no proof that the incident caused Lucy's heart attack.

VA disagreed.

"My mother was scared to death and no one will ever change my mind!"

While sifting through the large stack of sympathy cards, VA came across familiar handwriting on one envelope. With no return address, she opened it to find a beautiful sympathy card with lovely butterflies and a message that said:

"Take comfort, and find strength knowing you are thought of and cared about. You're not alone."

Signed,

One who Cares

CHAPTER 32

No More Tears

January 1962

$\mathcal{G}$abe was chosen to be the executor of his mother's will. The property and assets would be divided equally three ways, with VA continuing to live in the house on Mabry Drive. During the reading of the will, Ed and VA learned their mother had been living solely off interest from a secret trust Bill opened for her during his final leave.

Dr. Johannsen had a large stake in a now defunct oil drilling company in Louisiana and willed the ownership papers to Lucy. The oil wells dried up after the war, and the company went belly-up, but the money made before and after WB's death, made Lucy a wealthy woman. Gabe was amazed to find that Lucy still had all the assets left to her by WB.

Never owning stocks, they kept their wealth invested in real estate and cash hidden at home. There was no debt whatsoever. Also found inside the envelope with their mother's will was an old, worn, folded letter addressed to her four children.

As Gabe read the letter out loud, Lucy described the first time she met their father in 1910, and how much she loved him then. VA was shocked since she'd never heard her mother speak in such a loving way. She thought of how wonderful it must have been in those carefree days. She never believed it, but her mother really did love her father.

As her condition steadily declined, Susie was told of Lucy's death. Not knowing how she would react, Gabe and VA waited a little while, then left the bedroom. Immediately, Susie's live-in nurse, Cora Britt, ran out to bring them back. One large tear rolled down her cheek, and for the first time in a long while, Susie showed emotion.

Seven months had passed since Lucy's passing, and Cora seemed a little encouraged with Susie's appetite. Since the weekly meals from Lucy stopped, Cora stepped in and became the cook, housekeeper, and nurse.

Roast beef and potatoes seemed to be Susie's favorite and with more iron in her diet, she looked to be a little stronger, and her color seemed better. The doctor was pleased and allowed her to sit in front of a sunny window in her wheelchair once a day.

The days of encouragement were short lived. Susie developed pneumonia, and within a week, her condition turned grave. Gabe wanted everything humanly possible done for her. He had an oxygen tent moved into the bedroom. Round-the-clock nurses were hired to give Cora some needed rest, but she constantly stayed at Susie's bedside.

Susie Langdon Johannsen passed away in her sleep on February 7, 1962, at home. Gabe, being the only one beside Cora at the house, wept at her bedside. Steve was married, and Andy had entered his first year of college at the University of Alabama.

Susie's funeral was standing room only, and closed-circuit TV had to be set up at the Elmwood Cemetery Chapel for the mourners outside. She and Gabe knew almost everyone in town, and in her own way, Susie had touched each one.

With two deaths in a year, VA lost her mother and her best friend. The grieving for her mother had eased some, but now it was starting all over again.

Glancing around the full Chapel, many old and new friends were in attendance. Most of the relatives were at Lucy's funeral less than a year before.

After the service, and as the family filed out, VA noticed a face she hadn't seen in a long time. As she kept walking, she looked back, and the eyes followed her every move. She held Julia's hand, and kept Ginger close as the immense crowd outside kept stopping her to express their sympathy. Finally, wafting through the crowd, VA turned to see if she could see the person again, but it was too crowded.

They made it to the car to get in line for the short funeral procession to Elmwood Cemetery. While waiting in the car, she tried to look at each person as they exited. It was fruitless. That person had gotten lost in the crowd.

After the graveside service, the immediate family went to Gabe's house for lunch. VA couldn't eat. She had too many memories of Susie in that house and the emptiness of it was unbearable. After an hour, she made her polite goodbyes and left with the girls to sit in the emptiness of their own house.

A month after Susie's death, another envelope came in the mail with the same handwriting as before. This time it said, "Thinking of You." VA opened it and the message inside had been handwritten.

"May the memories that mean so much to you live forever."

Signed,

One who Cares

The script seemed so familiar. *Who was this?* It couldn't be Julian. She never could read his writing, and he wouldn't dare! She knew it wasn't Larry. He had a wife and way too much class. It didn't look like his writing, anyway. Maybe this person would send another one, but she wanted no more tears. She had grieved enough.

Susie had been gone six months, and the void in VA's life was huge. Mallory helped to fill that void since she and Peter Moore had gotten married a few months earlier, and always kept VA included in their group of friends. Mallory couldn't have made a better choice in husbands.

Gabe, on the other hand, was being chased by every woman over the mountain, available or not. It made VA nauseous. The female behavior hadn't changed since the last cocktail party she hosted for him. That had been HJHome's last party since Susie had fallen ill. Gabe left it up to the other real estate companies to do the "schmoozing."

VA continued to receive luncheon invitations and party invites of every kind from women trying to get close to Gabe. Each one went into the trash with no RSVP. She'd never give those tramps the satisfaction of a nod.

VA knew Gabe dated a few women from the Country Club, but she didn't know who. He volunteered no information. She stayed out of his business, but thought it seemed too soon after Susie's death. VA couldn't forget how Gabe talked down to her but now he seemed to be the topic of all the gossip. Although the men patted him on the back in affirmation, the bitches were just plain jealous.

While the same assholes labeled VA a tramp, it seemed Gabe's behavior deserved no such label. She noticed the new way he carried himself, and the change in his swagger. He was doing everything but walking around with his dong in his hand.

In December, 1962, Gabe announced his upcoming marriage to a widow, Janet Clay from the Country Club. They planned to get married at the end of January, at the Baptist chapel near his home. The announcement had been made at an informal get-together at Gabe's house.

A surprised VA had never seen Janet in her life, not even at the HJHome cocktail parties. Gabe glanced over at her, and she turned away in disbelief. After two hours, the party started to break up, and Gabe walked over to her.

Before he could utter a word, VA said under her breath, "Don't you *ever* criticize me! Susie hasn't been gone a full year, and you've let yourself fall into the bitch trap. You're unbelievable, and by the way, how can you even think of getting married in the same chapel as Susie?"

As she walked away from him it dawned on her that in two hours, Janet Clay never moved away from her little clique of women friends from the Country Club. To top it off, Gabe hadn't even tried to pry her away and introduce his fiancée to his sister.

There was an air about Janet Clay that didn't sit well with VA. A few weeks before the wedding, Gabe invited VA and the girls over for a cook-out at his house with his neighbors, and their children.

With a drink and cigarette in hand, Janet walked over to VA and said in an extremely loud southern drawl, "Vaa--ginia, I hate we didn't meet at our announcement party. Everything seemed so darn hectic. I tried to make my rounds and meet e-v-r-y-body."

VA rolled her eyes. "Since you were so involved with your own friends, I think there were a good many people you didn't meet. It was a casual party, it didn't seem very hectic to me. In fact, it was one of the most boring parties Gabe's ever given," VA said while getting a good look at her.

It was early January, and the bitch had a tan! That told VA she had to be a put-on fake and vain as well. She could pick one out in a crowd. Janet had all the hallmarks of "Bitchy" Abbott the first time they met years ago.

Janet had wild, frosted hair, and the style looked wiry and disheveled. She reminded her of the comedienne Phyllis Diller. There had to be something about her Gabe liked, but VA couldn't see it in her outward appearance.

The couple got married on January 26, 1963, in the small Baptist chapel. It was an intimate ceremony with only immediate family and close friends attending. VA remembered Gabe and Susie's wedding in 1939, and what a happy and loving occasion it was. She thought about how beautiful the same chapel looked that day so long ago, and the happy faces of Susie, Gabe, and both families.

This wedding was quite the opposite. It was nice, but there were no flowers, no music, and few smiles. There didn't seem to be any genuine happy feelings from the Johannsen side. Steve and Andy were emotionless, as well as some of Gabe's close friends.

Naturally, Janet's family was overjoyed. She had just married Birmingham's most affluent and distinguished catch of the year!

Throwing themselves at Gabe, the Clay family completely ignored Steve, Andy, and VA. Janet pulled Gabe away from them, and then went directly to the waiting car. No goodbye to his sons, his friends, or his sister. Janet Clay's plan to mold her brother into a different man had begun.

After the honeymoon, Janet demanded that Gabe sell his house and all the furnishings. She wanted nothing to do with his former life, and her demands were affecting nineteen-year-old Andy. The flared tempers between father and son were so bad, Andy rarely came home from college. When he did, he stayed at Steve's and seldom saw his father.

Janet wanted to build a new house and bring in her personal interior decorator to make it her own. This would cost Gabe a fortune, but he didn't seem to mind. He now had a healthy wife and sex life again. Nothing else seemed to matter.

After six months, the new house in affluent Cherokee Hills was finished. VA heard through mutual friends that Janet planned a huge housewarming party for all their friends and family. The party was a week away and she still hadn't heard from Gabe extending his invitation.

VA made it through the week and still hadn't heard from her brother. The party was the next night and she wanted to go, but if he let himself be swayed by his new wife, then she knew their close relationship was a thing of the past.

She never heard from her brother, which made her realize he had thrown away his past. It saddened her to know the brother she knew so well and respected, had let himself be molded into a different person. A person who had become shallow and superficial.

As VA sat in her den, the phone rang.

"Where were you last night, Auntie?" It was Steve. "I asked Dad if you were coming and he thought you were. He told Janet to call you two weeks ago."

"I didn't get the invitation," she said. "Gabe should've called me himself."

CHAPTER 33

Turbulent Times

Summer 1968

*N*ow that school was out for the summer, Gabe hired Ginger, 19, as the HJHome receptionist. VA remained at TSBB, and Julia, 15, was basically on her own. She wasn't old enough to remember the effect of her parent's divorce on Ginger and her mother, so she had a carefree personality, plenty of friends, and the boys were noticing her. With dark blonde hair and green eyes, she favored VA.

Sally Brookfield was Julia's best friend, and they were inseparable. They became friends in the fourth grade and had remained close ever since. Sally's parents thought Julia stayed home alone in the summer much too often and could be a bad influence on their daughter. They tried to control the amount of time the girls spent together.

Since Julia currently had a boyfriend, Will, Sally was restricted the entire summer from Julia's house.

Not allowed to date, Sally was whisked off to the family's beach house in Destin, Florida, for most of the summer. Sally's father, Freddy Brookfield, always stayed behind since he was the orchestra leader at one of the hot spots in town and worked every night.

VA had lunch every day with her friend and co-worker Dot Lucas. "VA, you know why they want to keep Sally and Julia separated during the summer, don't you? It's because you're divorced and work full time," she said. "Poor Sally's going to rebel one day, I can feel it. These ignorant people think being divorced is a label for a loose woman."

"That's just *wrong!* I have no social life," she replied, not meaning to raise her voice. "I remember Freddy Brookfield. He played the college circuit. His orchestra played for most of our sorority dances, and he couldn't keep his hands off the women!"

"Now that Julia has a boyfriend, they're giving her that label, too, and I know that's not true," said Dot. "There's nothing nicer than innocent 'summer love,' and it's normal for a teenage girl to go out on dates."

"I can find Julia with one phone call, any day of the week. She has more than one friend. I know each one of them and have their phone numbers. She knows what her restrictions are. Her boyfriend, Will, is a nice boy from a good family. His father is a federal judge. They might go to a movie once a week, and that's usually on the weekend. The only problem with them is they stay on the phone too much."

After talking to Dot on her lunch hour, VA walked back to her office and called home. Julia answered.

"I'm just calling to see what you're doing," VA said.

"Nothing, watching TV with Dawn from next door. We might walk down to the 'village' in a little while. We want to get something to eat at the drug store and see who's there. We're bored."

"Okay, I'll see you when I get home."

As VA hung up the phone, Bill "the weasel" Cunningham, strutted into her office with a small stack of papers. His arrogance and conceited gait turned her stomach.

"These employees have received a change in their hourly rate. By the end of the day, all changes need to be recorded for the next pay cycle," he said as he slinked out the door.

Being his payroll assistant, VA had also been put in charge of screening his calls and being the liaison between himself and Elias Steadman.

She wanted to inform Mr. Steadman about Bill's long lunches and how she had to address employee salary concerns when Cunningham didn't want to be bothered. With extra duties and responsibilities, she needed a raise. It had been two years since she received her last raise, and that had been a mere pittance.

Unannounced, VA walked into Bill's office and gave him an ultimatum. If she didn't get a raise, she would talk to Mr. Steadman. She was the sole provider for two teenagers. Even though Ginger was over 18, the small amount of child support for Julia didn't go very far, and she needed more money.

"I need a substantial raise now, since I've taken on more work, your work."

"The department can't afford it now, VA. I wish it could, but I only have so much to pay out per month."

"There are only three of us in the payroll department, and Tammy, our supposed secretary, doesn't do anything. We don't need her when you have me taking and screening your calls."

As VA spoke, Bill walked around her and shut his office door. Moving deliberately, he put his hands on her waist and turned her around to face him. Though only 5'4", VA still stood two inches taller. Bill brought his face close to hers while she reached back and put her hand on the office door knob. He caught her and kissed her before she could get out.

"What the hell, Bill? Get out of my way!" she yelled as she opened the door and stormed out. Grabbing a tissue from her desk drawer, she wiped off the feeling of that slime-ball's sad excuse for a kiss.

Tammy Rose, the worthless secretary she and Bill shared, sat at her desk reading a magazine as VA passed by. She let the magazine fall to her lap.

"Mrs. Morley? Are you okay?"

VA ignored her. Tammy looked to be in her forties, but dressed too young, wore too much makeup, and had long, teased bleached hair. She could be attractive if she tried, but now she looked like a blonde cow. Why Bill hired her wasn't a mystery. She was single.

She looked through the small stack of papers on her desk hoping to see her name with an increase. She saw Tammy's name, with an increase, but her own name wasn't included, and she felt the heat of rage rising from the pit of her stomach. Some of these employees had rate increases only six months earlier, plus a bonus, and now Tammy. VA hit the breaking point.

She went back to Bill's office, shut the door, and said through tight lips, "I have everything I need on you now. I'll go to Mr. Steadman after I leave this office and unload all I know pertaining to Bill Cunningham. You have made a big mistake!"

She stormed out of his office and caught the elevator to the fifth floor. "I can't stand him, I can't stand him," she said under her breath over and over.

After spilling all she knew to Mr. Steadman, Bill

Cunningham was called to his office.

"VA, I want you to be present while I speak to him," said Mr. Steadman.

She was more than happy to stay and see the little weasel squirm for a change. So many times, he had gotten too close to her, touched her inappropriately, and implied sexual innuendo not fit for the office.

"Would you like to see me, sir?" asked Bill. He saw VA sitting in Mr. Steadman's office and the expression on his face went from self-confident to arrogant.

"Bill, it's come to my attention that you've been behaving in a manner that's not suitable for this company. Is this true?"

"Well, I don't think so, Mr. Steadman. My department stays on top of the profit-sharing, payroll, insur--"

Not giving him time to complete his sentence, Mr. Steadman got up from his desk, walked around it, and stood in front of Bill. Being six feet, two inches tall, he towered over the little man.

"I will not abide any indecent behavior in my company. I don't have to explain to you the complaints that have come to my attention, and I will not tolerate any employee taking advantage of me, my company, or any of my co-workers," Mr. Steadman said, as he controlled his countenance. "You are officially terminated, effective immediately."

"Mr. Steadman, if you'll let me speak," said Bill, meek as a mouse.

"No, Bill. It's done. There's nothing else to say."

VA watched Bill, the slimy weasel, turn slowly in disbelief and leave the office. She remained seated as Mr. Steadman sat back down behind his large desk and let out a deep breath. He could tell she was a bit shaken.

"VA, this was not your fault. I've been hearing rumors about him for years. You're the only one who came forward personally and confirmed the alleged harassment and dishonesty. I appreciate it, and I'm deeply sorry for the pain it's caused."

She walked back to her office and thought about what had just transpired. It wasn't guilt she felt. The only reason she might feel a little remorse was that he lost his company benefits, and they added up to a substantial amount.

After Bill cleaned out his office and left the position he held for almost fifteen years, VA informed a puzzled Tammy Rose that Bill wouldn't be back.

"I'm glad. He always put his hands on me and he made me feel uncomfortable. I felt bad for you having to do his work. I've noticed it for a while."

"Now you and I are the payroll department. We'll

work together on everything," VA said.

"I'd like that, Mrs. Morley. I've never had enough to do."

VA felt bad about calling Tammy Rose a cow. She proved to be a hard worker, and with her help, the department ran like a fine-tuned machine. Mr. Steadman promoted VA to the Head of Payroll with a substantial raise, and Tammy now screened her calls. From that day, Tammy became a fine secretary and a true friend.

VA decided it was time to sell the house on Mabry Drive. Being a single mother and working full time, taking care of a house was next to impossible. Ed and Gabe agreed and after fourteen years, she could live with her girls in a home she selected on her own.

The house sold quickly, and VA chose a new apartment complex with a pool a few miles away from Mabry Drive, but sadly in another school district for Julia. At first, Julia was excited about the new high school, but then her attitude changed since she knew no one. She and Sally got together on weekends, but her parents still didn't trust Julia's home life or VA.

"What is it about me that these people don't trust?" VA asked herself. She went to work, came home, and that was the extent of it. Her daughter was being scrutinized for her mother's life; a life full of sadness and disappointment.

Julia had been forced to move away from her best friends and the only life she knew. Shy like her mother, she tried to make friends at Creek Valley High School, but most of the kids were in established cliques. Most days, Julia skipped the lunchroom and studied alone in the library. Those days were torture for her.

Mallory invited VA and the girls over for a weekend cookout since the sisters-in-law could never work out a time to meet during the week. Mallory always thought of VA as her sister, and Peter felt the same way. They had just built a new house, and VA and the girls would be their first guests.

Julia accompanied VA since she was bored, upset about her breakup with Will, and the move from the Shades Crest house.

Ginger, almost 20, stayed home. She had become rebellious, a hippie, and to VA's dismay, planned to move to California with a group of indigent people she had just met.

"What is it, Mallory? Why are my girls suffering for mistakes I made?"

"I don't know, but if Susie Johannsen were here, she could tell you. From the time you and the girls moved back from Atlanta, you were branded a woman divorced twice in four years. They don't know the circumstances, and that it was Julian who hurt you so. I don't know who started the gossip, but I'd love to find out."

"Why does anyone care about my life? It's because of Gabe. He told me once I had the appearance of a tramp when I went out with Payne Brown. These reports came from his 'friends'. We did nothing but go out to dinner and dance! Why is it that Gabe can go out, have women throw themselves at him and then marry a stuck-up bitch after Susie hadn't even been buried a year! I wasn't even invited to their housewarming party, were you?"

"No, and I wouldn't have gone if I had been."

As Julia helped Peter in the kitchen, she heard most of the conversation but said nothing.

The last few years had been turbulent for Ginger. She heard rumors about how her mother was pregnant, had to get married the first time to Julian then divorced him for no apparent reason.

They also said Julia came along from a tryst with Julian, and they had to get married again. Her mother never talked about it, but she knew it was all untrue. Ginger never told Julia and kept the painful feelings inside. She hoped to one day block it all out of her life.

These rumors were coming from some of her friend's mothers, and a few of these women were friends of Gabe and Janet's. What they didn't realize was they were talking about her and Julia too! They were the pregnancies that spawned the rumors. This caused her to become quiet and withdrawn during her teenage years and to stay in her room most of the time listening to music, seeing no one.

Ginger's relationship with her mother was strained, and loud arguments resulted from uncontrollable tempers.

The few times Ginger went out, it was usually to a "head" shop to buy incense or jewelry. There, she found a group of people she felt comfortable with. Jack, the manager of the shop, told her about a California trip the group was planning, and asked if she would be interested. She was. This was her way to escape. Ginger Morley made up her mind to get the hell out of Birmingham and never come back.

Ginger left for California on October 10, 1968, in an old, broken down Rambler station wagon owned by a girl named Anna. The old car was loaded down with luggage in the back with more suitcases crudely tied on top. The group consisted of two girls and two guys.

VA questioned how they would all fit in the small car, but Ginger, being vague and uncaring, told her they had it all figured out. She wanted no one to tell her how to live, or what to do, especially VA. She wanted to get away from scrutiny, and most of all, her mother.

VA only had a phone number for the mother of the girl named Anna. She called Anna's mother and voiced her concern over the trip since she had heard nothing from Ginger.

"Do you know about any of the other people that went on this trip? Ginger told me nothing."

"No, I'm like you. I'm worried to death," the mother said. "I hadn't heard from Anna since they left, two weeks ago, but she called me two days ago. All I know is that they made it out there."

VA hoped to receive a postcard, a letter, or anything from Ginger. She hadn't heard from her in three weeks and was having difficulty concentrating at work. Julia was no help since she stayed mad and unhappy all the time.

VA didn't know what to do. She needed her best friend. Susie always had time to listen and gave her non-judgmental advice. Gabe was no longer any help to her. She decided to call Ed.

"Ginger went to California with an unseemly group. They drove out there in a broken down old car and I haven't heard from her in three weeks," she said. "I can't get in touch with her and I'm worried to death."

"Now, Virginia, calm down. She's not underage, but if you're that worried, I think you should bring Julian into this. She's his daughter, too. I have a gut feeling that he'll help you out. All you can do is ask him.

Don't put it all on yourself."

"Okay, I guess I have to." VA hung up, but didn't know if Julian would help out or not. She wouldn't blame him if he hung up on her.

"I'm glad you still have the same phone number," she said, with a tremble in her voice. "I didn't want to involve you in this...."

"What is it VA?" Julian interrupted. "I'm surprised to hear from you. Did something happen to one of the girls?"

"Yes and no."

VA explained how unhappy Julia was, and that her usual pleasant demeanor had turned to anger and disdain. She felt Julia would be fine in time, but Ginger was her greatest concern. VA told him she hadn't heard from their daughter in three weeks and worried something had happened to her.

"What can I do? I haven't seen Ginger in four years. I just assumed my relationship with the girls was over."

"I understand why you feel that way," she said, "but I'm beginning to feel like she might be in deep trouble. I've been in contact with one of the other mothers and she finally heard from her daughter."

When Julian said, "I'm on my way to Birmingham," VA exhaled loudly with relief. Now she wasn't alone with worry. *Ed was right.*

As Julian Morley drove to Birmingham from Atlanta, he thought about how much he missed his daughters, and not having the chance to watch them grow up. He used to see them once a month, but those visits became fewer as the girls got older.

He hadn't seen them in four years, and now they were young ladies. *Why did she call me?* The reason VA included him in the scenario was a mystery to him. She had been hateful to him for so long, and now she needed him. *She must feel extremely alone.*

He never completely lost his feelings for VA. He would always love his girls, even though they had gotten too old for his short visits. When they were small, he could take them for the entire weekend, but as they grew, the visits became fewer and felt awkward. Now, though, Ginger was in trouble and VA needed him to help. He would do all he could. How could he refuse? He was doing this for Ginger, not VA.

Julian checked in to "The Parliament House," in Birmingham. VA offered to meet him after work at the hotel restaurant. When she entered the restaurant, he stood to greet her. She continued to be the lovely woman he knew years ago, and even though this meeting concerned their daughters, it would be a bittersweet one for him.

"Hello, VA," he said as he pulled out a chair for her. "Have you heard from Ginger since we spoke on the phone?"

"No," she said, as the waiter came to take the drink orders.

"What are you drinking now?"

"The same as always. A bourbon and water."

"I think the last time I ordered a drink for you, it was a gin and tonic. I don't remember; it's been so long ago."

Julian lit a cigarette for both and started the conversation about the girls. As he spoke, VA noticed how much he had aged. He was 62, and his hair, now gray, was styled the same way it had always been. Deep lines had formed on his forehead and around his eyes. She'd never seen Julian in glasses; now he wore them all the time.

"I called since I thought you should know about Ginger. Apparently, she heard rumors about you and me which aren't true. Gabe re-married soon after Susie died, and it seems that woman and her group of friends don't like me, and it is affecting both of the girls."

She told him what the rumors were and about Ginger's trip to California.

"I don't know if she's alive or dead," she said as her voice broke. "I need your help."

"I'll do all I can," he said sincerely. He felt a responsibility, too. "I can be away from Atlanta as long as I need to. I'll go to California and bring her home if you want me to, although I haven't seen her in a long time. She might not recognize me or let me bring her home. She might feel I have no right."

"What about your wife? You could've brought her with you."

"She divorced me a few years ago. I live alone in a nice apartment on West Peachtree Street."

He asked for the phone number of Anna's mother. Evidently, she'd heard from her daughter again, and knew of a location where three of the group, including Ginger, were staying in West Los Angeles. Julian took the next available flight determined to bring his daughter home.

After landing at 4:35 PM Pacific time, Julian gave the cab driver the address of the "West L.A. Motor Hotel." He arrived to find a seedy, dirty excuse for lodging. The unkempt woman at the counter gave him the room number for Ginger and her two friends. He knocked on the door and got no answer.

"Ginger?" he said as he knocked again. "Are you in there?"

The door slowly opened to a crack. "Who are you?"

"Is Ginger Morley here?"

The door opened to an untidy room with the TV on, and one person still sleeping. The stench was overwhelming. He wouldn't leave until he had his daughter with him.

"She's not here," said the girl. "She hasn't been here in two days."

Julian's heart sank. "Do you know where she went?"

"She might be at work. She got a job at the café down the street. Don't remember the name."

Julian left and had the cab driver help him look for the café.

"The Magnolia Café," two blocks away from the motel, was a diner boasting "Authentic Southern Cuisine." Julian told the cab driver to pull in. The odor of old grease permeated the painted concrete block building. He went into the dimly lit, greasy dive, hoping to find Ginger there. He sat down at a small table and looked around. The menu was written on a blackboard with chalk, and it wasn't long before a waitress with a slow, southern drawl approached him.

"What would you like, sir?" she asked politely.

Julian looked at his daughter. With a knot in his stomach, he tried not to overreact. He'd found her. He noticed her looking closely at him, a question in her eyes.

"Do you know me?" he asked. "I know you."

"Julian?"

"Yes. I heard you were out here, and I wanted to see you." He noticed her eyes filling with tears. "Will you allow me to take you home?"

Ginger, pale and thin, was still the pretty little girl he remembered, but she didn't look healthy. He stood and asked her to join him at the table.

"I can't They'll fire me."

"So, what? Let me take you back to Birmingham where you belong. Please?"

"I'm working here so I can save enough money for the flight back. Somebody I traveled out here with stole all the money I had and left. This has been holy hell since last week."

"Come on, let's go. I'll take care of your flight. Collect the money this place owes you, and we'll take the next plane home."

Ginger had nothing but the clothes on her back and her purse. Her wallet had a few dollars in it from tips, and her driver's license.

"Mama called you, didn't she? I'm shocked."

"Yes, she did. Your mother is worried sick about you. She hasn't heard from you in three weeks. Why haven't you contacted her?" Julian asked.

"We don't agree on anything. I had to get out. So much has been said about Julia and me. We've had to deal with gossip about you and Mama."

"We have all night to talk about that. Let's get back to the airport." Julian said.

As they waited at the airport for the next flight to Birmingham, Ginger explained to her father how great it had been when the group first arrived.

They lived in a commune in Laurel Canyon and made jewelry to sell on the streets. The group also spent time in Venice Beach where they met a new rock singer named Jim Morrison. He would play on the beach with his band, and she never felt so free! That was the highlight of the first few weeks.

She then told him how she fell for one of the boys in their group named "Roach," and thought he felt the same, but he did nothing but lie to her. One morning she woke up to find that all her money had been stolen, and he was gone. Deeply hurt, she went to the Pacific Ocean, and in a rage, threw her remaining possessions into the sea.

Her friends, Anna and Jack, still had around $35 and could afford the "West L.A. Motor Hotel" for three nights. With no money left, they didn't know where their next meal was coming from. Ginger saw "The Magnolia Café" and asked for a job. She was hired on the spot due to her southern accent.

She had to give most of her tips to the two 'friends' Julian saw at the motel. They wouldn't work, so the money went for the room and drugs. She wanted out of there, so her meals came from her employer. She offered to work twenty-four hour shifts, but it was against the law. The café owner offered the back-storage room to stay in until she found permanent lodging.

Julian called VA to let her know Ginger was with him, and the time they would land in Birmingham. He didn't go into detail, but told her Ginger would need medical attention when she got home.

The plane landed in Birmingham at 1:34 AM, and the cab took Julian and Ginger to the "Parliament House" where VA would pick her up.

Ginger slept through most of the flight and was quiet on the way to the hotel. While they waited for VA, she told him how her mother had been the brunt of rumors spread around the social set which included Janet Johannsen. She told him how fortunate he was to live in Atlanta and why she had to get out of Birmingham. The gossip affected Julia, too, but differently.

Julian didn't know how to comfort her. His daughter had been through hell, at home and in

California. Every rumor these women were spreading was false, and Ginger knew it but had no way to defend her mother or herself. The only way out was to leave, and he didn't blame her.

Julian made sure his daughter cleaned herself up and had a healthy meal, such as it was, at that late hour. VA arrived at 2:45 AM to pick Ginger up.

She saw VA and began to cry. "Mama, I didn't know what else to do!" The tears continued. "I'm sorry I hurt you, but I couldn't stand to live here anymore."

"I know. It's been hard on all of us. You owe your father a debt of gratitude."

Ginger gave her father a much-deserved hug, and a kiss on the cheek and said, "Thank you, Daddy, for saving me. Please don't go out of our lives again." She then walked to the car and waited for her mother.

"Thank you, Julian. You came through for us when I reached out to you for help. I appreciate it more than you know."

"She's my daughter, too, and I'm glad it ended this way. If you hadn't called me, we might have lost her, and we never would've known what happened to her."

VA agreed and tried to hold back tears of gratitude. "Julian, I have this to say," she stated with tears in her eyes. "As I quote our daughter, I didn't know what else to do." VA looked into his eyes and with a pause, she finally said, "I'm sorry we hurt each other so long ago." She took his hand in hers and squeezed it gently.

"I'm sorry, too," he said with the overwhelming feeling of regret. After he let her hand go, Julian watched her get in the car and drive away.

He wished she'd said those words years ago. Their lives and the lives of their daughters would have been completely different. He had gotten over VA a long time ago, but knowing there was a time she needed him again made his lonely life complete.

Part Four

I Can't Stop Loving You...

CHAPTER 34

Nothing Stays the Same

Late December 1984, Birmingham, Alabama

*J*o Stafford's recording of "You Belong to Me" instantly blared from the clock radio at 6:00 AM on December 26. VA had been lying awake for more than an hour waiting to get up. The holidays had given her four days off from work, and she dreaded the return of a back-to-normal work routine. After spending time with her girls and their families, she felt the usual letdown after the holidays. Now there would be nothing to look forward to. Going to the office, a beauty salon appointment on Saturdays, the grocery store visit, and a stop at the ABC package store for the weekly handle of bourbon, was the life VA Morley had made for herself.

While lying in bed, she thought how different this morning felt. There had been a dull ache in her right hip for a few days, but overnight, it had turned into a nagging pain. When she tried to get up, the pain became severe, and it concerned her since she had no one to call in case she couldn't walk. VA knew none of her neighbors, since she hated awkward conversation and didn't want to be bothered. She lived alone on the second floor of her old apartment building, and there was no elevator.

VA sat up slowly, waited a few minutes, and gingerly slid both legs over the side the bed. After lighting a cigarette, she grabbed the bedpost with one hand, and pushed down on the mattress with the other. While the cigarette dangled from her lips, her legs shook as she slowly stood.

She had always been in good health, but now her body felt its age. Sixty-five sounded old to her, but she still loved to sing and dance to the music of her life on the radio. Listening alone to her old favorites brought back painful memories, but she had good ones scattered in with the bad.

Steadying herself, she slowly limped to the bathroom. Her usual morning routine would be impossible. The worsening pain in her hip made standing for any period-of-time out of the question.

After flipping her cigarette into the toilet, VA held on to the sink and caught a quick glimpse of her reflection in the mirror.

Gone was the dark-haired beauty with the intoxicating deep emerald eyes from long ago. Gray now replaced the trademark black hair, and the lines on her face had deepened within the last six months. She washed her face, brushed her teeth, ran the hair pick through the stiff, teased hairdo, and thought of calling in sick.

As the clock radio played, a little smile came to her face as she remembered her "glamour days" during the 1930s, 40s and 50s. Those days were full of music, dancing, and most important of all, finding the love of her life. She also had two beautiful daughters and a husband. She had it all then, and life was as it should be.

After slowly getting dressed, and taking a last look in the mirror, she lit a cigarette and cursed the image. She thought of Mama Lucy and reminded herself, "I used to look like a million dollars. I'm glad she can't see me now."

After twenty-five years, she resigned from TSBB, and stayed home for a grueling six weeks with nowhere to go. TSBB had tripled in growth within the previous ten years, and VA felt overworked and underpaid.

Gabe created a position just for VA in his new HJHome, Inc. Mortgage Company. She was head of profit sharing and payroll. She had an office to herself where she usually sat with nothing to do.

After the turbulent years of the sixties, Gabe assured her he knew nothing about the rumors spread around about her. He always looked out for his little sister, and eventually found out Janet and her group of friends were to blame. He forced his wife to apologize and set all records straight, but it was too late. Irreversible damage had been done to VA and her daughters.

Janet thought she'd finally molded Gabe into the man she wanted him to be, but unknown to her, Gabe finally had enough of his wife's expensive tastes and ongoing snobbishness.

Without her knowledge, he continued to look out for his sister and help when she, or her girls, needed him. That was the way Gabe was raised, but he had to put up with the woman since there would never be a divorce. It would cost him a fortune, and in his elite group, it just wasn't done.

VA was never included in any of Gabe's social or family events, and she knew why. She knew almost everyone in his group of friends, but it was the snooty bitch he married who had the most to do with it. Though painful to her in the beginning, the hurt feelings were long gone. Nothing stays the same, and the last forty-five years impacted everything in both her life and Gabe's.

VA's closest friend, Gayle Forrester, died within the past year, so socializing with friends in Birmingham was nonexistent. Over the years, she and Mallory rarely got together, but she always looked forward to her annual trips to Dallas, though, to visit Ed and Mary. She let out a long sigh and closed her eyes as she felt the pain in her hip. She *had* to be able to go back to Texas.

After crushing out her cigarette in the ash tray, VA left the apartment and made her slow, painful way down the hall. She stood at the top of the staircase and looked down. Little did she know those stairs would change her life.

CHAPTER 35

Leave Me Alone

January 1985

The cold, late December morning brought sparkling frost on rooftops and a heavy coat of ice on the windshield. No way could VA scrape it off this morning. Grimacing, she got into the driver's seat to start the car and wait for the defroster to warm up.

Even though it was winter, VA still had a lovely drive to work. The canopy of icy tree branches hovered over the two-lane roads, and more surrounded the grand old homes built around the Country Club.

She had the car radio tuned to the local "oldies" station. It played songs from the 50s and 60s, and they always reminded her of Ginger and Julia.

VA turned in to the employee parking lot of HJHome and dreaded going in. "Gabe's only going to make things worse," she thought as she opened the car door. Slowly, and in excruciating pain, she made her way inside to the elevator. As she came out limping on the second floor, Dana, the receptionist, quickly got up and came toward her to help.

"I don't need any help," VA snapped. "When I do, I'll let you know."

Dana looked surprised, backed away, and returned to her desk. VA didn't mean to be hateful but hell, it was embarrassing to have to depend on someone just to walk to her desk. She was glad to be early since most of the employees weren't there.

As her co-workers trickled in, VA made sure she wouldn't have to get up from her desk until she needed a bathroom break.

She lit a cigarette and typed out checks for payroll and outgoing mail. As she worked, she heard Gabe's booming voice. He had that aristocratic southern drawl just like their father. Dana must have filled him in about her limp. He instantly appeared in the doorway of her small office.

"VA, I want to see you walk," he said.

"No, I can't. I'm in the middle of payroll, and it has to be finished before lunch," she argued.

"To hell with the payroll, VA. Get up and walk!"

Looking down at her hands on the desk, she shook her head and said, "I can't. It's too painful."

Gabe turned, then looked back and told her he would call Dr. Bob Wesley, his orthopedist. Hopefully, he could work her in.

She frowned as he walked out of her office. She knew he would do this. Maybe Dr. Wesley would be too busy and couldn't see her today. She hated doctors because of so many bad memories. They inflicted her life with pain in so many ways.

Soon her desk phone rang, and it was Gabe informing her that Dr. Wesley could work her in that day at 1:00. She knew Gabe would pull it off. He probably called on the doctor's private line. Her brother could pull strings when most people couldn't. She'd better be ready to leave at 12:30.

"Shit," VA said under her breath. She hung up the phone without another word. *Why has it always been his intention to run my life?"*

It was 12:20, and VA could hear Gabe leaving instructions and the phone number where he could be reached. Being a small office, it seemed large considering the amount of business conducted there. She would have to limp out in front of everyone and of course they all knew what was going on. "Little people" always spread the "big news."

Gabe entered her office and walked around the desk to help her up. She batted his hand away and slowly got up on her own. Holding tight to the edge of her desk, she managed to pick up her purse.

"Damn it, VA, why in hell haven't you had this taken care of?" he asked.

He grabbed one arm and put his other arm around her. She didn't fight him this time. Carefully, he led her out to the elevator as everyone pretended not to watch.

The friendly ones wished her well. A few of the men were nothing but sorry jackasses, and she didn't even look their way. Dana smiled and told VA she hoped all would be fine. VA didn't smile back but nodded a thank you.

Dr. Wesley's Southside office was busy, but there were a few seats available. Gabe checked her in with the receptionist and sat down next to her.

"I didn't think anything was wrong. I thought the pain would go away," VA said. "You know I hate doctors, and you know why."

As they sat, the next name called was hers. Gabe helped her up and led her back to the examining room. In a few minutes Dr. Wesley came in.

"Damn! VA Morley, I haven't seen you in years. I guess that's a good thing, huh," he said in his sissy, high-pitched drawl. "Gabe tells me you're in a lot of pain and having trouble walking. Tell me what's going on."

Dr. Wesley listened as she explained the pain she

had experienced within the last week and how she thought it must have happened by bumping a door to open it. He checked her vital signs, had her lay on the examining table, and asked her the general area of the pain. When she pointed to her right hip, he felt the area and VA flinched. He looked at Gabe and back to VA.

"I need to schedule a few tests on this hip. I don't think bumping a door open caused this. I think it's most likely osteoarthritis, but I want to be sure," he said. "After you leave here, go to St. Vincent's Hospital. I'll order the tests, and we should have our results today."

"Damn it," VA said to herself as she timidly agreed, wanting to know what tests he ordered. Tests usually were accompanied by some sort of pain.

Dr. Wesley ordered a complete blood work up, x-rays on the hip to determine osteoarthritis, measure bone mineral content, injury to the bone, and a bone biopsy. She could handle the x-rays but not the biopsy.

Her oldest friend, Gayle Forrester, had a bone biopsy and told her it had been painful. Gayle's biopsy came back positive for bone cancer, and she didn't recover.

They arrived at St. Vincent's and went directly to the second floor of the orthopedic wing. The nurse was expecting her and slowly guided her to the x-ray department. VA was frightened of the bone biopsy. She tried to be strong, but after Gayle's experience, she felt nothing but tension and fear.

When the tests were over, VA returned to the hospital waiting room to join Gabe. The test results would be reviewed by Dr. Wesley personally, the diagnosis made, and then treatment would be determined. In about an hour, VA and Gabe were called back to a small office and Dr. Wesley made his diagnosis.

"VA, I have good news and bad. To be honest, I thought the tests would determine cancer of the bone. They did not. That's the good news. The x-rays show you're suffering from osteoarthritis, and your right hip joint is deteriorating. I recommend a complete hip replacement, and we need to schedule it now. I'll prescribe pain medication for you to take until the surgery. It should help you until then."

As Virginia listened, all she could do was look down at her lap and shake her head. Did this mean she would be incapacitated for months? Would she have to get a live-in nurse? She couldn't afford that. Would she be bored and alone for the rest of her life? Worst of all, would she be able to stand the pain of it all?

"We'll figure it out. Don't worry about a thing. You have good insurance with the company," Gabe said noticing the worry in her face. "Okay, Bob, when the surgery is on the books, let me know. Thank you for working us in."

As VA slowly stood up, she murmured a low "thank you" and limped as her brother put his arm around her and helped her out.

Dr. Wesley scheduled the surgery for January 2. Ginger picked VA up on New Year's Day at 3:00. She helped her mother down to the car and carried her bag of essentials which included her clock radio.

While she waited in admissions, VA lit a cigarette, and thought about the pain she was about to go through. She had visions of her daddy taking her to his office in 1929 and Dr. Taylor waiting to yank her tonsils out. Dr. Johannsen explained it was a precautionary measure since sore throats and bad tonsils usually led to Scarlet Fever. She cried for two days and avoided him for a week.

After an hour, VA was taken to her room. Per instructions, she hadn't eaten since noon and could only have sips of water until midnight. After that, she could have nothing.

Ginger helped her mother settle in and called Julia so VA could talk to her. She wanted to be there, but Ginger told her to wait since their mother would be knocked out for a few days.

Early in the evening, while VA was alone in her room, Gabe dropped by to have a will signed that had been prepared for her by his attorney.

"Here you are," she mumbled under her breath,

"being businesslike and planning for me to die. I wish you would just leave me the hell alone."

"VA, sign this with no complaints. This is beneficial for you and the girls in case an unforeseen problem should occur," Gabe said. "I'll see you tomorrow."

VA didn't respond. She signed the document, and then he left. She remained upset with him on one hand and appreciative for all he did for her on the other.

With the radio playing low, VA leaned back on the pillow and began to reminisce about the past. So many memories flooded back.

She thought of the men in her life and when she was deemed "The Glamour Girl of West End." She thought of Larry and how much she still loved him. She hadn't heard anything about him in twenty years.

With raising the girls and working full-time, she'd lost touch with Mary Laura. She'd been her source of news about Larry. So much time had been wasted, and she still had many regrets about letting him go.

So many memories came back to her about her life with Julian. He'd always been there for her even after the hateful way she treated him all those years. They were both to blame for the result of their miserable life together. A gentle knock on her door caused her to open her eyes.

"Come in."

An attractive older man in a white doctor's coat came into her room, pulled up a chair next to her bed and sat down.

"Hello, VA," the doctor said. "I heard you were here, and I had to come in and see you."

"Hello," VA replied.

"You don't remember me, do you?"

"I haven't lost my entire mind yet, but you do look familiar," she said as she read out loud the embroidered name on his white coat. "Lawrence Abbott, MD." She looked up and sitting next to her was Larry, the man she would always love, the actual love of her life. "Larry, I can't believe it's you and you're sitting here with me."

"VA, I've wanted to get in touch with you for so long, but I was afraid to. The last time I saw you with that huge bruise on your thigh, and then at Gabe's cocktail party, you were married, and I had a wife."

As VA listened, she studied his face. He had aged, but it was still the handsome face she remembered from so long ago. The striking blue eyes hadn't dimmed, and that beautiful smile stayed the same. Completely grey now, the curl that always fell over his eye had now been combed back from his face.

"I'm having hip replacement surgery in the

morning. Dr. Wesley explained the procedure, but I'm afraid it's going to cripple me for the rest of my life."

"I know all about your surgery. You couldn't be in better hands. Dr. Wesley's a fine man and surgeon. You'll be back on your feet in a few months. But for now, you need your rest, so I'll check in on you tomorrow. I'm glad to see you again."

"Okay, I look forward to it."

Larry left and quietly closed the door behind him. She should've known he was on staff at St Vincent's since it was so convenient to his office. He'd be back to check on her tomorrow. She hoped to be awake when he came by.

She rested her head back on the pillow and smiled. "I Can't Stop Loving You" by Ray Charles was playing on her radio. She turned it up and listened to how true the lyrics were. The thoughts of seeing Larry again and hearing "their" music on the radio helped her to relax and fall asleep.

VA rested comfortably during the night, and the nurse on duty awakened her at 6:30 AM. Dr. Wesley came in, explained the surgery and what to expect afterward. He told her there were plenty of loved ones outside waiting to see her. *Who all was there?*

When the orderlies rolled her out, VA saw Ginger

and her husband John, Gabe, her nephew Steve, and his wife, Brenda. The only ones missing were Julia and Ed.

As the orderly wheeled VA into the operating room, she became anxious. The pain terrified her. As the assisting nurses prepared her for surgery, the anesthesiologist appeared. He quietly introduced himself and began to administer the anesthesia. He then asked her to count backwards from 100 and soon VA was out.

She slowly woke up to a nurse taking her blood pressure. She tried to say, "What the hell are you doing?" She couldn't speak because of the medication. *What was she doing in a hospital room?* She felt extremely weak, closed her eyes, and slept for another 24 hours.

After three days, VA was alert, but on strong pain medication. When she felt unbearable pain, the nurse would increase the morphine.

Gabe and Ginger were at the hospital with her when Dr. Wesley made his rounds. VA was to start on her first round of physical therapy the next day. The fastest way to recovery was to have VA on her feet as quickly as possible. After she became stable, and the therapist felt comfortable, she could go home.

VA couldn't climb stairs in the beginning and would need someone with her twenty-four hours a day. Ginger agreed the only answer was to bring VA to her house for rehabilitation. No way could Gabe volunteer his home.

Ginger and Gabe left after talking to Dr. Wesley; VA's lunch tray was brought in and placed on the table by the bed. She looked at it, ate a little Jell-O, drank some of the tea, then pushed the rest aside. She hated hospital food. It looked awful to her and she didn't think it was fit for a dog.

VA heard a light tap on the door, and Larry stepped in.

"I've been tied up and couldn't get back to see you until now. I'm sorry about that. I looked over your chart and saw that your recovery is right on schedule. Keep it up."

"I'll try. I start therapy tomorrow. I'm afraid I might fall."

"I don't think you will. Orthopedics isn't my specialty but I have full confidence in you."

VA looked deep into his eyes and swallowed hard before she spoke. "Are you still married to Nancy?" She couldn't help but blurt it out.

"Nancy died five years ago from liver cancer. It turned out to be a long, painful struggle for her. I tried to help all I could, but it was diagnosed as Stage 4, and she refused chemotherapy."

"I'm sorry to hear that," she said sincerely.

"Did you receive the cards I sent after your mother and Susie died?" Larry asked. "When I saw you at Susie's funeral, sending the card was all I could do to let you know I still cared."

"Those came from you? You're the 'One Who Cares'? I remember receiving them in the mail on my birthday for about ten years. They stopped around 1974, I think. I remember because that was about the time my daughter, Julia, got married and transferred to New Orleans."

"I couldn't let them be traced back to me. Nancy had become so paranoid after she met you at Gabe's cocktail party. I asked Ezra to sign and send them all for me, with Mary Laura's knowledge. Nancy was suspicious, so I stopped sending them."

"I knew I recognized the handwriting. Oh, Ezra. I read he passed away two years ago. How is Mary Laura?"

"Lonely but doing fine. I haven't seen her in a while since I stay so busy." Larry took VA's hand and said, "I need to continue my rounds, but I'll stop in again as soon as I can."

VA seemed to respond well to the physical therapy. She liked Jane, the therapist, because she was soft spoken and gentle. Jane looked to be 60ish, and they had a lot in common. Jane loved music and listened to the same radio station as VA. They talked about their lives during the war and how the music brought all their memories back.

After two weeks in the hospital, VA listened as Jane agreed with Dr. Wesley that it would be a long road to complete recovery for her, and it was essential to follow all post-op directions. Dr. Wesley thought it would be beneficial to her recovery to have her daughter and two grandsons close by.

VA was discharged on January 16, and the nurse wheeled her down to the car. VA immediately demanded a cigarette, so Ginger pulled in to a drug store and bought a carton of Virginia Slims.

VA took possession of the smokes and grinned. *"Like hell I'm convalescing at Ginger's for a few weeks. I'm going home in a day or two."*

"You know, Mama, John doesn't allow smoking in the house." Ginger said. "When you want a cigarette, I'll walk you outside."

VA shrugged and murmured to herself, "I'll do as I damn well please."

They arrived at Ginger's small, three-bedroom house in an eastern suburb of Birmingham. It would be tight, but they would make do. The minute VA got to the house, she lit a cigarette and found a comfortable chair she would claim as her own.

Two weeks of convalescing at Ginger's were a nightmare to VA. Ginger repeatedly read the post-op instructions over and over to her and she refused to follow any of them. She smoked in the house when she felt like it and didn't care if John was mad about it.

Sitting in the living room chair, she heard Ginger on the phone.

"Julia, you'll have to come up here," Ginger demanded. "Mama won't do anything she's supposed to. She's soiling the mattresses, smoking constantly in the house, and she refuses to exercise like she should. The boys are witnessing all of it. My family life is shot to hell."

"Okay, I'll be there Tuesday, make an appointment with Dr. Wesley on Wednesday. He'll guide us from there," Julia instructed.

Julia flew in to Birmingham on February 1. She met Ginger and VA at Dr. Wesley's office that afternoon. Seeing her defiant mother in a wheelchair and the actual reason for the visit made her feel sick inside. *Why are we having to do this?*

"VA, I'm not happy with your progress," said Dr. Wesley. "You should be up and using a walker."

"It still hurts too much to put any weight on the hip," she answered.

"I understand you aren't following the directions I sent with you when you were discharged."

"Oh yes I am. I've done everything you said to do."

Julia looked at her sister, then at Dr. Wesley.

"VA, as much as I hate to, I'm going to have to re-admit you to St. Vincent's to find out what's going on. Ginger tried to follow my instructions but you refused. Instead of two children, your daughter was taking care of three, and a husband."

Julia felt sick. Her mother looked down at the floor. She then looked up at her with a question in her eyes. Julia looked away and felt as if she and Ginger had taken away every bit of trust their mother had in them.

Once again, VA was admitted to St. Vincent's Hospital for observation, testing, and hopefully rehabilitation. She couldn't understand why. She thought the post-op instructions had been followed. *Why was she back in the hospital?* Her two girls had betrayed her. Why would they do this to her?

Once admitted back into the hospital, VA underwent more testing on the bone and another painful biopsy. After a week, Dr. Wesley dropped by with another doctor.

"VA, the results of all tests came out clear. No

cancer of the bone has been detected," he said. "This is one of my colleagues, Dr. Jack Graham. He's at the top of his field as a diagnostician."

Dr. Graham nodded and smiled. "Virginia, we want to find out the cause of your prolonged recovery. I have a few more tests I'd like to run and hopefully we can get to the bottom of this."

"Okay, if I have to," she said. "When can I go home?"

After the doctors left, a lunch tray was brought in and placed on her table. VA looked at it, made a face, and rolled it aside. It looked awful and there was no way in hell she would eat it.

CHAPTER 36

Always Cigarettes

Early March 1985

Weak and frail from not eating, VA lay in a hospital bed at St. Vincent's and thought a long time about her life. She had a good one despite the sad times and a few setbacks. Seeing Larry again when she was in the hospital the first time, seemed to make many of the bad memories disappear. He hadn't been to see her since she was re-admitted, so she just assumed he didn't know she was back in the hospital.

VA turned up her small bedside radio again to "I Can't Stop Loving You" by Ray Charles. That song seemed to come on a good bit, and she loved it. She lay her head back on the pillow and closed her eyes.

There was a faint knock on the door, and she thought it had to be another nurse coming in to probe her with something. The door slowly opened. Larry quietly came into her room, pulled up a chair next to her bed, and sat down.

"Hello, VA," he said. "I heard you were re-admitted, and I wanted to check on you."

"Larry, I'm glad to see you. Do you hear the song that's playing? It's one of my favorites. I heard "The Nearness of You" the other day. Do you remember it?"

"Of course I do. That was our song. I still have the original recording of Glenn Miller's version. I almost wore that record out."

"Are you able to stay a little while today? I get so bored in this room. There's nothing on TV and I love it when you visit."

"VA, I've missed you so, all these years. We missed out on so much time together."

"I'm so much older now, and my health isn't good. I'm sorry you have to see me like this."

"It doesn't matter. You're still beautiful to me."

Larry took VA's thin, frail hand in his and brought it to his cheek. "I never stopped loving you. I want to see you as much as you'll let me."

"Anytime, as you can see, I'm not going anywhere."

Larry got up, kissed her hand, and winked. "I'll see you tomorrow. Get some rest."

As he closed the door behind him, tears came to VA's eyes. Only Larry Abbott could make her cry.

Jane, the physical therapist, wasn't happy with VA's lack of progress, and her ongoing refusals to eat. VA was told the latest tests were still inconclusive; they had no idea what to treat, let alone how to treat it. There seemed to be no apparent reason for her swift decline. A feeding tube had been discussed, but that only made VA mad.

"Hell no! There'll be no feeding tube. If you want to do anything for me, I'd like a cigarette."

"You know there's no smoking allowed in the hospital. If you want a cigarette so badly, the nurse will take you downstairs to the smoking section," Dr. Wesley said. "Just remember, everyone will see you in a wheelchair without lipstick and your hair going in every direction. Also, you haven't had a manicure in months."

"Since when did they prohibit smoking everywhere? My daddy was a doctor and smoked all the time--and at the hospital! I've been smoking for 45 years!"

She knew smoking was forbidden in the hospital, but it made her mad because she couldn't get her way, not that she'd ever admit it.

After three weeks, Julia drove up from New Orleans to celebrate VA's 66th birthday on March 4th. It was hard to be festive in a hospital room, but Ginger planned a little party for their mother and brought in a small birthday cake. Upset at the sight of her mother and her severe decline, Julia walked out into the hallway and cried.

Ginger followed. "I thought you might get upset," she said. "Since you were here last, Mama hasn't eaten. She lies and says she eats a big breakfast every morning, but the nurses know otherwise. He's not positive, but Dr. Wesley thinks she might weigh eighty-five pounds at the most."

Julia slowly regained her composure and started back into the room. Gabe and Janet were on their way in and saw the tears on Julia's face.

"She looks so frail," Julia said. "They don't know what's wrong with her."

"Let's all go in," said Gabe. "We brought Golden Rule Barbeque. She loves that. Maybe she'll eat."

"Why is *she* here?" VA asked with disgust as she saw Janet.

"Mama, Gabe brought your favorite," Julia said, changing the subject. "Here, I fixed your plate."

"I'll eat when I'm ready," she snapped. "I had a huge breakfast this morning so I'm not very hungry." VA was confused, and defiant toward everyone.

Julia walked Gabe and Janet out of the room after the visit.

"Mama's not recovering, is she?"

"No," Gabe said while putting his hands in the pockets of his golf pants. "Dr. Wesley advised that we make plans to move your mother out of her apartment. She can't live on her own anymore, especially not on the second floor. He's looking into affordable nursing homes."

"Mama will never agree to that," Julia said. "She would rather die than be more humiliated than she is now."

Ginger met Julia at the hospital before she drove back to New Orleans. She hated to see her little sister leave, but she knew she had to get back to her one-year old little boy. Ginger saw Julia outside their mother's room crying.

"She's in there moaning," Julia said. "I can't stand to see her so helpless."

Ginger peeked in at her mother, came back to Julia and said, "I'm calling Gabe."

Gabe arrived in about fifteen minutes. Ginger told him their mother's condition.

"Your mother will never be able to go back to her apartment. She's declining quickly and you both need to arrange to move her out," he began, "Dr. Wesley has concluded there should be no reason Virginia isn't recovering, except for pure stubbornness."

Ginger felt this was the beginning of the end. As she thought about her mother and her unhappy life, she looked at Julia and said, "Now we're having to make life-altering plans for her. It's not fair to her."

Gabe took the girls to lunch and discussed their mother's financial condition.

"Your mother has good insurance with the company. Very seldom would she spend money on herself except for necessities." he said. "When Virginia signed her will before the surgery, she also gave me power of attorney for her medical and financial affairs. She has enough in her bank account to cover all final expenses."

"Thank God for you, Gabe," was all Julia could say.

Ginger was upset with Gabe for not filling Ed in on VA's actual condition and progress. He sugar-coated everything so Ed and Mary wouldn't worry. This upset her even more because Ed didn't find it necessary to travel to Birmingham until his sister was back on her feet. Ginger knew Gabe had made her mother's dire condition seem non-life threatening.

Julia went back to her mother's room and sat with her until time to leave. Ginger went home, and after a few minutes, an extremely weak VA woke up and was glad to have Julia all to herself.

"I have to leave today," Julia said. "Mama, why won't you eat? Is there something going on that you haven't told the doctors about?"

"No. I don't like the food here. It looks awful and tastes worse."

Julia took her mother's hand and held it as she went back to sleep.

VA woke up soon after Julia left and tried to reach over and turn up the radio to "That Sunday, That Summer," by Nat King Cole. It was a happy song, and one she always liked. As she listened, there was a light tap on the door and Larry walked in.

"I peeked in on your birthday, but you were sleeping. You had a nice crowd here to help you celebrate."

"I wish you'd come in," VA said barely above a whisper. "I could've introduced you to my daughters. I guess you saw Gabe and that woman."

Larry laughed. "I don't think you two get along very well."

"She's no Susie Johannsen, that's for sure," she said slowly. "Why don't you pull up a chair and sit down? I want to hear about everything you've been doing lately."

"I work most of the time; I don't have time for anything else," he said as he placed a chair next to the bed.

"Did you and Nancy ever have any children?"

"No, she never wanted them. I did, and brought it up to her frequently, but she always changed the subject. After a while, she wanted separate bedrooms and nothing to do with me. It was a sad situation," he said. "Well, I guess I'd better continue my rounds, so I'll stop in tomorrow." He bent down and kissed her cheek, then left.

"I could've had his children if I hadn't been such a fool...." VA leaned back on her pillow and dozed off.

CHAPTER 37

Holding the Eternal Grudge

Late March 1985

*W*hen Julia came back to town, the sisters went to their mother's apartment to inventory the furnishings and decide when to schedule moving day. Ginger was hesitant since she didn't like the idea of sifting through her mother's private things. She knew it had to be done, but she felt as if she had broken into someone's home and had to decide what to steal.

Each time Ginger walked into her mother's apartment building, the odor of cigarettes and old enamel paint permeated the hall. She never liked that musty 'old house' smell. She and her sister had to move their mother out of her home without her knowledge. *What did she ever do to deserve this?*

They walked into the apartment and found it just as VA left it. Nothing out of place, the familiar tick of the kitchen wall clock, and ashtrays running over. Ginger brought a notebook to record each significant item she and Julia found. She still felt an extreme feeling of guilt going through her mother's things.

She started in the spare bedroom and found the closet full of VA's old clothes from the 1960s and 70s and boxes full of old bank statements dating back to 1965. The dresser drawers didn't hold much of anything except old pajamas and underwear. Ginger jotted down each piece of furniture in the room and then joined Julia in the kitchen.

Julia went through the kitchen cabinets and drawers and called out their contents to Ginger. She remembered the old dishes, glassware, and the famous "bar-boy."

"This thing must be sixty years old," Julia said. "Mama always measured her liquor with it, remember?"

Julia continued to search through the pantry and saw the handle of bourbon. "I think Mama drank too much. I dreaded coming home and being here on Saturdays," she said. "She was always looped by 2:00."

"Don't talk about it," Ginger said. "Mama had my boys with her on the weekends sometimes, but I'm sure she behaved then. Let's go to her bedroom and see what's in there."

Julia went through their mother's dresser drawers, and found nothing but a few old girdles, old nightshirts, and perfume stained bras. She went through her mother's closet, and in addition to her clothes and shoes, there were more boxes full of recent bills, cancelled checks, and more bank statements. Her glass top vanity table held perfume bottles and a jewelry box full of old, tarnished costume jewelry.

As she searched the apartment, she had hoped to find a treasure trove of unanswered questions. The apartment held a lot of family history.

Their mother threw away most of their sentimental childhood mementos when they moved from the house on Mabry Drive, but Julia was determined to find something to explain what had never been revealed to them.

There were so many secrets to their mother and her past life. Julia continually asked questions, but VA never spoke of her younger days and rarely of their father unless it was something hateful.

Julia began to search the hall closet. As she searched, Ginger inventoried. There were boxes full of old photographs, record albums, and legal papers from the sale of the Mabry Drive house.

There were pictures of Gabe, Bill, and Edward in their World War II uniforms, and an assortment of old suitcases and war blankets. She came across a box of war medals that had to be their Uncle Bill's. Their mother never told them she had them in her possession. *Why had she always been so closed-mouthed and secretive about everything?*

Discouraged, Julia said, "I guess that's it." She went back to her mother's room and sat on the bed. She looked toward the open door of the closet and let out a loud sigh. "Wait! What's that?"

A small box was tucked away on the top shelf. It was partially covered by sheets and an old bedspread. *How did I miss this?*

Together, the girls opened it to find old letters and cards, faded flowers, a crudely fashioned twig made into a ring, a small box containing two beautiful diamond rings, and an envelope addressed to *"Ginger and Julia."*

"This is it! It has to be!" Julia screeched as she pulled Ginger down to sit beside her on the floor.

"Oh God," Ginger murmured. "What can be in it? I'm afraid to look."

Dear Ginger and Julia,

When you read this, I must be dead or close to it. I want you to know I dearly loved you both, and Julian did too. Your father was a good man although I never let you know it. I married him twice, and when we divorced for the second time, I had never seen a man so crushed, but my foolish pride always dictated my every move. He loved the two of you and me, but I pushed him away. We both made huge mistakes, and you were the ones to suffer the most. If a Clifford Morley ever contacts you, he is your half-brother. Your father had a former wife, and she is his mother.

I was engaged to a doctor before and during the war by the name of Lawrence Abbott. After forty-three years, I've never forgotten him and never will. Larry left me for someone else in Europe during the war, and your daddy saved me, and for that I have always been secretly indebted.

Your father died of heart failure on June 10, 1983, and I never told you. Since you both lost touch with him in his later years, I selfishly kept it to myself. Our old friend from Atlanta, Chloe Richmond, called and gave me the news. I'm responsible for you both not having a relationship with him. After all these years, it would've been best for all of us if you had.

Mama Lucy lost a baby between Gabe and me due to a fall in the middle of the night and was forced to carry the stillborn to term. She never emotionally recovered from it and blamed my father for the torture of having to carry that baby. Your grandfather was also a member of an organization that we wanted nothing to do with. I remember seeing him march in parades, but I was young and didn't know any better. I'm sure you can guess which one that was.

Your grandfather died in Blairsville, Alabama, attending a medical conference, but it was really the front for a tryst with his mistress at a boarding house owned by a Dr. Randall and his wife. Mama Lucy never discussed anything personal with us, and we only know because her sister, Aunt Pearl, told us all of this. Mama Lucy, we found out, never got over the loss of my father. A few days after my daddy's funeral, your uncle Bill visited Dr. Randall in Blairsville. Bill, so reserved and quiet, never got angry, or hit anyone in his life. After seeing Randall though, he left the boarding house with the doctor knocked out from a sock in the jaw. How did Bill know about it all? Mama Lucy confided in her eldest son.

It's also uncertain if Bill actually died from a German sniper's bullet. Aunt Pearl heard from other members of the family it could have been from friendly aircraft fire due to poor visibility during the postponed "Operation Cobra" advance in St. Lo, France, on July 24, 1944. We do know for a fact, Hitler was the cause of Bill's death, friendly fire or otherwise.

As Ginger knows, your father was always there for us when we needed him. He always wanted to have a relationship with "his girls," but my foolish pride always stood in the way. He was also the best dancer I ever had the privilege to dance with.

Even though I never showed it much, I love you both more than you'll ever know. My generation went through a horrific war and more heartbreak and loss than you can imagine. It molded our lives to the point of never outwardly showing our feelings or affection, and I apologize for that. I tried my best.

Mama

Julia put the letter back in the envelope. She wondered why her mother didn't let them have a life with their father. It wasn't fair. Their mother cursed him every chance she got and called him a jackass.

Ginger and VA decided never to tell Julia about Julian's trip to Los Angeles and how her father almost certainly saved her sister's life. Ginger never wanted to talk about that turbulent time again but one day soon, she would tell Julia.

After absorbing the contents of the letter, the sisters sat together on the floor and realized their most important question had now been answered.

"Do you think Mama's cold, bitter disposition was really because of the war?" Ginger asked.

"No, I think she feared rejection," Julia said. "I think that dictated her whole life. She rejected Larry and Julian. She always had to have the upper hand so that no one could leave her without it being her choice."

"I think the letter revealed something else when she wrote about Lucy's accident and the loss of the baby," Ginger said. "Remember how bitter and unaffectionate Lucy always was? Did she ever treat you with any kind of tenderness, like most grandmothers do? I never got anything from her in that regard. Just think how Mama had to live her whole life with no loving affection. When she thought Larry and Julian rejected her, she made the choice to be alone."

As Ginger continued to sit on the floor, she vaguely remembered her father living in the same house with them. "I think I remember hearing a fight between Mama and Julian. It was a long time before I ever saw him again. She held an eternal grudge against him."

They looked at each other and realized their mother was her own worst enemy.

Ginger and Julia went to the hospital the next day to find their mother in a catatonic state. After not eating for weeks, VA suffered from near starvation and had become almost comatose.

"Can't you hear 'I Can't Stop Loving You'?" VA asked in a weak whisper.

"No, Mama, I can't hear anything," Julia said.

With Ginger and Julia at her side, VA suddenly smiled, and a tear fell from her eye. The girls hurried out of the room to find the nurse. VA slowly opened her eyes, and Larry Abbott stood at her bedside.

"Good morning, VA. I hope you got plenty of rest last night. I didn't since I couldn't wait to see you today. Do you remember the first day I met you in English class at Southern? That was the day you captured my heart. When you wouldn't forgive me and take me back after the war, I, like you, wanted to die. Please say you'll come back to me now. I can't lose you again."

"Larry, can't you hear 'I Can't Stop Loving You'?"

"Yes, VA, I do hear it."

Another tear fell from VA's eye as she watched Larry leave the room. *"He must be on rounds now. I hope he comes back before he goes home."*

The girls returned with the nurse. With her eyes barely open, VA managed to say, "Larry was here."

They looked at each other with confusion since they were at the nurse's station five feet away, and no one had entered her room.

"What are you saying, Mama?" asked Julia.

"Larry Abbott was here." VA's whisper was barely audible.

"Mama, Dr. Larry Abbott died in 1973. Gabe told us. Didn't you know? We read your letter, and we know all about him," Ginger said tearfully.

That morning, March 31, 1985, Virginia Johannsen Morley passed away at 10:35 AM with her daughters at her side.

After taking her last breath, VA sat up and got out of bed as Larry Abbott opened the door to her room and held out his hand to her. His handsome young face, those wonderful lips, and the beautiful smile returned.

There stood the Larry she knew so long ago. When she looked down, her hands were young again, and she felt the smooth skin of her face. Her thick, dark hair barely touched her shoulders, just as it had years before. She looked up at him and smiled.

As her girls cried and called her name, VA took Larry's hand, then looked back at the frail old woman that remained.

"Hello, Beautiful," Larry said as he raised her hand to his lips.

Virginia Johannsen and the love of her life walked out the door and into eternity together. She looked back at her girls and lovingly said, "Please remember, I always did my best for you."

This has been a work of fiction, based on fact.

About the Author

Judith M. McManus is a former advertising artist and copywriter from Birmingham, Alabama. Her passion for history began with the study of family genealogy and published historical accounts passed down from her aunt and Alabama historian, Mattie Lou Teague Crow. She lives near Atlanta, Georgia with her husband. "The Music of her Life" is her debut novel.

Made in the USA
Columbia, SC
20 March 2019